KAREN CHANCE

Fury's Kiss

A MIDNIGHT'S DAUGHTER NOVEL

A SIGNET SELECT BOOK

SIGNET SELECT
Published by New American Library, a division of
Penguin Group (USA) Inc., 375 Hudson Street,
New York, New York 10014, USA
Penguin Group (Canada), 90 Eglinton Avenue East, Suite 700, Toronto,
Ontario M4P 2Y3, Canada (a division of Pearson Penguin Canada Inc.)
Penguin Books Ltd., 80 Strand, London WC2R 0RL, England
Penguin Ireland, 25 St. Stephen's Green, Dublin 2,
Ireland (a division of Penguin Books Ltd.)
Penguin Group (Australia), 250 Camberwell Road, Camberwell, Victoria 3124,
Australia (a division of Pearson Australia Group Pty. Ltd.)
Penguin Books India Pvt. Ltd., 11 Community Centre, Panchsheel Park,
New Delhi - 110 017, India
Penguin Group (NZ), 67 Apollo Drive, Rosedale, Auckland 0632,
New Zealand (a division of Pearson New Zealand Ltd.)
Penguin Books (South Africa) (Pty.) Ltd., 24 Sturdee Avenue,
Rosebank, Johannesburg 2196, South Africa

Penguin Books Ltd., Registered Offices:
80 Strand, London WC2R 0RL, England

First published by Signet Select, an imprint of New American Library,
a division of Penguin Group (USA) Inc.

First Printing, October 2012
10 9 8 7 6 5 4 3 2 1

PUBLISHER'S NOTE
This is a work of fiction. Names, characters, places, and incidents either are the product of the author's imagination or are used fictitiously, and any resemblance to actual persons, living or dead, business establishments, events, or locales is entirely coincidental.
The publisher does not have any control over and does not assume any responsibility for author or third-party Web sites or their content.

ALWAYS LEARNING

PEARSON

ACKNOWLEDGMENTS

Thanks to Anne Sowards and the entire Penguin production team for eternal patience in the production of this book.

Chapter One

It wasn't being shot that was the problem. Or the fact that someone had apparently decided to beat the crap out of me beforehand. Or afterward. Or, considering the way I felt, possibly both.

I wasn't sure, as I couldn't seem to remember the fight that had left me bloody and bruised, with a bullet hole in my right thigh and another in my left shoulder. I couldn't seem to remember much of anything else, either, including who the hell I was. But that still wasn't the problem.

No, the problem was that I'd woken up next to a vampire.

One who was maddeningly hard to kill.

"If you would but listen to me for a moment," he said, as I slammed his pretty red head against the concrete floor for *the sixth freaking time*.

"Okay," I panted, wondering what the hell his skull was made of. Granite? "Let's chat."

Of course, that would be difficult since I'd just changed tactics, grabbing his throat and squeezing for all I was worth.

I wasn't trying to choke him to death. That doesn't work with creatures who don't breathe, and the bastard's neck was too muscular for me to close my hands around anyway. But most vamps have instincts left over from their human days, and they don't like being grabbed there. It distracts them, messes up their concentration, makes them panic.

At least, I really hoped it did, since otherwise I was screwed.

He didn't have fangs in me yet, but he didn't need them. Because Hollywood had gotten it wrong. Even plain old vamps could leech blood molecules through the skin using a simple touch. As a master, this one could probably do it without even that, just by being in my vicinity, assuming he could concentrate. Which, judging by the bulging eyes, was probably not the case.

But then he got a leg over mine and flipped us.

Okay, then, I thought grimly. It looked like the choking thing wasn't providing enough of a distraction. Fortunately, he'd left me a hand free.

So I used it to break his nose.

"Damn it!" He actually looked surprised. "Stop fighting me!"

"Sure thing," I grunted, struggling for a foothold. "I'll just lie here and let you drain me."

"I'm not draining you!"

"Then why do I feel like shit?"

He stared down at me, exasperation and what looked weirdly like concern shimmering in liquid blue eyes. "Because you took two bullets in the last hour?"

Oh, yeah.

For a second, dizziness and an odd sense of familiarity combined to mess with my head. I stared up at the stranger, trying to place him. It should have been easy; he wasn't exactly the sort of guy you forgot.

The hair was actually more auburn than red, and there was an absurd amount of it for a man, flowing over his shoulders and my hands. It should have made him look girlie, but somehow it didn't. Maybe because it framed a strong, aristocratic face—high cheekbones, sensuous lips, hard jawline—that managed to be arresting even covered in blood from the broken nose. A nose that was already twitching back into place, like the smear of red was sinking back into the pale perfection of his skin, leaving him looking as if he'd never been injured at all and—

Damn it!

This is how they operate, I told myself harshly. They drain you until your brain doesn't work so well, then turn on the innocence or beauty or charm, confusing the hell out of you until you black out and they finish the job. Only that so wasn't happening this time.

Of course, that would be a lot easier to manage if I had a stake. Or a knife. Or anything remotely weapon-like, because hand-to-hand against this bastard was starting to look like a gesture in—

I paused, noticing the shackle dangling off my right wrist.

Oh, goodie.

"I'm trying to help you," he rasped, somehow getting a hand under the chain before it decapitated him.

"Sure you are." I grunted, really putting my back into it. "Next you'll be telling me you're my boyfriend, come to get me out of this."

He burst out laughing, since clearly he was off his head.

Or maybe that was me, because now I was hearing voices.

"Status." The word rang in my ear as clearly as if someone were looking over my shoulder. My head whipped around, but the only occupants of the iron-barred cage I'd woken up in were me, the vamp and a desiccated rat.

"I have . . . ugh . . . located her."

"Estimated extraction time?"

"That is . . . still being determined."

"There is a problem?"

The vamp's hand flailed out and grabbed one of the cage bars. I smashed my foot—the one in the steel-toed Cat—down on it. He cursed and let go. *"Yes, well . . . a few."*

"Show me."

And suddenly things went from weird to super-ultra-weird as a picture flashed through my head as vivid as a movie. It was upside down and jiggling, but the best I could tell it showed some chick wearing a blood-splattered tank and a crazed expression. Her short dark hair was spiky with sweat, her face was livid with bruises and her weird golden eyes were slitted with effort as she—

Oh. I guessed that was me.

Wow, I look like shit, I thought, right before I noticed something else. I looped the slack of the chain around the bar behind me for leverage and—

Oh, yeah. That worked better.

"What the hell is she doing?" That was someone new, a crabby voice with an English accent.

"With respect, Lord Marlowe," the vamp snapped, *"what does it look like?"*

"And she is trying to remove your head because . . . ?"

"She doesn't recognize me. I believe drugs may have been involved. She—"

"Drugs have no effect on dhampirs."

"I will be sure to tell her that, my lord. As soon as my vocal cords knit back together!"

"What about Lawrence?" That was the first voice again.

"I found him at the dock. He is dead."

"You are sure? He's first level—"

"Quite sure." The vamp's mental voice was dry. I got another flash—this time of a vampire, or what was left of one, the pieces arranged almost artistically on a patch of bloody concrete—and then it was gone.

Someone cursed. Maybe one of them, maybe me. I couldn't tell anymore. The longer they talked, the more my head ached. By now waves of pain were stabbing my brain with every word, like needles through the eye.

"Where are you?" the voice asked. *"We were tracking you, but lost the signal—"*

"Because they took her into one of their labs."

And suddenly I was in freaky visual number three, running through what looked like a time-lapse film of a city at night. For a couple of seconds, my brain took me on a crazy ride over mangled fences, under trash-strewn bridges and through a maze of alleyways that zipped by so fast, all the graffiti streamed together into one long, obscene snarl. It ended in what looked like a warehouse out of some dystopian nightmare, except even postapocalyptic ruins don't usually feature a bright orange hell-mouth swirling away in the middle of a wall.

"*What is* that?" the English guy demanded.

"*The other problem,*" the vamp rasped as the cage blinked into view again.

The transition left me dizzy and nauseous, and royally pissed off. Whatever kind of trick this was, it wasn't going to work. I growled and got serious.

"*That is why we have had difficulty finding their test sites,*" voice number one said. "*They've begun hiding them outside our world.*"

"*Yes,*" the vamp strangled out. "*It would appear that the Black Circle . . . is somewhat more inventive . . . than we had thought.*"

"*Are they folding space?*" the English guy asked. "*Or did you actually pass through to another—*"

"*Do you know, my lord, somehow I haven't had time to look!*"

"*Don't take that tone with me when we're trying to—*"

"*We will have operatives at your location in ten minutes,*" voice number one cut in smoothly. "*Attempt to contain the situation until then.*"

"*Under . . . stood.*"

Great. The guy was like freaking Teflon; every time I thought I had a grip, he slithered out of it. He should have been dead a couple times over by now, but he didn't even seem to be getting tired, while I was panting like a steam engine and sweating like a pig. And now he was about to have backup?

Of course, that might not matter, since I was going to be dead from an aneurysm soon if they didn't *shut the hell up.*

"*And Louis-Cesare—be careful.*" That was voice number one again, sounding grim. "*I can control her fits, but not until she reenters our world. And the fact that she does not recognize you is a bad sign—*"

"*Oh, do you really think so?*"

"*Listen to me! The two halves of her nature do not communicate. Therefore the fact that she does not know you may indicate that her vampire nature is perilously close to assuming control—"*

"Yes, I have seen it before. I can handle—"

"You have not *seen it before! You have seen it nearer the surface, perhaps, but still partly diluted by her human side, which tends to be—"*

"Lord Mircea—"

"—dominant mentally. But when she perceives herself in mortal danger, her vampire half—"

"Lord Mircea!" The vamp had somehow managed to croak that out loud, but it didn't help. The needle was an ice pick now, jabbing merrily around the inside of my skull. I made a sound between a snarl and a mewl, and smashed the vamp's head into the floor again.

It didn't help, either.

"—can assume full control and it is physically far stronger. It is also ruthless, cunning and five hundred years old. *You must not—"*

"What I must, my lord, is be able to concentrate!"

"Listen to him, you arrogant fool!" the English guy broke in. *"He's trying to tell you that nobody knows what a dhampir that old can do because they're always put down before then! But if you're not careful, you're going to find out the hard—"*

"GET OUT OF MY HEAD!" I screamed, unable to take it anymore. It was mental, because I didn't have enough breath left for anything else. But it had an effect anyway. I got a flash of a couple dark-haired vamps sitting at a table; one winced as if in pain, while the other let out a curse and stumbled backward, knocking his chair over.

But the biggest reaction came from the vamp beside me. He went suddenly, rigidly still. I didn't know if he was dead or just as freaked-out as I was, and right then I didn't care. I just wanted out of there.

Fortunately, the door of the cage we were in was hanging half off its hinges, the bars twisted in ways iron wasn't supposed to bend. I looped the chain around the vamp's neck another time, and through the sturdiest bar I could find. Then I pulled it tight, smashed it shut and ran like hell.

I couldn't see much; the windowless room was dim and there was a bunch of junk in the way—cargo crates, broken pieces of metal and machinery, and tarp-covered cages piled high and stacked like a maze. The only light came from a naked bulb swinging from a wire overhead, throwing leaping shadows against the walls. It would have been an accident waiting to happen even if I hadn't been staggering about like an old drunk.

As it was, it took about five seconds to stab myself in the side with something, and to bark my shin on something else. Not that it mattered; even breathing sent burning signals shooting along my nerves, lighting up a constellation of oh-shit points. I grabbed the side of a cage, pulse pounding fiercely, nausea roiling in my gut, and wondered if the light was really fading in and out or if that was me.

And then I saw it.

As a door, it left something to be desired. Like every thing, since it was just a dark rectangle set into a wall of peeling paint and rot. It would have looked perfect on one of those old B-movie sets, the kind with the dippy blonde edging slowly toward certain doom.

Only it looked like I was a brunette. And I'd already met the monster. And right now, I'd take it.

Or, you know, maybe not.

I pulled up abruptly after a couple seconds, but not because the vamp had caught me. That's just how long it took to round the side of the cage. And to find myself in the devil's own operating room.

The low light glinted off a rusty metal table sitting all alone in a cleared space near the door. It looked oddly like the trash heaps were trying to get away from it. I didn't blame them.

It had a high lip, presumably to catch slippery organs, and leather restraints heavy enough to have held Frankenstein. He wasn't on it at the moment, but there were weird stains on the restraints and around the drain underneath, and it reeked like a skunk dipped in sulfur. And if that wasn't enough to make the point, there were saws and clamps and assorted nasty things piled on one end. There were also more cages heaped around, many with clawlike gouges in the bars.

Oh, yeah. There were also some creatures.

It looked like whatever had been in the cages hadn't been too successful at getting out. Because jars of their not-so-spare body parts lined the room in shelf after shelf of formaldehyded nightmares. Most were just dark squiggles against the glass, or pale globules of what-the-hell preserved by somebody who probably slept with the lights on. But a few . . .

A few were staring back.

Ooookay, I thought, gawking at something that looked like an eye on a stalk. Dead things in jars were clearly a level seven on the creep-o-meter. But the operative word here was dead, and I didn't think that something bobbing about in formaldehyde was exactly a huge—

The eye abruptly spun and looked at me.

And then the milky iris turned black as the pupil blew wide.

And then I don't know what happened, because I and my suddenly full bladder were limping like mad for the door.

"Dory!" Somebody shouted a name behind me, but it didn't mean anything. Not when my brain was busy doing a montage of scenes from the kind of movies they show at two a.m. And apparently, whoever I was, I liked old monster flicks way more than was healthy, because it had a lot of fodder.

"Damn it! Listen to me!" The voice came at the same moment that a hand latched onto my ankle. I was moving too fast to stop, not that I would have anyway—there are worse things than hitting the floor chin first. But it still hurt like a bitch, and my bitten tongue flooded my mouth with copper.

That was oddly appropriate, since a red haze had descended over my eyes, like maybe I'd cut my forehead, too. But it didn't seem to interfere with my vision when I flipped over, jerked my foot back and then plowed it into the vamp's pretty face. And broke his nose.

Again.

He cursed and I cackled, because it was funny. And because I was a little tense. Which wasn't helped when I noticed the long white hand that was still wrapped around my ankle.

Well, shit.

The bastard gave a jerk, sliding me underneath him in a move so fast I barely realized what had happened. Until I looked up into the bloody face of death, swift and sure, glaring down at me. For a second, before I did the only thing I could.

And kneed death in the nuts.

Death, it turned out, knew a lot of French curse words. I was treated to most of them as we rolled around the floor, me trying to throw him off, him intent on draining me. And it looked like he was winning. At least, I assumed that was why the room kept trying to gray out at the edges, and why my attacks were batted aside like the antics of an overly energetic puppy.

Until I made a sudden lunge to the side, snatched a fire extinguisher off a trash pile, and smashed it into his stubborn head. Which would have been great, except that it gave Red a chance to get a foot on the floor. He did something balletic that was too fast for my eyes to track, but it ended with me flipping over his head and then him flipping over mine, only to land five or six yards away.

On his feet, facing me.

"Who the hell are you?" I demanded. "Spider-Man?"

"No." He swiped a hand across his bloody face. "Your boyfriend, come to get you out of this!"

"In your dreams!"

"Frequently," he growled—from all of an inch away.

Shit. I hadn't even seen him move. And then he fisted a hand in the front of my tank, jerked me up to his face and—

Kissed me?

As crazy as it sounds, that's what the lunatic was doing. In the middle of a mad scientist's lab, watched by all the creepy things in their little jars. And it looked like crazy was catching, because for a second there I was kissing him back, sucking on a bloody lower lip that tasted like heaven, tasted like candy, tasted like the best thing ever. Until I came to my senses and abruptly wrenched away, freaked-out and furious and turned on and—

"What the *hell* is wrong with you?"

"You are. *Tu me rends fou!*"

"What?"

"*Fou, fou!*" He made some weird gestures in the air. "You make me the crazy!"

I stared at him. "Buddy, I got news for you. I don't think you need any help."

The vampire looked offended, but he didn't get a chance to respond. Not with the place taking that moment to start coming apart. The ground rumbled under our feet, a bunch of little jars shook their way off the shelves and a big red light started revolving by the door.

Because, yeah. What this place had really needed was a bloody strobe.

But that wasn't half as bad as the ear-piercing alarm that split the air a second later. Or the fact that a nearby tarp-covered cage started shaking violently. Something in there *really* wanted out, and I *really* wanted to be gone before it managed it.

But it didn't look like the door was an option, since it was currently being used by a bunch of G.I. Joe look-alikes. Or they would have been, if Joe dressed in black body armor and slung bandoliers of potions over the parts of him that weren't already occupied by guns. *War mages,* I realized half a second before all hell broke loose.

Chapter Two

I dove for the operating table, since it was the only source of weapons, and grabbed a couple knives while sliding underneath. Meanwhile, the vamp was jumped by half the guards, who he promptly threw into the other half. Mages hit the deck, bullets started flying, jars started breaking and I hesitated, feeling conflicted.

The problem was that I didn't know if the mages were the bad guys, come to throw me back in my cage, or the good guys attempting a rescue. And then one who'd fallen nearby looked up and spotted me. And I barely had time to push the table over before a couple dozen bullet-shaped dents pinged out of the metal in front of my face.

Well, okay then.

The guy stopped firing after a few seconds, probably figuring out that whatever caliber he was using wasn't enough to punch through the thick old metal. So he used knives instead. And they must have been enchanted, because while the bullets had only pockmarked the surface, the knives sliced right on through.

But they didn't slice through me, because I wasn't there anymore. Bullets slammed into the wall over my head and sparked off the bars of the cages I dove behind. But only one hit me, and it was a minor wound in the calf that I barely noticed because I was too busy noticing the contents of one of the jars, which had been smashed by the earthquake or the bullets or who-the-hell-knew.

And, okay, maybe that hadn't been formaldehyde, I

thought, as the hand that landed in it went numb to the elbow. But it looked like the effect wore off fast. Because the creature that had been floundering around in it—something that looked like an octopus if they had six-inch fangs—suddenly perked up. And lunged for my face.

I screamed and slashed out with a knife, which didn't appear to do much more than piss it off. It came after me as I ran and stumbled and ducked behind this crate and that cage, not being picky, because *bullets* and *fangs*. And then I fell, tripping over something I never saw because I was too busy rolling to the side to avoid the creature, which hit the concrete beside me with a slimy, squelching sound that I thought might haunt my dreams, assuming I survived to have any.

And then it lunged for me again and I kicked it.

Although, no. To be fair, I *kicked* it, with enough force to have sent a football fifty yards to the end zone. Only there was no end zone, there was only the mage's face, which had popped up over the nearest cage with an anticipatory gleam in his eye right before the creature *gnawed it out*.

At least, that's what I assumed it was doing. It was kind of hard to see, considering that pale tentacles had wrapped around the man's entire head and neck. But the munching sounds would seem to indicate—

I blinked and stumbled back as something tiny skittered underfoot. It might have been a rat or a roach, but I wasn't in the mood to take chances. I was in the mood to make it out the damned door. Which I would have—if another flood of mages hadn't been blocking it as they poured inside, taking the odds from insane to just plain silly.

"Dory! Get out of here!" It took me a second to realize that the vamp had spoken, mainly because I was kind of surprised he was still alive. And even more so when he threw me a gun. "Go!"

I plucked it out of the air. It was a shiny black 9mm Glock 18. Nice.

And then I sprayed bullets—but not at the mages. Because pistol ammo probably wouldn't get through their body armor and because I wasn't feeling that charitable right now. *If you're going to be a bitch, might as well be a big bitch,* I thought, a little hysterically.

And took out the shelf behind them.

Suddenly, it was like the shooting gallery at the fair if the gun was fully automatic and the ducks never moved. I'm not going to say I broke every bottle, but if there were more than two or three remaining when I finished emptying the clip, I'd be surprised. Bullets ricocheted, jars exploded, bits of flying glass and shrapnel took out other jars, and not-formaldehyde rained down on the mages. Whose faces went saggy, and whose numb hands dropped their weapons, even as they looked around trying to find the source of the barrage. Which they never managed to do, since they rapidly went from confused and pissed off and homicidal to . . .

Well, whatever emotion can best be described as "lunch."

The only exceptions were the ones who had been spry enough to dodge back out the door before the fun started. Or the ones who had thrown themselves at the vampire, I guess under the impression that they'd last longer. Or the one who had been in front but who had ducked behind a bunch of crates.

You know, the one I hadn't seen.

He emerged shrieking a spell that blasted me off my feet and through the air, before slamming me into the wall hard enough to crack bone. Hard enough to liquefy my insides. Hard enough to cause the whole room to bleed—

Red.

I woke in the middle of a battle, which was not unusual.

A human was lunging at me with a knife, attempting to gut me, which was.

I blinked at him.

He was yelling something that I couldn't hear over the roaring in my ears, which always took a few moments to subside. But the sound bounced off the inside of my skull like rocks. It didn't hurt, but it was annoying, like an insect buzzing around my ears until I reached out and—

Yes.

That was better.

I peeled myself off the wall and looked around.

It was . . . colorful. The meaty smell of new blood painted the room in spatters, glowing crimson bright against the darkness. The stench of tainted magic came from a fire eating its way across the floor, flaring along the spectrum as it consumed old potion stains. And a familiar, skin-ruffling musk followed some of the humans, a sickly green that lingered like aftereffects every time one of them moved.

The combined stench was bad, but I had woken in worse, in battlefields days old, full of bloated corpses. No, it was all right.

But something else wasn't.

Something was wrong.

It wasn't the strange things running around underfoot. One started for me, then paused, lifting long crablike feelers out in front of it, before abruptly turning and scurrying away. I let it go.

Surprisingly, it also wasn't the vampire. There was one here, raising every hair on my body from the power he was radiating. First level. Old. Perhaps four hundred years, perhaps more. But the bloodlust was cool in him, his outline merely a vague blue shadow, only the pale mist steaming up from his body and the thin silvered veins under his skin showing any difference between him and the humans.

Satiated or gorged.

Irrelevant.

I let my eyes move on.

The room was cool, too—blues, grays, darkness in corners, one small source of light overhead. My nose twitched, calling it to me, only to be flooded with the ozone taste of electricity. I growled and then ignored it.

But something else gleamed, in brilliant flashes here and there. I walked through the writhing mass of humans toward it. One grabbed my arm; I tossed him against a wall. Another raised a weapon at me—slow, slow, they moved so slowly I could have ripped his throat out before he finished the motion. I settled for taking his rifle away and batting him across the room with it.

I reached the source of the light, but I still couldn't see it clearly. I growled again, and this time something answered. A strange, haunting cry, and then a hand, bright, bright like flame, emerged from nothingness. And started feeling around the floor.

I cocked my head to the side, nonplussed. I had seen many hands move about on their own, torn or cut off of vampires, or spasming from soon-to-be-dead humans. But they didn't glow.

Only I glowed.

I growled and grabbed it.

Something gave a shriek, and the hand jerked back. And there was muscle behind it, oh yes there was. Not like the humans, two of whom jumped me a second later and forced me to release the hand in order to crack their skulls together. And by the time I threw them aside and turned back, the hand was gone.

I growled.

Something whimpered.

Something else moved, and I caught a gleam again, like a candle behind a curtain.

I jerked at the fluttering thing and it slithered easily through my fingers. Cloth; waxed. I pulled some more and something on the other side grabbed it and pulled back. But I was stronger, and when I gave a jerk, it came away in my hands.

And the glow flooded the room.

Golden light, like looking into the sun, spilled everywhere, so bright I wanted to shield my eyes. It made it hard to see features—hard to see anything. But features didn't matter; I normally barely noticed them. Power I did.

I went down on my haunches and reached for it, but something was in the way.

Bars. Iron. New. I could still smell the solder. I pulled them aside and felt around in the box—why was it in a box?—and finally grasped it.

It bit my hand.

"No," I told it. "Bad."

And then I snatched it out.

I still couldn't see it very well; in fact it was harder up close where the light hurt my eyes. But it smelled wrong. I pulled it close and sniffed it, mentally filtering out the stink of blood and urine and peppery fear radiating off it, but for once, scent didn't help. I pawed at it, checking its limbs. It whimpered again, and the light flickered.

"Hurt?" I demanded, because I couldn't find any unclosed wounds.

It didn't reply.

"Hurt!" I said again, louder, because maybe it was deaf. But no. It flinched; it had heard me. And then some gunfire hit the cage, sparking off the bars, and it flinched again. And kept doing it, in little motions that flickered against the canvas like firelight.

Oh. It didn't like the noise. I stood up and tucked it under an arm. I would take it away from the sounds, and then it would be better.

I scanned the room.

The humans were dead or as good as. The vampire, of course, was not. Injured, but not mortally so, which made it more dangerous. I narrowed my eyes at it. There was a faint tinge of pink around the blue now, blended by the currents of its power into mauve tendrils that smoked up from the surface of its skin.

I kept the small thing close as I skirted the field of bodies. The vampire turned as we did, but made no forward movement. But the currents shivering through its veins increased, as its power surged.

I growled a warning.

The vampire was unhappy; I could feel it in the heat it suddenly gave off, in the way it charged the air with ozone. My nose wrinkled. I hated that smell. How humans lived in cities steeped in the scent of those who hunted them, I would never understand. How could they not know they were stalked, when every house reeked of the hunters? When every streetlight hummed like the stolen energy in their veins, making it almost impossible to tell the difference?

I would take the small thing somewhere with no false lights. With nothing but trees and wind and scurrying things even smaller than it was. With sounds of the earth that would not make it shiver and mewl.

The vampire hadn't moved.

I eyed it warily. Its power had faded, the silver current barely visible now, but it was only reined in. And its wounds were closing. The only serious one was on its stomach, where some potion had splattered and was eating through the flesh. But the vampire's healing abilities were faster than the poison's destructive ones. Soon it would be whole again. And if it fed from the few humans whose pulses still beat faintly, here and there, it would be back to full strength.

If I was going to attack, it should be now.

"Dory?" The vampire spoke, low and soft. The name wasn't mine, but it was looking at me. The eyes were limned in silver, too, like the veins. They stared at me, deep and empty and awful.

I growled and renewed my grip on the small thing, which was thrashing about. *I would kill the vampire if forced, but I was injured, too, and would also need to protect the small one. This was a fight I would avoid if I could.*

"Dory—" It held out a hand.

I backed up, jerking the small thing with me. "Mine," I said, low and guttural, and the vampire started as if surprised.

It probably was. They always assumed that I did not speak. That I could not. So many had plotted my death, discussed it, laughed about it, even while I was in the same room, because they assumed I was mindless. Like one of the failures of their kind, born mad.

But I was not a failure. I was what I was supposed to be. I was dhampir.

And they never lived to tell anyone they were wrong.

"Mine!" I said, challenge in the tone this time. If it wanted a fight, so be it.

But the vampire took several steps back, hands raised. "Oui—yes. Yours," it agreed. The words meant nothing, because vampires lied, but it also changed color. The pink faded to blue, to gray, to black as it went dim and almost seemed to collapse into itself. Dark and small suddenly, instead of bright with power. I watched it narrowly.

Unlike the young ones, those as old and strong as this could summon power in an instant, with little or no buildup required. It was backing down. It was refusing challenge.

But vampires lied.

My muscles tensed, adrenaline drowning my system, power and speed and—ripping, tearing, burning, yessss. The bloodlust flooded me as I prepared for fight not flight, always the preference, always the joy. And then I lunged—

—at the door, slamming it shut a second before something crashed into the other side.

The vampire jumped.

"You did not feel them change?" I challenged, pushing against the clawed hand that was caught in the gap between the door and the wall. It was longer than a man's, with huge, exaggerated knuckles under a covering of black hair, and thick yellowed talons that scored the heavy metal.

"I was . . . distracted."

"That kind of distraction can get you killed, vampire."

"So I see." It brought the butt end of a weapon down on the creature's fingers, hard enough to sever several of them, and the rest withdrew with a howl. "Shifters."

"Yes. I smelled their musk when I awoke. Did you not?"

"No." The voice was clipped. "They scented as human to me."

"Pity."

That must have stung, because power flashed through its veins for a split second before being reined in again. "There are thirteen, two of them injured," it said, showing off. "The odds are acceptable."

"Not with the small thing."

"The small—you mean the child?"

I looked down. The little one had grabbed onto my leg with a grip I would have defied even the vampire to break. That was good. It left my hands free.

"Child." I used language so seldom, sometimes the words wouldn't come. But this one . . . "Yes."

"I will protect her."

I didn't answer. I was looking at the claw marks on the door. They had the same foul stench as the creatures—wrong, unnatural—and they were bubbling the green paint as they dripped down the surface. A moment later, the lock on the door began to sizzle, smoking as if a blowtorch was on the other side.

I glanced up at the vampire. "You were saying?"

It scowled. It did that a lot. But a moment later, I joined it when the room lurched hard to the right, like a ship on the seas, and ugly cracks ran up the walls. One split the ceiling all the way to the light, causing it to flame out in a shower of sparks. But more light speared through the cracks, crisscrossing the gloom in slivers of hellish orange.

One lit on the bar of a cage, and the metal went as molten as in a furnace. But I had never seen a furnace turn a bar white-hot in an instant. Or boil it away to smoke in another.

I did not bother to see what the rest of the rays were doing. My eyes lit on a turned-over table not far away. It was in poor condition, but it had wheels. It would do.

I righted it and started piling things on top.

"What are you doing?" the vampire demanded. It looked like it might have interfered, but the lock was now gone and its back was against the door, keeping it closed. More or less.

"That will become apparent. Where are we?"

"Nowhere. The dark mages who used this place folded over a piece of a ley line, creating a pocket in non-space—" It broke off with a disgusted sound. "There is no time for this! We have to—"

"There is time," I said, poking my nose into a large jar. Little round balls of greasy metal. I added it to the pile.

The vampire made another displeased sound, but it answered. "A ley line is a river of great metaphysical power. Among other things, it separates worlds—"

"I know what a ley line is."

"Then you know that they are meant to be traveled

through very quickly—as when stepping through a portal. They are not designed to be used as a permanent residence!"

"Yet someone has done so."

"Those with an extensive knowledge of magic and a pressing need to hide have used the trick for centuries, but it carries great risk. If the spell they used as an anchor fails, the shield bubble keeping out the ley line's energy will fail, too, and in that case—" It gestured wildly at the room. "Do you understand?"

I glanced up. In the few seconds I had worked, the scene had changed. It now looked as if the room were made of glass and someone had thrown a ball at it. The impact point was a solid heart of flame, with boiling orange-red energy radiating outward in jagged rays. They lit the remaining pieces of the room like the sun through stained glass, causing the gunpowder in the air to shimmer like gold dust.

So much power.

It was beautiful.

I tore my eyes away. "I understand that we need to get out."

"Yes, yes! We need to get out! Therefore making a barrier will do us little—"

"I am not making a barrier."

The vampire looked at the heavy pieces of trash I had gathered on the table. "Then what is that?"

I didn't bother to answer. "Open the door," I said instead.

"Efin!" It threw up its hands, and then had to lower them quickly as the door buckled behind it. "Yes, yes, d'accord. Now you and the child, you stay behind me, do you understand?"

I looked at it. It liked to scowl, it liked to demand things, and it liked to talk. It reminded me of someone.

"I understand."

"Good." It took a breath. Then another, which made little sense as it did not breathe. And then it spun to the side.

The door crashed open and a snarl of fur and unbri-

dled savagery boiled into the room. And stopped, several yards in, slavering mouths agape. Which is what most creatures would do when faced with the solid field of flame the back half of the room had become.

They would have recovered in a second. I didn't give them one. I swung the table outward, putting all my strength behind it, and with the heaviness of the metal augmented by the tower of machinery on top. Machinery that spilled over when its base slammed into the shifters' backs, or stomachs for those with slightly better reflexes, not that it mattered; not that anything mattered. Not with a thousand pounds of falling steel and iron and tiny rolling metal bits sweeping them toward their doom.

And then I was jerked back by the vampire. Its teeth were out and its bloodlust was rising. But I did not think it was about to feed with the flames licking toward us. "Get on," I told it impatiently, shoving the table at it.

"You get on!" it snarled, and threw me and the small one onto the pitted tabletop. And then through the door. And then down a corridor, which was fast collapsing behind us.

I twisted around in time to see that several of the shifters had somehow made it out also, but they were uninterested in attacking us. They barreled into two of their own who had stayed behind, and then attacked them in their panic to get out. They went down in balls of fur and thrashing limbs and the next second were consumed by the gaping maw of energy behind us.

It was less like glass now, I thought, holding the whimpering small thing as the corridor curled up, concrete, brick and plaster, all the same. As if the scene were merely an image drawn on paper and held to a match.

It was oddly unreal, like the expression on the vampire's face as it ran, pushing us with inhuman speed, racing the impossible until fire lapped at its heels and I jerked it onto the table with us. The flames followed, crackling like lightning across the width of the tunnel, burning through the vampire's jacket and searing a wound in its arm. Smoke, stinking of burnt flesh and fabric, flooded the air. The corridor bucked and buckled. Electricity lifted the hair on my arms and prickled at my exposed skin, the space left to us sizzling with it as we scrambled backward, as the tunnel flamed out around us, as beautiful death reached fiery hands out for us—

—and missed.

The floor bucked wildly one last time, and suddenly we were bouncing into darkness, the table smoking like a flare, the portal behind us burning not orange but bright, incandescent white for one brief instant. Before it exploded like a bomb, picking us up and throwing us through the air and into a large group of people who were rushing through what looked like a warehouse door.

But they weren't people; they were vampires. Dozens of them, some getting out of the way in time, others somersaulting along with us as we hit the ground, as we rolled toward a street, as I reached for the small one the impact had torn out of my arms and a knife at the same time, because the fight was not over yet. No, the fight was just beginning as I rolled to a stop and surged to my feet and—

"NO!"

The voice tore through me like a hundred knives, plucking me out of the air halfway through a leap and sending me crashing to the ground. My body twisted, but the power wouldn't let me rise. Not the vampire's—not this vampire's. There was only one who could do this to me, and I looked up with no surprise at all to see the diffuse outline of a being made of moonlight, shimmering in the air above me.

"No," I told it. And "wait" and "child."

But it didn't listen. It never listened.

And then the glow faded, and there was nothing but darkness.

Chapter Three

Some days it doesn't pay to get out of bed. But when an earthquake is doing its best to shake your room apart, you don't have much of a choice. I blinked open my lashes to find sunlight poking cheerful fingers into my eyes, a wannabe Pavarotti in bird form outside my window, and at least a 5.0 on the Richter scale.

The jam jar of daisies on my dresser was dancing. Little puffs of plaster were sifting down from my ceiling. And my bed was slowly migrating across the worn wooden boards of my floor. I stared around in utter confusion because I was still half asleep, and because the pounding on the door almost exactly matched the pounding in my head. For a minute, I wasn't sure if it was the room shaking or me.

The room, I decided, when the jam jar danced to the edge of the dresser and leapt to its doom.

"Crap," I said, and fell out of bed.

The earthquake stopped.

A few seconds later, a gnarled, scarred hand, big as a bucket, squeezed around the doorframe. It was careful, because little things like solid oak doors are notoriously flimsy. But then it stopped without actually coming in.

The pain in my head was fairly astonishing, but it didn't stop me from recognizing the hand. It belonged to one of my roommates, because my living situation isn't any more normal than the rest of my life. Ymsi, the donator of daisies, had the slight disadvantage of being a troll. Not that it was a disadvantage to him, by all appearances, but it did cause the rest of us problems from time to time.

Like when he decided to wake us up by gently knocking on a door.

"Come in," I croaked, only to have nothing happen.

I hung my head. Of course not.

Ymsi had the usual troll love of beauty, and for some reason, he had decided that I fit the bill. And although he and his twin brother, Sven, had been on earth for a while now, they were still getting their feet wet when it came to the odder facets of human culture. Like the whole privacy thing.

This had resulted in my looking up in the middle of a bath one day to find Ymsi standing hunched in the doorway, staring at me with the same rapt look on his face that he used when encountering a new kind of flower. Or playing with the baby squirrel he had rescued from the backyard after a storm and kept as a pet. Or being introduced to the wonders of chocolate for the first time.

Apparently, in troll terms, that sort of thing was considered endearing.

Unfortunately for Ymsi, I am not a troll.

And I guess my reaction had been memorable. Or maybe Olga, a friend who was also of the troll persuasion, had had a talk with him. Because he had suddenly acquired a Victorian-era level of prudery where women were concerned. These days, he wouldn't dare to enter a lady's bedroom, my heavens no. Meaning that if I wanted to know what the deal was, I was going to have to get to the door.

Somehow.

I ended up crawling through daisy runoff, because it just seemed easier. I thought about trying to pull myself up by the knob, to answer the door like a normal person, but who the hell was I kidding? I settled for kicking it open with a foot instead, only to be confronted by a solid mountain of . . . well, mountain.

The acre or so of troll flesh not concealed by a tattered pair of shorts and a homespun shirt was greeny brown, with the consistency of caked earth if it had somehow petrified over time. I poked it—in the knee, which was as high as I could reach. The skin didn't do anything as normal as dimple, but the mountain did shuffle back a few feet, allowing a huge head to peer in the doorway.

It had floppy blond hair that fell over a prominent forehead, a nose the size and shape of a head of cauliflower, and small blue-pebble eyes. They squinted at me myopically.

"Yes?"

Ymsi didn't say anything.

I sighed and leaned my head against the wall.

Conversations with the twins could stretch over hours if not days, to the point that I often forgot what we'd been talking about. I sometimes wondered if the old legends were true, the ones that said that ancient folk in Scandinavia had sometimes been taken by surprise when the small hill they were camped beside suddenly got up and lumbered off. It had been a troll, waiting for a friend to show up, and slowly being covered by moss and grass in the meantime.

But Ymsi hadn't just clammed up. He'd also averted his eyes, which I found fairly odd. Until I looked down.

And saw what I was wearing.

With my brain trying to hammer its way through my skull and all, I hadn't noticed before, despite the fact that it was a lot nicer than my usual nightwear. Hell, it was nicer than my usual daywear, except I couldn't recall ever owning anything in that particular shade of . . . that kind of washed-out . . . that sort of not quite . . . Oh, hell. Who was I kidding?

It was pink.

For some god-awful reason, I was wearing a shell pink nightie.

I blinked blearily at it, but it didn't go away. It was still pink, still silky, and still frothy with what looked like handmade lace around the deep vee of the neckline. It had transparent sleeves, chiffon or something, big and voluminous and liberally tipped with lace. It also had a big floppy satin pussy bow under the vee, because 99.999 on the girlie meter had obviously not been good enough.

Did I mention it was pink?

I would have suspected that it belonged to my old roommate, Claire, who had been visiting for the past few weeks. Except that she was a redhead and hated pink in all its varied hues almost as much as I did. But it sure as hell wasn't mine.

It was, however, rather thin and rather short, which explained Ymsi's reaction. I snatched my old gray bathrobe off the back of the door, covered my wantonness, and tried again. "You wanted something?"

"Olga wants," Ymsi corrected, daring a glance at me.

I waited, but nothing else was forthcoming.

"Olga wants what?" I finally asked, but got nowhere. Ymsi's tiny eyes had fixated on the small amount of ankle I'd left exposed, with the scandalized expression of a nineteenth-century nanny. I quickly flipped over a bit of velour. "Ymsi, what about Olga?"

The eyes returned to mine, but no more information was forthcoming. Which was fair, since he'd already used up a week's worth of words for a troll. "You come," he added, in a grand display of loquaciousness, before rumbling back down the corridor, shaking a few pictures off the walls in the process.

I closed the door and slumped against it.

Olga clearly wanted something, but I had no idea what. And right then, I didn't care. The room was swimming in and out, I felt like I'd fallen down a set of stairs backward and my stomach was threatening an uprising. Worst of all, I couldn't seem to remember how I got this way.

Fey wine, at a guess. The lethal concoction from Faerie was the only thing I'd ever found that could knock even a dhampir squarely on her ass. I'd discovered this after my first-ever hangover a little over a week ago, which you'd think would have prevented the second.

But apparently not.

And this one was worse, because my memory hadn't been affected last time. Which was ironic, since dhampirs black out on a regular basis. Every time the train goes to crazy town, we lose all recall of what happened, waking up hours or days later, often in a bad way and usually surrounded by people in a worse one. Only I didn't think that was what had happened here. Because I didn't recall anything leading up to the blackout, either. In fact, I was drawing a blank on most of yesterday, which was pretty damned sad.

Five hundred years old is a hell of a time to discover that you can't hold your liquor.

I just lay there for a minute, staring at the one black sock I was wearing for some reason, and contemplated getting up. The floor was hard, but I didn't really feel like moving. Or breathing or living, not that I could do much about the last two. So I settled for fishing out the tag on my finery.

It wasn't doing anything so crass as to scratch my neck, of course, because it was silky, too. Which was what you'd expect from something bearing the name of a Parisian designer. A very famous Parisian designer who I hadn't even known made nighties, but I guess so.

I thought about that for a moment, and then panicked at the thought that I might easily have hurled all over something that probably cost more than my car.

I snatched it off and threw it on the bed, where it pulsed in and out with the rest of the room, looking a little surreal next to my well-washed duvet. But at least it covered up the oil stain from the last time I cleaned my guns. I supposed that was something.

There was no need to wonder where it had come from. It might as well have had Louis-Cesare's name embroidered on it, only they probably wouldn't have because that would be tacky. In the way that giant satin pussy bows weren't, apparently.

I stared at it blankly for another few moments, head pounding, gut churning. And decided that I was completely unable to handle the implications of the world's most awesome nightie right now. I crawled off to the bathroom instead, where I hugged porcelain and waited on my stomach to join the fun.

It was being a lazy little bastard today, content to just twist around under my ribs. But the light was dimmer in here, thanks to my forgetting to flip the switch when I came in. And while the tile was cold, the bathroom rug was thick and comfy and the robe I'd dragged in with me made a nice warm heap at my feet. My forehead found a cool spot along the rim that it liked and, overall, I decided, things were looking slightly—

"Dory!"

"Augghh!" I reacted before I thought, proving that split-second timing wasn't always a good thing. Like when it resulted in my leaping up and slamming another roommate against the bathroom wall.

Claire's wide green eyes regarded me over the arm I had shoved against her windpipe, but she didn't look afraid. Possibly because the slight redhead was perfectly capable of reversing our positions anytime she felt like it. "Are you all right?"

Considering that she was the one pinned to the wall, I thought that an odd question. But I wasn't having a great day, so I decided maybe it was me. "You startled me," I told her, letting go.

Claire did not seem to like this answer. "Ymsi said you're hurt!"

"What? No, just—" I stopped myself, barely in time, because Claire was not a fan of fey wine. Claire was, in fact, leaning heavily toward prohibition these days, so explaining that I'd somehow fallen off the wagon wasn't likely to result in my day getting any better.

"Just what?" she demanded.

"Just a little stiff," I substituted.

"A little stiff? You're black and blue!"

I looked down. And then I snatched up a towel, cursing my metabolism, which should have already smoothed out the evidence of whatever had happened last night. Fast healing was one of the few perks in a condition with a hell of a lot of negatives, only it was kind of hard to tell that at the moment.

"Well?" Claire demanded.

"Um," I said because my brain was still half baked.

Claire's hands went to her hips, never a good sign. "You told me you were going on a routine assignment.

You told me it was nothing to worry about. You told me not to wait up. And now I find you half dead—"

"I'm not half dead. It's just cosmetic—"

Claire grasped my shoulders and turned me toward the mirror. *"Cosmetic?"*

And okay. I had to admit, I'd looked better. My short hair was a matted wreck, there were dark circles under my eyes, and my usually pale skin was corpse white—the parts that weren't green or yellow or richly purple. More worryingly, my baby fangs were out, which usually happened only when I was perilously close to tipping over into Mr. Hyde territory.

I quickly drew them back in. It didn't help much. I still looked like Dracula's daughter.

Which was completely unfair, since he'd only been an uncle.

"Claire—"

"You promised me," she said, as I turned back to face her. Her tone was deadly quiet, but that was actually worse than one of her famous fits. The fits you could reason with; quiet Claire was laying down the law. "You promised you'd take better care of yourself—"

"I have been—"

"Yes, you really look like it!" Her gesture took in the whole sorry picture, which the towel wasn't doing a great job of hiding since it was only a hand variety. And since the mirror over the sink was busy reflecting my bruised ribs and backside.

But I was moving okay, and nothing inside was swelling or pinching or stabbing, or giving any of the other telltale signs of serious injury. I *had* healed; my body just tended to prioritize damage, and it hadn't gotten around to worrying about the pretty yet. But Claire didn't seem to get that.

Or maybe she did, because her forehead scrunched up, making her glasses skate down to the end of her nose. "Prioritize?"

Shit. Had I said that out loud?

"Then, if you look like this now . . ."

Shit shit.

"*—what kind of shape were you in last night?*"

Damn it. My head hurt, but I'd walked right into that one. And worse, I couldn't seem to think clearly enough to come up with a good lie.

"I'm fine," I said lamely.

"You could be lying in a puddle of blood, missing a head, and you'd say that!"

"Actually, if I was missing a head, I wouldn't be able—" I stopped, because Claire didn't look like she thought that was funny. I tried again. "You've seen me beat up before—"

"Not like this!"

"Yes, like this." I turned back to the sink, wetting a washcloth, hoping some of the stains on my face were just dirt. "I'm a mercenary for hire, Claire. I stick my nose in where people don't want it and they try to chop it off. It goes with the territory—"

"Bullshit!" she said furiously. "I lived with you for two years and saw you hurt less than in the last damn month. Two weeks ago, you were almost blown to pieces! A week after that, you were brought home in terrible shape by that vampire—"

"His name is Louis-Césare and I was mostly just hungover—"

"—and now I find you like *this*?"

The washcloth felt pretty good, but when I took it away, the face looked about the same. Still purple, but . . . moister. "Okay, I've had some bad luck lately."

"It isn't luck, Dory! It's those things."

"What things?" I asked, because I am stupid.

"You know what things! Vampires." It was just a word, but the tone made it an insult. I tended to forget that Claire was a teensy bit speciesist. She seemed willing to accept the fey in all their many types and permutations, but vamps were another matter.

Of course, a fey hadn't kidnapped and almost killed her, either. "The guys who grabbed you were on the wrong side," I reminded her.

"There is no side, Dory! Or if there is, it's their own—

their good, *their* interests. I don't even know how you got home like this!"

"I brought her," someone said quietly. And Claire and I both jumped, because neither of us had heard the approach of the handsome auburn-haired vamp in the doorway.

Claire also gave a little shriek, but it sounded more like outrage than shock. "How did you get in here?"

"I walked," Louis-Cesare said, not helping matters.

But he didn't look much like he cared. In fact, his expression was pretty scary, although fear wasn't really the primary emotion I was feeling as he came up behind me. A hand went to my face, turning it up to the light.

"There are wards," Claire said, glaring at him.

"Hm."

"And a garden full of fey!"

"So there are." The words themselves weren't insulting, but the tone had the same casual arrogance that regularly got him into trouble with all kinds of people. Like a certain redheaded half-fey, who looked like she was about to knock his hand away.

But she didn't, maybe because she saw the same thing I felt—the swelling in my bruised mouth going down as a calloused thumb swept across it, the lip returning more or less to its correct shape, the heat pooling low and intense in my—

Okay, maybe not that last part.

But it wasn't the excitement that worried me as our eyes met in the mirror. Hands came up to frame my face, big and warm and soothing, like the thumbs stroking along my cheekbones. It should have really ticked me off—the conceit of it, the more than a hint of possession, the presumption that he could just walk into my bathroom anytime he liked and—

And I didn't care. I wanted to turn in to the feel of those hands, wanted to sink into all that warmth, wanted to preen like a cat being stroked, wanted—

Wanted.

And it scared the hell out of me.

Chapter Four

I didn't notice when Claire left. I wasn't even sure *if* she left. I was finding it hard to concentrate with those big hands cupping my face, smoothing out my bruises as easily as someone wiping away makeup.

"Thought I took care of this last night," he murmured, warm, rough fingers gentling away the pain. "But I am not so good at this."

I wanted to ask what he meant, wanted to ask about last night, but I didn't. Because he was wrong. He was really, really good at this.

A swipe of his thumbs and I looked like I was wearing war paint in reverse, with swaths of paler skin showing through the eggplant. Another pass and only a faint mauve blush remained along my cheekbones. One more and even that was gone, my cheeks blooming pink with health—or maybe with something else.

The whole process should have been fascinating. I'd been healed a time or two in the past, but hadn't been in a state to notice the fine details. And they weren't getting my full attention now. I was too busy wanting to catch one of those talented fingers between my teeth, to bite down and feel the flesh give, to suck the sting away afterward, to—

To do a lot of stupid stuff that would only make a bad matter worse, I thought, catching sight of a spill of lustrous pink in the mirror.

The sun was streaming through the sheers over my windows, lighting up dust motes in the air and gleaming on the extravagant satin confection on my bed. Framed against the faded blue cotton of my comforter, it might as well have been lit in neon. *Damn it.*

Why lingerie? I thought resentfully. Of all the things he could have bought me, why did it have to be—

But of course, I knew why. It was the sort of gift a guy got a girl when he hoped he'd get a chance to see it on her. And then maybe to rip it off her. And that would have been fine; that would have been just dandy. A racy little red number, or a long slinky black thing, something cheap so I wouldn't care if it ended up in a couple pieces the next day? No problem-o.

But this?

This had expectations written all over it.

Expectations that I was going to fuck up royally because I wasn't the kind of gal who wore designer nightwear and knew what all the forks were for. I was the kind of gal who thought the nightgown drawer was where old T-shirts went to die and who had only started using forks in the last century. And who frankly still thought them kind of a waste when there were perfectly good knives handy.

Shit.

I swallowed and closed my eyes, but it didn't help. Maybe because the calloused thumbs were keeping up the slow caress, smoothing over my cheeks and down to my jaw, then back up into the hairline, massaging my throbbing head until the pain gave up and melted away. And then migrating to areas where there was no pain, where there never had been any, as if mapping my features: the arch of my brows, the sweep of my lashes, the bridge of my nose, and back down to catch on my lips.

Which was how I ended up sucking on a vampire's fingers when it was the last thing I ought to be doing.

How had I gotten myself into this?

Of course, I knew how. He'd caught me in a weak moment. I'd been hurt and he'd been kind, not to mention scorching hot, and for a minute there I'd actually let myself believe that this could sort of maybe kind of work, at least for a little while . . . maybe. . . .

Only it couldn't. Because dhampirs don't have relationships. Dhampirs have the occasional one-night stand in between bouts of madness, in which they hope their partner doesn't piss them off and they end up eating his face. I think my max "relationship" had lasted five days, and that had been an aberration. And this one had already lasted longer than that, if relationship was the term for two people who spent most of their time arguing and trying to kill each other.

Not that I was feeling particularly homicidal at the moment. I was feeling weirdly boneless, a strange, warm, drifting feeling, untethered, like I might just float away. Until he gripped my shoulders, grounding me.

When I opened my eyes again, my face was clear, my pupils dark, my skin flushed and my lips red and full. I looked drugged, but I'd been there enough times to know this wasn't it. This was better.

And it didn't help when the hands pulled me back against a warm, hard chest. I'd never thought of myself as delicate before I met Louis-Cesare, but I looked it next to six feet four inches of muscle barely contained by a navy sweater and jeans. The dark fabric made my paleness stand out starkly, like a reverse silhouette, and the hard lines of his body caused my curves to look softer, sweeter, strangely vulnerable—

And the record scratched again, because that wasn't me, that big-eyed waif in the mirror. I wasn't vulnerable. I never had been. I didn't need some guy to come along and take care of me, because I was perfectly capable of doing that myself, as I'd been proving for, oh, five centuries now. I didn't need outrageously expensive nightgowns that didn't even look like me. That looked completely *un*like me, in fact, like he hadn't even thought about it, like it hadn't crossed his mind how ridiculous I would look in a goddamn satin pussy bow and—

I didn't need *this*.

"What is it?" Louis-Cesare asked as I struggled out of his grasp, reaching for my robe.

"Nothing."

"Then why are you getting dressed?"

"Maybe I don't like being the only naked one in the room," I said sarcastically.

And immediately regretted it.

"That is easily remedied," he told me, and pulled off his sweater. And damn it, that wasn't what I'd meant.

But Louis-Cesare wasn't a guy who understood half measures. He was either all in or all out, and it was kind of obvious which side he'd taken on this particular question. Before I could say anything, he'd slipped off his belt, toed off his shoes and somehow managed to peel himself out of those tight-ass jeans—

And proved that it wasn't only the jeans that were tight. He bent over to drape his clothes across the tub, making my breath catch. It was a mouthwatering view, and then he turned around and gave me a better one. Completely unself-conscious in the way all vampires are after a few years, because when people can hear your every thought, modesty takes on a whole new meaning.

Not that he needed it.

Rumor had it that his father had actually been the Duke of Buckingham, instead of anybody with "de Bourbon" for a last name. This was the Buckingham who had started out as a plain old mister in James I's reign and ended up a freaking *duke*, the most powerful person in the country outside the royal family, mainly because of the way he filled out a pair of hose. He'd been called the best-looking man in England, something I hadn't heard until I met Louis-Cesare and started looking a few things up. But I had no trouble believing it.

No trouble at all.

Louis-Cesare was smiling, just a brief twist of his lips, but it was enough to set me off. "Are you listening to my thoughts again?" I demanded, because that was one side effect of fey wine—it tapped into my usually dormant mental abilities.

"No."

"Liar."

He stretched in a ripple of muscle, and flashed me an honest-to-God grin. "I don't need to read your mind when it is all over your face."

And okay, that's it, I decided, and started for the door, only to have him catch my hand and spin me back against him. "I like when it's on your face," he murmured.

"Well, you shouldn't," I said harshly, trying to drag the damned robe on.

"And why not?"

"You know why! This is a bad idea."

"Perhaps I like a challenge."

"Perhaps you're a glutton for punishment!"

"Perhaps I am in love."

I stopped knotting the tie of the robe and looked up. And met clear blue eyes, which were suddenly far more serious than I knew how to handle. "That's ... You ..." I stopped and licked my lips. "That's not how this is supposed to go."

"How is it supposed to go?" He looked genuinely curious.

"We trade witty banter for another minute and then I storm out."

"Do you wish to storm out?"

"Yes!" And it wasn't a lie. In that moment, I really, really wanted to get out of there. I wasn't in the headspace for this battle right now. I wasn't stupid; I'd known it was coming. But this wasn't the time. I hadn't figured out what I wanted to say yet. And I was tired and hurting and confused, and the arms he wrapped around me felt really good, like the hard chest he pulled me against, human warm under my cheek in defiance of all the legends.

"Then at least allow me to finish healing you."

I didn't say yes. But I didn't say no, either, and when he turned me back toward the mirror, I let him. And when his hands went to the robe, I let him manipulate that, too, unknotting the tie, pulling it out of the loops, parting the soft old velour, but leaving it hanging on my shoulders like a frame for my body.

Somehow that made me look even more nude, and as a barrier, the robe was less than worthless. The velvety folds caught and enhanced the warmth radiating from the body behind me, and the thin material did nothing to camouflage the hard lines of the chest and hips and legs pressed against mine. If anything, it magnified the differences between us, soft and hard, small and big, cold and oh, so warm.

Damn it, I should have grabbed a towel, I thought resentfully as big hands slid around my waist.

The darkest bruises lined my rib cage, like somebody had been stomping on it with a boot. And even with everything, it was still amazing to watch the skin change under his fingers, to see the prints they left behind in pale, perfect flesh when he moved them. Power, so like mine but so different, pushed into me with each touch, waves of it, as though he was massaging it straight into my skin. I could feel it mingling with my own, warm and tingling as it sped up a process that should have taken hours or days into bare moments, until he brushed the bruises away like cobwebs.

It shouldn't have surprised me. Louis-Cesare and I sprang from the same line—kissing cousins, in vampire terms—with his maker being the brother of my sire. And that line had always been known for its healing gifts. Among others, I thought, as those hands moved up the lattice of my ribs to cradle my breasts, to circle my nipples to aching hardness, to push back down my torso and frame my sex.

And suddenly, this wasn't feeling so soothing anymore.

I tried to turn around—to leave, or maybe to touch him, too, I wasn't real clear on motives right then—but he wouldn't let me. He pulled one of my arms around his neck, causing my body to arch outward. His eyes met mine in the mirror, daring me to look away as his fingers smoothed over my stomach, around my navel, and then began to card possessively through my curls.

He didn't say anything. Neither did I, even though I knew I should stop this. We were looking at a whole world of complicated here, and not just because of my varied hang-ups. I somehow didn't think the vampire community was going to be too pleased when their former golden boy showed up with a dhampir girlfriend. Not when he was already hanging by a thread.

Until a few weeks ago, Louis-Cesare had been a leading member of the European Senate, one of the ruling bodies for the vampire community, like the North American Senate was for ours. And he hadn't been just any old member, but their Enforcer, the position that did exactly what its name implied. Powerful, respected, even feared—in vampire terms he'd had it all.

Including a secret that, two weeks ago, brought it all down.

It turned out that the lover he'd had for centuries wasn't his lover at all. She was a revenant, a woman he had tried to save from an early death by making her a vampire, only to have the process go terribly, tragically wrong. It had left her dangerously mad and him with a legal obligation as her maker to end her life. Instead, wracked by guilt, he had kept her with him, violating one of the most important vampire laws in the process. And when her hatred of her own kind finally led her to try to destroy the Senate, the truth came out, and Louis-Cesare had been in a world of trouble.

A lesser vampire would have probably gotten the ax—literally. Louis-Cesare just got it figuratively, losing his position on the Senate and remaining under a cloud of suspicion. But in vampire terms, that was bad enough, because they aren't big on third chances. The last thing he needed was another unsuitable lover.

The last thing he needed was mc.

But it didn't look like he saw it that way, judging by how his grip had tightened. A knee spread my legs from behind, and a hand grasped my thigh, pulling it up and draping it over his, laying me open. His eyes darkened, blue shadowed to charcoal to almost black as his fingers began to fondle, to explore, making me watch as he pleasured me until my own eyes closed again in desperation.

The only reason dhampirs weren't the lowest rung of vampire society was that we weren't even on the ladder. We weren't supposed to exist—the whole dead thing playing hell with fertility—and were conceived only through some pretty bizarre circumstances. In my case, my father had been cursed with vampirism, rather than bitten, and the curse took a few days to complete the transformation. Leaving him plenty of time to sire an abomination that, like the hated revenants, was supposed to be put down as soon as he learned of its existence.

Luckily for me, Mircea had a major family fixation and a bad habit of ignoring rules he found inconvenient. He also had the devil's own luck at getting away with things others paid dearly for. Others like Louis-Cesare. Who had somehow managed to find the only girlfriend the Senate would hate more than his last one.

His hands slid over me, my breasts, my belly, my mound, moving easily across my sweat-slick skin. His tongue ran up my neck to my ear, hot breath ruffling my brain, teeth tugging on my lobe. He bit down just as his fingers made a move inside me that shot sparks straight up my spine. My body bucked against him, clenching desperately in unwanted pleasure.

I squirmed, my hand tightening in his hair, holding on as the turmoil in my mind and the pleasure in my body tried their best to drive me crazy. I wanted to shove him out the window for his own good; I wanted to drag him to the bed for mine. I wanted to shut the door in his face and never see him again; I wanted to sink my teeth into his neck, scarring him, putting a claim on him that everyone could see. I wanted to scream at him for being stupid, and stubborn, and for not understanding that, yes, it did matter what people thought if those people *could kill you.* That sometimes the rules did apply, even to ex-senators, maybe especially to ex-senators. I wanted to curl up with him under the covers and forget the world existed and whisper stupid shit that didn't matter because life wasn't a fucking fairy tale and it never had a goddamn happy ending and—and—

And my thoughts fractured, the room spun, and I came with a sound of pure desperation.

Which, in retrospect, probably wasn't the best idea when you live with a bunch of sensorially gifted creatures. Who, it seemed, couldn't tell the difference between a cry of passion and a cry of pain. As was demonstrated when the bedroom door suddenly blew off its hinges and Louis-Cesare flew backward and disappeared.

Leaving me blinking in confusion at the new, vampire-shaped hole in my dresser.

And my closet.

And my wall.

Which were less noticeable than you might think with an eight-hundred-pound dragon taking up most of the space in the room.

For a moment, it looked at me, and I looked at it, and the dozen or so blond-haired fey swarming into the room through the door looked at both of us. And then a slight tinge of amethyst slowly suffused the delicate scales covering the beast's cheekbones as it took in my lack of clothes—and blood and gore and missing limbs. "Oops?" it said gruffly, before melting back into my very embarrassed redheaded roommate.

I snatched my robe closed and plunged through my destroyed furniture and fluttering bits of wallpaper, into a closet that was now a wreck of plaster and hanging two-by-fours. And found that, yes, the hole did go completely through the house. Parts of my wardrobe were scattered all over the side lawn, with most of my bras for some reason decorating the neighbor's fence. But that was better than what had happened to my boyfriend, who had ended up—

Oh, *shit*.

"Dory, what—oh," Claire said in a small voice, coming to stand beside me.

Being two stories up, we had a perfect view of the car that had just pulled into the grassy drive along the side of the house, probably because it couldn't fit anywhere else since it was a stretch limo. A stretch limo that now had a naked vampire sticking out of the ruined windshield, firmly wedged between the wipers and the mirror. Right in front of a driver whose usual icy sangfroid had been shattered by an up-close-and-personal view of the world's greatest ass.

At least it can't get any worse, I thought, and then

three more vamps piled out of the backseat. And came around the car. And looked at Louis-Cesare, who was ignoring them in favor of staring up at me, an unreadable expression on his face.

"Should I apologize?" Claire asked, sounding worried.

"That ... probably wouldn't be the best idea right now," I said calmly, looking down at two Senate members and a senator's brother.

I was debating the odds that I could come up with some story to explain an underwear-strewn yard and a naked master vampire, when the brother looked up. "Oh, they do this sort of thing all the time," he said, responding to some question I hadn't heard. He shaded his eyes, and then a smile broke out over his handsome features. "Oh, there you are. Hello, Dory!"

He waved.

The other vampires turned to look at me, and I gave up. I went back into the bedroom, which had miraculously cleared of fey. Except for the one behind me, biting her lip.

"Dory—"

"It's okay."

"But the room—"

"It's fine."

"And your clothes—"

"I'll get them later."

"Later?" She frowned, watching me climb into the bed that I never should have left, earthquake be damned. "What are you going to do now?"

"Go back to sleep," I told her, dragging a pillow over my face.

And a moment later I heard her gently shut the door.

Chapter Five

Of course, I didn't really get any sleep. That would have been a little hard with a largish hole in the wall letting in the sounds of bass thumping out of a car radio, a neighbor mowing his lawn and a bunch of lilting fey voices laughing to each other as they chased my underwear. And somebody screaming bloody murder.

The pillow stayed over my face for a few minutes, anyway, because I really didn't want to know. But I finally faced reality. If I didn't go down soon, someone would come up, and I preferred to deal with whatever this was properly dressed.

I chose black—tank top, jeans, boots. Because that was what the cataclysm had left me and because it seemed appropriate. And then I had a drink, or two, from the bottle stashed under my bed, because this was going to be no kind of fun.

That had been a given from the moment I saw a certain curly-haired vamp climbing out of the back of the limo. The others might be explained away as family on a visit, although that was hardly a regular occurrence. But Kit Marlowe was the dreaded spymaster for the North American Vampire Senate, and he didn't pay social calls.

So I knew this was going to suck even before I found a smoking vampire in the hallway.

He wasn't Marlowe, or one of the other illustrious types who, by the sound of things, were camped out in the kitchen. He was about a foot too short, for one thing, and completely lacking in sartorial splendor for another.

And the overlarge nose and pointed face were a bit too ratlike.

And then there was the smoke, which wasn't coming from a cigarette.

He caught sight of me heading down the stairs and immediately turned around and showed me his rear. "Is my ass on fire?"

"Good morning to you, too."

"Screw that and look at my butt!"

"Do I have to?"

"Damn it, yes! I'm dying here!"

I checked out the part in question, because today was already shot to hell, and found it covered by a scorched pair of khakis. They looked a little weird, and I finally figured out why. The scorching was coming from the inside.

I grinned. It wasn't the worst predicament I'd seen him in. The vampire's name was Ray, and he'd been a slimy nightclub owner when I met him—and soon thereafter beheaded him—on the order of the Senate, who didn't care if he watered the drinks but did care very much about the illegal weapons he was smuggling in from Faerie. That should have been all she wrote, but one of the items he'd recently brought in happened to be the talisman now decorating the chubby body of Claire's young son.

It was why she was visiting. The talisman had been stolen from the royal house Claire was shortly to join, and she'd come chasing it—because it gave its wearer almost complete invincibility. And although we'd finally managed to get it back, for a while, Ray had been that owner. Only it looked like whatever residual help he'd gotten had worn off.

"Your butt's on fire," I agreed, and had an evil blue gaze aimed at me from over his shoulder.

"Well, don't just stand there! *Do something!*"

I edged around him and went into the kitchen, where, sure enough, four master vampires were hanging out, trying to pretend they belonged. That was despite the fact that one of them was wearing Claire's terry-cloth bathrobe, which was knee-length and roomy on her, but which hit him midthigh and showed a distractingly large wedge of chest. It didn't matter, since only one of them had a hope in hell of blending in anyway, and Louis-Cesare wasn't that guy.

Neither was the vamp he was glaring at for some reason. Kit Marlowe had the aforementioned curly brown hair, a pretentious little goatee and an attitude problem. He was currently leaning against the sink, arms crossed, face stuck in a snarl that showed a tiny bit of fang. That might have had something to do with the fact that he was visiting a dhampir, a creature he ranked slightly below rodentia. Or because the window he'd parked himself in front of was streaming sunlight onto the back of his head, slowly roasting his brains.

But he didn't move because he was badass like that.

"Is there a reason Ray is smelling up the hallway?" I asked, filling a jug from the tap.

"Because he's an idiot?" Marlowe snapped.

"I'm not the one who dragged me out here in the middle of the damned day!" came floating in the door.

"No, you're the one who panicked and ran screaming down the middle of the damned road."

"Because somebody broke the damned windshield!"

"With his body, which plugged the damned hole nicely," observed the fabulous creature at the kitchen table. Unlike Marlowe, he was sitting well out of the sun, because he wasn't badass at all and didn't care who knew it. He accepted a cup of coffee from Claire, who was looking faintly appalled. "Thank you, my dear."

I wasn't sure if Claire's expression had more to do with fear that a guest was about to combust or awe at the spectacle that was my uncle Radu. Because that blending-in thing? That really wasn't Radu's style.

Not that his current outfit was showing him to best advantage. He looked like he'd been plucked from his lab at vamp HQ, where he did nefarious things he wasn't allowed to talk about, without being given time to change. Because he was in boring old work clothes. Of course, for him, that translated into head-to-toe sapphire satin to complement his glossy dark hair, white silk hose to show off his fine calves, and no-doubt-genuine diamond buckles on his high-heeled shoes. He looked like the Blue Boy all grown up and fabulous.

His attire had been the height of male fashion in the mid-seventeenth century, which was the last time Radu had bothered to update his wardrobe. But sitting in a circa 1950s-era kitchen, drinking Sanka out of a chipped New York Giants mug, he was breathtakingly out of place. Like a curious peacock slumming with the pigeons in Central Park.

"And when he climbed out, what was I supposed to do then?" Ray demanded.

"Preferably something that did not involve running into the middle of a public highway to cower under your jacket with your ass in the air," Marlowe said drily.

"Hey! Not everybody is almighty first level, you know. Some of us still burn up in sunlight!"

"If only."

"Oh, sure. Insult me while I'm *on fire*. And while we wait for my master to come kill me. And if that don't work— "

"*I'm* going to kill you," Marlowe muttered.

"Hey, come at me, bro!" Ray said, appearing in the doorway, all spiky black hair and outraged expression. And then dodging back into the darkened hall, before anything else started smoldering. "What you got, huh? What you got?" drifted around the doorframe.

"You're only encouraging him," Mircea said, looking amused. And completely at home, because unlike the rest of our visitors, he never seemed out of place anywhere.

It was a good trick, since daddy dearest had the same dark coloring and handsome features as his brother, minus Radu's delicacy and stunning turquoise eyes. But Mircea stood out only when it would benefit him. Case in point: he'd left the car in a navy business suit similar to the russet one Marlowe was wearing. But one look at the dilapidated Victorian slowly moldering on its weed–choked lawn, and he'd realized that this Would Not Do.

The result was a missing jacket and tie, a popped collar, and sleeves pushed up to the elbows.

And the attitude matched the new look. Unlike Radu, who was peering around like a tourist at an exhibit on "The Habitat of the Modern American Brooklynite," Mircea could have been any corporate drone relaxing with family after a long day of cubicle sitting. It was an impression heightened when he swung Claire's young son into his lap.

To be fair, it had been the kid's idea. Aiden had toddled over from his nest of toys and blankie in the corner to tug on the new arrival's pant leg. And was now balancing on his thighs, looking at him with lively curiosity, two little fists bunched in what was no doubt a painfully expensive shirt.

It didn't surprise me; for some crazy reason, children liked Mircea. As did their mothers, as evidenced by the fact that Claire had yet to knock him through a wall despite his undoubted vampire-ness. What was odd was that Mircea genuinely liked them back.

The outfit adjustment was pure bullshit, but the indulgent smile he was aiming at the towheaded tot was the real deal. It made no sense at all because he was otherwise a ruthless, scheming son of a bitch with a take-no-prisoners attitude when it came to getting what he wanted. But there you go. Humans are weird, and vampires used to be human. And they sure as hell didn't lose any of their quirks when they transitioned.

"He's a fine boy," Mircea told Claire, who had stuffed her hands behind her back, probably to keep them from snatching her baby back. But then Mircea transferred the smile to her, all whiskey-dark eyes with little crinkles at the corners, and honest, self-deprecating humor—the kind that had made him the most successful negotiator the Senate had ever had. And Claire blinked.

It was funny, because she relaxed almost to the point of smiling. And then got angry at herself for it and tensed up again, only to bite her lip in confusion as two strong instincts battled it out. I thought there was a chance that the great negotiator might actually lose this round, because Claire had taken overprotectiveness to a whole new level. But then—

"Does anybody care that I'm dying out here?"

I sighed, turned off the water and went back into the hall, only to find Ray rubbing himself lewdly on the wallpaper. He'd already singed it in a long, dark streak, which was less of a concern than the eww factor. "Quit that!" I told him, and grabbed his tie.

"Don't start," he gasped. "I got hemorrhoids that don't hurt this bad."

"Vampires don't get hemorrhoids."

"We don't get 'em, no. But if we already got 'em when we die, they stick around, and I've been nursing these for four hundred years. So don't tell me I don't know pain, okay? I *know* pain, and this—"

"I won't tell you anything if you'll just *stop talking.*" I spun him around, bent him over and dumped half a gallon of water onto his smoking ass.

Which just made it smoke more, and start to sizzle. "Ow! Ow, ow, ow, ow, ow! What the hell are you doing?"

"Trying to put the fire out," I said, starting to get worried, because that should have worked. But then, what did I know? I'd set plenty of vamps ablaze through the years, but this was the first time I'd tried to extinguish one. And it didn't appear to be going well.

"A little help here," I said, sticking my head back into the kitchen.

"Try this," Claire said, grabbing something out of a cabinet. "I keep it around for kitchen burns and it's usually really—"

She stopped because she'd gotten close enough to catch sight of Ray, on the floor with his butt in the air, like the world's worst stripper. The khakis were still in place, thank God, but the seat had burnt out in two little moons, like assless chaps. The image was heightened by the fact that he was grinding and humping and wiggling in a way that would have gotten him a g-string full of exactly nothing because nobody was going to pay to see that.

"I told you to cut it out," I said, jerking him up.

"And I told you to *do* something, and I ain't seen—"
He paused when I shoved the small jar of ointment into
his hand. "What's this?"

"The cure for what ails you."

"Well, what are you waiting for? Spread it on." And
he turned his back and bent over again.

I looked hopefully at Claire, who had trained as a
nurse. But it looked like the Florence Nightingale gene
stopped just short, because she was in full-on retreat.
Great.

I regarded the gyrating moons, which were currently
as smooth as a baby's bottom since most of the hair had
singed off. *Just when you think the day can't get any
worse,* I thought grimly. And then I slapped on a palm-
ful of pale green goo.

"*OW!* What the hell?"

"Hold still," I told him, smacking on another blob.
The stuff was slippery and it kept oozing off the burnt
part.

"How can I hold still when you're beating on me?
Hey, hey, somebody, she's *beating me!*"

"Any moment now," I grumbled, and grabbed him
when he tried to run.

But he was smoking and panicked and now also slippery, and it was like trying to catch a greased pig. "Let
me go, you crazy bitch!"

"I'm trying to help you, you stupid— Oof!" I took a
heel in the stomach and an elbow to the chin before I
managed to wrestle him to the floor and sit on his legs.
Which gave me a chance to finish gooping him up while
he yelled and cursed and bucked like a rodeo bull.

And then suddenly stopped, and craned his head over
his shoulder to look at the damaged area. It was shiny
and pink and pimply, the parts that weren't faintly green.
But at least it was no longer smoking. "Hey. Hey, that
feels pretty good."

"So glad you approve."

"Yeah, it's okay." He thought about it for a moment.
"But I think I still feel a little bit of a burn. Maybe you
ought to massage it in some more. You know, really get

in there and—" He cut off, noticing the bare feet that had stopped in front of him. The ones attached to the strong calves and muscular thighs and terry-clothed torso of the guy glaring down at him. "Or, you know. Not."

I slapped the last of the salve on, just to hear him squeal, and then climbed off. "Your things are where you left them," I told Louis-Cesare, who nodded and edged past, giving me a hell of a view as he made his way up the stairs.

"No way he really looks like that," Ray said enviously. "It's probably just a glamourie. I bet he's really got zits and a potbelly and saggy buns."

I bit my lip. I could personally guarantee that absolutely no part of Louis-Cesare sagged. "You know he can hear you, right?"

"Like I care. I mean, what's he gonna do to me? What's anybody gonna do? I'm already a dead man."

"Yeah. You're a vampire."

"Not that kind of dead. Not the good kind—"

"There's a good kind?"

"Not lately. My life is hell," he said melodramatically. And then he paused, obviously waiting for me to ask why.

I let him wait.

The scene in the kitchen hadn't changed, except that my ward or son or possibly pet—the jury was still out—had also left the blankie and clambered up onto the seat next to Mircea. And was eyeing him suspiciously, like he didn't trust him.

Smart boy.

I sat down and scooped Stinky into my lap.

"And who is this ... young man?" Mircea guessed, because Stinky's brown fur was poking out of the sides of a diaper and a pale blue undershirt. The matching booties were nowhere to be seen, possibly eaten, or just left somewhere because they hadn't been designed to fit long monkey-like toes.

Claire noticed about the same time I did. "Where are your booties?" she demanded.

Stinky blinked huge gray baby eyes at her, and attempted to look innocent. But there was a self-satisfied air about him that did not bode well for the despised footwear. I stifled a smile.

"He likes being naked," I reminded her.

"Well, he's going to learn to like clothes," she said adamantly. Stinky and I exchanged glances. We had our doubts about that.

Mircea was still looking at me, so I shrugged. "You've met him before."

"I have?" An elegant eyebrow went up. Because Mircea was not accustomed to forgetting a face. Much less one like Stinky's.

"You were a bit out of it at the time," I said, and left it at that. Bringing up the events that had led to the death of his and Radu's other brother would ruin any mood, and this one was problematic enough as it was.

Fortunately Mircea didn't pursue it. "He is fey?"

"Duergar-Brownie," I said, my chin resting on the downy fur atop Stinky's head. "He's one of the hybrid crossbreeds the Dark Circle's been littering around. I found him at an auction a while ago—"

"Fascinating," Marlowe interrupted harshly. "But can we get on with this?"

"Depends on what this is," I said, pretty sure I didn't want to know. Mircea was being too nice. This was really going to suck.

If I'd had any doubts about that, the looks the others exchanged around the room would have clued me in. "On a scale of one to ten, how bad is it?" I asked Radu, because he was the least likely to lie to me.

He pursed sculpted lips. "Sevenish? Perhaps eight?" Wonderful.

But I might as well get it over with. "Lay it on me," I told him.

"Yes, well, it's a little involved. Perhaps you could start by telling us what you recall from last night—"

"She doesn't remember a damned thing," Marlowe said sharply. "She wouldn't have asked that question if she did. I told you—"

"Anything at all could be helpful," Radu added, ignoring Marlowe with aristocratic ease. "Even small details."

And then everybody looked at me.

Claire had set a glass of orange juice at my elbow, because the arrival of unwanted guests was not going to interrupt her morning routine. I took a moment to sip it, as if gathering my thoughts, which I wasn't really doing because there weren't any to gather. But I somehow didn't think that was going to go over well.

"We know you made it as far as the marina—" Radu began, before Marlowe cut him off.

"Don't help her! If you compromise the memories, they're of no use to us!"

"The marina," I repeated blankly, and then something did stir. Something about me and a vampire and a job we were supposed to— "Crap."

"What is it?" Claire asked.

"Headache." Which was putting it mildly. A stabbing pain had just run ear to ear, like an ice pick through the brain. And why did that sound familiar?

"We need whatever you can give us, Dory," Radu said. "The smugglers are bad enough, but with the Black Circle—"

"Damn it, Radu!" Marlowe exploded.

"Oh, pish. She already knows they're working together."

"But other people don't!"

"Such as?"

"Such as a yard full of fey, not one of whom we know a damn thing about!"

"They're my security," Claire said indignantly. "And part of the royal guard."

"Oh yes?" Dark eyes flashed. "And would that be the same royal guard who betrayed you and almost got your son killed—what? Two weeks ago?"

"I'll vouch for them!"

"And who will vouch for you?"

"Kit, please. This lovely young woman isn't going to say anything," Radu said, patting her hand. And thereby saving Marlowe a world of hurt without even knowing it.

Not that he was grateful. "How the bloody hell can you—"

"She is the daughter-in-law of one of our senior fey allies," Mircea murmured. "Is she not?"

Marlowe did not look pacified, maybe because the first time they'd met, Claire had thrown him out of the house. And judging by the narrowed emerald eyes, she was contemplating an encore. "Not to mention that this area isn't secured," he continued. "There could be listening devices all over the place!"

"Like the ones you left in here that we had to remove?" Claire snapped.

"Why bother to remove them if there was nothing to hear?" Marlowe snapped back.

Claire flushed almost as red as her hair. But before she could say anything, Radu broke in. "And what if people *are* listening? Our allies already know what we're doing and our enemies . . . Well, after last night, I think it's safe to say they have figured it out."

"All right. What happened last night?" I asked, dropping the pretense. Because it was starting to look like maybe I did need to know.

"Well, that's what you're supposed to tell us," Radu said reasonably. "But I'll see what I can do to jog your memory—without compromising anything," he added before Marlowe could intervene again.

He waited a moment, but the chief spy didn't say anything else. That had a little smirk flitting around the edges of Radu's mouth that shouldn't have been there, because Marlowe was perfectly capable of delivering a smackdown if he felt like it. But it looked like he wanted the info more than he wanted to bitch about security.

"Now," Radu said complacently, "you've been working with us on a task force to destroy a network of illegal portals—"

"I know that. I lost a day, not a month, 'Du."

"Hush." He leaned over to swat my knee. And then

proceeded to tell me a lot of other things I already knew, because the Great Portal Hunt, as I had started to think of it, was the biggest thing in otherworldly vice at the moment.

All sorts of dangerous crap from Faerie was being smuggled through portals that weren't supposed to exist. Only they did, and a bunch of fat cats had been getting noticeably fatter as a result. The fattest of them all had been a douche named Geminus, who had used his portals to smuggle in Dark Fey for a series of underground fights that had gotten him a lot of money and them a lot of dead. This had continued until he recently met his own maker, and not in the vampire sense of the word. Who was probably as skeeved out as the rest of us who had known him.

But as bad as Geminus had been, things weren't any better with him dead. In fact, the reverse was true, as would-be successors popped out of the woodwork to divvy up the very large pie he had left. Lately, the infighting had been getting pretty vicious, as every crook with delusions of grandeur struggled to become the new king of the hill.

There was just one problem, namely that Geminus hadn't been the trusting type, and had failed to share the location of his portals with the riffraff. And it wasn't like they could just go out and replace them. Even the few smugglers with money and connections enough to manage it had to contend with the fact that every time a new portal was brought into existence, it lit up the metaphysical skyline like a searchlight. Which tends to be bad for businesses that run on secrecy.

So, the criminal element was trying to find Geminus's portals in order to beat each other out in the smuggling game. The Black Circle, a group of dark mages, was trying to find them to bring in more weapons for the war they were waging on the Vampire Senate. And the Senate was trying to find them to shut them down before either of the other groups got lucky. But the only person who actually knew where they were was Geminus's lieutenant, who had been smart enough to guess how much fun life would be with everybody breathing down his neck.

"Varus," I said, interrupting Radu as my memory coughed up a name.

"Yes, well, I was getting there," 'Du said.

"What about him?" Mircea asked softly.

"He agreed to give the Senate the location of the portal system in return for immunity," I said, trying to focus on slippery-soft memories that slid out of reach every time I grabbed for one.

"But that did not occur."

"No. Because he was kidnapped last night."

"Yes!" Radu looked smugly at Marlowe. "Yes, he was. And naturally, as soon as we found out, we put together a task force to go after him. But our enemies had expected that and laid a trail full of red herrings in all directions, requiring us to field numerous teams. Like the one you were on."

"I was on a team?" I asked, because I usually work alone. And because I didn't recall that at all.

Radu nodded. "You know how it is these days. No one is allowed to go anywhere alone, particularly not for something like this. And Lawrence was assigned to you."

"Then why not ask him what happened?" I asked, afraid that I already knew the answer.

"Because he's dead," Marlowe said savagely. "They're all dead. Eleven fucking senior masters were sent out and exactly none came back. We found them hacked to pieces, those we got to before the sun took care of them. Butchered—every single one." Brown eyes bored into mine. "Everyone except you."

Chapter Six

I just sat there, stunned, while Claire lit into the chief spy. "What are you implying?"

"I'm not implying anything," Marlowe told her, his eyes never leaving mine. "I am stating it outright. Eleven masters and one dhampir went out, and only the dhampir returned. *And I want to know why.*"

"You know why." The voice was Louis-Cesare's, from the doorway. I didn't know how long he'd been standing there, but apparently it had been long enough, judging by his expression.

"No, I do not!" Marlowe said, turning on him. "I know how she got out of that hellhole. I don't know how she got *in*, or why. They kill Lawrence, someone with knowledge of the inner workings of my family, of the intelligence department, of the Senate itself, yet leave a *dhampir* alive?"

Angry dark eyes swerved back to mine, but I didn't respond because I was trying to comprehend that ridiculous number. *"Eleven?"* I repeated, certain I'd heard wrong.

"Kit is exaggerating," Mircea told me. "But only slightly. Most were found as he said, although two teams remain missing. But they did not report in and no one can contact them, including their former masters."

And that wasn't good. Mental communication within a family was a given, even after a Child reached a high enough status to be emancipated from his master's control. Their makers should have been able to reach them—if there was anything left to reach.

"By 'senior masters' you mean what?" I asked, still trying to wrap my head around it.

"None under second level. Most were first."

I just stared. "No."

"I didn't believe it either," Radu said quietly. "When they told me. It just seemed . . ." He trailed off with a flutter of his hand, because he didn't have adequate words for it.

Unfortunately, someone else did.

"Seems what?" Claire asked, looking around, obviously confused. "It's a tragedy, yes, but we're only talking about eleven—"

Marlowe made a retching sound, like someone had just kicked him in the stomach, probably because he couldn't attack her.

"Claire," I said. Provoking him right now was not a good idea. Not that I thought she would deliberately do that—she was normally far more sensitive to others' feelings than I was. But Marlowe was likely to take it that way. If brown eyes could burn, his were doing it.

But Claire either didn't notice or didn't understand. "But eleven men—"

"Not men," I told her, as Radu moved to Marlowe's side. "Senior masters."

"And that makes a difference?"

"I . . . Yes," I said helplessly, because trying to explain would take too long and I wanted to get back to the point.

But that clearly wasn't happening.

Something cracked, loud as a gunshot, and I jumped, before I realized it was the counter under Marlowe's hands. "Tell her," he said harshly.

"I don't think—"

"Tell her!"

I glanced at Mircea, who didn't see it because his eyes were on the chief spy. Like his brother's hand, which had slipped onto Marlowe's shoulder. Probably in case he lost his shit and tried to go for Claire across the table.

Not that that was likely. He wasn't an idiot, and despite appearances, he didn't really suffer from a lack of impulse control. He was just furious. And only one thing caused that kind of impotent rage in a senior master.

"Lawrence was one of yours," I guessed.

There was no spoken acknowledgment; Marlowe looked like he might be past it at this point. But his head jerked down in a half nod. And at least a few things started to make sense.

I glanced at Claire, who had figured out that she'd stepped in it, but wasn't sure how. "Senior masters are like . . . supernatural tanks," I told her, even though it was a lousy analogy. In a contest between the two, the tank would be toast. "They have abilities that are hard to explain—"

"I know what vampires can do," she said quietly.

"No. You really don't." I glanced around, but no one was stopping me—or helping, and this wasn't exactly easy to explain. The basics, yes, but conveying the scale . . . It was like trying to describe a trillion dollars. Newscasters threw that number around all the time, but it was hard to get a grip on it—until you were standing in the middle of a city block hip-deep in hundred-dollar bills.

"You know how a master vamp is stronger than a regular one, right?" I finally asked.

"Of course."

"A lot stronger."

"Yes."

"Well, take that difference, and increase it by an exponential amount, every time a master goes up a level. It's not just a step higher, it's . . . a different world," I said, floundering, because there really was no way to convey the difference.

But Claire seemed to understand something, because her eyes narrowed. "You're saying that—what's the next to lowest level of master? Sixth?"

I nodded.

"You're saying that a sixth-level master compared to a seventh is like a seventh-level compared to someone like . . . like Ray?"

"Hey!" Drifted in from the hall.

"No," I told her, biting my lip. "Ray is a master—"

"As hard as that is to believe," Radu murmured.

"—he's just not a very good one."

"Okay, that's enough!" Ray said, appearing in the doorway. And then dodging out again shouting, "Shit, shit!"

Claire looked after him, frowning slightly. Clearly, he was messing with the tidy little box in her mental file labeled VAMPIRE, which wasn't supposed to contain anything quite that pathetic. "Okay, so it would be like comparing a seventh-level to a regular old vampire?"

I thought about it, and decided that was actually pretty close. "Something like that."

"So each level . . ." Claire wrinkled her forehead. "It's like they're strong enough to be a master to the next level down?"

"That depends on the individual. Power varies a lot within levels, even before you get to first—"

"And what happens at first?"

"It isn't really a level. It's more a catchall for anyone who's too powerful to fit into the system anymore. It basically means, well—"

"Really, really powerful."

"Yes."

"So these masters you sent out last night, you're saying they were the equivalent of what? Eleven war mages?"

Louis-Cesare snorted.

Claire frowned.

"More like eleven armies," I said, since she was looking at me.

"Then why are they dead? If they were so strong—"

"That is the question," Mircea said, cutting Kit off, who had been about to say something rude, by the look of him. "We not only sent some of our best agents, but we sent them in pairs, with each selected to complement the other's strengths and weaknesses. They were ordered to locate Varus and then to call for assistance, if need be, from a group of additional operatives we had standing by. No one called."

"Then whatever happened, happened fast," I said, thinking about a vampire's lightning reflexes.

Mircea nodded. "I would assume a trap or snare, although there are few that would be sufficient. And our people have been trained to recognize and avoid those. But even if I am able to accept that both operatives on a team forgot their training, or were somehow overwhelmed in another way, I cannot believe it for all six! Nor can I account for why none of them managed to send a warning."

And yet, he was going to have to, I realized. Mircea was in charge of coordinating the Senate's anti-smuggling crusade, which drew assistance from other senators' families. Other senators who were probably already demanding to know what had happened to their people. And if he couldn't tell them . . . Well, I didn't actually know what would happen if he couldn't tell them, but I doubted it would be anything good.

I wondered what he planned to do about it.

"If they didn't send a warning, how did you know Dory was in trouble?" Claire asked.

"I didn't." Mircea glanced at Louis-Cesare.

"I heard her scream, in my mind," he said briefly. "It was cut off, almost immediately, but the voice was unmistakable. I knew approximately where she was from the last time her team had reported in, and was able to track her from there."

"But I thought you couldn't . . . not unless she was—" Claire looked at me, the frown growing. "I thought you weren't taking that stuff anymore."

There was no need to ask what "stuff" she meant, since there was only one thing that ramped up my mental abilities. It also helped to control my fits, but so did living with a magical null like Claire. And the wine had a lot of other side effects, like decreasing my edge in battle, that had me worried.

I hadn't worked out a long-term solution yet, like what I was going to do when she went back to Faerie. But my usage lately had gone way, way down. Too much so to explain how Louis-Cesare had been able to tune into my brain like a freaking shortwave radio.

"I am not able to read your mind," he said, reading my mind.

"What the hell!"

"But when you are in trouble, you project—"

"Not halfway across a city!"

"I was not halfway across a city," he said calmly. "I was leading the response team, which meant I was in Manhattan—"

"Okay, not across two miles, then!"

I didn't know why I was so upset, but suddenly it felt like the walls were closing in. I abruptly stood up, even though there was zero chance of going anywhere until they were finished with me. But it was like Marlowe and the counter; he'd had to crack it or someone's skull, and I had to move—now—or run screaming down the road like Ray.

Stinky snarled and spit in my arms, not because I was squeezing him too tight but because he was trying to get away. We had a lot in common, and he wanted to sink his teeth into somebody. Fey are formidable pretty much from the day they're born, as far as I can tell, but while he couldn't really hurt anyone in this group, the reverse wasn't true.

"It's okay," I told him, stroking his soft baby hair, but I wasn't sure who I was talking to—him or me.

"It is not 'okay.' You are upset," Louis-Cesare said, undoing whatever soothing qualities Stinky had imparted.

"Stop doing that!"

"I do not need to read your mind to know that, Dorina. You are backing away—"

"I am not!" I said, right before my butt bumped into the counter. "And how do I know you aren't?"

"Because I have just told you. And what difference would it make if I was? Why are you angry?"

"Maybe I don't like someone messing around in my head!"

"Messing around?" His forehead knitted.

"For God's sake!" He ran into English problems at the most convenient times. "It means—"

"I know what it means. What I do not understand is why it is a problem."

"Why?" I just stared at him. "Why wouldn't it be? Would you want me doing it to you?"

"I would not care," he said, and actually looked like he meant it. "And in any case, it has happened before—"

"Rarely! And not at will!"

"—and you do not need to do it to me. You have my memories. All of them."

I blinked, because I hadn't realized he knew about that. A metaphysical accident had resulted in a colossal info dump shortly after I met him—four hundred years of Louis-Cesare's memories straight into mine. I hadn't wanted them, hadn't asked for them, didn't want them now. I just didn't know how to get rid of them.

I also didn't know why he was just standing there like it was no big deal. If anything, he looked impatient, as if I was the one being weird here. He also looked like he wanted an answer, which was a little hard because I wasn't sure what the question was.

"That's . . . different," I finally said.

"How so?"

"That was an accident. And anyway, I never look at your memories."

"I know that you do not."

I took a second to yank Stinky back, who was still trying to scratch out the eyes of this strange creature who had offended me. "And how do you know that, if you're not in my head?"

"You did not know about Christine," he said, referring to the revenant who had landed him in his current mess. "You had my memories, all of them, at your fingertips. Yet you did not recognize her when you saw her."

And for some crazy reason, he looked almost insulted by that.

"They're *your* memories," I said, like I somehow needed to point this out. "I don't have the right—"

"You do," he said, coming toward me.

"I do not."

"I give it to you freely—"

"I don't want it!" I said, and my back hit the door.

Louis-Cesare stopped. For a moment we just looked at each other. And then he frowned.

"I was surprised," he finally said, "when I realized the truth. But I assumed it was due to your fear of intimacy—"

"I don't have a fear of intimacy!"

"—or your lack of desire for intimacy with me. But when you demonstrated that that was not the case—"

Claire made a little sound, whether of outrage or sympathy I couldn't tell.

"—naturally I wondered why you had not attempted to know me better. At the time, I put it down to living with humans and their secretive ways."

"Better than the reverse," Claire muttered, and tried to take Stinky, probably to leave my hands free in case I wanted to choke a certain vampire.

But I held on. Stinky's less-than-perfect social skills were keeping Louis-Cesare at arm's length. And right now, that was where I wanted him.

"But now I am forced to conclude that perhaps I was right in the beginning," he said stiffly. "Despite not objecting to physical intimacy—"

"Shut. Up," I begged, but of course he didn't. Vampires didn't have the same concept of privacy that humans did, and Louis-Cesare had obviously kept things bottled up as long as he was going to.

"—you do not wish anything more substantive than that. Or am I wrong?"

He stood there, arms crossed, blue eyes flashing. Completely oblivious to the audience, not one of whom was looking away or even pretending to mind his own business. Radu even looked like he might be taking mental notes.

"We're not talking about this now," I said, suppressing an impulse to grind my teeth.

"Then when?"

"*Some other time!* Right now we're talking about you

picking something out of my brain that you shouldn't have been able to hear."

"I naturally assumed it was because you had recently ingested fey wine," Louis-Cesare said. His expression made it clear that this wasn't over.

"She doesn't do that anymore," Claire said, glaring at him. Somehow she and I had ended up on one side of the room and the vampires on the other, a fact that was not lost on Louis-Cesare.

The frown tipped into a scowl. "Of course she does. Although I see no reason why it should concern you."

"It concerns me because I'm her friend! And it's dangerous!"

"And that has stopped Dorina when?" he demanded.

"Can we get back to the part about you reading my mind?" I asked, because this was veering into dangerous territory. "You say you can't, but a week ago you heard me all the way from Chinatown, and you were in Brooklyn."

I'd gotten involved in a dustup courtesy of Ray, and Louis-Cesare had come to help out. At the time, I'd been grateful. Of course, at the time I'd also been drunk off my ass, which didn't lead to great decision making.

"Which is my point," he said impatiently. "You had imbibed a large amount of fey wine that evening, which increased your mental abilities—"

"And that's *my* point, because I hadn't had any last night!"

"If you cannot recall last night, how do you know?"

Because I knew what the level had been in the bottle this morning. I didn't say, not needing that kind of hell. "Like Claire said, I don't do that anymore," I said sweetly.

He narrowed his eyes at me, but before he could say anything, Marlowe, of all people, came to my rescue.

"I have a squad of dead agents," he said harshly. "And a live dhampir. And I have yet to hear why."

"It is apparent why," Louis-Cesare said, his eyes on mine. "We have been pressing the smugglers harder of late, and they have decided to strike back. The more operatives they deprive us of, the longer it will take—"

"Then why leave *her*? In the right circumstances, she's as dangerous as another master. In some even more so, as she has abilities we lack!"

And that, I thought, was likely the closest thing to a compliment I would ever get from Marlowe.

Not that I was all that flattered when the next thing out of his mouth was: "They should have spilled her guts all over the pier, right beside Lawrence's!"

"Typical!" Claire said, looking disgusted. Louis-Cesare apparently didn't like the comment any better, because his face flushed and he rounded on the chief spy. But then Radu intervened.

"They may not have known what she is," he pointed out. "She scents as human, and the other telltale signs are difficult to spot. And why would they have been looking for them? There are so few dhampirs; they simply aren't what anyone expects—"

"It makes no difference!" Marlowe said, brushing that aside. "Whether they believed her to be human or mage or some mutant type of fey—"

Oh, yeah, I thought, watching Claire. This was going well.

"—why keep someone alive who could possibly identify them?"

"We don't know that she can identify them," Louis-Cesare argued. "She did not even know who I was when I found her. She may know nothing—"

"Oh, she knows," Marlowe said, turning implacable eyes on me. "And she's going to tell us, if I have to rip it out of her brain my—"

"Kit!" That was Radu again, but this time he was too late.

Chapter Seven

And suddenly it was like the old saying: you could have heard a pin drop. Which is a lot easier with vampire hearing anyway.

"Is that was this is about?" I asked, but Marlowe had clammed up. Not that it mattered; he wasn't the one running this show.

He never had been.

"Mind tricks don't work on me," I said, my eyes meeting Mircea's.

"Some do," he said quietly.

And yeah. Some did. Specifically, his did, because they worked on pretty much everyone.

There was one thing I hadn't gotten around to explaining to Claire in that twenty questions on vamps we'd been doing. Mainly because she wouldn't have believed me. No one did unless they saw it for themselves, and precious few outsiders ever did.

Every senior master, sometimes even before reaching first level, developed special abilities. It was the crazy stuff the old legends assigned to all vamps but that most never lived long enough or got powerful enough to see. Like turning into mist or morphing into an animal—the kind of things that impressed people at parties. The kind of stuff that was often less useful than spectacular or awe-inspiring or breathtaking.

Except in Mircea's case.

Mircea's gifts weren't like that. Mircea's gifts weren't showy at all—were, in fact, completely invisible, and all the more dangerous because of it. Mircea's talents lay with the mind.

"That's why you came here, why you had Louis-Cesare bring me back," I said. "You wanted me in familiar surroundings."

"It usually works best that way."

"You ought to know."

"What is it?" Claire asked, picking up on the sudden change in atmosphere. "What's going on?"

But this time Mircea didn't answer. This was the crunch point, and he knew it. His eyes never left mine. "Will you do it?"

I didn't say anything, because I was kind of surprised that he'd bothered to ask. Maybe whatever he was planning needed my cooperation. Maybe having me fight him would lessen the chance of getting anything useful. I actually wanted to believe that. Because believing the concern in those brown velvet eyes—*fake, fake, you know damned well it's fake*—was always a bad idea.

If I had a problem dealing with the flood of emotions Louis-Cesare stirred up, it was nothing compared to the tsunami named Mircea.

It had been this way as far back as I could remember, a strange dance toward and away from each other, a suspicious, snarling, snapping dance, which I guess made sense considering that we were genetically designed to tear each other's throat out. Lately, we'd been in one of the better cycles, circling closer, teeth still bared and claws still out because you never knew—*no, you never, ever knew*—but closer nonetheless. And I freely admitted that that had been mostly his doing.

I hadn't *wanted* to get closer. I hadn't needed one more ride on that merry-go-round, one more trip to that particular rodeo, when it always ended the same way. Why play when you can't win? Why try when you know ahead of time that it isn't going to work? When it *never* works? After centuries of the same old same old, I'd given up. I didn't want to dance anymore.

Which was when Mircea had decided that he did.

And I had to admit, he'd learned a few new steps

since last time. Maybe more than a few, and they hadn't been mere variations on a theme, either. When Mircea did something, he did it full throttle, and that included turning over a new leaf.

He'd started out by killing the creature who had killed my mother, despite the fact that the bastard in question was his own brother. He'd also told me a few things—very few—about the woman she had been, a commoner he'd married despite the fact that a match like that could only harm his ambitions. He had pulled me into his orbit by attaching me to the Senate's shiny new portal demolition squad, which he happened to head up. He had dangled Louis-Cesare—moody, unconventional, passionate Louis-Cesare—in front of me like bait in front of a starving fish.

Okay, maybe not that last one, since Louis-Cesare was a serious potential asset to the family, if he ever got his shit together. Which he wouldn't if he kept slumming around with me. So I didn't know what, if anything, Mircea had done there, and what had been coincidence. But that was the problem with Mircea—I never knew anything for certain.

He was sitting silently, waiting for me to work through it. Other people were talking—I heard Claire's bright tones, Radu's soothing murmur, a flash of Marlowe's thunder—but I couldn't concentrate on any of it. All I could see were those dark eyes, so like mine, yet so different. So very different.

Part of the reason I'd freaked out on Louis-Cesare hadn't had anything to do with him. He'd accidentally stumbled across one of my admittedly not insignificant number of hot spots, and this one was hotter than most. Or maybe sharper, because that's what it felt like, the broken edges sharp as glass where memories used to be.

Mircea had used his little gift on me when I was a child, sorting through my head, taking out my recollections of his brother, of what had happened to my mother, of who-knew-what-else, because I sure as hell didn't. But I could feel it, even now, the place where all those memories should have been, as conspicuous in its absence as a newly lost tooth.

Or a hole in the head. Because that's what it was: a hole, a wound, a fissure. I could feel the raw edges where my memories had been cut to pieces, the sudden blanks where the film broke and left me floundering on the brink of a thought. A diver walking to the edge of a cliff and looking over to see ... nothing.

Supposedly, the idea had been to keep me safe, since my baby dhampir mind had been set on revenge, and nobody in our family was an easy kill. Particularly not when surrounded by an army of guards bristling with weapons. True, they were human and I was not, but they'd also outnumbered me by a few hundred to one and Mircea hadn't liked the odds. He also hadn't liked the idea of a quick and easy death for his brother in case I got lucky.

Or so he said. But there was a problem with that. Because Mircea's idea of fitting punishment had been perpetual confinement, locking his crazed sibling away for centuries after making him a vampire so he couldn't die and get out of it. So he could never forget. It was a symphony of revenge instead of the few notes I'd planned to mete out, and it made perfect sense—except for one small detail.

No one under master status can make a vampire.

So Mircea had already made the leap to at least seventh-level master when he Changed Vlad, and I was a baby dhampir at the time, almost literally. And yet he couldn't have controlled me without the mental surgery? He couldn't have found another way without taking almost every damn memory I had of my early life, including all recollections of my mother? He couldn't have done something, anything, else?

I didn't buy it.

In fact, the more I thought about it, the less I bought it, which was why I was having problems with this whole reconciliation thing. And now he wanted back inside my head for round two? I stared at him silently and said nothing.

Neither did he.

Maybe because there wasn't anything to say. I didn't ask if they'd already checked other leads because I didn't have to. Mircea wouldn't have come here—not to me, not with this—unless he'd already tried everything else. Unless he was out of options.

So he was sitting there, bouncing Aiden on his knee, being patient with Claire, somehow keeping Marlowe in check, and waiting. For the deal. For the terms. For the bargains that were the only real heartbeat of vampire life.

And suddenly I was just sick of it, completely and utterly. There were things I could have asked for, things I could have used, but I didn't want anything from him. I never had.

Nothing that I was likely to get, anyway.

"All right," I heard myself say hoarsely.

And the dam burst.

Color, light, and the sound of raised voices surged around me. It felt like a veil had been lifted from over my head, leaving me blinking. And wincing, because Stinky had apparently been trying to get my attention by sinking wicked sharp nails into my thigh.

By the time I pried his toes out of my flesh, the party had moved to the living room, because it was darker. And Mircea needed his concentration for whatever he planned to do to my brain rather than putting out fires. I didn't follow because I needed a few minutes.

And because of Claire.

Claire was Not Happy.

"I don't like this," she hissed, not bothering to keep her voice down.

Not that it mattered. The living room was only across the hall and down a little ways. Which meant we may as well have been standing beside them as far as vampire hearing was concerned. But Claire didn't look like she cared.

"You don't understand," I told her, passing Stinky over so I could hold a paper towel to my leg. So much for another pair of jeans.

"Then explain it to me!" she said furiously, somehow managing to be intimidating despite balancing a baby on each hip. "Explain why you would even consider—"

"Because Varus wasn't among the corpses," I snapped. Damn, Stinky was developing freaking talons. "Which means he set us up—"

"He set *them* up. Not you! Why do you have to—"

"Claire, if the criminal element gets the idea that they can butcher the Senate's agents at will, we're all going to be in trouble. The Senate's got enough on its hands with the war; it doesn't need another front opening up here." Especially one that knew its weaknesses as well as Varus probably did.

The reason Geminus had gotten away with his little hobby for so long was that he hadn't been just any old vampire. He'd been a senator, and what was more, the Senate's weapons master, which had included locating and developing new ways to kill things. That had given him carte blanche to go into Faerie whenever he liked, and set up his network of portals. But it also meant that Varus, as his right-hand guy, had way too much knowledge about the Senate's inner workings—and its arsenal.

"We have to find him," I told Claire. "Finding Varus means finding his contacts, who may be some of the same people causing you problems back home."

"That isn't home."

"What?"

"Nothing." She shook her head, red hair flying everywhere. It was sunny today, but it had been raining a lot lately, and Claire's hair goes poufy when it rains. It was teetering on the edge of Afro territory right now, which wasn't a great look for her. But it was better than the dark circles under her eyes and the pinched skin at the corners of her mouth.

I'd been kind of out of it lately, recovering from one disaster and apparently getting into another, and hadn't really been paying attention. But maybe I should have; Claire looked like she could use it. "Are you all right?" I asked, wondering if we had a problem.

"This isn't about me!" she said shrilly, green eyes flashing.

And okay, yeah. A problem. Of course, maybe having her slam somebody through a wall should have clued me in to that already. Claire had the stereotypical redhead's temperament, but she usually stopped short of forcible redecoration.

"How can you let him do that, just . . . just tiptoe around in your brain like that?" she demanded.

"It won't be the first time."

"And that's even worse! He already altered your memories once. What's to say he won't do it again?"

It looked like Mircea had less success with fey than with humans, I thought, because Claire clearly wasn't a fan.

"It's like I told you," she said severely. "They only understand their own side, and it isn't yours!"

"I'm part vampire, Claire," I reminded her, since she seemed to keep forgetting that.

"You're part human, too. And I'm beginning to believe the human part is the best part--in all of us."

"What does that mean?"

She looked away. "Nothing. It's just . . . Lately it feels like everyone I love is hanging by a thread, while some madman runs around with scissors. And some days, I just want to—"

"Throw somebody through a wall?"

Her head whipped back around. "Damn it, Dory!"

"Okay, I'm sorry. I get that way, too, remember?"

"Then help me." Blazing emerald eyes met mine. "I can't take any more stress right now. I just want to know that you're safe. All right?"

"What are you stressed abou—"

"All right?"

I didn't say anything, because Louis-Cesare had appeared in the door. "They are ready."

Claire looked at me accusingly.

"I'll be fine," I told her firmly.

"Why do you even bother to say that?" she grumbled, and followed me across the hall.

The shades had all been pulled in the living room, and the curtains closed. The electricity was on, but it didn't help much since it only powered an old fixture that hung from the ceiling, the lamps having been carted off by the troll twins for their basement apartment. We didn't miss them much because we lived mostly in the kitchen and on the back porch, but it did make things a little gloomy at the moment.

I guess Ray had gotten tired of hanging out in the hall, and had come in here, only to be banished to a perch on the card table. I still didn't know what he was doing here, but this didn't seem like the time to ask, not with Marlowe glowering alongside, arms crossed, in almost the same pose he'd used in the kitchen. *Like a beam of sunshine,* I thought sourly.

Mircea and Radu had taken seats on the old-lady sofa, which Claire had inherited along with the house. It was red brocade with a high arched back, and always looked to me like it ought to be gracing a geriatric bordello. But with the two of them on it, its usual tattered garishness faded into the background.

A matching wingback chair had been pulled up in front of it, which I assumed was for me. I started toward it—which would have worked better if Louis-Cesare had let go of my arm. I looked up to find that the scowl he'd been wearing earlier had taken up permanent residence. It matched the shadow in his eyes, which the gloom had deepened to indigo.

"You don't have to do this," he told me shortly.

"Like hell she doesn't!" Marlowe snapped.

"You *don't*," Louis-Cesare reiterated, and Marlowe suddenly went very still.

That was probably because Louis-Cesare had just made what could have been interpreted as a direct challenge. And it might have, had he so much as glanced Marlowe's way. But his eyes were on me, and they were serious. I briefly closed mine.

When I opened them, he was still looking at me, still concerned. Still totally oblivious to the fact that he'd basically just challenged the Senate's chief spy to a duel. It was days like this that made me wonder how, even with his fighting ability, the guy had survived as long as he had.

He was honest and honorable and ethical and generous, in a culture that was exactly none of those things. That didn't even value those things, because "good" was a relative term and being a good vampire was to be like Marlowe: cunning, deceitful, ruthless, overwhelming. Or like Mircea: calm, patient, resourceful, relentless. "Kind" wasn't in the job description; "compassionate" even less so.

Damn it, the man needed a keeper.

Yeah, sure he did. A dark-haired, dimpled, dhampir keeper, which wasn't going to happen, so just *shut up*. Sometimes I didn't think it mattered what Mircea did in my head, because I was already crazy anyway.

"It's like someone invented you just to mess with me," I said resentfully.

"Quoi?"

I sighed. "I'm *fine*," I said, just wanting to get this over with.

"I see what you mean," he told Claire drily, and she blinked at him in what looked like surprise.

There was no point in stalling, so I walked over and sat down, really glad that I'd had that drink earlier. Even with Claire's presence leeching the manic energy off my skin, like some kind of supernatural magnet, I was still crawling with it. Any other time, I'd have been crawling the walls, too—or, more likely, punching through them. As it was, I wanted this *done*.

I cleared my throat. "Okay, so now what?" I asked . . . Radu, because just that fast everyone else was gone.

Chapter Eight

I don't know what I'd expected, but it wasn't that. Or having the lights go out. Or having the room suddenly be replaced by towering glass-covered skyscrapers on one side and rippling dark water on the other.

First-level masters, I reminded myself grimly. You never got anywhere underestimating them, and Mircea already knew my brain like the back of his hand. He ought to; he'd basically designed it.

But at least he hadn't had any trouble finding the right memory. The ripples frothed against an embankment like lace on a hem. Or maybe a neckline, because a few dozen ships rode the waves, glowing under the moonlight like a string of pearls.

The wind was fluttering real lace at Radu's throat and wrists when I looked back at him, and ruffling the long dark hair that he didn't always keep as tightly confined as his brother did. "What are you doing here?" I demanded, half expecting to hear my voice echo, since we were talking inside my head.

Radu didn't answer. He seemed a little preoccupied, possibly because the insanely realistic picture Mircea had conjured up had some holes in it. Literally, I realized, following 'Du's gaze to where pieces of things—buildings, the far end of a road, whole swaths of the sky—simply weren't there. The weirdest one was a nearby skyscraper that just disappeared halfway up, like King Kong had passed by and had a snack.

"What's wrong?" I asked, gripping his arm.

"I . . . Nothing." He looked a little paler than usual. "I suppose those are areas you simply didn't notice."

"What?"

"Well, we don't, do we?" he asked, a little more forcefully. "Even when we're on hyper alert, we can't notice everything."

"But my memory doesn't look like this!" I gestured at the moon, which was visible in the water but noticeably absent from the sky. Or maybe it was just behind some clouds; I wasn't enthusiastic about looking for it since the sky had the most gaps, with massive areas filled with nothing but boiling black mist.

"Well, it would," Radu said. "But your brain usually fills in the blanks."

"With what?"

"With guesswork. That's why many optical illusions work. Didn't you know?"

"No." And I could have lived without finding out. "Then why aren't I filling in the blanks now?"

Radu tilted his head slightly, like he was listening to something I couldn't hear. "Mircea said you would be, but he's cutting through all that. We can't have fantasy or mental manipulation filling in areas when it may fill them in wrong, do you see?"

"Yeah." I repressed an urge to hug my arms around myself. "Yeah, I guess." I sure as hell didn't want to have to do this again because I'd dreamed up the wrong information. I looked at him. "Why are you here again?"

"Mircea can't maintain the connection and also serve as your guide. That's my job."

"Okay, guide," I said, glancing around. "Where to?"

"Well, how should I know? It's your memory. I'm just here to pull you out if anything goes wrong."

I had been watching a nearby ship bobbing about on the waves, or should I say half a ship, since I'd apparently never gotten around to noticing the back half. But at that I turned my eyes on 'Du. "What could go wrong? I'm sitting in the living room. Right?"

"Well, yes, your body is. But it's your mind we're concerned with here, Dory."

I took a moment to process that. "You're telling me that something could go wrong with *my mind*?"

"No, no, not at all. Nothing like."

"Good." For a minute there, I'd been a little worried. I wasn't exactly the poster child for mental stability as it was. The last thing I needed—

"Of course, there have been a few incidents."

Radu was fiddling with the lace on his sleeve. "Incidents?"

"Of people who, well, went too far in. You can become lost, you see, wandering about from one old memory to the next, until you forget where you came in and—" He stopped, belatedly noticing my expression. "It almost never happens. And in any case, that's why I am here. To see that it doesn't."

"And you've done this how many times before?"

. . .

"'Du—"

"I know the theory, Dory," he said testily. "And I'm related to both of you, which makes me more . . . in sync . . . if you will, and a better bridge than anyone else could be. It's safer to have me do this than some stranger, however experienced. Which is why Mircea brought me along."

I stared at him. "That makes me feel so much better."

"Yes, I thought it would," Radu said. "But problems are more frequent when the subject is tired, and this sort of thing is fairly draining. We should get going."

Great. So not only was I in Wonderland, I was on a freaking timer. "How long do I have?"

"I don't know. That depends on you. A few minutes?"

"A few *minutes*? How am I supposed to find anything useful in—"

I stopped, because I'd just caught sight of the fairly odd image of myself, slipping through the shadows of the ships and pilings. I was wearing my usual work uniform of black leather jacket, black jeans and black boots, and managing to be almost invisible against the night. But I wasn't doing as good a job as whoever was with me.

Try as I might, I couldn't get a clear look at him. I

couldn't even manage to bring him into focus unless he was silhouetted against the ghostly outline of a hull. And even then he was just a vaguely man-shaped cloud, or a dim shadow of someone who wasn't actually—

"There." *Lawrence paused, the particles coalescing enough to allow speech. "The black one."*

I looked at the ship in question, a long, sleek, ebony torpedo in one of the larger berths, melding into the night almost as seamlessly as Lawrence did, looking exotic next to the flock of clunkier, paler specimens moored all around. But I didn't see anything else of interest. Or smell, since Lawrence had been following a scent trail.

"You're sure?" I asked, because all I could smell was brine and fish and gasoline, and the lingering scent of the cologne the now sleeping watchman had been wearing.

"No."

Lawrence sounded surprised, which made sense. Before he'd moved on to the illustrious heights of first-level master, he had been a Hound—a vampire gifted with even better olfactory senses than the norm, which were already pretty damned good. It was why he'd been chosen for this assignment, since it required tracing a tiny thread of a scent across half a city not known for the pristine quality of its air.

"What do you mean, 'no'?" I whispered, even though we were using a sound shield. It was just that kind of place, "Varus is either in there or he isn't."

Lawrence didn't answer, but he coalesced a little more, the misty particles of his being coming together into the shape of a tall, thin vampire with creepy red eyes. Not hay-fever red, not hungover red. Not even I-smoked-too-many-joints-tonight-oh-God red. They were the solid crimson of a stoplight, with the same faint glowing quality to them. Though stoplights didn't send shivers up my back when I looked at them.

Most vampires can pass for human even without a glamourie, but Lawrence clearly wasn't one of them. And he couldn't use a glamourie and his special sparkly master power at the same time, which left me running around with what looked like the spawn of Satan. Which would have been fine—if Satan's spawn had been able to do the job.

"He was," Lawrence told me, tipping his head back and then to the side, following some scent too faint for me to detect. "And he did not leave."

"He went in there and didn't leave, but he isn't there now?" I asked, for clarification.

Lawrence nodded.

"You mean, someone brought him here and killed him?"

"No. There is no stench of blood or decomposition."

"Then how does that work?"

"As I said, I do not know. But I am going to." And before I could stop him, he had disintegrated into what looked like a swarm of black bees, if the bees were too small to see and had no more substance than ash as they blew by my face. And onto the ship, where they disappeared under a door.

Damn it!

This was why I worked alone. Because stupid assholes with impulse control issues gave me a headache. For a minute there, I contemplated leaving him to look around on his own, since a cloud of mist or ash or whatever was a lot less likely to get holes blown through it than I was. And this was smelling more like a trap every second. But ironically, in his disjointed state Lawrence had less sensory perception than I did, his super nose apparently not able to do its job when dissolved into a million pieces.

So if this was a trap, he'd just gone in blind.

I slipped down the pier to the ship, which was bigger than it had seemed at a distance. There was no deck, just an ultramodern domed and gleaming expanse of obsidian Plexiglas, and no convenient gangplank left out Hollywood-like for me to use. So I backed up, as far as I could go without falling in the drink, ran and jumped—over the low railing running along the pier and onto the tiny area where the gangplank would have been if my life had a decent screenwriter.

Because it doesn't, I've had to develop some skills through the years, and I somehow stuck the landing. And then realized that it didn't do me much good since, of course, the damned door was locked. I stood there, balanced on the maybe half-inch lip, grumbling under my breath and sorting through my pockets for something that might get the door open since I couldn't just avoid it like some—

"Sorry to interrupt," a head said, poking out of the door. And causing me to jump back in surprise. Which would have been fine if there had been anything behind me.

I flailed out even as I fell, trying to find a handhold or a foothold or any kind of a hold to avoid cracking my head on the damned concrete dock. Or the pylons. Or whatever was under the water that I couldn't see but was about to experience the hard way, when my fingertips managed to snag the lip I'd been standing on. My body hit the side of the ship hard enough to rattle my teeth, while my fingers were almost wrenched out of their sockets trying to hold my entire weight.

I hung there for a second, watching little waves splash against the side of the ship and trying to convince myself that I shouldn't attempt to murder the guy whose long hair was almost brushing my face.

"What?" I said, glaring up at Radu. Who was looking fairly pleased for some reason.

"Oh, good. You should be able to see it from there."

"See what?"

"The name."

"The name?"

"Of the ship. We need to know—"

I said a bad word and started struggling to get back up. "There's only one black ship in the whole damned marina! How hard can it be—"

"But that's just it. There was no ship, of any color, in that slip this morning. And Kit wants—"

"Kit can kiss my ass," I grunted. Because fingertip chin-ups aren't fun even when you have more than half an inch to work with. "And if you want the ship's name, look for it yourself!"

"This is your memory, Dory," he told me, in a voice

that said he was overlooking my rudeness because he was generous like that. "I only see what you see. And by the way, Mircea says to tell you that you're getting tired. We need to hurry this up."

"I also . . . have a few things . . . you can tell Mircea," I panted, somehow getting back into position. And then having to practically rupture something to maintain my balance while checking out the hull in both directions. "Tell him there's no name."

"None whatsoever?"

"No! And if you want me to hurry this up, you need to—"

"What are you doing?"

"Augghh!"

A head shoved through the door at me, but I somehow kept my balance. Even with the sight of those evil red eyes staring into mine from all of an inch away. Which was less of an ick factor than the neck ending in a working black mass, like a million ants were trying to consume it.

I swallowed.

"If you'd given me a moment, I would have opened the door," Lawrence said mildly.

"Yeah, well. You failed to mention that."

"I wouldn't leave a partner behind," he told me. Which would have been more comforting if the ants hadn't taken that moment to swarm over his face, molding to the features until they were just nose- and mouth- and chin-shaped protrusions in a horrible, squirming mask. Until even that winked out and the door opened, so abruptly that I stumbled through his body on the other side.

It took everything I could do not to wipe frantically at my skin as the boiling black mass spun up around me. And then coalesced a few feet away into a vampire in a dark-colored suit. He looked like he had all the requisite parts, but my mouth still felt full of ash, my throat clogged with it, my heart beating double time because, damn.

"Take the back; I'll cover the front," he told me, as if nothing had happened. I just nodded. The sooner this was done, the better.

There wasn't much to see in the living area, which was

decorated in stark black and white. Plush white couches sat on gleaming black hardwood, which also supported a white baby grand. Black and white and red art prints were scattered over walls, although there weren't any of the kind of personal photos that might have been expected. There weren't any personal touches at all that I could see, except for a carved raven perched over a door, its gleaming obsidian feathers catching the light through a porthole.

Very literary, I thought, staring up at it. But not very reassuring. There also weren't any signs of a wanted ex-lieutenant, so I moved on.

Down a flight of stairs were the bedrooms, five of them facing each other along a short hall, with the master at the end. I tried to scent something out of place without actually going into the rooms, because if there was going to be a ward or trap, it would likely be inside. But all I smelled were teak and beeswax, bright lemon cleaner and vinegary nail polish, the tang of ozone and expensive perfume and—

Nothing.

I paused outside the door of one of the smaller cabins near the end of the hall. Unlike the others, it didn't appear to have been used recently, with no bright living scents cutting through a layer of dust. That wouldn't have been a big deal—maybe the owners used it for storage or just didn't have that many guests. Except for that Nothing: a gaping hole in the middle of the room's scent story, like someone had come along with a giant pair of scissors and simply cut it out.

There were a couple of things that could do that, including a shield that hid smells like the one I was using hid sounds. It was often employed by bad guys brewing up illegal potions and people storing otherworldly ingredients or merchandise, the smells of which were so distinctive that they'd tell anybody with a nose that something was up. And considering that we were after a bunch of smugglers, that was probably all it was, just a shield in case the local War Mage Corps got curious about somebody's stash.

But then, there was one other thing that left a big blank hole in the world.

I was about to call the expert when I felt an insubstantial hand materialize on my shoulder. "You found something."

"Maybe. It could just be somebody's cache of fey wine." Which I would, of course, have to confiscate to teach them proper respect for the law.

But Lawrence shook his head. *"No."*

"You're the expert," I said, and kicked in the door.

And okay. That wasn't wine. The problem was that I wasn't sure what it was, and judging by his caution as he walked over and knelt beside it, neither was Lawrence.

It didn't look particularly threatening—just a square hole in the floor, like a trapdoor. But this door was open, and a square column of strange underwater light was shooting out the top and puddling on the room's ceiling. Lawrence stuck his head in the hole, the light splashing his dark coat and thin features. I took my time, checking the room for nonexistent snares, before joining him.

The trapdoor turned out to be . . . a trapdoor. It was what was below that was interesting. A hole had been carved through the floor of the cabin and into a crawl space, and then kept on going right down to the hull. But instead of water gushing out to flood the room, there was only a film of light across the top, eerily similar to the waves outside in the way little ripples were chasing themselves across the surface.

It didn't really look like the portal I'd been halfway expecting, which should have been either invisible when closed or a swirling mass of color when opened. But it didn't look like anything else, either. It also still gave off no scent that I could name, but it looked like Lawrence might be having better luck. Because he'd jumped down and stuck his nose within an inch of the shining blue surface, which was ill-advised.

And then through it, which was crazy.

I followed and jerked him back. "What are you doing?"

He looked up in mild surprise, the first expression I'd seen him use. *"Going inside."*

"Going inside what?"

"This is a portal— "

"I got that."

"—through which Varus went along with three others, two vampires and a human. The last was a mage, by the smell."

Great. That was all we needed, to have one of them involved. "Dark or light?"

"It isn't easy to tell. The differences are not as great as humans would have you believe. There was no stink of blood magic on him, meaning that he could be a light mage— "

"Or a dark one who just hasn't slit anybody's throat recently."

"Not within the last ten days," he agreed. "Which is as far back as my scent record goes."

I just looked at him, but he wasn't kidding. And then he wasn't there anymore, either. Because the bat shit crazy loon had dissolved and flowed straight through the portal.

"Lawrence!" I hissed, but it was too late.

He was gone.

Not being insane—well, not at the moment—I jerked my coat open and dragged out my key chain. I snapped off an Eye of Argos charm, threaded it through my belt and broke the surface with that, trying to peer around. On the plus side, the belt didn't catch fire or get chopped off, shredded, or otherwise destroyed. On the negative, I couldn't see shit, even after adjusting the charm, except for a few tumbled rocks. The portal's light on the other end was blocking everything else.

I sat there on my heels for a second. If it had been just the two vamps we were talking about, I wouldn't have been too worried. Anything a vampire—well, anything a normal vampire—could survive, so could I. But the presence of the mage made it hinky. Mages had tricks and spells and wards and traps and a whole host of other nastiness at their disposal, and that was just the light kind. I really, really didn't like the idea of going through an unknown portal into a dark who-the-hell-knew with a possible black mage running around.

But I liked leaving Lawrence to face him on his own

*even less. I could call in, explain what had happened and wait for backup—*which is what sane people did, Lawrence—*but by the time it got here, he would have already dealt with or been dealt with by whoever was down there. There would be nothing left but picking up the pieces, assuming we could find them all, which in his case wasn't that likely.*

"I never leave a partner behind," *he'd said. Except when he did. Or when he assumed the crazy dhampir would be right on his heels. And I guess he was right, because the next thing I knew, I was slipping down through the middle of the portal and feeling the not-water closing over my head.*

Chapter Nine

"What are you doing?" a voice demanded, causing me to bite my tongue on a scream. It was extraordinarily bad timing, because I hit the ground a second later, jarring my jawbone and causing my fangs to pop out. And then plunging them into my own flesh.

Which was just as well, as it kept me from uttering any of the comments that were trembling on the tip of my mangled tongue. I pried my teeth out and spat blood. It took a few seconds, because there was a lot of it, and then I looked up to find Radu hovering over me.

Literally, since his feet weren't touching the floor. "How are you doing that?" I demanded when I could talk.

"How should I know?" he asked, looking like a testy angel with that long dark hair floating around that beautiful face. "I told you, this is new to me, too. But at a guess, the laws of physics don't work when it's all in your head."

"Tell that to my jaw," I said, rubbing it.

"Well, I'm sorry, but Mircea wants—" He stopped, tilting his head. "Mircea wants me to take you out, but Kit is arguing against it." He winced.

"What is it?"

"Louis-Cesare is ... objecting ... to something Kit said," Radu told me diplomatically.

I hoped the objecting hadn't involved any thumps, because the day that happened I damned well wanted to be there to see it. But right now there was something I wanted more. "I need to finish this."

Radu shook his head. "It isn't a good idea, Dory. We can come back—"

"And the missing vampires?"

"You know they're . . ." Radu looked uncomfortable. "Well, you know the odds."

"And you know how tricky first- and second-level masters can be."

He sighed. Considering who his brother was, yes, he did. "It would be best to be able to go after them sooner rather than later," he admitted. "But—"

"Then get out of here." I'd gotten to my feet and now I tried to push past him, but a pale, long-fingered hand gripped my arm. It was always surprising to remember that 'Du was a vampire, too, and also second-level. He didn't look it, didn't act it. But the strength of that hand was unmistakable.

"There are four missing men, 'Du," I said, because I couldn't break his grip. I might have, on a good day, since fighting isn't only about strength and I know a hell of a lot more about it than Radu ever bothered to learn. But he was right—I was getting tired. Trying to fight my way out would just end this all the sooner.

But Radu didn't let go. "When did they become men?" he asked softly.

"What?"

"They're vampires, Dory. Not too long ago, they would have been things to you. We were all merely things."

"No."

"Yes." The wavering beams of light threw odd shadows across that handsome face, making it hard to read his expression. "You killed our kind—"

"I killed the bad guys, 'Du," I said impatiently, because I really was tired. And in pain. All the little aches Louis-Cesare had soothed away were coming back, not at full strength, but enough to remind me that he was better at killing things than healing them. "I never went after anybody who didn't deserve it."

"Not hurting is a different thing from saving," he replied quietly. "There was a time when you would have let

Raymond burn up in your hallway. When you would not have cared if four strange vampires died. When you would have been like your friend Claire, who says all the right things but looks at us as if we were roaches crawling across her kitchen floor."

"You . . . didn't act like you noticed that."

"Of course not. I am charming," Radu pointed out.

"Yeah," I said, because in his own, extremely weird way, he sort of was. He was also sort of right, but I didn't think now was the time to go into it.

"Can you go Oprah on me later?" I asked. "If I'm going to do this, I really need—"

"Shit!"

The drop was a bitch. Fourteen feet isn't fun anyway, but landing on a lot of pointy rocks is even less so. Fortunately, the points were fairly small, leaving me beat up and bloody instead of impaled. Unfortunately, they were also hot as fuck.

"Shit! Shit!"

I jumped up, getting hard boot leather between me and the floor. It looked perfectly normal—beige and rocky, except for clearer bits here and there covered with sand—but the Ray impression I was currently doing said otherwise. The knees of my jeans were burnt out, one sleeve of the leather jacket I'd been wearing was melted to my arm, and my hands—

"Damn it!" The portal's light showed me palms full of blisters, which wouldn't have been so bad except for the half ton of gravel embedded in them. And the damned stuff was continuing to blister the areas around it even as my body tried to heal. It was like picking up a handful of embers, only these didn't seem inclined to go out.

After a second, I bit the bullet and wiped my hands on my jeans, leaving blood and skin behind along with the gravel, because I didn't have time to pick out every individual piece. My soles were already starting to smoke, and when they went, it was time's up. And since it looked like that would take all of another minute or so, I faced reality and pulled out the big guns.

Or, to be more precise, the big cheat.

Being a dhampir has certain advantages—better senses, rapid healing, greater strength, speed, etc. What it does not have is magic, of any type, kind or variety, which is a problem considering many of the things I fight. But as flat-chested girls and balding guys learned a long time ago, what nature didn't give you, you can often buy. And mages have to make a living, too.

But the cool toys don't come cheap. I mentally tacked another grand onto the tally for tonight's little outing, and pulled a Baggie out of an inner coat pocket. Inside was a cheap-looking bracelet, bronze and cuff style, like the magnetic crap shysters are always trying to pawn off on arthritis sufferers at the mall. Only this one actually worked.

Not for healing, but for making sure you didn't need any. The thing was a temporary shield, fine as any a war mage could project, which was fair, since I'd bought it off one. But like all shields, it ate magic like candy. And it wasn't like I could generate more when the reservoir ran dry. A plastic strip on the side showed the drain—fifteen minutes under ideal conditions, which was stupid when the whole point of having the damned thing was that you weren't in ideal conditions.

Anyway, I could hope for maybe five here. I also hoped that nobody with superfine hearing was paying attention, because the big boy didn't play well with others. Specifically, it required dropping all other shields, which interfered with it for some reason I didn't understand since magic theory made my head hurt. But the mage's instructions had been specific, so the sound shield had to go.

The new spell closed over me, a cool bubble of protection molding to my scorched skin like air-conditioned glass. I gave a—very brief—sigh of relief as the temp dropped a good fifty degrees, allowing me to breathe. I also took a few precious seconds to shoot a line with a grappling hook back through the portal and onto the boat, making sure it caught. It was retractable, so as long as I managed to get back here, and the line hadn't burnt up, and nobody was shooting at me on the way up, I'd be fine.

Yeah.

So.

The only good thing was that I didn't have to choose directions. Behind me was a wall, and while there was a chance that Lawrence had found a way through it, I wasn't going to. He was either somewhere ahead or he wasn't, and I had about four and a half minutes left to find out. I started moving.

SOP in cases like this is to take a couple steps, check for snares, take another couple steps, repeat as needed. But (a) that would get me all of ten yards before my protection gave out, (b) I didn't see Lawrence's mangled body anywhere and (c) why the hell bother to put a snare in here? The corridor of the damned was enough of a barrier all on its own.

And not just because of the heat. The tunnel was naturally occurring by the look of it, with some lofty areas — like the one the portal had let out on — but up ahead the ceiling ducked low enough that it looked like I might have to crawl. It was also lumpy and hot and completely lacking in partners, bad guys, or anything else of interest except some fireflies zipping around the darkness over my head.

They weren't the only source of light. Once I got away from the portal, I started noticing glowing patches in the walls, like mold if it was the color of fire and sent off heat waves so intense they were almost visible. I found that out when I ran into one, causing the line on the shield's meter to drop like a stone. I hit the ground and flipped over to see the room wavering through the intense band of heat above me.

Fun.

I was a little more cautious after that, ducking and dodging to avoid draining the shield even faster, until I hit the crawling part. It didn't have as much of the freaky mold but also didn't have a floor after a dozen yards or so, thanks to letting out straight into an enormous cavern. Which was when everything started to speed up.

In rapid succession I saw Lawrence all the way at the bottom, near crevices filled with some type of round things in clumps, like golden caviar. A man — or a mannequin, *judging by the way the head fell off when Lawrence touched it—was on a chair in front of him. And a huge swarm of what I guess weren't fireflies, after all, was flowing out of openings in the walls and fissures in the rocks into a spinning, glowing tornado in the air between us.*

I showed up right before it dove—straight at Lawrence.

I had a half second to see him turn, his face and body illuminated with hundreds of swirling golden dots, like a disco ball. And then he shattered, coming apart in the time it took to blink. And damn, that was impressive. So much so that for a second I thought he was going to be okay. But then the golden cloud noticed the darker one rising through its middle.

And tightened up like a closing fist.

For an instant, there were two swirls, dark and light, circling each other in a graceful ballet in midair, a living yin and yang. And then Lawrence pulled away, scattering himself in a wide arc, which I didn't understand until I noticed. The dark ashes were burning.

It was like a fire in reverse—ash catching alight and burning gold, then orange, then red and then nothing as it flamed out, disintegrating entirely. Lawrence scattered further, maybe losing control, maybe trying to minimize the damage, I couldn't tell. But even if it was the latter, there were too many of them and he had too far to go and—

He wasn't going to make it.

I tore the cuff off my wrist, glanced at the bar—and shit. It looked like even my cynical estimate had been a little optimistic. Because there was all of thirty seconds left when I hurled it into the heart of the swarm and yelled, "Lawrence!"

I didn't wait to see if he caught it; I was already turning the instant it left my hand. I'd done what I could and my only job now was to report in and let the other groups know what they were walking into. But for that, I had to get out. Or crawl and scurry and flail and stumble out, because without the shield—

God. It wasn't like an oven. Ovens had even heat and this wasn't even close. That damned lichen or whatever it was formed a deadly lattice across the tunnel, shimmering in lines where the 130-degree air suddenly shot up, 20, 50, 100 degrees in almost invisible waves.

There weren't as many in the low area of the tunnel, but there was also less room to avoid them. I took one of the "cooler" bands across the face and felt it sear my skin, didn't quite miss one of the hotter ones and smelled my hair start to burn. But I didn't bother to put it out because there was no time. I reached the part of the corridor where I could finally stand up straight and tore ahead, my half-melted soles barely touching the ground.

I didn't try for pretty; didn't care about form. I ducked and rolled and ran halfway up one wall before throwing myself to the hateful floor and rolling another few yards forward, under the worst of the bands. Not that it seemed to help.

In seconds, my hands were a mass of blisters, my jacket was smoking, my eyes were watering so badly I could barely see the deadly heat shimmers. Hell, the whole room was shimmering. Including a watery patch of ground up ahead, glowing like a beacon and wavering like a mirage in the middle of the desert.

My burning hand closed on the burning cord I'd left behind, and a second later I was flying through the portal and smacking face-first into the gently rocking hull. And staggering off. And realizing that anything I could pass through, something else could, too, which was a problem since I didn't know how to shut this particular portal down.

I didn't waste time waiting for Lawrence. If he was going to make it out, he'd be right on my heels. And if he wasn't—

Then he wasn't. Partner or no, releasing that burning swarm on the city wasn't in the job plan. I wouldn't have expected him to risk it for me, and I wasn't going to do it for him.

There are explosives that work specifically on portals, but I didn't have any. What I did have was a sawed-off shotgun and a lot of spare clips, and I used them, shooting the boards around the portal with slug after slug, at almost *point-blank range. Plexiglas flew, some kind of Styrofoam-looking guts were gouged out and my ears felt like they might be bleeding. But within moments, water started bubbling through and then spilling over. Faster than I would have believed possible, I was up to my knees and there was what looked like a sinkhole doing its best to siphon the Atlantic into wherever-the-hell.*

Which was good, because something was doing its best to come through from the other side. I scrambled out of the trapdoor, watching as something bloomed under the water, something massive and glowing. But while passing through a portal is usually instantaneous, whatever it was seemed to be having a little trouble. Maybe because of the tsunami currently slapping it in the face.

Burn that, I thought viciously, and fired again, sending both barrels straight into the glowing heart.

And then tried to duck as something flew out at me, something huge and black and smoking. I staggered back, hitting the flooded hallway with a splash and a yelp, because whatever was on me was hot, hot, so fucking hot. But I couldn't see because steam was rising from the water and the damned boat was sinking and the explosion must have done something to the electrical, because the lights were blinking on and off—

But I didn't need them when I found myself staring into a pair of glowing red eyes.

"Lawrence!"

"Did you have to fucking shoot me?" he snarled, and then we were running and splashing and half drowning—at least I was—back down the hall and through the living area, and out onto the dock, which was within easy reach now that half the craft was underwater.

I pulled up, gasping and choking, having swallowed almost as much as the portal, and dragged myself onto the pier. My half-melted jacket was still smoking, but at least the dunking had put out my hair. I ripped the damned leather off, what parts weren't already welded to my hide, as Lawrence collapsed beside me.

"It was a trap," he gasped.

No shit, I didn't say, because he looked bad. Not bullet-

wound-bad, which he didn't have because he'd still been half dissolved when I shot him. But he was gasping and retching and generally looking like a guy who might have left some important bits behind.

And carried a few others along for the ride. The suit had mostly burnt away, allowing me to see bright spots moving under pale skin, as if someone was shining tiny flashlights through him. One thigh disintegrated in a cascade of black ash, isolating something that twitched and writhed in a puddle of seawater for an instant before flaming out. Others blinked out inside him, probably choked by the fluids in his body, but one—

A brief burning scent was all the warning I had before something burst out of the flesh on his arm. It shone against the blue darkness like a living ember for a second, still smoking from the blood sizzling on its body. I jumped up, getting a glimpse of fine, fire-lit traceries of wings, a solid golden carapace and black, opaque eyes—before it disintegrated under what remained of my left boot heel.

"Fuck!" I said, breathing heavily as Lawrence struggled to sit up.

"Those were . . . Varus's clothes . . ." he rasped. "But on . . . a dummy. We were . . ."

"Shut up," I told him, checking my cell phone because he was in no shape to call for help himself. And neither was I, thanks to the latest in a long line of busted pieces of crap having drowned along with me.

"Have to . . . warn the others—"

"I said shut up!" I rasped. He needed his strength if he was going to last until I got back. "I'm going to find a phone and call in. Just stay—"

"Dorina!"

I didn't need the warning. The look on his face told me it wasn't good even before a bullet slammed into my shoulder. It was large enough caliber to send me sprawling over Lawrence for half a second, before I was rolling, trying to raise a gun with an arm that no longer worked, and then switching hands and still not getting a slug off because the powder was—

Another bullet tore the gun out of my hand as I scrambled back, trying with my left hand to find a weapon that wasn't soaked, which would have been easier if I could have reached my damned jacket. But I couldn't even see it; someone had a light blazing in my eyes, bright as a—

"Dory!"

—searchlight, blinding me as I grabbed Lawrence, trying to drag him into the water because if he was able to disintegrate again he'd have done it already and we needed—

"Take her out!"

—to buy time. But red was blooming on Lawrence's shirt, two, three, four places, as they concentrated fire on him because they weren't stupid, no, no, not stupid, just fucking assholes—

"Radu, take her out!"

"I'm trying!"

—and I was out of usable weapons, except for the knife in my boot, which I threw almost blind, just zeroing in on the location of those shots. I heard someone curse—

"Now, Radu!"

—and didn't hear the sound of another gunshot—too deaf—but I felt when it hit home, shredding my thigh, which hurt less than someone's boot to my face—

"Radu!"

—and there was no time—

"Dorina!"

—no time—

—"Lawrence—"

Chapter Ten

I ended up back in bed, after all. I woke up sprawled on familiar lumps, pillow gone, sheets gone, quilt wadded into a pillow-like ball that I was hugging instead. It was dark, and for a minute I didn't know what the hell had happened.

And then I swam back to full consciousness, and I still didn't.

The sound of water was coming from somewhere nearby . . . faint, gentle, horrible. I stared around, still half convinced I was being carved to pieces on that bloody wharf. Until I finally realized it was gurgling through the wall behind my head.

I flopped back against the bed, breathing hard.

It was just somebody doing dishes or trying to take a bath. And sounding like they were trying to fill a swimming pool, because it took forever around here for water to heat up. It was a ridiculous waste anytime somebody wanted to get clean, but when this house was built, they hadn't worried about things like environmental friendliness. When this house was built, they were closer to worrying about Indian attacks and this was Brooklyn.

The Indian attacks had slacked off these days, unless you counted Bawa's curry at the takeaway place down the road—and having experienced it, I saw no reason why you *shouldn't*. But the plumbing remained. Intact and inefficient, it took its own sweet time and probably always would because I lived in a magic house.

Well, technically, it wasn't the house that was magic,

but the ley lines that ran underneath it. Rivers of metaphysical power, they crossed and pooled right under the foundation, providing the juice for a housekeeping spell that kept things exactly as they had been when it was laid, lo these many years ago. I think the idea had been to clean the house and *then* lay the spell, but I suppose the bachelor who had owned the place had thought it looked good enough.

Of course, good enough meant that the stains on my ceiling were never going to go away no matter how many times I painted over them. The scuffs on the hardwood floors were never getting buffed out. And if I tried doing something radical like changing out the yellowed sheers for something that might actually block sunlight, some of my personal belongings would shortly thereafter end up missing.

The house was vindictive like that.

But the spell also meant that I didn't need to bother with things like scrubbing the ring in the tub, because it was never going to go away anyway, or sweeping the floor, which always stayed exactly as dusty as it always had and always would. Or fixing the wall that I suddenly remembered was supposed to have a hole in it but which the light of a passing car showed to be as solid and depressingly covered with cabbage roses as ever.

A flash of another scene—crimson and black and blinding, incandescent white—blazed across my eyes for a second. Until I shoved it away, along with the damned roses. And got up so I wouldn't have to look at them.

The dresser had a heap of bras on it, some complete with grassy bits and sandspurs. I spent a few minutes sorting them out to give myself something to do. To drown out Lawrence's voice screaming my name on the wharf, its tone saying he already knew there was nothing either of us could do.

I swallowed and told myself the usual crap: Lawrence had been a professional. Lawrence had known what he was getting into. Lawrence had taken what he felt was an acceptable risk.

And as always, it was exactly no damned comfort at

all. And neither was my usual postmission dissection, going over every missed opportunity, every tiny mistake, every "should have." Because this time, none of it would have made any difference.

I should have called in. But we'd only been in that other place for a few minutes, and one vampire power I've never heard of was teleportation. Even if I'd called for backup as soon as we set eyes on the portal, they wouldn't have made it there in time.

I should have prevented Lawrence from going inside in the first place, or followed him quicker. Except that there had been nothing tangible to grab onto once he did his disappearing routine, and going into an unknown portal without any idea of what was on the other side was beyond crazy. It was slightly less so for him, given his ability, but I could have been walking into a volcano or off a cliff.

I should have figured out that, yeah, anybody who bothered to set a trap that carefully might have also designed a Plan B. Except that I'd have acted no differently, even if I had known. In the end, there had been more danger in not closing the portal than in worrying about a possible ambush.

I should have . . .

Done exactly what I did. It had been textbook. And it had failed spectacularly, anyway.

How do you kill a senior master the easy way? By not killing him yourself. By trapping him somewhere with a hostile atmosphere, where if he stays in one piece too long or hits the wrong patch of air, he'll burn up without anything attacking him at all. And then by making sure that something damn well does attack him by putting your trap right down in the middle of—what? Those creatures' eggs?

I didn't know. But something had set them off, something had made them go for him like a stirred-up hornet's nest. And how do you fight something you've never even seen with all of thirty seconds to figure it out? While you're fucking on fire?

The answer was, you didn't. You ran like hell, if you

had any brains at all, which is what Lawrence had done. What we'd both done, which is what they'd expected. They'd probably hoped those things would catch us before we made it back into our world, but hey, no sweat either way. Even if we got out, we were sure to be weak and hurting and confused, and a much easier target than should ever have been the case.

I felt nails digging into my palm, hard enough to break skin, and didn't even try to pull them out. It was what infuriated me the most. Not that he'd died—we'd all known that was a possibility on this kind of thing. But to die like that? Not able to defend yourself, or to get away, or to do anything but lie there and be butchered like an animal by some cowardly sons of bitches who didn't have the guts to face you—

It was the main reason I worked alone. So if I didn't come back, there was only myself to blame. And there was no partner to leave on the ground behind me.

I didn't bother with a bath, since the only place I'd gone was inside my head. I ran fingers through my hair in lieu of a brush, changed to a slightly less rumpled tank top and decided to view the rips in my jeans as a fashion statement. Then I went downstairs.

It couldn't have been too late, because the kids were still up, and Claire was a stickler for a nine p.m. bedtime. They were on the floor in the living room, wedged between two lumps of troll, since no way was the sofa holding all of that. I stuck my head in to say hi, but didn't get much of a reply because SpongeBob was on and SpongeBob is the shit.

I didn't join them—my stomach was starting to protest the lack of breakfast. And lunch. And from the shriveled-up way it felt right now, possibly dinner yesterday, too.

I padded into the kitchen, and found Claire at the stove. She was stirring something in the huge pot she used to cook for her fey bodyguards, who looked like lithe young gazelles and ate like starving hippos. She had her hair up in a bright red ponytail, had a fifties-era apron on and the whole scene looked like *I Love Lucy* in a domestic mood. It was a charming, old-fashioned picture—or it would have been if a vampire hadn't been perched on the stool beside her.

"What are you still doing here?" I asked Ray, who was scowling into the pot.

"Trying to tell your friend that that's too much pepper."

"It's chicken and rice," Claire said, pushing his big nose out of the way so she could stir. "It's supposed to be peppery."

"Peppery, yeah. Sear your tongue off, no."

"What would you know about it? Your kind doesn't eat."

"My kind eats just fine, and I'm a master, sweetheart. I can even taste it. Not that I'm gonna taste that because you're ruining it."

"You're just tired of grinding the pepper."

He didn't deny it.

Ray glanced at me as I came up alongside, drawn by the wonderful smell. His hands were dusted with little black flecks, like he'd been at the firing range all day. "It's about time you showed up. I was starting to think you were dead."

"No, just starved." I peered over Claire's shoulder and my stomach growled agreement. "How long till we eat?"

"Not long," she said, giving me the once-over. I guess I must have passed muster because all she said was: "I'm thinking maybe add some peas?"

"Peas are good." Right now anything sounded good. I might actually eat almost as much as a fey.

I walked over to the sink to wash up, even though I didn't need it, because Claire was a stickler for that, too. "Your father asked you to call him when you woke up," she told me. "You know, if you survived." A bag of frozen peas hit the counter, a little harder than necessary.

"Here we go again," Ray said with a sigh.

"He's a *dick*," Claire said forcefully.

"He's a senator." Ray shrugged. "They're all dicks. It's a job requirement."

"Well, he should have job security, then!"

"I didn't notice you throwing him out of the house like the other one," Ray said archly.

"What other one?" I asked.

"Marlowe," Claire said, spinning around. "He's not getting back in here, Dory. I've had enough. I mean it. That man is—" She muttered something that I must have misheard because Claire didn't talk that way.

I blinked. "What did he do now?"

"Oh, nothing! He just wanted to put you back in!"

"Back in?"

"Back inside your memory! After they almost lost you and you were so exhausted you couldn't even sit up, he wanted to put you back!"

"Why didn't they?" I asked, because last night had gone a bit fuzzy again, but I knew I hadn't gotten a look at anyone's face. Not even the guy who had stepped on mine. That damned searchlight had ensured as much, or whatever they had been using. Probably some new kind of spell that I was going to have to look out for because it might be—

"What?" I asked, because Claire was glaring at me.

"Why not?"

"Claire, we need to know—"

"The dick wouldn't let him," Ray broke in. "I guess it's why he just got escorted to the door instead of thrown out."

I stopped, my hands all soapy. "Mircea ... got escorted to the door?" I repeated, not sure I'd heard right.

"I should have thrown them all out when they showed up!" Claire said severely.

Damn. I would have paid money to see that, I thought in awe. Like, a *lot* of money.

"You need to stay away from those vampires, Dory," she told me, scowling. Because obviously I wasn't taking this seriously enough. "You need to stay away from all of them.

"That's a little hard when I'm working for them," I pointed out.

"Maybe it's about to get easier."

"What?"

"Nothing." She turned back to the stove. "Just . . . something your father said."

"Something like . . ."

"Like he plans to fire your ass," Ray informed me, digging through the fridge. "What? You guys got no beer?"

"What?"

"Beer. Alcohol. Booze. Hell, I'm desperate. I'll even drink that light crap — "

"Not you," I said, and jerked him out before he found the Guinness. And turned back to see Claire looking mulish.

"Want to run that by me again?"

"He didn't say . . . he just agreed with me."

"About what?"

"About the fact that you could have died, Dory!" she said, slamming her wooden spoon down. "If they can kill a master, they can kill you!"

"'They' didn't kill a master. 'They' ambushed us like the pathetic wastes of flesh — "

"They arranged it," Claire said, thrusting out her chin.

"Yeah. And I'm going to arrange a little something as soon as I figure out — "

"He said you'd say that."

"Gonna be hard to go on a rampage without backup," Ray pointed out, climbing back onto his stool with one of my longnecks.

"I'll have backup," I said grimly, reaching for my phone before I remembered: mine was currently waterlogged. So I grabbed the house phone off the wall and punched in a number I'm not supposed to have.

"What the hell?" I demanded.

The vampire on the other end of the connection snorted. At least, that's what the sound would have been called if I had uttered it. But when you wore Brioni tuxedos because Armani was too common, it was called "expressing disapproval."

"Dorina. How did you obtain this number?"

"I got tired of going through your boys. According to them, you're always out or you're always busy."

"Which is frequently the case. And you did not answer the question."

"How about you answer one first."

"Such as?"

"Such as I let you into my head and now I'm *fired*?"

"Of course not."

"Good. Because I have a few ideas about—"

"You're suspended."

"I'm—what?"

"It is merely temporary."

"Why?" I asked harshly. "Because I let Lawrence get killed?"

"You didn't 'let' Lawrence do anything. Lawrence was the senior member of that team. If anything, he let you down—"

"How? By dying?"

"By allowing overconfidence in his abilities to blind him to the dangers of the situation," Mircea said, a little bite creeping into his tone. "Having three master abilities made him unusual, but not invincible. As he discovered—*after* he put you in the untenable position of abandoning him or rushing in after him. And of course, you chose the latter—"

"What was I supposed to do?"

"You weren't supposed to be in that position in the first place. And you will not be again, not until—"

"Okay, let me see if I've got this straight. I'm being fired for not leaving Lawrence to die?"

"You're not being fired—"

"Funny, that's what it sounds like."

"You're being suspended until we determine—"

"Determine what?"

"Why you're still alive!" Mircea snapped.

Okay, that was a new record. It usually took me a full two minutes to get under his skin. Fair enough; it took him about that many seconds to work his way under mine.

"You want to explain that?" I asked, after a pause.

"If you give me a chance," he said curtly. "However poor Kit's choice of phrasing may have been, what he said this afternoon had merit—in any scenario I can envision, you should have been killed as well as Lawrence. That was the point, it would seem, of that whole exercise—to deprive us of as many agents as possible—"

"Like Radu said, maybe they didn't—"

"—and clearly, we were not likely to send anything less than our best after a witness as important as Varus. Whether they knew what you are or not, you should have died last night. They had no reason whatsoever to keep you alive—and yet they did."

"Maybe they—"

"And not just bleeding out on the pier. They *took* you. They picked you up and took you away, to some misbegotten hole in the wall where we could not find you. You are Mine, but not as a Child born of blood would be. I cannot trace you, and I foolishly did not think to put a trace on you—"

"Wait. I don't remember any—"

"I know that you do not! But I saw. Through Louis-Cesare's eyes, I saw it all, and it was very clear that they had some sort of plan for you. And until I know what that plan was, it is too much of a risk—"

"Like it's not for everybody? From what you're saying, it seems like I'm in less danger than anyone else. Wherever I ended up, I'm alive—"

"And so you shall remain."

It was implacable—dry, cold, and hard as steel—in the tone I hated most from him. It was the one that said he wasn't even listening to me, that he never had been, that he wasn't going to. It was the one that said I might as well hang up right now, because this conversation was going exactly nowhere. But some of Mircea's ungodly bullheadedness had dripped down the family line to me, and I wasn't done yet.

"My partner is dead," I said flatly. "Do you really expect me to—"

"Your partner. Whom you knew for all of an hour,

and whose existence you had completely forgotten until this afternoon?"

"You know damned well that doesn't—"

"Lawrence was Kit's man. He was only the third Child he ever made. If you think someone will not bleed for this, many someones, you do not know him as I do."

"Then let me help!"

"No."

"If you were short on agents before, it's twice as bad now! Why in the name of—"

"Because you are *Mine*." The voice snapped like a whip. "As Lawrence was Kit's. Closer, even, born not only of blood but of flesh and bone, and I will not risk—"

"You're not risking anything!"

"That is correct. I am not. Not this time."

"Damn it, Mircea!" I hung on to the phone, mad as hell but not able to give this up. I needed this job. And not just for the money, although a steady income was something I thought I could get used to. I needed it because of what I was.

I couldn't just not hunt. It didn't work that way. Even with Claire here it didn't. Her presence made it easier to postpone episodes, to maintain some level of control. But I was what I was. A life lacking in violence might be the norm for most people, but for me it was a one-way ticket to the crazy house, and not just for a brief visit. The creature that lived inside my veins demanded blood; the only thing I'd ever been able to decide was whose.

And now he was taking that away.

"That Duergar mix of yours," Mircea said after a moment. "You are fond of him, are you not?"

"What does that have to do with anything?"

"How would you like to see him walking headlong into a danger you cannot even name?"

"That's not . . ." I gripped the phone tightly so I wouldn't shove it through the wall. "That's different. He's a child."

"And when he is not?" Mircea asked softly. "When he is an adult, when he has developed whatever abilities fate has decided for him, do you think you will feel one whit differently than you do today? Do you think you will suddenly not mind if someone takes him from you, if they threaten him, if they hurt him?"

"You never . . ." I swallowed, because he was doing it to me again. Just like every fucking . . . Goddamn it. "You never cared before."

"I have always cared."

"Then let me *hunt*."

"No."

"Mircea. I can find the ones who did this. I can—"

"What you can do is obey me," the voice said, going cold again. "For once in your life, you will do as I say!" And the phone went dead.

Chapter Eleven

"That went well," Ray said, sipping beer.

Claire came up behind me, saying nothing but sliding a slim white hand onto my shoulder. And reminding me that her usual passive abilities were nothing compared to what she could really do. Like when she abruptly pulled the rage off me, as fast as someone whipping off a cloak.

"Stop it," I choked out. I didn't want to feel better. I wanted to break something. But instead, I saw myself slowly replacing the receiver, and my hand didn't even shake.

"It's better than having you burst a blood vessel," she said drily, her own hand sliding away. Her cheeks were a little pink, but otherwise she looked perfectly normal. I tried to work up some annoyance about that, but it fizzled out, too. When she was making an effort, Claire was like a dozen Prozac in a shot of whiskey. If I'd been wearing a mood ring, it would have just flipped to mellow, stoner blue.

"Damn it, Claire," I said, trying for heat and getting only warm fuzzies.

"He's right," she said simply. "You know he is."

"I don't know anything of the kind."

"You can hunt other things."

"I don't *want* to hunt other things."

"You'll get used to it," she told me, with zero sympathy. Claire wasn't big on sympathy. Claire was big on getting your shit together and getting on with it, as demonstrated when she took a stack of plates off the counter and pushed them into my stomach. "Can you set the tables?"

I glared at her, black eyes into green, and she narrowed hers back. She didn't budge. But the plates poked me in the stomach again, a little harder this time. I bit my lip on a smile, amused and pissed off at the same time because I shouldn't be feeling amused.

"You're gonna need more plates than that," Ray piped up.

Claire glanced at him. "Why?"

"You got company."

I took the damned plates to the window, and spotted a parade coming at us from across the road. "What company?" Claire asked. She was blind as a bat without her glasses, which as usual she'd misplaced.

"It's just the guys from next door."

There was a similar Victorian monstrosity wilting across the road, only it was even larger than ours, a relic from when people around here could afford servants' quarters. That made it a hard sell these days, with too much to air-condition and too much to heat—not that the house appeared to have either. But the artists who had taken it over didn't seem to care, and the many little rooms were perfect for communal living.

"*Just* the guys?" Claire asked sharply.

"No, some of the girls are with them." A couple blondes, a redhead and two brunettes were bearing casseroles and covered plates that looked like they might contain cookies—or, if I was lucky, some medicinal brownies.

But Claire didn't seem so enthused. "Crap!" she said, searching around in her clothes for the missing glasses.

"What's the problem? Throw another bag of rice in the pot, maybe a few more peas—"

"It's not the food I'm worried about, Dory!"

"What then?"

"They're . . . women of questionable morals."

I laughed out loud at that one. "What?"

"You heard me."

"Claire. You do realize what century it is, don't you?"

"And you do realize what we have in the backyard, don't you?" she snapped back.

"What? You mean your bodyguards?" The fey had pitched tents back there rather than stay in the house, because there wasn't enough room inside for everyone and it was some kind of no-no in their culture to not treat people of the same rank equally. Luckily, they seemed to enjoy outdoor living. No reason not to. Retrieving my underwear had been the most work they'd done in two weeks.

"No," she said, finally locating the glasses in a pocket of her apron. "I mean a bunch of young male fey who are currently without supervision."

"Where's Heidar?" I asked, talking about Claire's fiancé, who was supposed to be in charge of the motley crew.

"He went back this morning. Something his father wanted—I don't know. But that leaves us—damn it!" She'd gone to the kitchen door in time to see the group being greeted warmly by what looked like the Norwegian male swim team. A dozen tall, well-built guys with long blond hair were hanging over the back fence, grinning like Christmas had come early.

The artists were grinning back. "We keep hearing this crazy music," Jacob said, holding up a guitar. He was the tall one with the Jewfro and the Grizzly Adams beard. "Do you guys play?"

"Yes. We will play with you," one of the fey told him, his eyes on the pretty Hispanic girl at Jacob's side.

"Oh, I love your accent," one of the other girls told the nearest noble of the Royal House Blarestri of the High Court of the Fey. "Are you Swedish?"

"Yes," he assured her solemnly. "I am of the Swedish."

"Oh, cool."

Claire rolled her eyes.

"They're not children," I reminded her, grinning.

"That's what I'm worried about."

"Don't you think you're overreacting just a—"

"Why do you think there are all those legends about

the fey kidnapping human women?" she demanded, whirling on me. "What do you think they did with them?"

"I know, but—"

"Fertile females are like gold in Faerie, Dory—rarer even. And the fey can smell them coming. It's like ... bees to honey. You haven't seen it—I have."

"Well, so what? They're all adults. If they want to—"

"*Fertile* females."

"Oh. *Oh*," I said, finally getting it. "Is that what you're—"

"Yes! I know what it's like to be caught between worlds. I wouldn't wish that on ... well, certainly not a bunch of helpless children!"

"But even if ... I mean, the fey are notoriously infertile, right?"

"With their own women, yes. *These are not their own women!*"

"Okay, Claire, okay. Calm down," I told her, feeling a little strange because that was her line. "You're their commander's fiancée. Just order them—"

She was already shaking her head. "On something else—anything else—yes. I could. But not on this. Why do you think I've kept them so closely confined? Why Heidar has? They'll just sneak out tonight when I'm asleep. It's like babysitting twelve randy teenagers, and I can't watch them all the—"

"So why not get 'em some condoms?" Ray piped up.

Claire stopped. And then turned to look at him. "I ... don't think they know what those are," she said doubtfully. "They don't have them in Faerie. The birth rate is low enough as it is; there's no reason to develop something to lower it even further."

"Well, it ain't rocket science," he pointed out. "They could learn, right?"

Claire was nodding, obviously liking this new idea. "Yes. Yes, they can." She looked at me. "How many condoms do you have?"

"What?"

"Condoms, condoms! You must have some!"

"Why must I?" I didn't think sex once a decade warranted it. And anyway, the only guy I was into at the moment wasn't the type to need them. Not that we would have anyway, considering that I'd spent much of the last two weeks recuperating. And that probably wasn't going to change, since it would only make it harder when—

"Dory!"

"I'm fresh out," I told her.

"Well, go to the store," Claire said, grabbing her purse and shoving it at me. "I—I'll take the food out. They'll have to eat first. And by the time they're finished, you'll be back."

"With the condoms."

"Right."

"For the giant orgy you're convinced we're about to have in the backyard."

"Dory! Just go!"

"I'll go with," Ray said, getting up. "I need a snack."

Which was how I ended up condom shopping with a vampire.

"She always that tense?" Ray asked, as we pulled away from the house in my old Firebird.

"No. She's just . . . under a lot of pressure right now."

"What pressure? Her kid's okay, right?"

I nodded. Actually, I had no idea what Claire's problem was. Maybe it was just residual. In about a year, she'd gone from underpaid auction-house employee to fey princess to new mother to woman on the run with her endangered child, who also happened to be the heir to the Blarestri throne. It was enough to put anyone on edge.

But Aiden really was okay, with the conspiracy that had threatened his life over and the instigator dead. And he was now in possession of a talisman that pretty much ensured that he'd stay that way, even if someone managed to get past the wards, the phalanx in the garden, and the tense, half-dragon mother. Frankly, I didn't fancy anyone's chances.

"She'll calm down eventually," I told Ray. "So what are you doing here again?"

"Living," he said, which I'd have taken for a smart remark, except he sounded pretty emphatic. But I didn't have time to follow up on it. The nearest store was only a couple blocks away, and we'd already arrived.

Sanjay, brother to Bawa of the world's deadliest curry, ran it, but he went home at six and some new girl was on duty. We skirted the aisles of Ramen, cards of press-on nails and towers of hairspray that constituted daily essentials in Brooklyn, and finally located the condom aisle. It also housed the diapers and the baby food. I wasn't sure if that was random product placement or brilliant advertising, but either way, there was a good selection.

"So what kind are we talking about here?" Ray asked, surveying a neatly stacked display.

"I don't know. Just pick one."

"Well, there's a lot of choice. I mean, you got your flavored, your ridged, your pre-lubed, your thin, your super-ultra-thin, your super-ultra-thin-pre-lubed, your ... Huh."

"Huh what?"

"Would you look at this?" he asked, examining a small box. "It says it glows in the dark."

"So?"

"So what use is that to anybody? I mean, what am I supposed to do? Write her name in the air with it?"

"I'd rather not think of you doing anything with it," I said honestly.

"Besides, the fey already glow, so you gotta think it's a waste of—"

"Ray!" I glanced around, but there was nobody within earshot.

"Well, excuse me if I'm not used to buying condoms for aliens," he said more softly.

"They're not aliens."

"Well, they're not human. I mean, they could have anything under those tunics, you know?"

"Like what?"

"Like . . . I don't know. It could be barbed or some-thing."

"Barbed?"

"Well, I don't know." He slanted me a glance. "Do you?"

I just looked at him.

"No, of course not. You're too uptight."

"I am not uptight."

"You're the definition of uptight. I bet you and Mr. Muscle Bound haven't even done it yet."

"Okay, enough with the personal—"

"Nailed it." He nodded. "You wouldn't have freaked out on him this afternoon otherwise. 'Oh, no, somebody's in my head for five seconds, even if it did save my life—'"

I scowled. "You don't get it. He's not supposed to be able to do that."

"He's a senior master. They got skills." Ray shrugged. "Anyway, I don't know what you're complaining about. As soon as a baby vamp wakes up, he's got all kinds of people in his head."

"I'm not a vampire," I said, but Ray wasn't listening.

"There's his master, poking around, telling him what's what and that he better toe the line. There's the senior vamps in the family, checking out the new talent, just in case they want to recruit him for one of their cliques later on. There's the slightly older babies, trying to dig up some dirt to make sure he stays on the bottom of the heap, and so on. And they *never shut up*. Yak, yak, yak, yak, yak, yak, yak. It drove me crazy for years."

"Is that what happened?"

"But I got used to it. So will you."

"Maybe I don't want to get used to it," I muttered, examining a box that promised to vibrate. I thought that was my job. I put it back.

"Oh, you want it, all right," Ray said. "The two of you practically melt the walls every time you get within three feet of—"

"That's not the same thing," I told him irritably. It wasn't the sex that worried me. I'd had sex; I'd never had a relationship with a vampire unless you counted Mircea, and look how well that had turned out. If I couldn't even manage the usual father-daughter stuff, how was I supposed to handle something much more complex with someone I didn't know half as well?

Relationships weren't my best thing. They never had been. Even the easy ones. And nothing about Louis-Cesare was easy.

"It is when you're dating a master. You gotta take the whole package, you know?" Ray said. And then he stopped, and turned to look at me. "Hey, that's it, isn't it?"

"What is?"

"You never dated a master before."

"I've been with vampires."

"Yeah, sure. Any regular old vamp—I can see that. I mean, you're stronger than him; you're the one calling the shots; you're the one who says when you've had enough and it's time to head out."

"Shut up and pick something."

"But it's not the same with a senior master, is it? Somebody who might be stronger than you. Somebody who might want to take the lead sometimes, too. Somebody you can't just dump whenever you—"

I tipped the whole display into the basket he'd picked up by the door. He blinked. "Well, that oughta do it."

I grabbed the basket o' condoms and went to wait in line, ignoring the looks from a couple people ahead of me, who were apparently not used to seeing someone buying twenty boxes at once. Ray went to lean on the counter, supposedly enthralled by an awesome display of toenail clippers, but in fact snacking on the salesclerk.

And, predictably, my stomach curled into a knot.

It was one of the things—one of the very, very many things—about dating a master that wasn't going to work. Ray made it sound so easy, like this was just some kind of tug-of-war, some weird power play, that I needed to get past and I'd be fine. Like all the other humans who eagerly lined up to attach themselves to the great houses. Mircea probably turned away fifty a month, and those were just the ones arrogant enough to try. Louis-Cesare, as the longtime darling of the European Senate, could hardly have attracted any fewer.

Ray probably thought I should feel honored to have caught his eye. That I should feel grateful. That I should feel . . . whatever those other humans felt.

He forgot one thing.

I wasn't human.

There had always been a love/hate—okay, mostly hate—thing going on with me and the vampire community. I'd tried to stay away; I'd spent years trying. Like Claire said, there were other things to hunt and most of them were much less likely to hunt me back. But there was nothing that made my blood sing, my senses reel, my heart pound quite like chasing my natural prey.

Except maybe fucking it.

It was crude, but it was the truth. Vampires weren't just prey to me; they never had been. There was this weird kind of yearning underneath it all, and resentment and jealousy and a bone-deep ache that I didn't understand. Not completely. I just knew that, every once in a while, the craving got too deep and it was either fight or fuck, and mostly it was the former but sometimes . . . sometimes it had been the latter. Just long enough to get it out of my system, to keep myself from going crazier than I already was.

And then, yeah, I moved on. Why the hell wouldn't I? If I stayed around, it always ended the same way, and crazy or not, I didn't particularly like the idea of staking a former lover. No matter how much a few of them had deserved it.

But this wasn't a one-night stand. This was . . . well, I didn't really know what this was, since I'd been avoiding discussing it. Talking about it meant facing the fact that this weird little interlude or experiment or whatever the hell I thought I'd been doing had run its course. Because how could you care about someone when his very means of existence made your stomach hurt?

Not that Louis-Cesare needed to snack on random clerks when he probably had a whole stable lined up and eager to be used. I knew that. But still. It was what he *was*.

And I killed what he was.

"What size you think they take?" Ray asked.

I looked up, blinking, to see that it was my turn. "Does it matter? We have plenty."

"Well, yeah. But they're all different sizes," he said, piling boxes on the counter. "And what if the—what if they need something like extra small? You got enough extra smalls?"

"They're not extra small," I told him irritably. "They don't need extra smalls."

"I thought you said you didn't know."

"They're seven feet tall!"

"Don't matter," he argued. "Plenty of big guys got a Tiny Tim. Sometimes I think they all do. I mean, why else spend all that time in the gym? Why get all those muscles? If you got it where it counts, the ladies know. You don't gotta advertise."

The mocha-skinned clerk, who could easily have made two of Ray, snorted.

"Well, there's no way to know," I told him, "so we're just going to have to chance it."

"You could call her and ask."

"Call—" I stopped. "You mean Claire?"

"Well, it was her idea."

I had a sudden flash of Claire's face if I called to ask what size condom her fiancé took. It was kind of breathtaking.

"You want me to ring these up or not?" the cashier asked.

"If they don't fit, can we bring them back?"

"No refunds on condoms."

"Just call her," Ray said.

"I am not calling Claire and asking . . . I'm not calling Claire."

"Okay by me. I mean, I don't care. But you get 'em too small and they pop off, and you get 'em too big and they slide off, and either way, it's pointy-eared babies all ar—"

"Ray!"

"I mean, I guess they'd go over pretty well at a *Star Trek* convention, but the rest of the time—"

"All right! Stop it! All right!"

"It's not just Claire who's a little tense," he said, as I dug around for a cell phone I didn't have, and then commandeered his. I didn't waste time trying to figure out how to phrase this because some things are better just winged.

"If you're not buying anything, you gotta get out of line," the cashier told me.

"There's nobody else in the store."

"Don't matter—there's rules. Somebody could come in, and I'm the only one on."

"Start ringing things up, then. This won't take long."

"Which ones?"

"I don't care." I pushed some at her. "These."

"These?" She looked dubious.

The phone was still ringing, but nobody was picking up. "Why not those?"

She glanced at Ray. "'Cause if that's your man, I'd say you can leave these off," and she pushed the three biggest sizes to the side.

"Oh, no, you didn't," Ray said.

"It's your own fault," I told him. She might have thought it, but she probably wouldn't have said it if he hadn't been snacking earlier. But that sort of thing puts some people in a bad mood—usually those with enough magical blood to recognize the theft but not to name it. And the anger tends to resolve itself into a generalized dislike of the vamp in question.

And then someone picked up. *"Oui?"*

Damn. I thought about hanging up, pretending to be a wrong number, as cowardly as that would have been. But I guess he recognized my breathing or something—which was disturbing enough right there—because he said, "Dory?"

"What are you doing there?" I asked, harsher than I'd intended.

"I was about to ask you the same. Where are you?"

"Buying condoms," I said, watching the salesclerk ring up a box of mediums and hand them to Ray.

"Why?"

"Is there more than one reason?" I asked, because "we have a garden full of randy fey" wasn't on the approved-conversation list.

There was silence on the other end of the phone.

"What's this shit?" Ray demanded, looking at the salesclerk.

"Honey, truth hurts, but ain't no way you're a Magnum."

"Well, I ain't no medium!"

The clerk smiled. "Yeah, but I was being generous."

"Dorina," Louis-Cesare finally said. "You do realize . . . I thought you had been with our kind before."

"I have."

"Then why . . ." He stopped. And when he spoke again, his voice had changed. "Who are they for?"

"What are you doing?" the cashier demanded, as Ray grabbed another box. "I ain't rung those up yet."

Ray pulled out a foil package and tossed the box back on the counter. "So ring it up."

She arched an eyebrow, but didn't bother, maybe because she was watching him unbutton his fly. I caught his wrist. "What are you doing?"

"Proving a point."

"Not in the middle of the store, you're not."

"Ain't nobody here," the cashier reminded me, grinning. "And ain't no way he's filling that thing out."

"Dorina?" Louis-Cesare's voice was loud in my ear. The one I had squeezed against the phone, which was squeezed against my sore shoulder, because I was using both hands to keep Ray's point in his pants.

"The fey, damn it!" I told him. "They're for the fey!"

"Which one?" Louis-Cesare asked, his voice going velvety soft.

"All of them— No, Ray! Ray, cut it out!"

"*All* of them?"

"No, that's not what I—"

Ray gave a sudden twist, and the phone went sliding

across the floor. And I went sliding after it, because it was that or risk an Interspecies Incident. But I didn't pick it up. Because my hand landed on it about the same time that a foot did—a foot in a size sixteen boot belonging to a guy big enough to need it.

No, not a guy, I thought, looking up when the phone didn't budge. A vampire. And not one of the nicer ones.

Chapter Twelve

"Mm-hmm. Now *that's* a Magnum," the clerk said behind me. She sounded impressed.

I was, too, but for a different reason. "I didn't hear you come in," I accused, standing up. And then getting a few feet between us.

The vamp grinned, all big white teeth in a handsome Asian face, which upset the tiger tat sleeping on his left cheek. It uncurled, stretched, and muscled down to the open neck of his black polo, watching me the whole time through narrowed emerald eyes. It looked like it was thinking about going for my jugular. Unlike its owner, who was in a worryingly good mood.

He switched the toothpick he'd been chewing to the other side of his mouth. "Takes talent," he said mildly. And then he lunged.

A fist with enough force behind it to punch through a wall went whistling toward my face. But it didn't punch a wall — or anything else — because I did a limbo-like maneuver that had me bent almost double in the wrong direction. And that much momentum doesn't stop on a dime. It took him a half second to recover, and that was a half second too long.

I whirled, got my boot in his ass and *pushed*. He went barreling straight into the cash register, causing the clerk to jump back, the machine to hit the ground and the drawer to pop open. Change scattered, bills fluttered and he turned, grinning, because he was nuts and always had been.

I tried to remember his name, since it helps if you're

trying to talk somebody down. But "Scarface" was the only thing coming to mind. It was the nickname I'd given him the first time we met—you know, a couple of minutes after I tried to blow him up.

In fairness to me, he'd been trying to kill me at the time. In fairness to him, I'd been trying to steal something that belonged to his master, namely Ray, who the Senate had wanted to squeal on his boss's White Tiger triad and its network of illegal portals. So you could say we had been about even on the fault scale when the bomb decided matters—temporarily, because the guy was a first-level master.

A little thing like a bomb going off practically on top of him hadn't slowed him down for long. It had left him with a face full of scars, however, and an attitude. The scars had faded, and I thought the attitude had, too, when we ended up on the same side—sort of—a little later. So I wasn't exactly facing an enemy.

Of course, he wasn't a friend, either. At least, not in the conventional sense. Like in the not ripping the ICEE machine off the wall and chucking it at my head sense.

I ducked, which avoided decapitation but did nothing to prevent cold neon blue sludge from drenching me when the tank burst against the wall. He grinned. "Not your color."

"What is your problem?" I asked, scooping the freezing mess out of my cleavage.

"We got unfinished business," he reminded me.

"My name's not Bill."

He chuckled. "Yeah, I loved that movie. Shoulda brought a katana, but it seemed like an unfair advantage."

And then he pulled out a shotgun and blew the shit out of the fixture behind me.

It would have blown a hole through me, too, but I'd already been on my way to the ground. I rolled, slipped in the guts of a shampoo bottle, got to my feet and slid behind a row of fixtures. Which went up in a line of explosions right on my heels, because vampire reflexes on reload made almost any gun an automatic.

Until the crazy bastard firing it runs out of shells, anyway.

I crouched behind a bunch of mirrors on a pegboard, which were making a lot of *oh, shit* faces at me. I debated shooting back, but it wouldn't have done any good. I had an M1911 .45 under my arm and a 9mm Glock 17 in a concealed holster at my waist, plus a cute little .22 I kept as a backup in my boot. None of which would do more to this joker than piss him off.

But it looked like I'd better come up with something, judging by the gun butt that obliterated the mirrors a second later.

I launched myself backward, flipped and sent three knives into his heart, one right after the other. Which didn't buy me any time, unless you count the second he took to do an Arnold Schwarzenegger impression and flex a pec at me. And pop the damned things out.

"Don't you hate it when they do that?" he asked sympathetically.

"They ... don't usually do that," I admitted.

"Yeah." He looked smug. "But I been getting a lot of practice lately. You know the games are on."

"So I heard."

Everybody had heard. Everybody in the vampire community, anyway. Thanks to the war—and Geminus's recent demise—the Senate was currently missing seven members out of thirteen. It left them vulnerable as all hell and seriously overworked, but it was an unprecedented opportunity for ambitious first-level masters. Because by tradition the seats went, as Alexander the Great had once said about his empire, "to the strongest." There was a series of duels, with the winners—aka the survivors—taking all.

To the vamp world, it was the Olympics, the World Cup and the Super Bowl all rolled into one, with contenders like Scarface having the time of their deaths advancing through the ranks. And since he was still here, I assumed he was advancing just fine. It didn't surprise me; I hadn't managed to kill him, and I'd given it a damned good try.

"You seen any of the matches?" he asked, holding up on my demise long enough to get his ego stroked.

"My invitation got lost in the mail."

He chuckled. "Too bad. I'd bet on you next to some of those jokers. Can't even take a punch, but think they ought to be a senator."

"It's a scandal."

"Damn right." He shook his head. "You know, I was gutting this loser the other day, and I thought, *It'd be more fun fighting that little dhampir. I wonder if she's recovered yet.* And here you are."

"Lucky me," I said.

Scarface grinned. "You know, I might even let you live. You're funny."

I had a good comeback for that, but didn't get to use it, being too busy dodging left, right, left a dozen or so times, as rapid-fire fists punched the air all around me, like some kind of automatic hammer. At least, they did until—

"This is a damned shame right here," someone said, and another shotgun blast tore through the shop.

It wasn't from Scarface's gun, which he'd abandoned when he started trying to use me for a punching bag. I looked behind him to find the clerk standing there, 12-gauge in hand, and eyes huge. Maybe because we were looking at each other through the hole she'd just blown in Scarface's sternum.

He looked down at it and then back over his shoulder at her. "That stings," he said. She didn't answer, being too busy staring at him with her mouth hanging open. He turned around and closed it for her with a finger. "You got a name?"

"D-Delisha."

He checked her out. "Yes, you are. You got a man, Delisha?"

"Had one. Fool cheated on me so I kicked his ass to the curb."

Scarface got out a card and tucked it in the pocket of a truly magnificent pair of jeans. "Save me the trouble." Then he took the shotgun away from her, turned the butt

sideways like a paddle and smacked her ample rear with
it. "Get," he told her.

She got.

He turned his attention back on me. "Where were
we?"

"You can't do stuff like that in front of norms," I reminded him.

He shrugged. "She works for Singh. He rents half the
damned shop out to trolls."

And yes, yes, he did. Olga and a partner ran a beauty
parlor/weapons emporium out of the back room, because trolls like one-stop shopping. For some crazy reason, that had slipped my fevered brain. But come to
think of it, it might turn out to be—

I didn't get to finish the thought, being too busy avoid-
ing another swipe with the shotgun—Delisha's, because
Scarface had tossed his. In the middle of a cross aisle.
Not five yards from me.

He saw the direction of my gaze and grinned. "What
are you gonna do? Club me with it?"

"Seems to be a popular choice."

"Yeah, but that won't hurt me. Any more than that
little peashooter at your waist will. And the shotgun's out
of ammo, sweet cheeks."

I didn't answer. I just lunged for it. He didn't even
come after me, so sure I didn't have ammo for a gun I
wasn't carrying.

But only because it was on a dock somewhere, or
more likely at the bottom of the ocean. Which it hadn't
been when I'd packed this jacket a few days ago. My
fingers closed on the gun, the shells slammed home and
I turned, still on the floor.

"Well, I'll be damned," he said.

And then I blew his face off.

At least, I assumed so, although I didn't wait around
to find out. If a bomb hadn't stopped him, that wouldn't
either, not for long. I ran for the door, not screaming for
Ray because I figured he was long gone by now.

Or rather, I did until he ran into me coming back inside.

"What the—"

"Aughhh!" he said, which didn't explain anything, and then I looked over his shoulder and saw a bunch more tiger-tatted guys, which did.

It looked like they'd been loitering out front, smoking cigarettes and waiting for their buddy to finish trashing me. Now they were standing around with those cigarettes hanging out of their mouths, since clearly my survival hadn't been in the game plan. And still might not be, because there were five of them and while I doubted they were on Scarface's level, they were masters. And, right now, that would be good enough.

"Um," I said creatively.

They didn't say anything.

I licked my lips, trying to think. And finding it really hard for some reason. Maybe the same reason I was all but swaying on my feet.

"What is wrong with you?" Ray hissed, because we weren't presenting much of an intimidating front right now.

"Missed dinner," I muttered, hoping I hadn't skipped out on my last meal. And the one before that. And the one before—

"What?"

"I didn't eat."

"What difference does that make?"

"I'm not like you. I can't recharge by feeding off of someone. I need food."

"I know that! When was the last time you ate?"

"Yesterday?"

"Yester—*why the hell didn't you eat?*"

"We had to go buy condoms, remember?"

"And you couldn't grab something on the way out?" he said hysterically. "I'm gonna die because you couldn't grab a sandwich?"

"No, you're going to die because you wanted a snack. You could have stayed home."

"Well, excuse the hell out of me! The Senate didn't feed me, okay? I hadn't eaten either, in like two weeks! And what was I gonna eat at the house? All you have is fey and part fey and they all taste like shit. And their blood doesn't even do any—"

"May I say something?" one of the vamps asked politely.

The voice was cultured, with a faint British accent. It sounded a little odd coming from a guy with white-blond hair done up in eighties punk spikes, a leather jacket with more zippers even than mine and eyes so pale they looked blind. If he was going for disturbing, he was right on the money. But I guessed he was pretty important, because Ray's grip on my wrist had suddenly turned painful.

"Sure," I told him.

"This contest, it is between you and the Exalted Zheng-zi. We are not here to interfere."

"Really." Good to know. Well, possibly good. "So . . . why are you here?"

"For the traitor." Those colorless eyes swiveled to Ray, who probably didn't see them because he was busy trying to hide behind my back. "Give him to us and you may go."

"He's lying," Ray said rapidly. "Zheng's going for a Senate seat. He's not gonna let this go. He can't. You made him look bad and he can't afford—"

"Silence!" the other vamp hissed, and there must have been some power behind it, because Ray made a little hiccuping sound and shut up.

"I wish I knew how to do that," I told the vamp honestly.

He smiled, and it was surprisingly attractive. Or not so surprisingly. Most vamps could turn on the charm when they wanted something.

Only I couldn't figure out what he wanted with Ray.

"So what do you want with Ray?" I asked, because what the hell. "He's already coughed up everything he knows about your operation. The Senate wouldn't have released him otherwise."

"Perhaps we wish to repay him for that," the vamp said, baring some teeth. Which had all been filed to wicked-looking points.

Okay, then. That was one way to hide fangs, I guessed.

"Not to call you a liar," I said, "but bullshit. I don't doubt your boss wants revenge, but this bad? Five senior masters and a tank, after . . . after Ray?" I amended, because if the guy was about to get shredded, no need to insult him first.

"Perhaps we knew he was with you."

"Thanks for the compliment, but bullshit again. I didn't know he was going to be with me. You couldn't have guessed it before you came out looking for him. So how about the truth?" Preferably quickly, considering that Zheng was making some not-so-dead noises behind the fixture.

They must have distracted the vamp, too, because Ray suddenly regained the power of speech. And boy, did he use it. "They want me to hack a portal for them, only I can't. I told them I can't 'cause the Senate said one more thing, you know, just one more thing and they were gonna stake me for sure. And I told Lord Cheung and he said—"

"He said that you are a sniveling, worthless, waste of flesh and he regrets the day he took you on!" the vamp snapped, talking about his and Zheng's boss.

"Tough shit," Ray told him. Which would have been more impressive if he hadn't dodged back behind me. "'Cause I'm here now."

"Not for long."

"Yeah, well. Dory might have something to say about that!"

"Do you?" the vamp asked, arching a thin white eyebrow at me.

"Of course she does!" Ray said, poking me in the back.

I didn't say anything. Because something interesting had just been mentioned—for the second time. And, finally, my energy-starved brain had managed to latch onto it.

Olga had been tapping into the ley line sink that powered the house's spells to make it easier for her people to get around. Most species can pass for human with a cheap glamourie, but that gets harder when you're a walking mountain. There are still spells that work, of course, but they're expensive, and they add up after a while. Whereas a portal powered by a ley line sink that nobody knew about was free.

And, of course, one of the first places Olga had linked to was her place of business.

Her place of business in the back room of this store.

"All you have to do is stand aside," the vamp murmured, putting power behind it. He probably thought he was influencing me, which he wasn't nearly strong enough to do. I don't know if my resistance comes from my nature or from dealing with Mircea's shit for so long, but I'm not that easy to manipulate.

But I guess Ray must have thought otherwise, because he stomped on my instep. "What the hell?" I yelped.

"Don't listen to him! He's trying to—"

"I know what he's trying to do!" I said, resisting the urge to cut a bitch. Damn, that had hurt.

"Give him to us!" the albino told me, and a wave of suggestion hit me like a club. Or, more accurately, like a hundred barbs trying to sink into my brain. I shook them off, snarling.

"Bite me!"

"I think I shall let Master Zheng do that," he said sweetly, as his buddy lurched out from behind a mangled fixture.

How he was on his feet, I don't know. His hair was on fire, his face was a blackened mess, and one eye was hanging down his mostly missing left cheek. But at least the name fit again, I thought hysterically, as Ray's fingers dug into my wrist.

"Oh, shit," he said, very, very quietly.

"Run," I told him.

"What?"

"Run!"

"Where? They're guarding the rear, too. I already checked!"

"Portal," I said, shoving him as Scarface grabbed my jacket.

From about twelve feet away.

The *fuck*?

"Portal?" Ray said, like he'd never heard of such a thing.

I didn't answer. I was too busy absorbing the sight of the hugely elongated arm that, Gumby-like, had just snaked across the room. It had all the usual arm parts, including muscle, judging by the grip it had on the front of my jacket. But it was ... well, it was just stupid. Like being jerked across the shop by something that couldn't be real but obviously was. Like the cast-iron fist that waited for me if I didn't manage to—

I twisted in midair, unable to stop but just able to get my feet up. So that I hit him with steel-tipped boots instead of my face. Which would have worked better if the bastard had lost his grip.

"What portal?" Ray yelled.

"Olga's—in the back!" I gasped, trying to break free and getting hauled back by my jacket.

"Oh. She has—oh!" He turned and fled. And I got a hand on one of my dozen or so zippers, which weren't so much a fashion statement as a save-my-neck statement, as demonstrated when I pulled the one on the right shoulder down and the whole sleeve came off. It left Scarface holding leather and me burning it as I scrambled away.

For about a second, until something wrapped around my waist like a particularly hairy python.

I didn't try to shake it off; it probably wouldn't have worked anyway, and besides, there was no time. Because the son of a bitch was draining me, healing himself by sapping whatever energy I had left, and if I didn't get away now, now, right freaking *now*, it was going to all be over. So I kept going, dragging the elastic snake of an arm with me, around a pillar and over some shelves, then hitting the main aisle and running hell-bent for leather for the back door.

Along the way, I got a glimpse of the vamps outside. They had dropped the cool poses in order to press their noses to the glass in the front of the store, their faces in turn eager and astonished and worried as I just. Kept. Going. And then pulsing in and out along with my heartbeat as the room started to gray out and the door seemed to recede into the distance and it began to feel like maybe some bastard had snuck up and somehow encased my feet in cement, and—

And then Scarface let go.

But not of me.

I don't know if it was on purpose, or if the tension that had been building up had just gotten too much. But whatever the reason, a six-foot-five, two-hundred-sixty-pound vampire makes a hell of a projectile when he suddenly comes shooting at you. As the pole found out when he burst through it, taking down a good section of the ceiling. And then went pinballing between some heavy fixtures. And then whipped around a second pole and—

Whummmp!

I didn't have time to brace myself, didn't have time to do anything before he hit me, hard enough to knock the breath out of my lungs and send both of us careening through the air and past the swinging door and down a short hall and through another door that Ray had thankfully left open because otherwise I'd have been a small smear on the wood. But he had and I wasn't and a second later the portal caught me, just a big gold swirl on a scuffed white wall that had never looked more welcoming.

At least it did until I slammed into something halfway through.

The opening to a portal doesn't just give access to the no-space between worlds. It also violently propels you through it, grabbing you and giving you a heck of a push as soon as you break the surface. I'd always assumed that was so you didn't end up trapped halfway, with nothing to provide enough traction to get you to your destination. That was still the theory, but it obviously didn't work all the time.

Because the something I'd just run into turned out to be some*body.*

But the violence of the push I'd received was fresh and not particularly bothered by a little thing like picking up a two-hundred-pound passenger. The midportal collision was only a hiccup on the journey; it didn't even slow me down. I had a half second to glimpse a stranger's slack-jawed face, and then he and I were bursting out the other side, straight into the almost-dark of the twins' basement bedroom.

Ray was there, staring at me with blue eyes made neon bright by the reflected light of the portal. But the twins weren't. Which was a shame, since I could really have used an anchor right about then.

Because the stubborn SOB behind me wasn't letting go.

Scarface must have grabbed something—maybe one of the hair dryers along the wall, maybe the wall itself, I didn't know, but something solid—back in the salon. Because instead of tumbling to the ground along with the hitchhiker I'd locked desperate legs around, I bulleted out of the golden swirl, stared at Ray for half a second, and was then jerked backward with enough force to give me whiplash.

Which I guess had been the point, but what with the holey sternum and the half-missing face and the Gumby impression, my opponent wasn't able to seize the moment. At least, I don't think it was his plan to still be in place when me and whoever I'd picked up came barreling back through the tunnel. And hit the other side. And trampolined off a membrane of elastic vampire flesh before abruptly reversing course again.

I was getting a little seasick and more than a little dizzy, but I managed to get disentangled from my passenger before I shot out into the twins' room again. That left me emerging butt first, which wasn't ideal as far as landing, but it was good enough to allow Ray to get an improvised lasso around one of my ankles. Only I wasn't sure if that was a good thing or not when I ended up jerked back into the vortex, where a half-crazed vampire was lying in wait.

And judging by the expression on his rapidly healing face, I thought he might be reevaluating that whole letting-me-live thing. But then he got a look at my former passenger, who the current had wafted back to us from somewhere above. I knew it was the current, because this guy clearly wasn't going anywhere under his own steam ever again.

Shoulder-length black hair drifted around a dead white face, its eyes given the illusion of life by the portal's glowing bands of psychedelic light. But illusion was all it was, judging from the slash of black across his throat. It was crusty and he was either bled out or so close it made no difference, so I was assuming this wasn't recent. Also, either he was a vampire or somebody had decided to be thorough, because there was a stake buried hilt-deep in his chest.

He looked vaguely familiar, but I couldn't place him. Something that obviously wasn't true for Scarface. "Shit," he croaked.

And then "Varus."

And then he let me go.

Chapter Thirteen

"You are certain he said 'Varus'?" Marlowe demanded, and then stuck his head into the portal before I could say anything.

Not that I'd been planning on it. I'd already answered that question, and a bunch of others, the best I could. Yes, I thought that's what Scarface had said. No, I wasn't one hundred percent sure. Yes, the dead guy had resembled the briefing pic I'd been given the night before. No, I couldn't positively ID. I'd had all of a second to look at him, and he hadn't exactly been at his best.

And for that matter, neither was I.

I was slumped at the bottom of the basement stairs, clutching a glass of whiskey and wishing it were stronger—or something else entirely. Yeah, something else would have been good, because even decent Bushmills was pretty much useless against whole-body whiplash. Every joint I had felt like it had been pulled out of place by a vengeful giant and then popped back in—more or less—to the point that just *sitting* hurt like a bitch.

Much less sitting and having to listen to Marlowe.

But I didn't have much choice, since he and a couple of his servants had shown up right on the heels of the excitement, so soon that they must have been on their way here anyway. That wasn't much of a surprise—I hadn't really thought he was through with the Senate's only eyewitness. But I had to admit to curiosity on one point.

I rotated my body to keep from having to move my

neck, and looked at Claire, who was standing on the step above me. "I thought you weren't letting him back in."

She didn't answer. She just looked at me, eyes wide and shocked, the way they'd been ever since I'd gotten back. Claire didn't appear to find me funny right now.

That was okay; I wasn't finding me too funny, either.

Or maybe she just couldn't understand me. My voice sounded perfectly clear in my head, but what had come out of my mouth was a lot closer to the *wah-wah-wah* sound *Peanuts* characters hear when an adult is speaking. That probably had something to do with the crack my jaw had taken when Ray hauled me out of the portal's gravity, which was pretty much nonexistent, and back into ours, which dislikes hovering humans for some reason.

My body had hit a pile of the twins' dirty laundry, but my jaw had hit concrete. So along with whiplash I was now impersonating Popeye on the right-hand side. That wouldn't have been so bad, given what could have happened tonight, except that it ensured that I still couldn't eat. So in addition to weakness from the blood loss and generalized *oww* through every joint, I also had the bonus of clawing stomach pains.

So I wasn't real thrilled when Marlowe pulled back inside and glared at me. "Describe him!"

"Leave her alone! Can't you see she's hurt?" Claire said, putting a hand on my shoulder. Which would have been more comforting if not for all the bruises.

"Ow," I said indistinctly, and she snatched it back.

Marlowe was still looking at me, and he didn't look much better than I did. At a guess, he'd been up for something like forty-eight hours, and unlike most vamps, he wasn't bothering to hide it. His clothes were rumpled, his shoes were covered in caked mud, and his usually curly mop was sticking up in a way that would have been comical if not for the fierce white face below. He looked like he might have been leading the search for Varus ever since he'd left here, and now I was telling him that the guy had been dead the whole time.

But I couldn't help that.

"I've already told you everything I know," I said, as clearly as I could manage. "If you don't believe—"

"I believe you," he snarled. "That's the problem."

"Come again?"

"You aren't the first person to find a body today," he told me, trying to pace. But the twins hadn't quite grasped the concept of housecleaning, and he almost immediately ran into another pile of random stuff. Which he kicked violently against a wall. "They've been turning up like flotsam in portals all over the city!"

"What?"

"I opened one at my own flat not two hours ago, only to find a corpse plastered against the security shield. Like a bloody bug on a windshield!"

I blinked. "Who was it?"

"One of Varus's chief competitors. As were the others. We've retrieved members from three different families so far—that we know of." His lips twisted. "The owners of the illegal portals have yet to report in."

I frowned. "So you're saying what? That Varus was cleaning house? Attacking us last night and then going after—"

"That was the initial theory, yes. It was thought that he was taking advantage of the Senate's preoccupation with the war to set himself up as the undisputed leader of the smuggling world. And that the . . . calling cards . . . he shoved into the portal system were his way of announcing that fact."

My frown grew. "How does that work? Even if the Senate ignored a slap in the face like last night—"

"That was not a slap. It was a direct challenge, and it will be answered!"

"But that's the point. Did he think you would just let him get away with—"

"We don't know what he was thinking," Marlowe said, sweetly vicious. "We intended to ask him, but somehow, I do not think he will be answering many questions now!"

No, I guessed not. I also guessed that I knew what Olga had wanted to talk to me about earlier. Probably wondering who the dead body was that I'd tossed into the portal.

"So what's the theory?" I asked. "That there's a new game in town? Or that one of his subordinates—"

Marlowe's eyes flashed. "Thanks to you, we don't have a theory!"

I started to point out that Varus's death was hardly my fault, but I didn't. Because Marlowe had thrown out a hand as if to punctuate his sentence, and something hit the wall like a shot. I jumped and Claire yelped, and then we both watched a two-inch crack run up and down, floor to ceiling, from an impact point the size of a cannonball made by absolutely nothing because nothing was there.

I stared at it blankly. The cellar had been built back when people took that shit seriously, and the walls were at least two feet thick. I knew that because that's how far the impression into the bricks went.

Allllll righty then.

My mouth closed with a little pop. My jaw hurt like a bitch, anyway, and hey, I could ask questions later. But apparently someone else wasn't feeling quite as intimidated.

"I want to know what you're going to do about those men who attacked Dory!" Claire said hotly.

"They weren't men," Marlowe corrected, crossing his arms. Probably so he wouldn't finish demolishing the house.

"Vampires, then!"

"Senior masters."

"And that means what?"

"That means you have your answer."

"Like hell I do!" she said, leaving the stairs to get in his face.

"Um, Claire . . ." I said, only to be completely ignored.

"You have witnesses!"

I started to get up, because Marlowe was in a scary mood. But to my surprise, his eyes softened slightly at the sight of the infuriated redhead invading his personal space, and his shoulders unclenched a trifle. "Your loyalty to your friend does you credit," he told her shortly. "But it does not alter the facts."

"Which are?"

"That my only witnesses are a human who left early and a vampire already under interdict for a variety of crimes. And that is hardly—"

"You have Dory!"

"A dhampir has no standing under the law. She is neither vampire nor human nor mage nor any other recognized creature—"

"You're saying no one would believe her?" Claire demanded incredulously.

"I'm saying she would never be allowed to testify. Under vampire law, she isn't a person—"

"The *hell* she—"

"—while on the other side are a first-level master and a handful of second- and third-levels—from a different court, I might add, making it far harder to put pressure on them. None of whom will likely remember anything of this evening's activities."

"They were in a *jiffy store*," Claire said mulishly. "There has to be surveillance—"

I choked out a laugh. And for the first time Marlowe glanced at me with something akin to understanding. He and I both knew what SOP was in these cases.

I hoped Singh had insurance.

"Destroyed," Marlowe confirmed. "And even had it not been, it would allow the owner to bring a claim for damages, nothing more. A dhampir has no protection under the law. She cannot—"

"Then anyone can just attack her on sight?" Claire said in disbelief.

"Yes. Which is why her father wanted her out of this." He shot me a resentful look. "But she seems incapable of managing to go a single day without—"

"*They* attacked *her*!" Claire said, furious all over again. "What the hell are you thinking?"

Marlowe's brows lowered once more, and for a moment he looked like he was considering telling her. Which was why they didn't let him handle the diplomatic stuff. I decided I could live without seeing what would happen if those two ever really got into it.

"Uh, one question," I said, pulling those dark eyes to me.

"What?"

"You said the bodies have been showing up in portals all over the city, like flotsam."

"Yes?"

"But portals aren't like ... like a river system, are they? They're self-contained units. So how did the bodies get in there?"

He just looked at me. And his expression said plainly that he didn't know how he got stuck working with such incompetents. I scowled, because it was a valid question.

"Someone must have gone to each portal to plant them," I persisted. "So maybe someone saw—"

"They didn't have to plant them."

"What does that mean?"

"Ask your servant," he said sardonically.

"My what?"

I didn't get an answer, because the door at the top of the stairs banged open and Ray staggered in. At least, I assumed it was Ray. All I saw was a shock of dark hair over a pile of dishes that smelled so good they had me tearing up.

"Oh, for— Go eat!" Marlowe said in disgust, and turned back to yell at an unfortunate vamp who had just been spit out by the portal.

"Come on," Ray said. "I'm setting up on the porch."

He and his tottering mound of dishes departed, and I got to my feet, joints creaking in protest. Sitting for that long had left me stove up, and when I tried to crack my back, it went off like another shot, scaring the shit out of the vamp. Claire's expression teetered closer to open tears.

I sighed. "It's not as bad as it looks."

"Of course it's not! You wouldn't be able to stand otherwise!"

"You shoulda seen the other guy," I said, grinning slightly at the thought of Zheng-zi's messed-up face.

And then almost choked on something. After a second of hacking, I spat part of a tooth out into my palm.

Damn. I hated when that happened.

I looked up to find Claire staring at me with something approaching horror.

I started to say something, but the horror turned to a glare so bright, I swear I could see little flames in her pupils. "If you say you're fine," she told me tremulously, "I'll kill you!"

My mouth closed abruptly, and I meekly let her lead me off to the porch.

Ray, for some reason, had gone all out. The little table we used for snacks now had a bright white drape that someone had doubled over to hide Stinky's latest artwork. In the middle was a vase with a bunch of the neighbor's purple hydrangeas stuffed in the top. A chair had been pulled up along one side, near the ratty old swing. It was even rattier old wicker, but a pillow had been stuffed into the seat and a chenille throw had been folded over the top.

It was surprisingly comfy, but I wouldn't have cared if I'd been sitting on the floor, not with the things Ray was piling on the table and on the broad porch railing when he ran out of room. "I can't eat all this," I said, unsure that I could eat at all.

"You haven't tried," he pointed out. "Besides, I picked soft stuff."

And he had. The night's extravagance included leftover chicken and rice, mushy peas, squashy white dinner rolls, beer and some kind of mixed-berry pie. I stared at it in a kind of wonder.

"We'll call your father," Claire told me, as I started slathering butter on a roll. "We'll see what he has to say about—"

"Claire. There's nothing to prosecute for, okay?" I said, with difficulty.

"Nothing—look at you!"

I glanced helplessly at Ray, because I wasn't up to explaining the intricacies of vampire life right at the moment. He sighed. "It's like this," he told her. "Zheng-zi, well, he kind of paid Dory a compliment tonight."

"What?"

"Look. He had his guys with him. He coulda turned 'em loose on us, and it woulda been over. Dory's good and I'm . . . well, Dory's good, but no way was she taking on that many senior masters with a couple little guns and no food. It wasn't happening, okay?"

"Well, obviously it did happen. She's alive!"

"She's alive because he told 'em not to interfere. She's alive because he showed her the respect of dueling her like he would have another master, with rules and shit."

"He still tried to kill her!"

"Masters try to kill each other all the time," Ray pointed out. "They're dueling each other every night up at the consul's place. It's one of the big bummers about being locked away; I haven't gotten to see any of the matches."

"Could you even get tickets?" I asked, my mouth full of buttery goodness.

"Hey, I know people," Ray said.

"Like who?"

"Like sharks who want an arm and a leg," he admitted. "I was gonna ask you if your father's box had any extra seats."

I shook my head. "Full up."

"Damn. I mean, I'd buy 'em and all—"

"Can we talk about the fact that Dory almost *died*?" Claire asked, livid.

"But she didn't, did she?" Ray pointed out. "She won. And Zheng probably wouldn't have killed her anyway. He said—"

"Probably?" Claire's green eyes flashed.

I thought Ray should be careful. Claire was kind of looking like she wanted an excuse. But he just cocked his head sideways. "Hey, is that the baby crying?"

"No!" she told him. Right before a distinct wail was heard echoing through the night. "Damn it!" she said. And then she bit her lip. And then she bustled off.

"You have the devil's own luck," I told him.

"You may as well not bother," he told me back. "Nobody can understand you, and your tongue keeps flopping out and it's kind of off-putting."

I responded with a gesture, because my tongue was busy with chicken at the moment. I found that if I chewed, very carefully, on the opposite side of my mouth, it was only painful instead of excruciating. Although it would have been totally worth it, anyway. If there was a heaven, it was made of this stuff.

"And it's not luck," Ray told me, pouring my beer into a glass. I usually didn't bother, but it was nice, all frosty and chilled and stuff. He handed it to me and my fingers made little heat prints on the sides. "There's a party in the backyard and Marlowe's got a dozen men coming in and out, slamming doors and clomping around downstairs. Who could sleep through all that?"

"That's smart," I said, surprised.

"I can be smart." He looked offended. "And I told you, don't talk."

I decided that might be best, and settled for watching him try to clean up the kids' chess game. He'd set it on the floor in order to have a place to put the grub, which would have been fine if this were a normal game. But this was one Olga had enchanted for the kids, and troll magic tended to be a little ... peculiar.

The pieces, which looked like miniature trolls and ogres, were fine as long as they stayed on the board. It enclosed them in their own little world, where they could stalk and ambush and whack the heck out of each other to their hearts' content. But Ray had managed to knock a few of them off the board when he moved it, and they were now milling around in confusion.

One had wandered into one of Claire's gardening clogs, where it was setting up what looked like a defensive position. Another was floundering around in the clutches of a mop, slashing at the gray threads with a tiny sword. And a third, a little mottled-looking fellow with wild hair, a crazed expression and just a ragged pair of pants left from his once nice uniform, was making a break for the stairs.

Ray clapped a clear plastic cup over the wild man with one hand, and grabbed the one battling the mop monster with the other. And promptly snatched that hand back. A tiny bead of blood was welling up on one finger.

He held it out to me. "What the hell is this?"

"You've got to keep them on the board," I told him in between bites.

"Or what?"

"Or they get . . . feisty."

"Screw that!" he said, grabbing the mop guy. "They're going back in the box."

I shrugged. I mostly just left them out anymore. It was easier.

But Ray managed to get two of the three back in their ogre- and troll-shaped cutouts, where the enchantment froze them in place. And then he turned to the wild man under the cup, who was making a series of familiar gestures. Ray got down on eye level and blinked at it.

A tiny face pressed against the side of the plastic, distorting tinier features for a moment, as the two of them sized each other up. Small fists were raised, and then the little creature turned around and something else was lowered. And a couple other things were pressed firmly against the plastic.

"Is that . . . what is he . . . is he *mooning* me?" Ray demanded.

I grinned, and then quit because it hurt. "That one's a little weird," I told him.

"That one's about to be mush!" he said, grabbing it out of its temporary prison. "What's wrong with it anyway? It looks like it's been painted."

"Something like that," I said drily.

"What?"

"Stinky swallowed it a couple weeks ago."

"Swallowed?" His lip curled. "Then how—"

"It came through okay, but it's never been quite right since."

Ray dropped it like it was hot. "You have a weird house," he told me, smacking the cup back over it and wiping his hand on his pants.

I shrugged. I really couldn't argue the point. He put a brick on the cup, got a beer and propped up on the swing, watching me stuff my face. The creak of the chain blended with the sound of music and light laughter from the garden, which I couldn't see too well because of the glow from the house behind me. But it was nice.

"So," he said casually, after a few minutes. "You're, uh, you're in a better mood now, right?"

I was, I thought, looking up suspiciously. "Why?"

"'Cause, uh, there might be some stuff we need to talk about."

"Like what?"

"Oh, this and, uh . . ."

"Good stuff?" I asked, knowing damned well it wasn't. My life didn't work like that.

"Well, you know. . . ."

Crap.

Chapter Fourteen

The table and the glass and the freaking *flowers* should have clued me in, I thought sourly. "What?"

"See, you're already mad. I knew that was gonna happen," Ray complained.

"Then why bring it up?"

"'Cause I don't have a choice. We *have* to talk. But I'm not good at it and I don't want to piss you off, 'cause you're already looking a little ... tense. So this probably isn't the right time, but if I don't get to it soon, someone else will and that could be bad depending on who we're talking about—"

"Pencil," I said, as distinctly as I could, which apparently wasn't distinct enough.

"What?"

"Pen. Cil."

"Oh. I don't—wait. I got a pen," he said, pulling one out of his jacket.

I took it and wrote *SHUT UP* on the tablecloth.

"Oh, well, that's nice," he said, twisting his head around to look at it. "Pen don't come out, you know, and that was one of the last decent tablecloths you guys had. And anyway, I just told you, I *can't*. I gotta figure out how to start this, and you're not helping with the shut ups. I know you're probably tired, but there's some stuff you need to know and—what's that?"

He twisted his head some more to look at my latest doodle.

"Is that a butt? Are you calling me a butthead? Because that's great; that's real mature. I'm trying to be serious here and you're—"

"Portal," I said, around a mouthful of roll.

"What?"

I swallowed. "It's a *portal*, damn it."

"That's a portal?" He squinted. "Then why does it have that crack up the middle?"

"That's a person. Coming through."

"A person?" He transferred the squint from the doodle to me. "Where's the head? Where's the legs? I think you're shitting with—"

"It's abstract!"

"Yeah. You know who does abstract art? People who can't draw, that's who."

Ray, I decided, really did have the devil's own luck, because I needed the fork too much to stab him through the eye with it. "Tell me about the hacking Cheung wants you to do," I said.

"Oh. Yeah, well, that's ... yeah. I guess that could work," he said. "We can start with that."

"Start?" I asked, but he ignored me.

"So okay. You know about portals, right? Like how when you open 'em you get that big whoosh of power?"

I shrugged and went back to eating.

"Yeah, yeah. You wouldn't," he said enviously. "You keep yours open all the time, wasting a ton of energy because you got a damned ley line sink under the house and don't care. But it took the smuggling community years to figure that out."

"To figure what out?"

"That if you keep your portals open all the time, you don't get that big burst. Or, you do, but you only get it the first time, and if there's lots of ley lines in an area spewing out lots of magical energy, the Corps ain't so good about tracking you down on the first go. It's the third or the fourth or the tenth when they get you, narrowing it down a little more each time, see?"

"But most people can't keep a portal open all the time," I said, draining my glass and grabbing the bottle.

I was more a bottle kind of gal, anyway.

"We're not talking about most people," Ray said, looking at me disapprovingly. "And you guys aren't the only ones to have a ley line sink. They show up every time two lines cross. And they cross all the time around here. Ley lines don't like New York, they love it, especially Manhattan. They're snaking around all over the place like a subway map on acid."

"Yeah, I—"

"Leave it to norms not to wonder why there's this huge, overcrowded city on a tiny island barely two miles long," he said, shaking his head. "Which also happens to be one of the hardest places to build in the world. I mean, it's crazy. Manhattan's traffic is a nightmare 'cause it's an island, which is bad enough, but then every new subway tunnel has to bore through a slab of solid granite that eats drill bits like candy."

"Ray. I know all this."

"Yeah, but I'm getting to stuff maybe you don't know. Just eat your pie."

I didn't think I could hold the pie. I pulled it over anyway. Mmm, flaky.

"But norms are attracted to ley lines," he continued, "even though they don't know it, and so cities tend to grow up where you got a lot of 'em. But unlike most places with this many lines, Manhattan doesn't have a damned vortex. The lines cross, sure, but they don't puddle up in one big snarl. That kind of thing's useless 'cause it puts out too much power. Every time you try to open a portal around one of those, you get kerblammy—"

"Kerblammy?"

"—and that's not good for business. But around here, the lines are more like . . . like this." He held his hands up, interlacing the fingers. "They cross, but not all at one place. So you get lots of lines, lots of ley line sinks to power portals, and lots of background energy, making finding them a nightmare for the so-called good guys."

"So-called?"

He shot me a look. "Come on. You like your wine, don't you? Who you think brings that in?"

"We're not after the portals because of the wine," I reminded him.

"Not now, maybe, not with the war on. And not because of the Senate; they don't care about stuff like that. But the Corps?" He scowled. "They're a huge pain in my ass."

"They also have a point. A lot of bad stuff comes through those things—"

"And so does a lot of good stuff. And so does a lot of stuff that can be bad or good, depending on how it's used, but that the Circle just outlawed all together, 'cause it's easier that way."

I didn't say anything, because I kind of agreed with him there. The Silver Circle was the light magic organization that governed the mages like the Senate did the vamps. The Corps were their police unit, and overall, they did a pretty good job of countering the Black Circle's shysters, crooks and hoodlums. But they did tend to be a little . . . anal . . . about some things.

Including most things that came through illegal portals.

"I mean, it's complete bullshit," Ray bitched. "When the fey got mad way back when and yanked all the portals, nobody thought about the little guy, did they? Nobody thought about all the people on both sides that had friends and businesses and lives that depended on being able to come and go. Some of their leaders get in a snit for some reason, and all of a sudden—nothing. And they don't get over being butt hurt after a while, like normal people. It's been thousands of years and the pathways are still blocked and trade's still in the shitter and nobody seems to give a damn!"

"Except for the heroic smugglers."

"Sure, be that way. But when you want something— when the damned *mages* want something—that ain't supposed to be available outside Faerie, who do you come to see?"

"So you're the good guys?"

"Yeah," Ray said defiantly. And then he shifted in his seat. "Sort of. Anyway, my point is, Manhattan is the shit. If you're a smuggler, this is where you want to be."

I thought about that while I gummed pie. "So you're telling me you can just cut a new portal here, and nobody will notice?" I was pretty sure that hadn't been in the briefing I'd had.

He shook his head. "Not if you're trying to slice all the way through to Faerie, no. Takes too much power. But smaller stuff, yeah, you can get away with that. It sort of melds into the background noise. Like Olga's portal—that didn't raise any eyebrows, right?"

"Because it goes all of two blocks. And that wouldn't do you any good."

"See, that's what most people would think," he said, leaning forward. "But I been in the business a long time. And one day, the portal we were using got discovered by the damned Corps and shut down—right before a big shipment was due to come through."

"That's rough," I said, wondering if there was more pie.

"You ain't just kidding that's rough. The boss don't care about my problems. The boss just wants his stuff. He's promised it to some pretty big-time people and he's gonna look bad if he can't deliver. So I get to thinking."

"Uh-oh."

"Yeah, as it turned out. But at the time, I don't think 'uh-oh.' At the time, I think, hey, I gotta figure a way out of this problem. So I start to wonder, what would happen if I cut a portal, but not to Faerie? What would happen if I cut it—get this—into another portal?"

It took a moment for that to sink in, because he'd said it so casually. And because my mind was mostly occupied by important things, like pie. And because it was stupid.

Really, really stupid.

I'd always thought of ley lines the way most people view nuclear energy. They could be useful—ley line sinks powered all kinds of things, and the currents inside the lines were strong enough to make for quick transport virtually anywhere. But that convenience came with a steep price tag for anybody who didn't show it the proper respect.

Not that there were too many of those. The dangers involved intimidated even war mages, who had a reputation for badassery that bordered on lunacy. But they hazarded the lines only with the heaviest of shields, and any portals they cut into them were done extremely gingerly.

Vampires—the sane kind, anyway—avoided them almost entirely. If something went wrong, their flammability ensured that they wouldn't even have the few seconds the mages would to find a way out. Human transport was slower, but it came without the possibility of your own personal Chernobyl if something went wrong.

But my jaw ached every time I tried to talk, so I settled for summing up the obvious. "You can't do that."

Ray grinned. "Wanna bet?"

"No, I mean, you *can't*—"

I broke off, because one of the fey was coming up the steps. He wasn't glowing, having dimmed the light shadows their kind shed in our world down for our guests. But he managed to look fairly otherworldly anyway, the long white-blond hair holding a shimmer of moonlight; the bone structure subtly different from a human's; the almond-shaped eyes hinting of other shores, except for their startling, almost vivid blueness.

He was holding a small, grubby creature that was kicking and flailing and giving every appearance of trying to murder the two long fingers gripping it by the scruff of the neck. "Have you perhaps misplaced something?" he asked, arching an elegant brow.

"Damn it," Ray said, sitting up. "I thought I—shit."

I assumed he was referring to the plastic cup, which was still weighed down by the piece of garden edging he'd placed on top. But which now had a mouseholesized piece cut out of the side. Presumably by the tiny sword the escape artist was waving around menacingly.

"It appears to be defective," the fey said drily. "Would you like a new enchantment?"

"A new enchantment?" Ray looked up from examining the cup. "What's that do?"

"It replaces the old."

"Replaces how?"

The fey looked at me. "Obliterates. Is that the right word?"

Damned if I knew. Claire had been helping them with their English, but she knew enough of their language to be able to figure out what they were trying to say. "It's a word," I agreed.

"You mean kill it?" Ray looked horrified.

"It isn't alive, therefore it cannot die," the fey reasoned. "But it would have a new ... personality, if you like."

"I don't like," Ray said, grabbing it. "It's fine." The fey's eyes danced in the light from the house, obviously amused. Particularly when the wild man suddenly stabbed Ray in the palm. "Damn it!"

The fey shook his head and started to go. But then he paused on the stairs and looked back at me. "Oh, and you may tell the Lady Claire that her ... gifts ... while thoughtful, will not be needed."

"Gifts?"

"The condoms," Ray said, sucking his palm.

"You managed to get those?" I asked, incredulously.

"Hey, it's what we went for. I don't know if I grabbed the right sizes, though."

We both looked at the fey, whose grin widened. But he only said: "There are enchantments for that. And in any case, the ladies appear to have ... come prepared."

"Well, have fun," I told him.

His smile was blinding. "I shall."

He left and Ray dragged his two-inch captive over to the chessboard. "They creep me out," he told me in a low voice, after a moment.

"Who?"

"The fey. Always did. 'New personality' my ass."

"They're okay," I said, because it was true, and because I wouldn't put it past those ears to still be able to hear us. "What are you doing?" I asked, watching him struggle to stuff his prisoner into the felt-lined indentation.

"Putting him back!" he said, as the wild man popped up again, mad as hell. Ray had confiscated the sword, but his prisoner was resourceful. And bit the end of his thumb.

"Son of a—"

"That won't work," I told him, as Ray pushed the squirming thing down again and fitted the plastic cover on top. It was clear and molded to the shape of the pieces, which left the little guy effectively trapped. Until he wormed a knife out of his boot and started sawing away at it.

"Why is he doing that?" Ray demanded.

"He doesn't turn off anymore."

"What? Not at all?"

I shook my head. "It's why we usually leave the game out. The boys like for him to have company."

"Then why didn't you say so?" he demanded.

Because I didn't think you'd care about a child's toy, I didn't say, helping Ray remove my dishes so he could set the game up again on the table.

We finished and he went to nurse his wounds on the swing. The pieces were back to exploring their little world, which I guess was what Faerie looked like. Or at least the part Olga was from. The board had started out a plain old chess type, if oversized. But the familiar checkerboard was invisible now, overgrown by grass and trees and caves and a miniature stream.

The whole setting was too big to fit on the board, so the scenery changed as they moved around, setting up ambushes and defensive positions, polishing armor and weapons, or just squatting on a rock, in the case of the wild man. Some of the other little ogres were starting a campfire over by a copse of trees, and they kept shooting him looks, but he didn't appear to notice. He was too busy staring at the sky.

"They don't seem like much company to me," Ray said, watching the scene. "Look—they don't like him now."

"I don't think that's the problem," I murmured.

What was it Plato had said? Something about a bunch of guys born in a cave, who had never seen the outside world. Just shadows of things reflected on the walls sometimes, distorted and unreal. Until one of them broke out one day, and started exploring a larger world. He could go back to his old life, but he wasn't the same person anymore.

His world had gotten bigger, and things were never going to be quite the same again.

But Ray didn't agree. "Naw, he's different now," he told me. "People don't like different."

There was something in his tone that made me look up. He was draped over the seat, wrapped in gloom since the porch light wasn't on and the light from the house had diminished, thanks to someone shutting off the fixture in the hall. The main illumination came from the lanterns the fey had lit around camp, just little pinpricks in the darkness, and the flickering blue-white of the cartoon channel from the living room that nobody had bothered to turn off.

He'd lit a cigarette, and with just the reddened end lighting up his face, he should have looked sinister. But Ray's features just didn't run to it. The eyes were too big and too blue and too oddly guileless. The cheeks were too round, and the chin was tilted just a bit too defiantly outward. Like he expected to get belted at any moment, but wasn't going to duck his head anyway.

It was the face of a guy who'd been beaten up before and who had every expectation of being beaten up again, but who wasn't going to cower. And he'd had plenty of opportunities to learn. I didn't know a lot about his background, but I knew enough to guess that he hadn't found the vampire lifestyle to be all fun and games.

He'd been born the half-breed son of a Dutch sailor and an Indonesian village woman during the bad old days of colonialism. The sailor had decamped before Ray made an appearance and his mother had died when he was a teenager. Leaving him a blue-eyed freak among the villagers, and one who reminded people a bit too much of their hated colonial masters.

It hadn't taken them long to drive him out, leaving him to fend for himself. Which he had done by joining a group of pirates right before they decided to attack a fat-looking prize. That might have been an okay plan, if said prize hadn't been the flagship of one Zheng Zhilong, the leader of one of the greatest pirate fleets ever to sail the seas.

Zheng—no relation that I knew of to our tiger-tatted friend—had spared Ray's life, only to turn around and take it when he decided to make him a vampire. Maybe he thought that having someone who could pass for a European in a pinch might come in useful. But apparently that hadn't worked out so great, because he'd traded Ray to a fellow pirate only a few years later. Who had traded him in turn, because looking sort of European didn't automatically confer a knowledge of languages Ray had never heard or customs he'd never experienced.

Somehow, he'd eventually ended up with Cheung. Who instead of trading him, had promptly shipped him off to the family's outpost in New York. Which seemed less strange to me now that I'd had Ray's rundown on the importance of the place for otherworldly smuggling.

What remained weird was that he was still here.

Despite being middling in looks, middling in power— he'd never advanced beyond fifth-level master status— and middling in ability of any kind, he'd done okay. He'd succeeded when those with far more impressive résumés had failed. He'd survived when those with far more power had died.

He was like the cockroach of the vampire world.

Of course, come to think of it, so was I. People might not like us, might even detest us. But we'd still be here when they were dust.

There were worse things.

"Different can be okay," I said and passed him another beer. "Now tell me about your portals."

Chapter Fifteen

Ray flipped the cap off with his thumb—an advantage to having vampire-tough nails—and took a swig. "It's like I told you. I figured out how to hack into 'em."

"So you said." But that made no sense, so obviously I'd missed something. "Are you talking about just using the same entrance for different portals?" Because people did that all the time. Olga had tinkered with the one in the basement until it could go three or four places now, along two different lines, and I didn't think she was done.

But Ray shook his head. "You can only do that if you're at a conjunction of a bunch of different lines. Olga's got two that cross here, so she can cycle 'em if she wants rather than having two gates cluttering up the place. But you still need access to the gate to do that."

"Okay. Following you so far."

"Well, it's like I said. I needed to get into Faerie, but everybody guards their gates like mad. So how was I going to get to one? Much less bring a ton of stuff through without anybody noticing? It'd be like needing to get on the Internet and deciding to break into some high-security building to use one of their computers. Not worth it, is it?"

"But you still needed to get on the Internet," I said slowly.

"Yeah. So I did what everybody else does."

"You hacked into a signal?"

He nodded. "Only the signal in this case was a portal

somebody else had already cut into Faerie. I just cut into theirs. It's easy once you know where the thing is—"

"But you didn't know!" I said, getting pissed. "None of us know. That's why we've been running all over the city like a bunch of crazed—"

"Yeah, but I knew the other players, right?" he interrupted. "The Circle, the Senate, they don't always know who's doing what. But I knew the competition. So I had my boys spy on 'em and figure out where they were bringing their stuff in. And honestly, it wasn't even that hard. Most of 'em had their gateway in a warehouse or something, so they didn't have to transport the merchandise too far."

I glared at him. "And once you knew where they were—"

"I knew which ley line they were using. And after that, it was pie."

"Define 'pie,'" I demanded.

"It was easy," Ray said, trying to blow a smoke ring and failing. He frowned at the wobbly thing for a moment, and then glanced at me. "Portals kind of look like that in the lines. Just tiny ripples you can see through, so they're almost invisible. They're really hard to detect, especially if you have mile after mile to explore and you have no idea where they are. It's why the Corps never tried to shut 'em down that way—it's like a needle in a haystack, if the needle was transparent and the haystack was an ocean."

"But once you do know where they are—"

He shrugged. "You just make another gateway. Only instead of cutting through the line, you cut into the portal that's already cutting through the line. Minimal outlay of power; minimal chance to get caught."

"Unless the owners figure out what you're doing and kill you!"

"Yeah, but that don't happen. Plenty of people try to attack other people's gates; it's how most turf wars get started, and why the damned things are guarded so heavy. But this—they don't even know they're supposed to be looking for this. It's not a thing—"

"It's not a thing because it's stupid!" I said harshly. "What if you'd missed the portal? What if you'd hacked into the middle of a ley line, and ended up getting nuked? What if—"

"What if we'd shot ourselves in the head?" he said sarcastically. "I mean, come on. We were careful. The only real problem was that there was no way to know where a particular portal was going. It wasn't like I could just ask: hey, that illegal portal you're running, so where does it go again? No. And a lot of 'em didn't go where we wanted."

He was completely sincere, like that was literally all he'd had to worry about. The sheer audacity was . . . well, it was almost breathtaking. Which was probably why he'd gotten away with it, I realized. Someone, somewhere, through the centuries must have had the same thought, possibly even several someones. But right on its heels had been a what-am-I-thinking slap to the head, and that had been it

Until Ray. Ray had just thought, *Cool*. Ray had thought, *Let's do this and get me out of trouble with my boss*. That was like . . . like getting a thorn in your toe and deciding to cut off the foot. It solved one problem, but boy, did it open up a ton more.

But Ray didn't see that. Ray was looking smug. Ray was proud of himself.

Ray was quite possibly insane.

"So you cut some more," I said, because of course he had.

He nodded. "Yeah, and then some more and—well, it took a while to find one near enough to our old location to work. And even then, we ended up in this creepy-looking swamp on the other end. And ran into all kinds of problems."

"Like what?"

Ray didn't answer. But I received a sudden flash of a swamp, old and fetid and dark as night, except for a few random beams of light spearing down from far overhead. They highlighted still black water, mold-covered bark and a bunch of silent shadows zipping through the trees.

We were running alongside the shadows, who I guessed were the vamps Ray had brought with him. Although I wasn't sure quite what we were running on. Or why the trees seemed to be growing sideways for some—

And then I realized that we were sprinting along the trunks, hitting the ground only occasionally on a rock or a root or who-knew-what because we were moving almost too fast to see, as was everyone else. Like they were playing some crazy kind of swamp parkour. And they were damned good. Not a single foot touched the dark water below.

Until we did. Our foot hit a particularly slimy rock and slid out of control—just for a second, and just barely stirring the water. But a second was enough.

Something huge and old and cracked like the trunk of an oak, broke the surface, too fast for me to see much besides a few tons' worth of terror coming right at us. A massive tail slashed down, sending an arc of greenish water ten feet into the air; huge yellowed teeth gleamed and lunged; and we came within a hairbreadth of losing a foot before another vamp caught us, swinging us high, high out over the water—

And then I was back, breathing hard, although I hadn't moved an inch.

"Oh," I swallowed. "Those kind of problems."

Ray's eyes widened. "Hey. Did you just see—"

"So how many portals did you make?" I interrupted. Because I didn't like to talk about the glimpses the wine occasionally gave me into other people's heads. Ray might act like it was no big deal, but I wasn't used to it and I didn't like it.

"I—" Ray stopped. "You mean, like total or just that time?"

"*That time?* How many times were there?"

"Well, it's like this."

"Shit."

"Once I got the shipment in, of course the boss wanted to know how. I mean, you would, wouldn't you?"

"And you told him. And he thought, why stop with one?"

"Right. Because the fey, they don't travel much. Not

the ones you got around here, they're freaky or some-thing, I don't know. But most fey, they don't want to move much from where they were born. So if you want their stuff, you gotta go to them. And the boss wanted, oh, a lot of stuff."

"So he had you cutting portals like a mad weasel," I said grimly.

And why not? Ray wasn't exactly high in the power structure at Cheung enterprises. So Cheung wasn't really risking anything. Ray gets vaporized and it's no big loss. Ray gets caught and Cheung disavows all knowledge of his activities.

Which was probably exactly what he had done, or the Senate would have nabbed him already. The last people they wanted to have taking some of those vacant Senate seats were Cheung and his buddy with the messed-up face. They were an unknown quantity with possible ties to the Chinese empress, the leader of the East Asian Senate. Who just happened to be the biggest rival for power that the North American Consul had.

No, if Ray had given the Senate anything on Cheung, they'd have used it. On the other hand, it was in Cheung's best interest to stay as far from his disgraced servant as possible at this vital juncture. Yet here he was, trying to lure him back into the fold.

I didn't know what Cheung was planning to bring in, but obviously he wanted it pretty bad.

I looked up to find Ray sulking. "What?"

"Can we stop it with the names?" he demanded.

"I didn't call you any names."

"What about 'weasel'? That supposed to be compli-mentary?"

"It was more of an expression."

"And 'butthead'?"

"That was you. You called yourself—" I shut my eyes. "Never mind. Just tell me what happened."

"What you think happened?" he asked grumpily. "I kept cutting portals and making deals with the people I found on the other end."

"And nobody ever noticed anything? None of those

other smugglers ever saw a bunch of people lugging out truckloads full of suspicious-looking merchandise right across the street from them?"

"Well, sure, they might have. If we'd been dumb enough to *be* across the street."

"But you just said—"

"I said I had to be near their portal to hack into it. I didn't say I had to stay there."

"Then how did you—" I stopped. Because a horrible suspicion had just formed. A really, really horrible suspicion. But I had to be wrong. I had to be. Because not even Ray would have. . . . Would he?

"Ray," I said carefully. "How did you get the stuff out?"

He looked up from contemplating his navel or whatever he'd been doing, and blinked at me. "Same way I got it in. Some masters have more guys, you know? So they can patrol more. I couldn't be seen moving a lot of stuff right by where they had a portal. These guys aren't too bright, most of 'em anyway, but they are paranoid. If they caught me with a bunch of stuff near their gate, they might have gotten suspicious."

"So . . ."

"So sometimes I had to link another portal to the first one," he said, oh so reasonably. "So I could cut into another line and divert the stuff away from the area."

"You cut a hack, *from the hack you'd just made*, into another portal?" I asked, sure I'd gotten it wrong.

"Yeah," he said brightly. "Or sometimes two, because it's like the subway, every train isn't going where you need. But link enough of 'em, and sooner or later—"

"*Link enough of them?* How many of the portals in Manhattan have you drawn into this bastardized system of yours?"

"I don't know. Maybe half?"

"*Half?*" I stared at him in disbelief.

"Well, it's not like I used all of 'em, but like I said, it wasn't always possible to know where a portal was going when I hacked into it. There was a certain amount of trial and error in—"

"Does the Senate know?" I interrupted.

"Of course they do. I mean, I had to tell 'em, right? They were planning to blow up the illegal portals, but some of them were linked to legal ones through some of my hacks, and that could have caused . . . oh, a lot of problems. I mean, can you see their faces if they'd blown up one of theirs?"

I didn't even react to that. I wasn't even surprised anymore. Maybe I was going numb.

I drained the rest of my beer.

"You hacked into the Senate's portals," I said flatly.

"Well, it wasn't like I was using their gateways, was it?" he said, frowning. Like he'd expected to be patted on the back for his ingenuity, and all he was getting was dull-eyed horror. "They got so many protections on those things, a guy'd have to be crazy to try to break in. And even say you did, whaddya got? A bunch of pissed-off masters who'll end you before you can blink. And I didn't need their gateways anyway, just some of the space in between. You know, to bridge the gap between some of my other lines."

I just stared at him for a moment, actually speechless. *"Why are you still alive?"* I finally demanded.

"'Cause that was the deal. I tell 'em everything, spill my guts, not hold anything back. And then they don't kill me. And they had to deal; they never would have found all of 'em on their own. I mean, seriously, we're talking years—"

"And they just let you walk."

He rolled his eyes. "Of course. Why not? They assumed Cheung was gonna kill me as soon as they tossed me out onto the sidewalk anyway. Save 'em the trouble."

"But they didn't toss you out," I said, remembering a certain limo ride from this morning. True, nobody had seemed too interested in helping Ray not to go up in flames. But considering everything, I'd have expected them to be pouring on gasoline and lighting a match.

But he wasn't listening.

"It really bites my ass, you know?" he told me. "I'm why Cheung ended up a big-time player in the smuggling trade in the first place, when we used to be small potatoes.

It was me. It was all me. But did I get any credit, any respect, for any of it? Hell no. I'm still Ray the screwup, Ray the joke, Ray the butthead. Only the joke's on him now, 'cause I got a new master, and he can *bite me*."

"A new master?" I frowned. "I thought you've been in the Senate's custody this whole time."

"Yeah, well." He fidgeted and stubbed out his cigarette, even though it was only halfway down. "You know how it was. I wanted to just go home. Go back to the way things were. But that's a little hard with the master trying to kill me so I couldn't give away the locations of all the hacks I'd done. And possibly incriminate him in the bargain. So where was I gonna go? I had to go to the Senate."

"Yeah, you said you were going to sing like a canary," I recalled.

Cheung had only allowed Raymond to fall into the Senate's hands in the first place because he'd assumed that his erstwhile employee, who had been sans head at the time, wasn't going to last long enough to tell anyone anything. But once he realized that Ray, who'd turned out to be unusually hardy thanks to Claire's missing talisman, was still alive, the hunt had been on. He'd caught up with him a week or so ago, and Ray had used me to get him out of trouble.

The last thing I'd seen, other than the bird he'd shot me as a thank-you, was him pelting for the Senate's dubious protection as fast as his legs could carry him. It had been a smart move. Not that the Senate was any kinder than his old boss, but they'd had a reason to keep Ray alive and Cheung hadn't. At least not then. And, as the old saying goes, life means hope—and schemes and intrigue and wiggle room. Which I guessed Ray had used, since he was still here.

"Oh, yeah," he confirmed. "I kept my part of the bargain. The way I figured it, if I didn't talk, the boss'd kill me to make sure I never did, and if I did talk, he'd kill me for betraying him. Either way, it ended with me dead. And since the Senate had me ... well, they won that round."

"And then one of them decided to pick you up?" I

asked in disbelief. I was having a hard time seeing a senator—any senator—taking on a train wreck like Ray.

"Hell no," he said bitterly. "They laughed in my face when I brought it up! Anyway, they said they had to send me back to my master. Cheung never emancipated me, so I was still his property, and if they weren't going to execute me, they had to return me. That's the law."

And yes, it was. It was the sort of thing that often failed to get mentioned to all those hopeful humans lining up to join the eternity club: that the majority of its members never made it to the upper levels. That most of them stayed essentially slaves for life, and nobody cared much what a master did with his slaves—or, by vampire law, could do anything about it if they did.

"But they didn't return you," I said, wondering why I suddenly had a weird feeling.

"Damned right, they didn't. But only because I figured a way out. Just like with the portal mess." He sat back, scowling, setting the swing to rocking madly. "You know, when you're a low-level master, you keep hoping that, one of these days, you're gonna go up a rank. It's like a short guy who keeps looking at basketball players and thinking, one of these days, that'll be me. I might be five-two right now, but in a year, or two, or three, I'm Michael Jordan. Only in a year, or two or three, you're still five-two. And one day, it dawns on you, that it's all you're ever gonna be."

"Ray—"

"So, you learn to deal with it. You say, okay, maybe I won't ever be a basketball star. But maybe I can be Bill Gates and make more money than all of them. Or maybe—"

"Ray—"

"—I'll be somebody else, somebody important. 'Cause size isn't everything and power isn't everything, no matter how much the big guys think it is. And so I learned to use my head."

I tried to break in again, but Ray was on a roll, the words flooding out of him now.

"That's something the big guys don't have to do—like

Zheng-zi. He's got more power in his little finger than I got in my whole body, but it hurts as much as it helps. Look at tonight. He don't bother to think, how am I gonna take down this chick who already kicked my butt a couple times. He don't worry about it because he's Zheng-freaking-zi and he don't have to. He assumes he'll just overpower you. But you're like me; you use your head. And so who ended up in pieces and who didn't? We got a lot in common, you and me." He finally stopped, dead still, and stared at the ground. "Maybe that's what made me think of it."

"Think of what?"

"That the Senate couldn't turn me over to Cheung, 'cause he wasn't really my master anymore. 'Cause a master can sell a servant to somebody who needs their talents, or trade 'em for somebody they like more, or, hell, lose 'em in a freaking card game." He looked up, and blue eyes met mine. "Or . . . he can give them away."

"Give them away?" I repeated, feeling a little dizzy. But I was wrong; I wasn't thinking clearly either, because he couldn't be saying what I thought he was.

Ray didn't answer. He just got up and picked up my now empty beer bottle. "You're out. Shall I get another one of those for you . . . master?"

Chapter Sixteen

Twenty minutes or so later, I was sitting with my head in my hands, a second empty beer bottle by my side and a throbbing headache at my temples. I felt rather than heard someone come up behind me and I didn't have to wonder who. My vagina had just gotten a heartbeat.

Big palms spread out large and warm on my shoulders and I dropped my head forward, because it seemed like something nice might happen if I did.

"Hard night?" Louis-Cesare murmured, thumbs going unerringly to the worst spots with just the right amount of pressure.

"I seem to have acquired a vampire servant," I mumbled into the tabletop. "Who made a Frankenportal system all over the city. That somebody's using as a dumping ground for dead smugglers."

He had been working his way up the back of my neck, making gooseflesh rise all over my arms. But at that he stopped. "I beg your pardon?"

I sighed.

"You have a vampire servant?" he asked, apparently deciding to break it down.

"Ray," I confirmed, without lifting my head. Because I was kind of hoping he'd start up again. "You know how Cheung said we could take him, for all he cared, and he never wanted to see him again?"

"Vaguely."

"Well, Ray remembered it verbatim. And convinced

the Senate that it meant Cheung had given him away. To me."

"But . . . you are not a vampire."

"Yeah, I mentioned that. But Ray checked on it and there's nothing in the rule books about what species the giftee has to be."

"Possibly due to it being understood."

"Mm-hmm," I said, because he'd started the massage again, and it felt really, really good. Sinfully good. "But understood isn't stated, which means the Senate can interpret the rule however they like."

"And they chose to interpret it in Raymond's favor due to his knowledge of the portal system."

"Which they thought they might possibly need again. Yeah." Sticking me on unpaid babysitting duty so Cheung couldn't reclaim his property.

Typical.

Louis-Cesare was silent for a moment. "Where is Raymond now?"

I shrugged. "Marlowe dragged him off a few minutes ago."

"But he just released him this morning."

"Yeah, but that was before bodies started showing up in people's basements. The Senate wants Ray to help them trace the currents and figure out where they were dumped into the system. They're hoping for an eyewitness."

"That seems . . . unlikely."

"Uh-huh." Not least of which because I didn't think Ray really remembered all his tunnels. He didn't strike me as an organized kind of guy. He struck me as the kind of guy who'd make a good stoner if he didn't like money and bitching so much.

Louis-Cesare didn't ask any more questions, which was fine with me since I didn't feel like talking. Not with his knuckles pushing gobs of fiery pain up each side of my neck. Up and out, leaving behind a streak of absence-of-pain that was better than pleasure.

And he groaned right along with me.

It should have pissed me off, because it almost certainly meant he was picking up on my feelings, if not more. But I was having trouble getting worked up about it. Maybe because it was dark and the fey were singing something soft and sweet on the far side of the yard and the scent of weed was drifting on the air, probably from the same source. Or because the muscles along my spine were slowly liquefying as more pain I hadn't even known I had was ruthlessly hunted down and pushed out.

I stayed put.

That was even true when a hand made its way up through my hair and over to my hurt cheek. I froze in anticipation of more pain, but the touch was so light, there wasn't any. And he didn't move his fingers, so there was no friction. They were cooler than my skin tonight, maybe because he hadn't fed recently, or because the wound was hotter than my normal body temperature. Either way, they felt good.

They stayed in place for a long moment, as though he was gathering information by touch. And for all I knew, he could do that now. Then, without moving them, he bent his head over my shoulder and kissed the side of my neck.

"No," I whispered, with no conviction whatsoever.

I wasn't too surprised when he ignored me.

He kissed another spot, and then another, none of them too close to the swelling, all of them desperately sensitive and long ignored, because there were a lot of things you could do for yourself, but you couldn't nibble your own neck. None of it was designed to be arousing—soft lips, no tongue, sticking close to some comfort boundary he'd intuited—but it was anyway. It was also odd, for some reason I couldn't quite name, until it suddenly hit me.

People didn't just come up and *touch* a dhampir.

Sure, enemies grabbed me in combat, and Claire touched me in emergencies. But casual, friendly contact had always been in short supply. Even my former lovers had been cautious, and not just the vampire ones. Humans could feel it, too—that there was something strange about me, something different, something off. And they tended to keep their distance.

The only creature who had just never seemed to notice was Stinky. His long, stick-like fingers and toes allowed him to climb people as easily as trees, furniture and anything else that didn't run off fast enough. And he liked human contact—even mine. Maybe especially mine, because he regularly crawled into my lap or invaded my bed, with the unconscious arrogance of children and puppies everywhere.

Louis-Cesare wasn't a child. Or a puppy. But he kept doing it anyway. And not just on intimate occasions like this morning. He touched the small of my back when I preceded him through a door. He touched my hand or my shoulder when we were talking. He randomly smoothed a hand down my hair just anytime he felt like it and then acted like nothing had happened.

And it threw me off balance every damned time. It wasn't aggressive; it wasn't painful; it wasn't a challenge. It was just *there*, subtle and unconscious and quietly devastating because it also wasn't unwanted.

The worst of it was that I'd found myself slowing down when we came near a door. Not for any good reason, just to make sure I got that touch. Or standing a little closer to make a random brush that much more likely. Or—and this was when I really knew I was in trouble—actually considering growing my hair out, just because I knew he'd like it. Even though the reason for keeping it short—denying the bad guys an easy handle— was significantly more important *to my fucking survival*.

So, we had a problem. And I didn't think that the method I used with Stinky, that is, letting him get away with it, was a great idea here. Louis-Cesare wasn't a neglected child or a puppy I'd found in a Dumpster. He was a master vampire and master vampires didn't follow you home and hang out on your back porch.

Okay, except for Ray. But he was clearly demented and anyway, he was fifth-level and had a good reason. Whereas Louis-Cesare was first-level with his own family and his own court, probably every bit as lavish as Mircea's since he'd been a senator, too, until a few weeks ago.

And that made our worlds about as far apart as they could possibly get.

I didn't want him here.

I didn't *need* him here.

I needed him gone. Out of my life before I got used to having him around. Before it hurt more than it was already going to when I finally womaned up and—

"You don't relax easily," he murmured.

"I'm a dhampir. This *is* relaxed," I said. It was supposed to be harsh, a verbal hands-off, but instead it came out tired and kind of sleepy.

Louis-Cesare didn't comment. He just cupped those big hands around my face, and slowed way, *way* down. Running parted lips over my cheek and jaw as if just being permitted to touch my skin was a privilege.

And okay, that wasn't helping. And neither were the arms that wrapped around me, pulling me off the table and back against a warm body inside a fuzzy sweater. Or the mouth that found my ear and my cheek, which had deflated at some point I hadn't noticed. Or the way his breath caught when he finally met my lips.

And then the back door banged open and a flood of yellow light hit us. And a familiar voice said, "Oh. Sorry."

I looked up to see Claire, silhouetted in the light, not looking even a tiny bit sorry. Maybe because her hair was frazzled and her apron was drenched and she smelled like dish soap. And she had a big black plastic tub in her hand, the type we used for cleaning off the tables in the garden.

Which, I belatedly realized, hadn't been done yet.

And she wasn't going to get any help from the fey. Their warriors might lay down their lives for Claire, but they wouldn't do dishes for her. Or peel potatoes, or carry out the trash, or help with any of the other household chores that had multiplied in number and difficulty with a dozen extra mouths to feed.

The twins were more easygoing, but trolls aren't known for a light touch, and we preferred not to have to replace all the dishes. Again. So every night we traded off, and it was my turn to clear the tables, only with everything that had happened, I'd managed to forget.

"Give me that," I said, reaching for the tub as she tried to edge around us. And had it snatched away.

"You're not doing it tonight," she told me, pushing sweaty hair off her face.

"Why not? You got stuck with the dishes."

"I'm not half dead!"

"Neither am I." I was actually feeling a lot better now that I had some food inside me. Hunger was always a bigger problem than some pulled muscles or a bruised jaw. My metabolism could take care of those pretty fast on its own, even without vampire assistance. But it couldn't feed itself. And healing took a lot of energy.

"You need to get some sleep," she said crossly.

"I slept most of the day. And I'm not leaving you with all the cleaning up to do."

"You are if I say so," she told me. Because Claire never met a person she didn't try to boss around.

And most of the time, it worked. But not tonight. "It's tables or dishes, Claire. One or the other."

She sighed suddenly, and gave up. Too tired to argue, probably. "Tables, then. No need for both of us to get soaked."

But Louis-Cesare didn't like that idea. "I will do it, if you will rest," he told me.

Claire blinked at him, as if she must have heard wrong, and I laughed. "*You* will do it?"

"Why not?"

I licked my lips, so very, very many comments warring to be the first one out. But Claire looked him over critically. Of course, he wasn't dressed for housework.

He was wearing the same khaki trousers and blue sweater as this afternoon. He wore sweaters a lot; I didn't know why. Vampires could regulate their temperature a lot better than humans, but a sweater in August looked strange. I guessed maybe he liked the way it felt against his skin.

It was understandable. The fabric—some kind of ungodly soft angora—just enhanced the hard muscle below, and proved almost impossible not to touch. I didn't even realize I'd been doing it until I felt a nipple harden abruptly under my hand.

And until a dishcloth hit me in the face.

"I've changed my mind," Claire told me drily. "You're on kitchen duty."

"Why?"

"You need to cool off."

"I'm fine," I said, feeling my cheeks heat, and tossed the towel back.

"Of course you are," she said, rolling her eyes. But then she left us to it.

The back of the house is one of the reasons the old place is preferable to any slick new apartment. Yes, the water had to run for ten minutes to get remotely close to hot. Yes, half the outlets would shock the hell out of you if you did anything so radical as try to plug anything in. Yes, the garden gate screamed like a murder victim at the slightest touch.

But then there was this.

It was a relic from a time when people actually used backyards for things like hanging up laundry and planting a garden and, hell, playing major-league baseball, given the size. But then the fey had moved in. The front of the house had had to remain the same, since it faced the street and people might have wondered had it suddenly turned into a literal fairyland. But the back was fenced and fairly private, and the fey had been bored and . . . well.

The old fence had been close to falling down, with rotten and/or missing boards and choked with weeds. But now the weeds had been replaced by vines that had braided themselves together, filling holes and then flowing along the old boards like waves. The illusion was heightened by sprays of some kind of white flower that foamed up here and there, like breaking water.

There were more flowers dotting the yard, despite the fact that most of them weren't in season. One of those that was, the neighbor's purple hydrangeas, had really gotten into the spirit of things. The usually sickly-looking bush had all but burst out of the ground, cascading over the fence like a waterfall and forming a waving purple puddle along one side of the yard.

In the middle of it all a miniature city had sprung up, a half circle of vaguely medieval-looking tents splashed with gold by the chains of lanterns strung between them. A bunch of huge roots had pushed up from the ground in the center, making a sitting area around a fire pit, where the artists and the fey were talking and singing and laughing and apparently getting along like gangbusters. Of course, that might have had something to do with the aforementioned cloud of weed.

That wouldn't affect the fey, who were pretty much immune to weak old human plants. But it ensured that their guests didn't notice certain things. Like the nearby patch of not-bluebells, which chimed with a faint tune whenever the breeze rustled through them. Or the strings of fireflies that festooned the bushes and sparkled in the trees, like tiny Christmas lights. Or the old lawn table and chairs that were living up to the name, having been completely covered, down to the individual slats in the seats, by a fuzzy blanket of bright green moss.

It was beautiful and weird and kind of disturbing and—

"Enchanting," Louis-Cesare said, looking around as we approached three new picnic tables set up halfway between the house and the camp.

"Yeah, literally," I said, plopping the tray on the end of the nearest table and shaking out the trash bag folded inside.

The tables sat six each, which was normally plenty, even when family and fey all ate together. But tonight there had been more people than usual, and mismatched chairs, extra place settings and visitors' casserole dishes littered the area, making cleanup more of a job than usual. I closed up a couple folding chairs and stacked them against a tree, and then turned to table number one, only to have Louis-Cesare take the first plate out of my hand.

"I said I would do that."

"Except we need our dishes in one piece," I said, taking it back. "Thanks."

"You think I do not know how?" he asked, and the dreaded eyebrow of doom went north.

"I think you do not know how," I agreed.

And the next thing I knew, my hand was empty. And eight plates, bowls and glasses were in the bin, each in its own perfect little stack, with eight sets of silverware piled alongside. And a vampire was leaning against the side of the table, looking smug.

"I thought you had servants to do that," I said, trying not to look impressed. Because his ego was already big enough.

"Now. But there were years when I did not."

Yeah, I always forgot that about him. Because of a weird set of circumstances I didn't completely understand, Louis-Cesare hadn't spent his formative years in the bosom of a vampire family, being bullied and picked on and ordered around, but also being taught the ropes. Maybe it was why he was a pretty unconventional vampire even now.

Well, that and stubbornness. Somewhere in all those masterless years, he'd formed his own ideas about how the world worked. And by the time anybody got around to pointing out to him that, for example, senior masters did *not* bus tables, he'd been past caring.

"But I am surprised your friend does not," Louis-Cesare said. "Do fey princesses not rate help?"

"If by 'help' you mean wilting noblewomen who wrinkle their noses at everything and don't lift a hand." They'd lasted less than a day. Claire didn't play like that.

"The fey do not have kitchen help?"

I sighed. "Yes. But it's the whole hierarchy thing. The soldiers were okay with the noblewomen being housed inside, since apparently they're too delicate to face the rigors of the backyard." He grinned. "But the regular servants couldn't be put in better housing than the soldiers, because the soldiers outrank them. And we couldn't fit the soldiers in the house, even if they doubled up, since there aren't enough free rooms. So—"

"So no help."

"No."

Louis-Cesare looked thoughtful.

"Well, except for the twins."

"The twins?"

"Sven and Ymsi. But while they're good at picking up the couch so we can vacuum, they aren't so good with the more delicate tasks. We lost eight windows when they tried to wash them and ended up obliterating them instead. And they're not any better at cooking."

"Given their size, I find that surprising," he said drily.

"Yes, well. It's not so much that they can't cook, as *what* they cook. Trolls eat, well, I've never found anything they *don't* eat, at least not so far."

"Do I want to know what that means?"

I thought of a memorable dinner a few weeks ago. And shuddered. "No."

Thankfully, he didn't ask, just moved on to table number two. Which didn't last any longer than table one. In a blink, the new plates were stacked neatly on top of the old ones, with the assorted accoutrements wedged perfectly alongside. If the whole master vampire thing didn't work out, I knew some restaurants that would snap him up in a second. And then he got cocky and moved the overflowing bin to table number three.

As if.

"Where are your servants?" I asked with a grin, wondering if there was a whole family of crazy vamps out there.

"Some are working with Lord Marlowe. The Senate is shorthanded, and I was asked to have my masters lend a hand."

"And the others?"

"Some are at Les Pléiades, my court in France. And some are here, in New York."

"Here? Then why haven't I seen any?"

"They have been busy looking for a house for me."

"You're buying a house here?"

"Hm. For some reason, I find New York to be more . . . attractive . . . than I remembered."

I wasn't sure how to respond to that, so I didn't say anything. I just followed behind him, stuffing paper goods in the garbage bag and closing up half-eaten trays of bakery rolls. Some of them hadn't even been opened, but the others would probably be stale by tomorrow. Not that that was a bad thing. Claire's bread pudding with whiskey sauce was almost as good as an orgasm.

Almost.

I grinned at that, and Louis-Cesare saw it. "What is it?"

"Nothing."

And it wasn't. Nothing important, anyway. Or dangerous. Or death-defying or, well, anything. And that was the point.

Is this how normal people live all the time? I wondered. I didn't know. I'd never been normal. I would never be normal. But I got to visit it once in a while, and it was . . . nice.

"By the way," he told me, "my majordomo would like to know your favorite color."

I blinked. Both because that was kind of out of the blue and because he'd somehow just stacked every damned dish off the third table onto the teetering pile.

"Why?"

"I informed him that I would like the decor to be pleasing to you."

I just stood there, getting further behind on the trash as I attempted to process that. "Why?" I finally repeated.

"For when you visit," he said, like of course I would. And like I would care about the decor if I did. I'd never even owned *furniture*, and he was worried that I wouldn't like the color scheme?

It was bizarre.

But he was standing there, looking at me like he expected an answer. Which I didn't have because I'd never thought about it. "I . . . don't have one."

He frowned. "But everyone has one. Mine is blue; Radu's is yellow. Your friend Claire's is green, judging by the amount she wears it."

And yes, it sounded reasonable when he put it like that, but it still didn't change the fact I didn't know. And clothing choices weren't likely to help me, because mine had always been more about expediency than anything else. I wasn't worried about looking good. I was worried about what I could afford, because my lifestyle tended to be hard on clothes. I was worried about the best possible camouflage to do the job, because the harder you are to see, the harder you are to hit. Or shoot. Or stab. And that usually boiled down to dark blue, which is actually more difficult to see at night than any other color, or black, because it's the urban uniform pretty much everywhere.

"Dory?"

"I . . . Black?" I guessed, because I had to say something. Or God help me, he might decide it was pink.

"Black?"

"What's wrong with black?"

His lips twitched. "Nothing. And it should provide Georges with an . . . interesting challenge."

He'd finished piling up the rest of the dishes as he spoke, into a towering, trembling mountain, like the preparation for some weird kind of circus act. Somehow, they were all in there—or on there, since most weren't actually touching anything but other dishes and air. But it wasn't going to do us any good, since they clearly weren't going anywhere else.

Louis-Cesare saw my expression. "You think I can't get them safely into the house?"

"I know you can't." For one thing, I doubted they'd fit through the door.

The eyebrow made a reappearance. "Are you willing to bet on that?"

"Bet what?"

He gave me a slow smile, the kind that said that money wasn't likely to be involved here.

Which was just as well, since Mircea had just fired me. But that wasn't the point, since I could afford other things even less.

"I don't think so," I opened my mouth to say, only my tongue had other ideas. My tongue chirped a cheerful "okay" before I could stop it.

And Louis-Cesare didn't give me a chance to recant.

He took off for the house, weaving through the yard's obstacles like a dancer—or what he was, an expert swordsman—with that ridiculous pile of dishes on one shoulder. And somehow he didn't drop a single one.

I hadn't really expected him to.

Chapter Seventeen

He was gone a long time. Well, okay, it was probably more like five minutes, but it felt like a long time when you're busy arguing with yourself about how stupid you're being and not getting anywhere. My brain was pissed, but my body clearly wasn't on board. My toes kept trying to tap and my face kept trying to grin and on the whole, I thought the body might be winning.

I decided to go stand near the fey, so I'd at least have a reason for looking like an idiot.

Things had gotten to the jam stage, and they were really going at it. The neighbors had brought the usual—drums, a tambourine and Jacob's guitar. The fey instruments were a little different, but still sort of familiar—flute-type things, lute-type things, and one collection of oddness that looked like an octopus had mated with some bag-pipes.

What took me a few minutes to notice was that the fey without instruments were playing, too.

The breeze rustled through the treetops like a brush on cymbals. Water dripped out of a bamboo fountain with the regularity of a metronome. Wind chimes tinkled on the edge of the house with a suspiciously convenient rhythm. The flapping of a neighbor's flag, the rumble of distant thunder, and the crickets sounding off in the hedge all got in on the act. Even the annoying bird from this morning, which should have been long asleep, was busy warbling out a tune.

It wasn't obvious, not at first. But after standing there

a few minutes, it was hard not to notice. The whole yard had become an instrument.

"How are they doing that?" I asked Claire, who had come up beside me, the tired lines in her face smoothing out as she watched the dancers.

She shook her head helplessly. "Magic?"

And yeah, it was. Not the kind I was used to, the kind bought from shady dealers in back alleys, the kind used to hurt. But magic nonetheless. Happy and joyful and humming over my skin. It cut through the fatigue, making me want to dance like some of the girls were already doing, their bodies blocking out the firelight in intervals, flickering like images on a silent-film reel.

Only they weren't faded pictures in black and white, but glorious, living color. Bright scarves fluttered, long hair flowed, eyes sparkled, and jewelry caught the light in dazzling flashes that also, somehow, seemed to be in time to the music. Or the magic, because the whole yard breathed with it, in and out, in and out, like the heartbeat of a giant creature laughing and spinning and whirling in the night—

And then so was I. Someone slid an arm around my waist and I looked up to see Louis-Cesare's eyes gleaming down at me, bright as sapphires—for a second. And then we were off.

And it *was* magic, or something very like it. My feet seemed to know the steps, complicated as they were, and the rhythm that was pounding up through the ground instead of the other way around, like the earth itself was directing the dance. And the earth seemed to be in a good mood, because soon almost everyone was caught up in it, even Claire, who was laughing and shaking her head and pulling back from the fey trying to coax her into the dance.

Which only ensured that she fell into the arms of the one behind her.

He swept her into the widening circle before she could tell him no, not that she looked like she wanted to. Her bright red hair bounced around her shoulders as she laughed and spun and leapt in steps I don't think she knew, either, but that were suddenly instinctive. It was like breathing or—no, I realized.

It was like we were part of the music.

The magic that had the garden in thrall had pulled us in, too, adding us to the beat without missing a note. Our pounding feet, our laughter, even our thudding pulses— everything fed into the melody, as if it had been intended all along. As if that was how it had been written.

And then it changed, slowing from vibrant energy to a thrumming, heavy rhythm that shivered up through my feet, raising goose bumps over my entire body. The other would have been hard to transcribe, to take all the myriad sensations and put them on a page. This would have been impossible.

No notes could capture the feel of Louis-Cesare tensing and relaxing against me, the slow grind of skin on cloth and skin on skin that I swear I could feel everywhere, even the places where we didn't touch. Or the hand on my hip, guiding us both, or the chest warm and hard against mine, or the open-mouthed kiss that stole my breath before giving it back, all in time to the beat of the music.

I'd like to blame it on the magic, but it wasn't a spell that had my arms looping around his neck, drawing him into another slow kiss, or my body arching against him, with every shift of our muscles sending sparks up my spine. It wasn't magic, although it felt a bit like it. But this was better, pushing back to see eyes dilated dark and hungry with real emotion.

My arms had been around his neck, but now they dropped so my hands could stroke through his hair, my nails skim down his cheek, before pulling away, fingers twined in his. I drew him out of the flickering circle of light, and into the darkness under a small group of trees. I didn't have to pull very hard.

The trees were ornamental and not very big, but one was a willow and gave good shade. And I decided that was good enough. I pulled Louis-Cesare into its shadow, and the next thing I knew, I was pressed against the trunk, a hungry vampire licking a stripe up the side of my throat, sucking a kiss below my ear, catching the lobe between his teeth.

I drew in a sharp breath, but it wasn't a vampire bite. It was the nip of a human lover who had lost a bit of control, and that was okay. I was feeling a little reckless myself. Or maybe more than a little.

My hands ran up his chest, ghosting over ribs and pecs and skin too fine for a soldier. He pulled back, just long enough to strip the sweater off, before attacking my neck again. And whether by luck or design, he'd found exactly the approach I liked best.

It was part of why I'd been attracted to vampires in the past; the edge of danger, the knowledge of what they could do adding thrill to thrill. Louis-Cesare wouldn't hurt me; I knew that. But he could. A senior master that close? Inside my defenses? I groaned and hooked a leg around him, drawing him closer.

His body was heavy, and huge and warm. None of which was news. The guy was well over six feet tall, and solid as a rock. But it felt like news, felt new, with all that strength pressing against me, all that power thrumming from his skin into mine.

And that was before the images hit.

His mouth crushing against hers, parting her lips in a bruising kiss that she returns with equal intensity. His hands on her waist, unzipping those so-tight jeans, the ones he swore she wore just to drive him mad. Fingers gentle on her thighs as he strips the material down, the heat of her mouth fading as he follows it, dropping to his knees, nimble fingers sliding beneath her underwear and pausing to caress her tautness. Before stripping them away, too. And then the sweet wetness between her legs, chased by his tongue, feeling her back arch off the tree, hearing her come with his name on her lips . . .

I blinked and snapped out of it, panting and breathless. And unsure what had just happened, since my jeans were still on. "I . . . what was *that*?"

Mischievous dark blue eyes met mine as my shirt fluttered to the ground. "I am the waiter tonight, am I not?"

It took me a second, but I got it. "And that was the menu?"

"For the first course. Unless mademoiselle has another preference . . ."

"No, I think . . . I think that will do fine," I said, my voice a little high. Maybe because my bra had just been unhooked and warm lips had begun licking a trail down to my breast. Where a wicked tongue circled a taut nipple with agonizing slowness. I started to ask if this was the appetizer, but it was lost in the groan when he finally took the aching nub into his mouth. And then flicked his tongue back and forth until I was panting in approval.

I am . . . definitely going to have to compliment the chef, I thought wildly, and pushed into the sensation.

He laughed. "And to think I almost did not come back."

"Come back?" I repeated blankly, before I remembered. I'd been on the phone with him when Scarface showed up. He'd been at the house.

"I thought you would be asleep," he murmured, scraping the barest edge of fangs along delicate skin.

"W-where did you go?"

"I am currently able to tell you everywhere to purchase condoms within a five-mile radius," he said wryly.

"You went looking for me?"

"After our conversation terminated so abruptly? Of course." He slid across to the nub's neglected twin. "But unlike you seem to believe, I cannot read your mind at will, particularly at a distance. And Claire had no idea where you had gone."

"We always go to Singh's."

"Yes. But it is linked to this house by a portal and you had taken your car. I therefore assumed—"

"I don't like portals."

"As I discovered . . . eventually. I called Claire when I could not locate you, and was informed that you had just arrived back here. She also told me something of what had happened, but she did not know details."

"But . . . that must be two hours ago. Where did you go in the meantime?"

"To obtain the details," he said, coming up for a kiss.

I splayed a hand on his chest. "What?"

"I merely went to his house—"

I blinked. "Whose house?"

"Zheng-zi's."

"You went to Scarface's *house*?"

"Scarface," he mused. "It is a good name for him. At least, for now."

"What did you do?" I asked—fearfully—because the last thing Louis-Cesare needed was to get into another unauthorized fight. Especially with someone heavily favored to become a senator. Who would then be in a position to cause him a world of hurt.

"Tell me you didn't attack him."

He smiled grimly. "The temptation was . . . severe. But judging by appearances, you had already taken care of that."

"So what? You just went by to say hello?"

"I went to inform him that the next time he duels you, I shall stand as second."

"Then he won't duel me!"

"That was rather the idea," he said, starting to frown. As it finally registered that something was wrong.

And it was; I just didn't know what.

It wasn't like I wanted Scarface out there, dogging my footsteps, waiting for another chance. And my win tonight had been about luck as much as skill, and luck was a fickle bitch who didn't always like me much. I should be pleased that Louis-Cesare had handled this in a way that worked for everyone.

It was a diplomatic feat worthy of Mircea. I got protection, Louis-Cesare avoided strike three with the Senate, and Scarface didn't lose any more face than he already had. Because no one wanted to duel Louis-Cesare. That was a death sentence and everybody knew it. No one would blame Zheng for backing off.

I should be happy. Hell, I should be thrilled.

So why was I so angry that my hands were shaking?

It felt almost like it did before I tipped over into Hulk mode. My breath had started coming faster, my heartbeat had become a visible pulse around my vision, and my fangs had dropped, piercing my lower lip. But it was different this time, too.

A minute ago, the fey camp had been shrouded in shadows, the only people really visible those in the fire's stuttering ring. But suddenly I could see everyone, even those who, like us, had already disappeared into the shadows or snuck away into the tents. The fey were blinding columns of white; the humans darker, redder, more varied. But all were perfectly visible, the heat rising from their bodies giving away their location as accurately as a searchlight.

I didn't have vision like that. I never had. But it was hard to concentrate on it with anger surging through my veins.

"Your eyes," Louis-Cesare said, his voice sounding far off even though he was right there.

"My *blood*," I snarled, my voice going guttural, my hands digging into his flesh. *"My kill."*

"Dorina—"

"Dory, I'm going to bed," Claire said, coming through the trees. "Can you check—"

She stopped dead, to the point that it looked almost like she'd run into a wall. And I don't know what she saw, but the next second she was running at me, even as I was trying to back away. I didn't want anyone to touch me, not even her. I was afraid, because I didn't know what was happening. And I was angry, so fucking angry I could barely see.

And then the landscape flooded red, like a bucket of blood had been splashed over a camera lens. And oh God, that wasn't good. Claire grabbed my arm, but I barely felt it, the usual calming current of her power all but lost in the gathering storm.

"What did you do to her?" she demanded, whirling on Louis-Cesare.

"I made a mistake," he said, his voice hollow. Or maybe that was me. Sounds were distorting, too, magnifying. A girl's laughter from near the fire, some wood popping, tiny shush-shushings of wind rustling the trees—all were equally clear, equally audible. The garden was suddenly deafening.

"What kind of a mistake?" Claire said, her voice harsh. *"What did you do?"*

"I . . . It is difficult to explain to a human—"

"Try," Claire gritted out, exerting real power now, trying to pull the rage off me. But this time, for the first time, it didn't work. Or, rather it did, I could feel it leaving my body, like a hot wind pouring into the blessed coolness of her being, pouring in and being absorbed. But while that usually left me pale and weak and very, very calm, tonight it was barely noticeable. Just enough to keep me on this side of sanity, fighting and clawing and teetering on the very edge.

Some of the fey appeared through the trees, and here and there the bright blade of a sword caught the bloody light from the lanterns, gleaming seductively. I had a sudden impulse, a mad desire to fly at them, to find out if they were as good with an edged weapon as I'd always heard, to see if they could blood me before I—

What the hell was wrong with me?

"What did you do?" Claire shouted.

"I . . . wasn't thinking," Louis-Cesare said. "I was furious that he would dare . . . I wanted to protect her."

"Then why is she like this?"

"I did not ask permission."

"What?"

"To champion her. I did not ask."

"Why does that matter?"

"Because, in doing so, I treated her in a way I would not have my own kind," he said bleakly. "To assume that she needed protection was to imply that she is inferior, that she cannot protect herself. It . . . ." He licked his lips. "Another first-level master would have eviscerated me for that."

"But Dory isn't a master—she isn't a vampire at all!"

"Part of her is. And that part recognized the insult."

More fey had gathered around as they spoke, and despite what some crazy part of my brain thought, I *had* seen them fight before, and I definitely wasn't interested in seeing it again. But I was glad they were here; if I went off, if I lost the inner struggle, I wasn't sure Louis-Cesare could hold alone. Not that he didn't have the ability, but the monster that lived in my veins didn't know pity, didn't understand compassion. He did.

It could prove a fatal weakness.

And not just for him.

"Get away from me," I told Claire, my voice thickening.

"I don't understand," she said frantically. "I should be able to absorb this, I should be able to help—"

"Get away!" I grabbed her arms, shaking her hard enough to cause the ponytail to collapse and spill bright red curls around her face. Hard enough to make her *listen*. "Get in the house. Get to the kids. . . . Don't let me in. Promise!"

She nodded, her green eyes wild and frightened. Because I'd never before hurt her. Because she'd never before understood that I *could*.

I shoved her away, abruptly enough that it sent her staggering. And as soon as I lost that touch, the clouds that had been building on the edge of my vision rushed in. I wasn't going to win this. I'd been here too often not to know. I wasn't going to—

"My apologies."

The soft words cut through the storm about to overtake me, like someone had hit a pause button. The rage was still there, a seething, boiling mass, just at the edge of my vision. And that's where it stayed, long enough, at least, for me to look down and see Louis-Cesare kneeling—kneeling?—on one knee on the ground in front of me.

He looked like some kind of medieval warrior, waiting to be knighted. Or maybe a particularly brawny Renaissance angel. His head was bowed, the gleaming auburn hair falling on each side of the strong shoulders, the nape left vulnerable and unprotected. It was the archaic vampire sign of penitence, left over from some time when they'd liked to get dramatic about things. It had never been altered, although it wasn't seen much these days. When it was, it was done by a servant to a master, if the master was particularly old or particularly traditional.

Or between equals, when the offense was particularly severe.

It was, in essence, giving the other a distinct advantage if he or she wanted to hurt you, or even kill you. Because the neck was one of the few vulnerable spots that vampires and humans shared. But I didn't want to hurt him, I thought, even as my eyes fixed on that defenseless flesh. I could practically feel the blood running through it, could all but taste it, warm and fresh and coppery sweet on my—

God!

I stumbled back a step, but Louis-Cesare didn't move. He stayed in the same position, head down, eyes lowered. "Zheng-zi treated you with more respect tonight than I did," he said quietly. "And he is supposed to be your enemy. You are right to be angry. It was your blood and I should not have interfered." He finally looked up, blue eyes dark and somber and completely sincere. "I will not make such an error again."

And just like that, the world slammed back to normal, so fast it left me gasping.

And I wasn't the only one.

"What the hell just happened?" Claire yelled. Right before she fell to the ground, clutching at the soil that swelled up under her fingertips. And then kept on swelling, a boiling mass of dirt and grass and leaves, and one lone plastic cup being fast churned to pieces.

I didn't understand what was going on until light started shining through the cracks in the earth, bright beams that stabbed the darkness and lit up the overhanging canopy of trees in spots, like tiny strobes. But it wasn't electric, wasn't anything I'd ever seen before. Except, I realized, in the ley lines.

It was power, pure magical energy, and since nulls didn't make any, there was no need to guess whose. Dhampirs don't make magic, but we *are* magic, as much magical beings as the creatures that spawned us. Only I'd never have guessed that that much was inside me—or had been, before Claire decided to try to swallow an ocean.

And failed. It was getting bigger, that roiling ball of power, leaking out of her because she couldn't absorb it all. And I guess she realized that, too, because she suddenly screamed and lost her grip, and something huge boiled away under the ground, like a torpedo through water.

Headed straight for the fey camp.

People screamed, bodies dove or jumped or were snatched out of the way, and the fire pit went up like a bomb, exploding into burning chunks as whatever-it-was raced underneath. It kept on going for another dozen yards, looking for all the world like some kind of huge, radioactive mole. Right up until it slammed into the fence.

I don't know why it stopped there, why it didn't just keep on going, doing no telling what kind of damage in the neighborhood. Maybe it was because the fey had enchanted the fence, or at least the vines flowing along it. Or maybe it had just hit exactly right, like lightning to a rod. But whatever the cause, it crashed into the fence like a freight train, in one burst of sound and violent white light.

And then the whole thing exploded.

But not in the normal sense.

Vines swelled like inflating balloons, going from the size of a finger to the size of tree trunks in an instant. The flower bunches dotting them here and there detonated all in a line, like living firecrackers. We were suddenly showered with what looked like confetti, covering half the yard in fluttering, flying petals. The part that wasn't already covered in smoldering wood or burning tents.

I stared at Claire, who stared back at me, and then we both looked at the visitors, who were standing in a swirling snowstorm, looking around in wonder. And didn't say anything. It was left to Jacob to sum up the evening.

"Whoa," he said, eyes wide behind his glasses. "You folks really know how to party."

Chapter Eighteen

Darkness, angry clouds boiling between buildings, and no electric lights that hadn't been shot out long ago. Not a good part of town. Not a part where people liked light being shed on their activities.

Didn't matter. Nature thumbed its nose at human preferences, sending the lightning that flashed overhead, strobing the dark street and the small alley that branched off from it with searing white. And causing the graffiti on the walls to practically leap off the old bricks.

The aftereffects lingered, crowding the small space with strange symbols in brilliant neon. They hung in the air for a moment, like bright banners, beautiful, ethereal, almost tangible. And then slowly faded.

I didn't mind.

I didn't need them.

The alley wasn't dark to me. Mold grew over the old bricks, etching them with patches of teal luminescence that were slowly consuming the paint, blurring the letters with a more subtle message. A trail of muddy water ran down the middle, like a ribbon of emerald light. The edges of garbage cans, stacked outside a restaurant, glowed in a rainbow of colors, with layers of decomposing food stretching back for days. The cat huddled under some steps was a vibrant blob of crimson. The streaks some human in a hurry had dribbled on one wall were a smoking purple, like the rooftops of the buildings on either side, slowly releasing the last heat of the day.

All was visible, all was light.

But nothing was as bright as the small, glowing footsteps, like puddles of gold, that I was following.

They wove across the muddy width of the alley, so clear, I thought I could have reached out and touched one. Could have picked it up out of the muck and held it in my hand. Could have—

A door opened up ahead, sending a bright, artificial beam into the night, a river of smelly ozone that drowned all the other, fainter lights. Like a wash of acid across a floor. It made me want to flinch, to hiss like the cat under some stairs was doing, before it turned its bushy tail and leapt into the night.

But I didn't. I didn't move at all. I was hugging a wall, already in shadow, and the light served only to increase it. The wedge of deep blue-gray around me deepened to inky black, the open door providing additional contrast.

Not that it mattered. The human standing silhouetted in the rectangle of light was as night-blind as they all were, and cocky. So much so that a cigarette dangled from his lips, its deep red tip bright even against the electric field behind him. He may as well have had a target on his chest.

But I didn't take advantage of it. He wasn't the one I wanted. But he smelled like him.

A memory stirred.

A hand gripped my chin, cold, hard, alien. I hissed and tried to bite, and it was snatched away. Someone scowled; I couldn't see it, but I could hear it in his voice. "What is this? Are you mad?"

"I thought you might find it . . . exotic."

"Exotic?" The voice was incredulous now. "What are you trying to pull?"

"Nothing, my lord, nothing. But you always say you want the unusual, to keep an eye out—"

"For fighters, warriors. Someone to tease the crowds away from that damned Geminus. Not children!"

"But I thought—"

"Leave the thinking to me. Sell it to the pimp and be done with it, and show me something I can use!"

The cage door had clanged down, and they had gone.

But the scent had remained. The same scent that was clinging to the guard's skin now.

Fodder, then. Sent out to make sure the master's many enemies weren't lying in wait. Or if they were, to act like one of the canaries the humans used to put down their mine shafts. Nothing more than a walking early-warning signal, someone whose spilt blood would serve as an alarm no vampire could ignore.

Minutes passed. A car pulled up at the end of the alley, headlights off, and glided to a stop. The human raised a hand in greeting and went down the few short steps to the alley floor.

The car door opened; the driver got out and leaned against the side of the vehicle, legs crossed, body relaxed. "Got a spare?"

He was human, too. The voice harsh, discordant. Not the real driver, then. Just someone who brought the car around and was now waiting to hand it over.

"Sure." The first guard flicked half a pack of cigarettes through the air, the cellophane side flashing for a second in the light from the door.

"Funny man," the other said. "What am I supposed to light it with? My finger?"

"You don't come too prepared, do you?" the first guard groused, reaching for something in his pocket.

"Trying to quit."

And then, for a split second, both men were watching a lighter follow the same arc as the cigarettes. And I moved, in the instant before it was caught, just a blur against the night, unseen, unheard. Through the door behind the human, and into the brightness beyond.

Strange but true; those creatures that most liked the night, that preferred to shroud their deeds in secret, wanted brilliant light around them. Even those whose eyes didn't need it. Maybe they didn't trust their partners, and wanted to see every hand's turn. Or perhaps it went deeper. An instinctive knowledge that they weren't the only things that hide in shadow.

Like the one I melted into as a tall figure came down the stairs.

He was human-slow, with a heavy tread: another guard. He sent a disinterested glance around the room, checking everything, seeing nothing. "Clear," he said, and I mouthed it with him.

Old trick, my heartbeat synced with his, our breathing in time, the same slow, steady aspiration. A clock ticked on a wall, heavy, loud. Outside, the smoking human finished his cigarette and crushed it underfoot, scattering a stale chemical scent on the breeze.

Then there were more footsteps on the stairs, quiet this time, light. Almost silent. Three, the two in front young, bright, warm. The one in back old, dark, like a pool of deep, cold water.

And strangely hesitant, as if he knew something was wrong.

They didn't get that old by being stupid.

The two vampire guards stopped abruptly, halfway between one step and the next. But nobody spoke, nobody moved. It was as if time itself stood still.

One second, two.

"Master?" the human said, confused.

The master didn't answer.

I had done nothing wrong, made no mistakes. But sometimes it didn't matter. The clock ticked.

Outside, the clouds cracked open and rain began to fall. Light at first, and then heavier, pattering against the roof, plinking off the metal trash cans, causing one of the waiting humans to curse. Inside, the master spoke.

"Danil."

The human guard looked up. "Master?"

"Leave us."

The man's confusion increased. "But, master, the car—"

"Now."

Danil left.

The two vampire guards leapt over the stairs and, a second later, hit the floor. One still wearing a snarl; the other with a strangely blank expression. Surprised.

Like the master when he spoke again. "Someone paid well. Tell me who it was, and I will make this—"

He cut off as my hand found his throat. From his expression, he hadn't seen me move. I gripped his flesh, my nails breaking the skin. Thick blood, so red it was almost black, oozed down his neck in rivulets, over my fingers. Didn't matter.

There was no one left to scent it.

"Painless?" I breathed, and he blanched. His fear flooded my nostrils as he recognized me—not who I was but what. I smiled. I liked that. Wanted more, wanted to close my hand, to jerk back, to tear out his throat in the same moment that I stabbed UP—

But not yet.

"I will make you the same offer," I hissed, jerking him close. "Name him, and this will be quick."

"Name? Name who? I don't—"

I put it into his mind, the whole scene. His face as the cage door slammed shut, and the face of the one making the offer. The one I needed.

"But, that's all?" He looked incredulous. "That's why you're—"

The nails sank in more, up to the first knuckle. I was enjoying this. He saw.

He saw and it broke him.

"I don't know! I never had a name. They don't—"

"A location, then."

"A warehouse, in Jersey. I can give you the address, but it won't help. We only meet there a few times a year, to bid on the more unusual lots, and only when we receive a call—"

I stripped the location from his mind. An old place, abandoned, overgrown. Useless. I growled.

"Please! I don't know any more—"

"That is . . . unfortunate."

"—but I can give you whatever you want!"

"No," I said, looking into the shadows. Where something gold glimmered against the dark. "You can't."

I came to, thrashing around, caught in a trap that threatened to smother me. And halfway through a scream. I cut it off abruptly, but it echoed in my ears, like the pulse in my throat as I fought to free myself from the clutches of—

My overstuffed comforter?

The old squashy thing hit the floor like a body, and I sat up, breathing hard.

My eyes darted around, trying to find the source of the threat, only there wasn't one. Just my bedroom, the pile of bras still on the dresser, along with a gun belt and more of Ymsi's wilting flowers. All lit by dust-filled beams of sunlight.

Which was wrong.... Wasn't it? It had been dark. It had been—

I had a fleeting image of a slice of blood hitting a wall, a cigarette falling onto dirty concrete, and small golden footprints glowing against a dark street. And then a blast of pain hit me, hard enough to wrench a cry from my throat. Son of a—

I jerked violently, grabbing for my temples.

And fell out of bed for the second morning in a row.

My ass hit wood, hard enough to bruise, because I'd managed to miss the comforter. Of course. I dragged it over, but otherwise I didn't move. I just lay there for a few minutes, clutching familiar softness, feeling weak and disoriented and listening to that damned bird again.

My head was pounding like the world's worst hangover, and the cheerful little trills weren't helping. I blearily thought about shooting it, but our fey visitors would probably object. I decided it wasn't worth it and started trying to squint the alarm clock on my nightstand into view.

And got a second shock: 3:45.

Not so much a cheerful morning, then, as a cheerful afternoon.

I stared at the clock and it stared stubbornly back, insisting that yes, it really was that late. That I really had slept for something like sixteen hours. And yet I didn't feel particularly well rested. In fact, I felt a lot like crawling back into bed.

Until I remembered last night.

The tendrils of whatever I'd been dreaming about had

dissipated, but my little freak show yesterday was clear as crystal. My forehead was halfway to the floor anyway, so I just let it sink the rest of the way down. Oh, God. *Why?*

God apparently did not have an opinion on the matter. Neither did the floor. But the smooth old boards were cool against my flushed cheek, so I stayed there anyway, working through the embarrassment and the guilt and the general fucked-up-ness of my life. Which you'd think I'd be used to after centuries of that sort of thing.

But I wasn't.

Because I wasn't supposed to remember.

I'd always blacked out during my little episodes. Always. I'd wake up, sometimes weeks or months later in different freaking *countries*, with no idea where I was or how I'd gotten there. Or what I'd done in the meantime.

And that was scary; that was bad. But I'd just discovered something worse: going along for the ride. Staying awake for the whole terrifying scene, knowing just how out of control I'd been, just how close I'd come—

I broke off, breathing hard.

One of the few things I'd always been able to say about my condition was that it was constant. I'd sometimes railed about that, about the fact that age hadn't granted me any of the extra powers and privileges that it did the vamps. Years had passed, but my fits had never become the slightest bit less frequent, never the tiniest amount more controlled.

But then, they had never gotten worse, either.

Until now.

And the really scary part of it was that I had no one to ask, no way to find out what the hell was going on. Because nobody knew anything about dhampirs. And they didn't want to know, since experimenting on something that could go ballistic and kill you at any moment wasn't high on most people's priority lists.

Healers had slammed doors in my face or cowered until I went away. Shysters had sold me the magical equivalent of snake oil and then run for the hills. The few unorthodox mages with enough cred for me to bother hunting them down had given up in disgust when their enchantments slid right off me. And nobody had really known what the hell they were doing anyway.

And that included other dhampirs.

Not that I'd met many, since we were a rare breed. And most of those I did stumble across either weren't sane enough or hadn't lived long enough to wonder why we were the way we were. The only exception had been some Indian guru-type I finally tracked down in the deserts of Rajasthan. He was also the only one I'd met who'd lasted as long as me—by meditating the rage away, or so he claimed. I'd sort of suspected that living hundreds of miles from any possible prey might have helped.

And yet he'd proven as useless as all the rest. He'd suggested that I learn meditation to improve my karma. And that I get the hell out of his territory before he ripped my head off and ruined his. He hadn't offered any advice on how to solve my problem.

I stared at the dust bunnies under my bed and wondered if this was how it ended. If this was why I'd never met any really old dhampirs. If maybe we self-destructed, assuming we didn't manage to check out early, like some kind of metaphysical time bomb.

I didn't know. I'd always just assumed that I would follow the vampire example and go on living until I pissed off the wrong person. But maybe not. Because I was half human, too. And human aging had all kinds of issues attached to it, didn't it?

Like mental illnesses that got worse over time, for example.

Fear clawed at my belly, as all the elements of my worst nightmares rolled together into one. The sense of powerlessness I hated, of not being able to control what I did, who I hurt. The dread of becoming like the things I hunted, of seeing the horror on people's faces as I destroyed everything they loved, needlessly, uselessly. The terror of descending into a cage of my own mind, shouting, begging to be let out, while something else took control.

And forced me to watch.

I shuddered hard and sat up, wrapping my arms around myself. I wanted to shove the thoughts away, but I couldn't afford it. Not now. Not when I didn't know what had caused this.

And not when it had happened twice now.

The first time had been during a fight six weeks ago. I'd been hit with a stunner designed to take out a platoon of war mages, which should have taken me out, too. But my alter ego is stronger and I guess it had decided that taking a nap right then might not be a great idea, since we probably wouldn't have woken up.

My dhampir nature had been in control for only a few seconds, but that had been enough to allow us to fight through the spell. And to freak me the hell out. But then, seeing myself in full-on Hulk mode wasn't anything like the strangest thing that happened that day. And afterward, I'd managed to shrug it off, putting it down to extreme stress, or luck, or desperation.

That theory had been reinforced when weeks passed and it hadn't happened again. I'd filed it away as a one-off, just another weird thing in a life not entirely devoid of the bizarre. Only apparently not. Apparently my control had had less to do with a stable psyche and more to do with other things. Like Claire coming back.

Or like my new favorite beverage.

I could see it now, due to my never having understood the point of a bed skirt. The bottle was thick blue glass, bumpy and bubbly and almost opaque, like the kind that puddles at the bottom of stained-glass windows. It had rolled next to one of the foot posts at some point, leaving a little trail in the dust. I reached underneath and pulled it out, and some liquid sloshed against the side.

It didn't look like much, clear as vodka without the tint provided by the bottle. And it tasted like even less, just vaguely of the flowers and herbs it was made from—if flowers and herbs were in the habit of tasting you back. And drinking you down. And standing you on your head because fey fauna might be scary, but I honestly thought fey flora gave it a run for its money.

But while the wine had a kick like an enraged hippo, it was also the only thing I'd found that helped to control my fits. Or no, that wasn't exactly right. It didn't *help*. Help was what human hooch, Mary Jane, and living with a powerful null had done for me. Help was giving me fewer episodes, or helping them to be shorter, or giving me more time to get away from innocent people who didn't need to meet Hurricane Dory whenever I felt one coming on.

Fey wine didn't do that. Fey wine turned them off, stopped them cold, shut them down. It was the magic elixir I'd been searching for most of my life, and it had seemed like a dream come true when I first discovered it earlier this summer.

Until I'd started to notice a few things.

Like how it let vamps spy on my thoughts. Or how it eroded my edge in combat, almost getting me killed a few times. Or how I was fast growing dependent on the stuff. I'd cut way back after seeing how, even after Claire returned and I didn't really need it anymore, I'd still wanted it.

Like, really, really wanted it.

Like right now, in fact.

I pulled the stopper out of the bottle, which wasn't cork because the stuff ate right through it, and slammed back a couple shots' worth. I can chug straight whiskey and not bat an eye, but a swallow of this stuff was enough to have me tearing up, to leave me gasping. But I hit it again right after, anyway.

And it was good. Not the taste, but the feeling it spread down my torso, through my limbs, throughout my body was just a huge relief. Not because it took away the pain—it didn't—but because it ensured that, at least for a little while, I wasn't going to be inflicting some on anyone else.

I shoved the stopper back in, dragged myself up and went to the closet. My clothes had been returned by whoever had retrieved them after the cataclysm. Meaning that half had been carefully folded and hung back up (Claire) and half were piled in a colorful wad on the floor (the fey). I shoved the wad aside, popped the door over my weapons stash and dumped most of what I had on hand into the big duffel I used for missions. Then I stuffed some clothes on top, stuck the wine bottle in the side, grabbed a jacket on my way across the bedroom and flung open the door.

And almost ran into the angry person standing on the other side.

Chapter Nineteen

"Going somewhere?" Claire asked grimly.

"Damned right!" I tried to push past her, and got slammed into the wall for my trouble.

"I don't think so."

I stared at her over the thin, paisley-covered arm that had me pinned, because Claire didn't do a lot of slamming. Of course, she didn't usually glare daggers at me, either, so today was obviously about new experiences. Too bad I didn't have time for them.

I threw off her hold and took a step toward the stairs.

And promptly ended up making the acquaintance of Mr. Wall again.

My eyes narrowed; hers narrowed back. I dropped the duffel, which had ended up in between us, giving me room to slip under her grasp. And that worked great — for about a second. Which was how long it took for a scale-covered gauntlet to grab my shoulder and for the slamming to recommence, this time with a little more gusto.

"That's cheating," I told my still mostly human-looking roommate.

Claire scowled at me, or possibly at the remains of the sleeve on her once nice wrap dress, which hadn't been designed to accommodate a dragon's forearm. "And what you were trying to do wasn't?"

"I was trying to get out of here —"

"Yes, I got that!"

"You know it's necessary," I said, struggling—uselessly, because when one of the dragon-kind puts you somewhere, you stay there.

"Like hell it is! You have a crazed vampire after you—"

"Not anymore." Probably.

"—*and* a bunch of smugglers or whoever kidnapped you all of two days ago! Are you *trying* to get yourself killed?"

"I'm trying to do what you should have last night!" I snapped, starting to get angry.

"And what was that?"

"Throw me out! Instead you leave me here, inside the damned wards, where I might easily have—"

"Done what? Hurt me?" She looked incredulous.

"You aren't the only one here!"

"I think your boyfriend can take care of himself," she said drily.

"He isn't my—that's not who I meant!"

"As can the guards."

"Damn it, Claire. You know who I mean!"

"No, I really—" I saw when it hit, when her eyes widened. As if it had literally not occurred to her despite my all but spelling it out last night.

"You're sane when you transform," I gritted out. "I'm not. And since I can't guarantee I won't attack someone who *can't* defend themselves, I'm out of—"

I cut off because something had just zipped by us, moving so fast it was merely a blur of color.

I started to ask what the hell, but before I could get the words out, the blur had knocked a mirror off the wall, caught it a couple inches off the floor, put it back where it belonged, zipped the rest of the way down the hall and finally resolved itself into a small man with a smaller mustache. He was of medium height and slender, with dark eyes, slicked-back black hair, and a sharp dark outfit. It made him look like the maître d' at one of the kind of restaurants that don't take reservations, because if you're not important enough for them to recognize you, you aren't getting in anyway.

It looked a little incongruous next to the overflowing laundry hamper he had tucked under one arm.

"Who—" I tried again.

"The other reason I have a headache," Claire muttered, as the maître d' hoisted the basket of laundry—meticulously folded sheets and towels, by the look of it—and rapid-fired them into a linen closet, like a veteran poker player dealing cards.

If I'd tried that, they'd have ended up in a crumpled mess, and probably piled in the bottom of the closet. In his case, they obediently formed themselves into perfectly square piles with military precision, allowing him to kick the door shut with one mirror-bright patent leather shoe, zip back down the hall, tuck something into Claire's apron pocket, and disappear down the stairs.

The whole thing had taken maybe ten seconds.

"That . . . was a vampire," I said stupidly.

Claire sighed. "Tell me something I don't know."

"What did he give you?" I asked, because she'd fished it out.

She opened her palm to show me a little packet of pills. "It's like they know what I need before I need it."

"Not unless you're going to dry-swallow. You don't have any—" I stopped because I'd blinked. And now she was holding a glass of water.

"They even folded the fitted sheets," she said. And then she let me go in order to knock back the aspirin.

"That's impossible."

"That's what I always thought, but it can be done. And the old copper cookware—you know, the ones that had that lovely patina?"

"I guess," I said, because I cooked about once a decade.

"Well, they're bright and shiny now," she said sourly. "At least they were the last time I was allowed into my own kitchen, which was about an hour ago, so God knows what's been done in—"

"Who are they?'"

"You said it," she grimaced. "Vampires."

"But whose?"

"Whose do you think?"

Damn.

"I'll talk to Ray," I told her. "I know his people probably need somewhere to crash until I get this mess sorted out, but I never told him they could—"

"They aren't Ray's," Claire said, looking at me funny.

"Whose then?"

She put her hands, both of which were back to normal, I was relieved to see, on her hips. "Did you or did you not tell Louis-Cesare that I needed domestic help?"

"I . . . Not in so many words, no."

"Well, he interpreted it that way. They showed up a couple hours ago and took over. So far, they've done the laundry, mowed the yard, cleaned the house to within an inch of its life—despite my telling them that the spell would just return everything to the way it was, anyway—shampooed the cats and replanted my marigolds!"

"Your marigolds?"

"They said the lines weren't straight enough!" She looked pissed. No one gets points for telling a Virgo that she doesn't know how to keep house.

"Why didn't you just dismiss them?" I asked.

"Oh, now why didn't I think of that? Because they wouldn't let me! That vampire sent them to you and you're the only one who can tell them to go. And that's exactly what you're going to do! And then you're going to march yourself back up here and get a bath—"

"I'm doing nothing of the—"

"—and then you're going to get dressed and unpack that ridiculous bag and come downstairs again and *we're all going to have a nice meal, okay?*"

"No, it's not okay. It's not safe—"

"Bullshit." Claire swearing was odd enough to shut me up. "We lived together for almost two years, didn't we?"

"Yes, but—"

"And how many times did something like last night happen?"

"Once is enough! And it also happened a month ago—"

"And what *else* happened a month ago?"

"What are you—"

"Damn it, Dory!" Her eyes had focused on my bag, which was still on the floor, and she leaned over and jerked something out. "You've got it on you!"

"Of course I've got it on me," I said, wrestling her for my little blue bottle. "What did you expect after—"

"I expected you to take a moment and wonder if this wasn't the problem!" Claire said, and threw it viciously at the wall.

It didn't shatter into a thousand pieces, but only because the glass was so thick. It did, however, stick halfway into the wall and stay there. I turned my eyes from the new hallway decoration and back to Claire, who was practically incandescent.

"My abilities draw out your power, release it, destroy it!" she told me angrily. "That's what a null *is*. But the wine isn't a null."

"Well, it's doing something."

"Yes! Yes, it is! It stops your fits, but it *doesn't remove the cause*. It's like closing the valve on a steam engine. It might keep the steam from escaping, but it doesn't do anything about the *pressure*."

I'd been about to say something, but at that I stopped. And just stared at her for a moment. "That's what you think is happening?"

"I don't know," she said, exasperated. "That's what I've been trying to tell you. Nobody knows what that stuff does when ingested by a dhampir. All we know is that it brings out latent magical abilities in humans. But you're not human."

"But you believe it's been putting a kind of stopper in my fits."

She shoved frazzled red hair off her forehead. "Well, it makes sense, doesn't it? You drink it, and it stops your fits, because it shuts off any escape valve for that part of you. But it doesn't do anything to let off the pressure. So it just keeps building and building. And sooner or later—"

"Pow."

"Very much pow."

I nodded. "Thank you," I told her, and meant it. I pried the bottle out of the wall.

"What are you doing?"

"Even if you're right, it can still be useful in emergencies," I told her, shoving it back in my pack.

"But ... where are you going?" she demanded, as I started for the stairs again.

"The same place I was going before. Away."

"But I've just explained—"

"That the wine doesn't work, not over the long haul."

"Dory!" She grabbed for my arm again, but this time I was ready, and spun out of her reach. "Damn it, get back here!"

"I *can't.*"

She reached for me again, but I grabbed her this time, pushing her into the wall face-first. It wasn't hard enough to hurt, but she didn't look too happy. Of course, neither was I.

"It's getting worse, all right," I told her harshly. "Let's face it. You can't control me anymore. And the wine is a stopgap at best. Meaning I'm not—"

I broke off because my back suddenly hit the wall. On the other side of the corridor. Which was a surprise, since I didn't recall moving.

"You know what's not safe?" Claire demanded furiously, stalking toward me. "*I* am not safe. You're not the only one dealing with pressure right now. I'm under it all day, every day, with no end in sight! And no matter what I try to tell anyone, they never—"

She cut off abruptly, and looked away. "What is it?" I demanded.

She didn't say anything.

"Claire—"

"No," she said, looking back at me, her eyes shuttered. "You have enough problems of your own. I can't solve them for you, but I can keep from piling any more on."

"But I can help—"

Red hair tossed. "How? I thought you were leaving."

I just looked at her, because Claire never stayed mad

for long. And this proved to be no exception. She deflated suddenly, looking miserable. "You won't like it."

"If it has you looking like that, I already don't like it."

"No, I mean—" She stopped, and licked her lips. And then she stiffened her shoulders and met my eyes squarely. And dropped the bombshell.

"Æsubrand hasn't been seen in almost a week."

I blinked. Okay, if anything could distract me from my own private hell, that was it. Æsubrand was a little bit of hell all on his own.

And, as irony would have it, he was also soon to be Claire's cousin by marriage. It seemed that the fey family she was about to marry into was almost as messed up as mine. In fact, it might just take the prize, since none of my relatives were actively trying to kill each other.

Well, not at the moment.

Unfortunately, that wasn't true for Claire. Her father-in-law was Caedmon, king of the Blarestri, one of the three main divisions of the Light Fey. He had a sister, Efridís, who had been married off to the Svarestri king, the leader of one of the other great houses, to seal a treaty or something. I wasn't real clear on the details. What I was clear on was that she'd had a son, who had turned out to be a homicidal son of a bitch.

He was also ambitious as hell, to the point that merely inheriting one throne wasn't good enough for him. Oh, no. Æsubrand wanted two. Specifically, he wanted Caedmon's, which he'd had a claim to—right up until Heidar, aka Caedmon Jr., met a certain redheaded half dragon. And they had a son.

Heidar hadn't been a problem for Æsubrand, because Blarestri law required its kings to have a majority of fey blood and his mother had been plain old human. But Claire, who was more than fifty percent fey, had tipped their son straight into the line of succession. And the line of fire.

Aiden's existence had seriously messed up his cousin's fey-unifying, dynasty-building, Æsubrand-glorifying plans, and he hadn't taken it well. As in, he'd tried to kill Claire while she was still pregnant, and when that didn't work, he'd gone after baby Aiden. But—lucky me—I'd managed to get in his way not once, but twice. Not that I'd been the only reason he failed, or even the main one, but for some reason, he seemed to blame me.

One of these days, I was going to have to work on my people skills.

"You think he's here?" I asked, because that was just all we needed.

"Caedmon doesn't know," Claire said distractedly, running a hand through already messy curls. "But he didn't seem . . . He said he'd be more inclined to think that Æsubrand was back here if it didn't look like he was."

I tried to parse that, and failed utterly. "Come again?"

"You know his mother's ability with glamourie?"

I nodded. Most fey could change their appearance to some degree, even without the potions they sometimes sold to us. But Efridís was said to be especially gifted, to the point of even being able to fool her fellow fey. She'd used her skills to impersonate her darling boy, helping him break out of the fey version of jail, last time I'd heard.

And then I finally realized what Claire was saying. "You think she'd be covering for him."

"*Caedmon* thinks so," she said, frowning. "He said the Svarestri know we spy on them, just like they do on us. And that if Æsubrand *was* here, his mother would be doing everything in her power to make it look like he was still at court. He'd be seen riding, hunting, hawking—anything to make him highly visible. But he isn't."

"Which means what?"

"That's just it—I don't know! Caedmon thinks Æsubrand probably *is* away from court, just not here. So he doesn't need anyone to cover for him. He said he could be patrolling the border, or leading war games, or on a freaking trade mission—" She threw up her hands in disgust.

"But you're assuming the worst."

"Do I have a choice?" she asked wildly. "After everything?"

No. She really didn't. Aiden's talisman protected him,

but only to a degree. It meant that someone might not be able to just walk up and kill him, as they'd tried once before. But it wouldn't do a damned thing to stop a kidnapping. And if Æsubrand ever got Aiden into his elegant hands, I didn't think it would be long before he'd find a way to dispose of the problem—permanently.

It was, I suspected, why Claire was still here instead of back in Faerie. She'd recovered the talisman two weeks ago but had shown no signs of leaving. Maybe because Æsubrand didn't know Earth all that well, which put him at a disadvantage here.

Not that he hadn't managed to compensate before, at least somewhat, but Faerie had proven no safer. Some of Caedmon's own courtiers seemed to think that a full Light Fey king sounded better than a part-human, part–Dark Fey mutt. It was probably what had Claire looking like she was about to explode.

"There must be some way to verify—" I began.

"Heidar's trying." Her hands twisted in her apron, and for all her power, she was suddenly just another anxious mother, desperate to ensure her child's safety. "That's why he went back. He's doing a reconnaissance into the Svarestri lands—"

"What?"

She nodded, frantically. "I begged him not to, but he said he used to do it for fun as a boy. That he knew some old trails, had some contacts. That he might be able to alleviate my fears . . ."

And instead he'd doubled them. Now Claire was left worrying about her son *and* her fiancé. No wonder she'd been going out of her mind.

And I really wasn't helping, was I?

"What can I do?" I asked simply.

"You can let me return the favor you did me," she said severely. "When I came here in the middle of the night with a baby on my hip and half of Faerie after me! The smart thing would have been to throw me out—"

"It's your house."

"—and leave me to handle my own problems, but you

didn't. You refused to let me run off and possibly get myself and my child killed. You did what friends do when other friends are acting stupid and panicked and you *told me so*. Like I'm telling you."

"That was a completely different situation, and you know it. Your enemies were outside—"

"You're not an enemy, Dory!"

"I'm not an enemy *now*."

Claire didn't like that. "Last night, the only person in danger was you! Louis-Cesare—"

"Isn't here all the time." And might not be again. "Your eyes," he'd said, looking a little freaked-out. And yeah, I guessed so. I'd only glimpsed myself in full-on dhampir mode once before, in that fight a month ago, and it hadn't been pretty. Hadn't, in fact, looked particularly human—snarling face, gleaming fangs, and glowing, demonic eyes . . .

Shit.

"He doesn't need to be!" Claire said forcefully. "I was going to say that if he hadn't been able to take care of it, *we have a garden full of fey*. And the elite of the royal guard at that!"

"Who might not have been enough."

"Oh, please!" She looked me up and down critically, and didn't seem impressed. "If they can't handle one lone dhampir, I'll kick their asses. And then I will."

"You will what?"

"Handle you."

"*You'll* handle me."

"You think I can't?" she asked, her chin lifting.

"I think you *won't*."

"Then you don't know me that well."

I rolled my eyes. "I know you plenty. You're a *vegan*. Cutting up meat for the fey's meals almost makes you sick. You have all those marigolds because you don't even like hurting bugs!"

"Faerie changes a person."

"Not that much. And my other half is a ruthless—"

"So am I. I've had to learn to be. And if it will make

you feel any better, if you go crazy, and for some unfathomable reason decide to attack Aiden or Stinky—and for the love of *God* give that child a better name—"

"I told you, Duergars have to earn—"

"—then I'll kill you myself."

I stopped. Because Claire had sounded like she meant it. She looked like it, too, with those usually soft green eyes hard and steady on mine.

"You will?"

"Yes. I will."

"You'd hesitate."

"No. Not with a child's life at stake. Not with Aiden's life. I'll kill anyone who touches him."

And that last was so cold, so implacable, that it actually sent a chill up my spine. In that moment I honestly believed my gentle roommate to be capable of murder. Even mine.

"Good," I told her.

She nodded, letting out a breath. "Good," she agreed, wiping her hands on her apron. "Now get down there and get rid of those damned vamps!"

Chapter Twenty

I found the vamps in the formal dining room we never used, which was usually musty and full of dust, but now smelled like a truck full of lemons had crashed into the side of the house. There were five of them. And I'd been wrong. They didn't look like they'd just stepped out of a high-end restaurant, unless the high end restaurant was in the nineteenth century.

There were three men and two women, all with smooth, dark hair, perfectly shined shoes, and proper black maid or butler attire. They looked like Mattel had put out a country house collector's set: servant's edition. Only somebody had gotten sloppy with the faces, because the perfect servants were looking a little weirded out.

Maybe because they were all bunched around the troll twins.

Or, no, it was really more of a line than a bunch. The vamp by the gleaming sideboard, who had covered his snappy outfit with a long white chef's apron, passed a dish to the one next to him. Who passed it on to the next and so on, until it reached the boys. Who consumed it like they always did—in one gulp. And then politely waited for more.

The vamps were apparently not used to seeing a Bundt cake be wolfed down like a doughnut—hence the big eyes. Which got even bigger when one of them glanced up and saw me. And then they were all looking, heads coming up like puppets on a string as the news flashed silently between them.

And then one of them smiled.

Which was when things got a little surreal.

Not that they were difficult. Oh, no. I womaned up and went in to explain the situation, and they quickly agreed to "take their leave" as soon as they finished stuffing the twins. But they said it with smiles all around. Big, genuine smiles that made dark eyes light up and dimples pop.

It made my teeth hurt.

Broadly smiling vamps weren't exactly common in my experience, unless they had a knife ready to slide between my ribs. So I thought I could be forgiven for flinching slightly every time one of them moved. Which, to give them credit, they caught on to pretty fast. But while most vamps would have had a little fun at my expense, like moving to different parts of the room so that I'd have trouble keeping them all in sight, these just seemed perplexed. And chagrined. Like they thought maybe they were doing something wrong.

So they tried to fix it by slowing down—way down. And by making very deliberate motions and only when they had to, which creeped me out even more, because vamps don't move like that. And so it went until they almost weren't moving at all, until it was like talking to a group of determinedly smiling statues.

"I, uh." I licked my lips. "I have to go," I told them, a little desperately. And then fled to find some lunch before I passed out.

I didn't know why I was so hungry, considering I'd eaten enough last night for a dozen longshoremen, or one fey. But I was. Unfortunately, the kitchen wasn't looking too promising.

In fact, it was just as well that the vamps had been keeping Claire out, because she was going to go ballistic when she saw this. Empty cabinets hung open everywhere, the sink was piled with dirty dishes, and more of the same were stacked high on every available surface. Except for the end of the table. It was covered by a dwindling pile of food, mostly desserts, ready for sacrifice to the two bottomless pits out there.

My metabolism doesn't run so well on sugar, so I passed them up in favor of a trip to the fridge. Which was usually stuffed full, considering the number of mouths we had to feed. But today it looked more like the bad old days, when Claire had been gone and I'd been living the life of the carefree—and hungry—bachelorette.

I'd once considered myself lucky if I had a can of tuna fish and a couple of those little mayo packets in the house, but Claire had spoiled me. My stomach rumbled in dismay at the almost empty shelves. But a look in the freezer yielded a bit more bounty, and old scavenger instincts took over.

In fact, I was so busy assembling lunch or supper or lupper or whatever it was called at four p.m. that I barely noticed the chef guy coming into the kitchen. Until I turned around from the toaster to grab something from the depleted fridge and almost ran into him. He was a little shorter than the maître d' and a little pudgier, with a double chin and a happy belly under all that painfully starched linen. Which must have been just for show, because despite the state of the kitchen, there wasn't a speck on him. But something had upset him; the guy appeared to be on the verge of tears.

"Zere is no more bread," he confessed tragically, like someone admitting witchcraft to the Inquisition.

"That's okay." My waffles dinged. I took them out, threw on some cold cuts and a couple pickle slices I'd fished out of a mostly empty jar and smushed it into a sandwich. And looked up to find the vamp struck dumb in horror.

"You . . . you cannot eat zat," he whispered, obviously appalled.

I looked at it. "You're right." But there wasn't any butter, so I grabbed the mayo and slathered up one of the still-hot waffles. It melted nicely into all the cracks, but my creation still needed something. I got an inspiration and stuck my head back in the fridge, opened a drawer and—

Success. I turned back to my sandwich, only to find that it wasn't there anymore. Maybe because it had been hijacked.

"Give me that!" I told the vamp, who was holding it firmly against his chest, a determined look on his face.

"What ees zat?" he demanded, eyeing my prize.

"Cheese." I held it up.

"Zat ees not cheese."

"How do you know?"

"Eet is *orange*."

"A lot of cheese is orange."

"*Non!* No cheese ees that color. Cheese comes from zee milk. Zee milk, eet ees white. When 'ave you seen milk that looks like zat?"

I held up the square of little slices and pointed at the bold-faced label. "Processed American Cheese."

He snatched the package, without letting go of his hostage. And eyed it warily. "Eet says 'cheese food.'" He looked up, obviously perplexed. "What ees thees? Zee cheese, it does not eat."

"I think the idea is that you eat it."

"*Non!*" It was emphatic. "My master, 'ee would ne-vair forgive—"

I made a grab for the cheese, but the guy was faster than he looked. He dodged around the table. I dodged after him.

"Give me that!"

"You cannot eat zees swill!"

"Watch me!"

"*Non, non,* eet ees moldy!"

"Nice try," I snarled. That stuff didn't grow mold. I think mold was afraid of it.

I made a feint and then another one, and finally snatched my sandwich back. It was a little smushed, but it was okay. I took a defiant bite.

"Please." He resorted to big brown puppy dog eyes. "I beg of you."

I swallowed, but it wasn't easy. I remembered my foraging skills as being better than this. "Well, I have to eat something," I pointed out. "Where did all the food go?"

"Zee fey," he whispered, looking over his shoulder. "Zey are . . . zey are not human."

"Can't argue with that."

"*Non*, you do not understand. We feed zee ones out in zee garden, yes? And zey eat." He rolled his eyes. "Oh, zey eat! But finally, zey stop."

"And then you got cocky and decided to fill up the twins," I guessed.

He nodded. "But zere ees something wrong wiz zem. Zey eat and eat, and zey do not stop."

"I could have told you that."

"*Mais c'est ne pas possible!* Where do zey put it all?"

"Hollow leg?" I offered, sniffing my sandwich. There was definitely something rank in there. Maybe the olive loaf . . .

The chef was looking at me cunningly. "Eef you do not eat zat," he wheedled, "I weel make you somesing better."

"Out of what?"

"Out of . . ." he looked around in desperation. And spied a half-empty carton of eggs. "Out of *les oeufs*. I weel make an omelet!"

"An omelet?"

"Yes, yes! Such an omelet I weel make for you!" He waved the hand with the despised cheese in it. "As has nevair been seen. It shall be an omelet of the gods!"

"Will you use that?"

He looked at the small package in his hand. His face crumpled.

"Just kidding," I told him. "How can I turn down a divine omelet?"

I don't think I've ever seen a happier vamp in my life.

And then I turned around and saw his opposite, peering suspiciously through the glass panes in the kitchen door. I sighed. I briefly considered turning the hose on him, like we used to do for the neighbor's dog, who kept digging up Claire's herb garden. But I doubted it would work in this case.

I opened the door instead and stuck my head out. "What?"

"Let me in!" Marlowe said, trying to push past me. And getting the shit zapped out of him by the wards. "Fuck!"

"Language," I admonished. "There are children in the house."

"Then come outside," he said evilly.

I considered that. "You know, I'm kind of comfortable where I am."

He looked past me. "What is Verrell doing here?"

"Who?"

"Louis-Cesare's chef!"

"Oh." I looked over my shoulder at the vamp, who was humming happily to himself and whisking the hell out of some eggs. I turned back to Marlowe. "Making me an omelet."

"Why?"

"He didn't like my sandwich."

"He didn't—" Marlowe stopped and looked skyward, forgetting that it was still daylight out. Which I guess must have burned his retinas, because he cursed viciously.

"If you keep that up," I told him, "I'm going to have to ask you to—"

"Who is this?" he demanded, shoving a photo in my face.

I didn't answer, because it was all of a millimeter away from my eyeball. But I stepped back a pace and checked it out, because it seemed the easiest way to get rid of him. It showed a guy who looked like a cross between the maître d' and the chef, only not as pleasant-looking. He had a little black mustache that was vainly trying to add character to a round pudding face, bushy black brows and small, suspicious eyes that he'd focused with loathing on whoever had taken the photo.

"No idea," I told Marlowe.

"You're sure?"

"As sure as I can be from a photo. Why?"

"Because you were on his yacht two days ago."

I thought about that for a second. And then I let him in. Because his temper was short enough when his brains weren't frying, and I doubted I'd get any info otherwise.

"The one at the bottom of the sea?" I asked, as he pushed past me.

"It's not on the sea bottom any longer," he said, batting at slightly steaming curls. "It must have been sucked in by that damned portal."

"Then how do you know it belonged to this guy?" I asked.

Marlowe tucked the photo back under his jacket, which was steaming slightly, too. That was weird for someone at his level, unless he still hadn't gotten any sleep. Which would also explain the mood.

"It had something better," he told me shortly. "Or did you make up the raven over the doorjamb?"

It took me a second to remember the ugly statue cheapening an otherwise tasteful room. "No, it was there."

"Then unless there are two black yachts with raven mascots, it was the *Corvus.*"

"That's Latin for 'raven,' isn't it?"

"Yes," Marlowe said, looking vaguely surprised that I'd know that. "More to the point, it was the name bestowed by Roman soldiers on the planks they used to board the ships they were attacking. It had a 'beak' on one end to grab hold and bite into the other ship's deck."

"So that guy was Roman?" He hadn't looked it.

"No, but the person who sold it to him was. The yacht used to belong to Geminus, before he sized up a few years ago. He sold his old one to his good friend Slava—who I want you to ID. If you saw him at that pier, it could be the break we need."

"But I didn't."

"You don't know what you saw!" Marlowe said testily. "Mircea pulled you out at the worst possible time and is refusing to put you back in."

"And you expect me to convince him otherwise?" I asked skeptically. Because I wasn't having a lot of luck with that sort of thing lately.

"No. I expect you to come with me to Slava's tonight, and see if anything jogs your memory. A scent, a gesture, a—"

"Tonight?"

"Yes, tonight! Unless you have a prior engagement?"

The sarcasm dripped. I ignored it, because the omelet of the gods had just been slid under my nose.

I sat down and took a bite. My eyes widened. "It is good, no?" Verrell asked, looking smug.

"How do you do this with just eggs?" I asked, stuffing my face.

"Oh, there are other things, too," he said loftily. "Olive oil, some chives, a bit of pepper—just a touch, you understand—"

Marlowe's hand came down on the table and Verrell jumped. "What is the problem with tonight?" he demanded.

I swallowed egg. "Nothing. If I hadn't been fired."

"You aren't working for us. You are merely identifying a suspect."

"So, you've cleared it with Mircea, then?"

He looked shifty.

Yeah, I'd thought so.

"You have a reputation for a certain . . . lack of concern . . . for your father's wishes," Marlowe pointed out.

This was true. It was also true that I had a vested interest in this smuggling mess. But I didn't think it would help my bank account much to admit it.

"Say I was to find myself free," I said. "What's the occasion?"

"Just wear a dress. Something sexy."

I raised an eyebrow at him. "I don't have any dresses, sexy or otherwise."

"You don't—why not?"

"They trip me up in combat. One almost got me killed recently, so I threw the rest out."

"Then borrow one from your roommate!"

I pursed my lips. Claire was six feet tall. Her shortest dress would drag the floor on me. Not to mention being completely not my style.

"So we're going to a Ren faire, then?"

Marlowe ran a hand through his hair and muttered something. And then he eyed me up and down. "What are you? A two?"

"Depends on the dress. Mostly I'm a four, but it depends how snug they fit across—"

"The bust, yes," he said thoughtfully.

I blinked. "That is ... deeply disturbing ... coming from you."

He scowled. "I'll send something over! Just be at Central at nine!" he told me, referring to the local office of the Vampire Senate.

"Give me one good reason why I should help you."

"I'll pay triple."

I smiled and ate omelet. "That's a good reason."

Chapter Twenty-one

"I can't believe I waxed for this," I said, eight hours later. And picked a banana peel out of my hair.

Marlowe didn't even bother to tell me to shut up, which wasn't a great sign. Not that I thought he was in any real danger. Slava's guys knew the penalty for killing a senator, and they weren't going to risk it, orders or no. But he was looking a little under the weather.

I, on the other hand, didn't have a scratch on me, unless you counted the ladder in my hose. I guess they'd assumed I was just his evening snack pack or something. Because they hadn't even bothered to rough me up before they threw us both in the Dumpster.

Which was kind of where they lost me.

Slava had been on Marlowe's radar long before he bought a yacht from the wrong guy. He was infamous for providing a smorgasbord of vice to the local paranormal community, including running one of the biggest prostitution rings in Manhattan. And for operating a notorious sex club, appropriately named the Aerie, in the penthouse above.

Of course, that wasn't what had annoyed the Senate. They weren't in the habit of policing vice and believed that what two adults did privately—or not so privately, in the right venue—was up to them. Unless said adults weren't exactly human, weren't exactly here legally, and weren't exactly willing.

Slava was rumored to have reversed the usual fey-enslaving-humans thing to provide unusual delights to his more jaded—and well-heeled—customers. Which definitely *was* illegal, only nobody had ever been able to pin anything on him. Which was the part I didn't get. Why did a guy who'd stared down both the Senate and the Circle for decades suddenly go nuts when Marlowe showed up to ask a few questions? Sure, a visit from the chief spy didn't make anybody happy, especially somebody who was guilty as hell. But if half the rumors were true, Slava had been living that way for years. Why panic now?

I dug coffee grounds out of my décolletage and slid another glance Marlowe's way. But he didn't look like he wanted to discuss it. He was just sitting there, like the Buddha of Trash, his burgundy velvet evening coat splattered with blood and mustard, the latter from somebody's day old Reuben, by the smell. I wrinkled my nose and tossed one of the five-inch black satin torture devices he'd provided over the side of the Dumpster.

It bounced off the curb and landed in a puddle of something nasty.

Of course it did.

I sighed and heaved myself out after it. That was harder than it sounds, thanks to the Ace bandage in dress form that constituted Marlowe's idea of sexy. But at least the color was nice. Crimson wasn't my usual thing, but it covered a multitude of sins, not to mention ketchup.

Although I couldn't help but notice that I smelled a little . . . unusual.

Chanel No. 5 obviously wasn't meant for the trenches.

I brushed myself down, rescued the shoe, and looked up to find the Buddha making faces at the sky. I couldn't see him that well—lower Manhattan is fairly well lit at night, but we were in the shadow of a building. But he looked like he was having a stroke.

Or it would have, if he'd been human. Since he was a vampire, I assumed he was having a conversation with some of his boys, doing the telepathic equivalent of tearing them a new one. So it was no real shock when less than a minute later a bunch of little cat feet came running down the sidewalk, and resolved themselves into a group of silent, black-suited vamps.

One of them made the mistake of trying to help the boss out of the Dumpster, only to have a fist knotted in his collar. "Well?" Marlowe snarled.

"No portal activity, my lord. If Slava has one on the premises, it is not active at present."

"Then he doesn't have one." Marlowe jumped out and landed on the street beside me.

Someone else must have said something, because he responded. But he was the only one who bothered to articulate for the little dhampir. So I got only his side of the conversation as he stripped down, the mustard-covered shirt following the Reubenized coat back into the Dumpster.

"Of course I'm bloody sure! He knows we'll be coming for him. If he had an easy out, he'd use it! . . . Damn it, I said no! A mass stampede would be the perfect diversion. We're not going to give him that. . . . I want this building sealed, do you understand? Every door, every window, every crack. We have him, and we're damned well going to keep him!"

Marlowe had stripped replacement garments off the vamp closest to his size and threw them on while he looked me over. "I'm going back in. Are you up for it?"

"We just got kicked out."

"That's not what I asked," he snapped, shoving studs through the holes in his shirt cuffs.

"But relevant. We never made it past the lobby. And now he's probably got people watching the exits, too. How do you expect—"

I stopped, because a fire engine chose that moment to sling around a corner. That wouldn't have been all that unusual, except that its lights were flashing, its siren was blaring, and it was skidding on what looked like only half its wheels. And then it straightened up and came barreling down the street. And onto the sidewalk. And through the double doors of the swanky building Slava called home in a burst of light and sound and shattering glass.

Which was either the biggest coincidence ever or Marlowe's attempt at a distraction.

All right, points for effort, I thought, watching the

truck's rear wheels burn rubber on the sidewalk, kicking up a cloud of smoke as they tried to shove the bulky back end the rest of the way through the opening. But I didn't see how that was going to—

And then it exploded.

Okay, yeah. That's better, I thought, ducking behind the Dumpster to avoid the mass of flaming flying debris that was currently lighting up half the block. Marlowe said something, but I couldn't hear him over the ringing in my ears—and the blaring siren, which was somehow still going. "What?"

"In or out?" he yelled, holding out a hand.

What the hell. "In." And the next thing I knew, we were flying down the sidewalk, past a burning vamp running the other way, up some shallow stairs and through a fiery hole that used to be the doorway.

And straight into a wall of smoke. The damned truck must have been loaded with gasoline, because the whole lobby was burning. Not that I could see much of it, but the heat was phenomenal and there was virtually no breathable air.

Of course, that last didn't bother the vamps lunging at us through the clouds. They looked like something out of a nightmare: just dark, smoldering outlines and glowing eyes. But it didn't look like they'd been hurt too badly, because three jumped Marlowe, and a bunch more surged past us to attack his boys coming in the front door.

I was starting to feel neglected when an iron hand closed around my wrist.

I clamped my own hand down over it, wrenched up the thumb and twisted sharply, until there was a grunt and the thud of knees hitting tile. I looked down to see a confused vamp staring up at me. He wasn't one of the stronger ones, maybe sixth-level at a guess, which was why he'd decided to be brave and jump the human. His eyes went from his broken hand to me and back again, as if he couldn't figure out why he couldn't stand.

Until I helped him out, by baring baby fangs.

His eyes widened, and when I let him go, he scrambled away without even standing up—straight through a wall of glass.

And then Marlowe grabbed my hand and we were off again.

We ran through the wreck of the front desk, past a wall with assorted truck parts sticking out of it, down a hall and into an elevator that was just opening. A confused young couple got off, only to hesitate at the sight of the inferno behind us. "Get them out!" Marlowe snapped, confusing me for a moment, until I noticed that one of his boys was right on our heels.

And then we were inside and off.

"How do I look?" Marlowe demanded, slinging a borrowed tie around his neck.

"Like hell," I choked. Between smoke and powdered drywall, we were both pretty grimy.

I started to hit the stop button, but he grabbed my wrist. "No time."

"Well, we can't ... go in there ... like this," I gasped, and then coughed again to clear my lungs. "Not if the idea is to grab Slava without anybody noticing."

"It is." Marlowe brushed down his coat savagely. "The bastard has too many prominent guests. A few of the wrong people get caught in the cross fire and the fallout won't be pretty."

"Well, right now neither are we."

"Do the best you can," he told me stubbornly. "If I'd known he was likely to run, I'd have set this up differently. But we're stuck with it now."

"Maybe not. If he doesn't have a portal, he's trapped. We could—"

"There are other ways out than a portal!"

"Such as?"

"Such as the helicopter he called for five minutes ago."

"And how do you know that?"

He just tapped an ear before bending over and shaking both hands through his curly mop, sending dust flying everywhere—including all over me. But I didn't take time to bitch, since I assumed that the ear thing meant he'd bugged Slava's place at some point. Which reminded me.

I needed to check the kitchen when I got home.

I repaired the damage as best I could with only the shiny metal doors for a mirror. Luckily, the dust didn't stick to the slick material any more than the trash had. Damn, I needed to get me some of this.

Marlowe straightened up and looked me over. "You'll do. What about me?"

He still looked a little dusty and a little rumpled, and the guy he'd borrowed the clothes from had been a good deal thinner across the chest. So neither the shirt nor the coat fit properly. Marlowe had solved that problem by letting them both gape open, and by leaving the tie askew under one ear. And by subtly altering his expression.

A minute before, he'd been a focused, furious master vamp jonesing for some payback. Now he was a jolly, slightly inebriated playboy, ready to finish his night of debauchery with a spot of . . . well, whatever Slava had on the menu. It was actually pretty impressive.

Especially since he wasn't using a glamourie. The features were the same—the stubborn chin, the too-sharp nose, the dark brown eyes that usually looked small due to being narrowed in suspicion. Now they were big and slightly glazed, the nose and high cheekbones were flushed a rosy color, and the brown curls were artfully unkempt. In a matter of a few seconds, and without any magic that I was able to detect, he'd gone from 007 to Arthur.

"Not bad," I admitted. "*If* nobody gets too close. We both smell like we fell into the grill at a barbecue."

"Not for long," he said, pulling a flask out of his hip pocket. He took a swig, and then threw a palm full of whiskey all over me.

Great.

He sprinkled some on his coat, and slapped more on his face like cologne. "How about now?"

"Now we smell like a drunk barbecue."

"Have to do," he told me, as the elevator slid to a halt.

I started for the door, but Marlowe hit the button, keeping the doors closed.

"What happened to no time?" I asked, as he put out an arm, trapping me in a corner.

He didn't answer, and his dark eyes were serious. "Remember—no mistakes."

"Get out of my way."

I started to push past, but he grabbed my arm. "I mean it."

"And you think I don't?"

"I think you are good at killing things. But he's no good to me dead. I need to know who's behind this, and it isn't a two-bit pimp like Slava."

"His boys will know—"

"He was always a suspicious little shit," said the Paranoid King, cutting me off. "We can't know what, if anything, he shared with his people. He dies and we could get sod all."

"Okay, I get it."

"For your sake, I hope so. Help me get him out of here—alive—and there will be a nice bonus in it for you. Kill him, I will make it a personal project to see that you never work for us again."

"Let go of me," I said flatly, because I didn't feel like trying to explain to Marlowe that this wasn't just about the money. "This isn't just about the money," I added, because I'm perverse like that.

"Then what is it about?"

"You know what."

"Must have slipped my mind."

I scowled. Revisiting personal failures isn't my favorite thing. Particularly not personal failures that had gotten someone killed.

And all right, yes, I hadn't actually gotten Lawrence killed. I knew that. He was an upper-level master and they did what they damned well pleased.

But it still felt like my fault.

It had ever since Mircea let me relive it in glorious color in my head. Maybe that was why I couldn't shake it. I could see it as vividly as if it had just happened: the blue-black dock, the dark red blood, and Lawrence's bright, desperate eyes as I tried to drag him to the water, to get him out of the line of fire.

Tried and failed.

So, yeah, it felt like my fault. And I didn't like that feeling. I didn't know if I would feel any better once I ripped into the guys who had ripped into him, but I was looking forward to finding out.

At least, I would be if Marlowe ever got out of my way.

"Well?" he demanded.

"Lawrence, all right?" I snapped.

Marlowe's face abruptly blanked, and something shifted behind his eyes. For a moment, I thought he was actually going to attack me. I think maybe he did, too, because he froze, and when he spoke again, his voice had changed, deepened, roughened. "I'm supposed to believe you give a *damn* about a vampire you barely knew?"

"He was my partner—"

"He was a *vampire*. Just like a thousand others you've killed. Don't insult my intelligence—"

"Is that possible?"

"—by telling me you're here for him!"

"Fine. I won't." Why the hell I ever tried to explain anything to Marlowe, I didn't know, I must be going senile. I started for the door again, but the arm didn't budge.

"You may have Mircea fooled," he told me, getting in my face. "May have won over Radu, may have seduced Louis-Cesare. But I *know what you are*."

"Then you know better than to piss me off."

"Damn it! I want an answer!"

"About *what*?" I demanded. "About the fact that I should have kept him from going in there? Or followed him in faster? Or done *something* other than stand there while they blasted him full of holes? Because I know that, all right?"

I jerked out of Marlowe's grip.

"If he'd been with a vampire he knew—hell, even one

he didn't—he wouldn't have gone off like that," I said bitterly. "He'd have waited for her, explained what he was doing, *included* her. But he wasn't with another vampire, was he? He was with a dhampir. And he didn't expect me to have his back anyway, so why not go off on his own? He probably thought he'd be safer that way. Probably thought you had it in for him, to partner him up with a creature as dangerous as whatever he was hunting!"

I pushed past him, furious, guilty, humiliated—and found myself hauled back. I was about to register my displeasure—forcibly—when Marlowe stopped me by saying the last words I expected to hear. "He requested you."

I glared at him. "What?"

"He requested to be assigned to you. Several of them did."

"Why?"

"You'd have to ask them. My guess would be ... curiosity. Until recently, many of them didn't even believe that dhampirs existed. Thought your kind were merely myth. Then they find out that not only do they exist but that one is in their midst, and of Mircea's family line at that...."

"Then curiosity got him killed!"

"No. Pride got him killed. He should have waited for you, he should have—" His jaw clenched. "I knew it was trouble when he received a second major gift before reaching first level.... That is rarely a good thing."

"He was powerful—"

"Not enough! As I tried to tell him, on more than one occasion. But he'd never been in a position that his abilities couldn't overcome. What the physical couldn't handle, the mental got him out of, and vice versa. He never had his back against a wall. He never—"

He broke off but I knew what he meant. "He never failed."

"No. And sometimes, they need to fail. They need the lessons it teaches. Or the first time they do may be their last!" He looked at me, his eyes dark and implacable. "But not tonight. We don't fail tonight."

"You'll have Slava alive," I told him simply.

He looked at me for a few long seconds, searching my face for something that I guess he found. Or maybe we were just out of time. "Then let's go get him."

Chapter Twenty-two

The elevator doors opened and we stumbled out—onto the wrong floor. At least, that's what I thought at first. Because whatever I'd been expecting, this wasn't it.

The human S&M community may occasionally get tired of the Gothic stereotype, but they play into it often enough. Lots of black and red, lots of whips and chains, lots of deliberately scary props wielded by deliberately scary people. Which made sense, I supposed. If the idea was to test limits, to push boundaries, to ride the knife edge between pain and fear and pleasure, then you went with whatever worked.

Unless you were Slava, apparently.

Slava had gone with highly polished blond woods, chrome modernist furniture and art glass, with pretty white and gold fixtures hovering over a reception desk and a water feature trickling away on the opposite wall. It looked like a Norwegian day spa. And the weird thing was, his version was actually more intimidating. Like he was saying "I don't need the props; I have the real thing."

Only the real thing must have been inside, because the guy standing up behind the desk wasn't scary at all.

He also wasn't vampire. He was garden-variety human—a nice, reassuringly bland presence to welcome the more skittish types—but I was betting there was a call button conveniently located under the desk. And what would respond wouldn't be nice, human or particularly welcoming.

But the button didn't get pushed because Marlowe

staggered through the lobby with his arm around my waist, flashing some kind of card at the guy. He did it so fast that I didn't see what it was, and I doubt the guy did, either. But enough of a suggestion rippled through the air along with it to have him settling back against his chair, unconcerned.

And then we were pushing past some frosted-glass doors and into—

Damn.

The penthouse had either come with a full semicircle of fifteen-foot windows, or they'd been added later. Probably at the same time that it had been gutted, leaving a huge open area for maybe a couple hundred guests. And a group of performers in the place of chandeliers, executing flowing, sensual acrobatics in body sequins and some not-so-strategically-placed feathers.

The birds in the Aerie, I assumed.

Anywhere else, they would have been the main draw, and then some. But at Slava's they apparently counted as decoration. The real show was taking place below, on a rotating platform surrounded by a crowd of people who all looked like they were attending the opera.

I guess PVC cat suits would have clashed with the decor, because there wasn't one in sight. Instead, tuxes and glittery evening dresses seemed to be the norm, with a few expensive lounge suits and LBDs on the younger sort. The guests were sipping champagne against a breathtaking hundred-eighty-degree view of Manhattan, including a tiny Lady Liberty off to the far left, who also appeared to be watching the show.

Only "watching" wasn't quite the right word, I realized a second later.

This was very definitely audience participation.

A heavy whip cracked and a powerful body flinched. But the groan that emanated from the perfectly sculpted lips wasn't pain. I could tell because I felt it right along with him: the biting caress of the lash, the sweet sting of sweat trickling into the wound, the dark ache of arousal.

"Harder." The low growl caused the two PVC-clad doms on either side of the platform to exchange glances.

Maybe because they'd already striped their subject's smooth bronze skin from the heavily corded back to the muscular, straining thighs.

It was pretty impressive, considering the wings that kept getting in the way.

"Bugger," Marlowe said, under his breath.

I didn't say anything. I was busy tamping down a visceral response that had my skin tightening, my breath shortening and sweat starting to bead my skin underneath the silky fabric of the dress. And because I couldn't have anyway.

The majority of Slava's family were downstairs, dealing with the disaster, but there were enough up here to make even whispered conversation out of the question. Specifically, there were two of them guarding a door on the far right of the room. And since it was the only one with accessories, I didn't need Marlowe's nod to know that it was our target.

There was no reason not to stare as I made my way around the room, since that was what everyone else was doing. You'd think they'd never seen an eight-foot-tall naked guy with long black and silver wings getting the crap beaten out of him before. And either he'd said something to piss off the doms, or they were just in the habit of giving value for the money.

Because they were really working him over.

One of the girls had switched from a regular whip to a cat, and a flick of her wrist sent the straps slicing through the air to land almost gently against the broad back. But the crack echoed around the room, and a spread of livid welts bloomed against the sun-kissed flesh. Her subject murmured approval and leaned into the blows that followed, until they crisscrossed his back and decorated his sides. When the platform rotated back around and she started to similarly adorn his abs, he trembled slightly, but still didn't cry out.

But the rest of us did.

The whip cracked again, this time reaching around the side to flick over a tender nipple, and the blaze of sensation was enough to have me sucking in a startled breath. And the whole room gasped right along with me. The Irin smiled grimly, his lower lip splitting under his teeth, blood seeping out. He touched it with his tongue, reveling in the delicious wetness of it. And a nearby guy shuddered and slid down the wall.

And that was why the Fallen, aka the Watchers, aka the Irin, were high on my avoid-at-all-costs list.

I didn't know if they really were fallen angels, as they claimed, or if they were just another demon race with better-than-average PR. But their power was as scary as it was odd, something close enough to mind control to make me really unhappy. But I couldn't do anything about it now except stay well out of the creature's line of sight as I worked around to my target.

I didn't have to worry about anyone else's.

By the time I got through the crowd, it had ceased to be a group of individuals watching a performance and had transformed into a single entity that moaned and writhed and sweated out the experience right along with the Irin. It was like he was a conductor and we were his orchestra, only what was playing wasn't notes on a page but sensations on skin. And he was damned good at it.

I had to stop and give myself a mental shakedown before approaching the guards, sloughing off the tendrils of sensation that wanted to wrap me up, to pull me back, to sink me into the collective wave of pleasure building behind me. And force myself to face the job ahead. Because the vamps guarding the door were both masters.

Not that it mattered in this case. Even a baby vamp can sense the presence of another, especially one as powerful as Marlowe. Which was why he was hanging back, waiting for me to get the door open before moving up.

Since I had to manage it in full view of the main salon, the idea was to split one guard away from the other and deal with them separately. The dress should have helped with that, being cut up to here and down to there and fitting me like a glove. Along with the extras I'd spent half a day on—short, sleek dark hair, heavily lined black eyes and shiny red lips—I'd expected it to provide a decent enough distraction.

I'd expected wrong. Thanks to the show the Irin was providing, no one was paying me the slightest attention, including the two guards. I actually had to tap one on the shoulder to get noticed.

"Got a cigarette?" I asked, a little more harshly than normal. But, damn it, I could have worn jeans.

"What? Oh, yeah." He dug a case out of his trousers and passed it over, his eyes never leaving the show.

I hiked the dress up and put a stiletto-clad foot on a nearby chair, flashing more than a little thigh. "How about a light?" I asked huskily.

"In a bowl on the bar."

"How about you get one for me?"

"How about you get it yourself?"

"How about I knock your teeth in?"

"What?"

I sighed and gave up. I put the cigarette case back in his pocket, took out the passkey and let myself in through the door. The guy never even blinked.

My new phone rang. I dug it out of my purse and checked the readout. Marlowe.

Of course.

"What the hell was that?" he demanded.

"You wanted in, we're in. Now come on, or I'm going to do this myself."

I didn't get an answer, except for an irritated click in my ear. But a few seconds later he slipped through the door I was holding open with one aching foot. And a second after that, I was shoved against the wall, a hard body was pressed against me and a practiced mouth came down on mine.

For a second, I just froze.

The kiss was crazy enough all on its own. But then there was the knee pushing between my legs and the hand moving up my thigh, sliding the slick material of the dress out of the way so he could wrap my leg around his. His hair was cool and soft, his mouth was hot and hard, and he smelled like whiskey and smoke and electricity. And he could kiss; not as well as Louis-Cesare, but more than competently.

Which was going to do fuck all to preserve his manhood in three, two—

A wedge of sound pushed out into the quiet corridor: tinned laughter from some TV show, the buzz of a drink machine, the scrape of a heel against a doorframe. And then—

"Hey," someone said. "You can't be back here."

Marlowe didn't respond, and I couldn't, since it looked like he was going for authenticity. Which worried me less than the fact that it was doing exactly nothing for me. And okay, it was Marlowe, but still. Considering the, uh, intensity of the situation, I'd have expected to feel something.

But I didn't. Not a damned thing. Nothing but anger and annoyance and a weird sort of sadness, because he wasn't the one I wanted.

Oh, God, I thought in horror. Louis-Cesare's ruined me for other men.

"Hey, I'm talking to you!"

Marlowe didn't react, since the voice was still too far away. And neither did I, except to freak out a little and wrap my other leg around him, climbing his body and grabbing his hair and sticking my tongue down his throat, all at the same time. He made a strangled *urk* sound, but manfully hung in there, bracing his legs and gripping my thighs. And yet I still felt exactly zip.

Until he suddenly pinched the hell out of me.

"Who let you back here?" another voice asked, from closer in. It was a man's—literally. Because neither he nor his buddy was vampire.

There was no tingle coming from them, no itch, none of the telltale electricity that the vamp pressed against me was shedding like little bursts of lightning. It hurt—like being groped by an electric porcupine. But not as much as when the bastard pinched me again.

I broke off, out of breath and furious. "Son of a bitch!"

"This is a restricted area," the first of two business suits informed us.

"So is my thigh," I snarled, wrenching my head around so I could examine my left leg. And sure enough, under the ladder in my hose was a red mark as long as my thumb. It was definitely going to bruise. "Son of a bitch."

"You already said that," Marlowe said smarmily. "And I don't see anything. Do you?" He glanced at Suit #2. Who came around to check it out.

"These hose cost forty bucks," I said furiously. "I'm adding them to the bill!"

"And I will take them off again."

"On what grounds?"

"On the grounds that they were already ripped down-stairs."

"You two need to go back out front," Suit #1 said, coming up on my right.

I glared at Marlowe. "If it's on your time, it's on your dime."

"And who decided that?"

"It's called expenses!"

He looked at me consideringly as he let me down. "I'll go halves."

"Done." They'd only cost me twenty, anyway.

"Did you hear me?" Suit #1 demanded, finally coming within arm's length.

And getting coldcocked by my fist upside his jaw.

"Loud and clear," I said, watching Marlowe extricate his knuckles from the face of Suit #2. "What was with all the pinching?" I demanded.

"No blood."

"What?"

"I wanted to remind you to make sure to bruise rather than bloody him. This corridor is protected by a sound shield, but they do not block odors. And nothing is cal-culated to get a vampire's attention faster than—" He noticed my expression and stopped.

"Thank you, Captain Obvious."

"I'm on the Senate," he reminded me. "It's Lord Ob-vious. And I don't want any mistakes tonight."

I could have said a lot of things to that, but we didn't have time. "I'll see what I can do," I said sweetly, and squatted by my guy to frisk him.

But other than a .45 that I tucked into the front of my

dress, there was nothing of interest. Like detailed plans of the smugglers' intentions. Or a map of their portal system. Or even a photo ID, none of which the bad guys I met ever seemed thoughtful enough to provide.

"Nothing," Marlowe said in disgust, throwing his man alongside and then crouching beside him.

"But human."

"Mages," he confirmed.

"Dark or light?"

He concentrated for a second, then shook his head. "Can't tell."

"There's a lot of that going around." I met his eyes, and his expression darkened. And I knew we were both thinking about Lawrence and the mage he'd followed into hell. "Mages, demons, vampires, smugglers—what's next?"

"Let's go find out," he growled.

Finding out meant finding Slava's office, which was a process of elimination involving a lot of rooms that looked like they ought to have interesting activities going on—hence the silence spell, I assumed—but that were inexplicably empty. Like the door the men had been coming out of, which proved to be a break room. And the corridor. And everything except a door at the very end of the hall with a light on under it.

I scowled at it.

We'd been up here six, maybe seven minutes by now, with another couple in the elevator. That was plenty of time for Slava to have prepared a welcome, even if he hadn't already had something in place. And since this had been his base of operations for years, that seemed unlikely.

He knew we were here. He knew there was a chance we would get past his men. Yet there were no guards, no traps, nothing to keep us from waltzing right into his office except a couple of clueless mages who hadn't even had shields up. It was enough to give me stomach cramps.

"Hold up," I said.

We were plastered to either side of the office door, about to break in, so Marlowe didn't look happy at the interruption. "What now?" he demanded, like the previous delays had been my fault.

"I'm not sure," I admitted. But it wasn't just paranoia coming out to play. Something had triggered an "oh, crap" response in the back of my mind.

I couldn't pin it down any more than that, because there was nothing to see but empty corridor and, thanks to the spell, nothing to hear. And the only odors coming from the room ahead were pretty standard for an office: printer ink, industrial cleaner, a full ashtray, and feline, because apparently even evil pimps keep pets. There was nothing to explain why the hair had suddenly risen all along the back of my neck.

But it had, and it was a problem. Particularly as my big bag o' tricks had been confiscated on the first go-round. All I had was a purloined gun with no extra clips and no idea what was behind that damned door.

And I was suddenly finding myself less than curious.

"For fuck's sake!" Marlowe hissed, as I just stood there. "You're supposed to be a professional!"

"I am," I said. "And in my professional opinion, there's something—"

But Marlowe didn't want my opinion, professional or otherwise. Marlowe wanted inside that room. "Remember—alive," he snarled. And before I could stop him, he'd grasped the knob, flung open the door and bolted inside with vampire swiftness.

Which was when things got a little confusing.

A blur even my eyes couldn't track shot out of the room and then shot back in, slamming the door behind it. It took less time than it takes to say, almost less than it takes to think—maybe a second in all. It took me another to notice that Marlowe was now across the hall, splayed against the wall.

Nailed to the tasteful gold wallpaper by the knife buried in his heart.

It would have killed a human, and seriously inconvenienced a regular vampire. But that sort of thing doesn't work so well on senior masters. Not even with wood, and Marlowe's bloody hands were slipping on a metal hilt. But it didn't look like it had done him any good, either.

A thin ribbon of blood trickled out of the side of his mouth as he opened it to gasp, "Wha'?"

I didn't answer, because I didn't know. And because the door suddenly opened again, if you can call it that when a body is flung through it, splintering the wood and sending someone flying back into Marlowe. And plunging the knife he'd just jerked out of his rib cage right back inside.

Judging by his expression, that hadn't been too healthy, but I didn't have time to worry about it. Or about the fact that the vamp who had smashed into him was no longer in one piece, or even two. Or that one of those pieces was screaming in a high-pitched wheeze, like a little girl.

Because the thing in the room was now the thing on me.

What followed wasn't exactly a fight, since a fight implies planning and strategy and execution and this was just the last step, fueled by pure instinct because there was no time for anything else. I blocked a flurry of knives that was really only one but was wielded by a slashing maniac with unearthly speed that I'd only ever encountered from a first-level vamp. But this wasn't one, because the feel was wrong; the feel was strange, but it was oddly familiar, too, in a way I didn't have time to grasp before—

Before I had him.

I feinted left and then jerked right with a liquid movement that I guess my assailant hadn't been expecting. Because it allowed me to grab the neck that was following the knife headed for my heart. I held on to it with one hand while holding the damn knife away from me with the other. And looked past it to see—

Shit.

The shiny side of the knife trembling between us reflected a coldly handsome face, so pale that it didn't look human—which was fair, since it wasn't. A mass of silver-blond hair obscured most of the features, but I didn't need them. The eyes glittering between the strands were

more than enough. Like twin stars, they were the most
unusual color I'd ever seen—solid opaque pewter. And
narrowed and angry and terribly familiar as they met
mine.

For a split second, until he threw off my hold, vaulted
back into the office and slid across the desk.

"What the hell?" Marlowe cursed—from behind me,
because I was already moving, hurling myself across the
room and reaching out—

And missing, because the damned cat ran underneath
my feet. *"Shit!"*

"I asked you a question!" Marlowe barked, and a
bloody hand fell on my shoulder as I leaned out the
window—the one his attacker had just thrown himself
through. And either Marlowe had forgotten that he
wasn't handling another vamp, or he didn't care if he
cracked bone.

Luckily for him, I was too busy scanning the street far,
far below to do more than shake him off. But there was
no badly dented car, no body painting the sidewalk red,
no sign of his attacker at all. Until I looked up.

And was clipped on the chin by the hard end of someone's boot.

Son of a bitch.

I went staggering back into the desk, bounced off and
started for the window again. Only to stop at the sight of
a fey perched on top of a struggling pork chop doing a
Superman impression. The pork chop was Slava. The fey
was Æsubrand. And they were levitating outside the
window like it was no big thing.

Chapter Twenty-three

For a moment, I just stared. Not because of the hovering in midair thing. Levitation charms aren't exactly rare, although using them in full view of norms is a no-no. But human laws aren't so easy to apply to a prince of the fey, and anyway, that wasn't the problem.

No, the problem was that this particular prince hadn't stuck his charm on a chair, a bookcase or a rug à la Aladdin. No, he'd stuck it on *Slava*. Which meant that both of them were about to be roadkill because the magic they were using didn't work that way.

But Æsubrand obviously didn't know enough about human charms to realize that. Or that he would need a propulsion system, or at least a good push, if he wanted to go anywhere. Which he hadn't gotten because he'd been too busy kicking me in the head.

Leaving them stranded—for the moment.

I stopped staring up at them and started looking around the office, hoping for a grappling hook—preferably one attached to an M16. But I guess Slava kept the weapons elsewhere, because I didn't see one. Of course, there was another option.

"Pull us in when I grab him," I told Marlowe, who had just staggered up behind me.

"Grab who?" he rasped, and then stopped, staring in disbelief at the insanity outside the window.

"Æsubrand," I said shortly, jerking down the office blinds and stripping off the cord. And thankfully, Slava's impressively tall windows extended in here, and they had cords to match.

"What? There are *fey* now?" Marlowe demanded, outraged.

And I had to admit, it did seem a little unfair.

"Looks that way," I said and threw myself out the window.

I ignored the stream of cursing from behind me because I had about a second to time this right or I'd be a greasy spot on the sidewalk. Luckily, it looked like Æsubrand hadn't expected company. At least he hadn't until I grabbed tubby's belt and held on for dear life.

A pair of silver-bright eyes met mine over a pin-striped mountain for a second, before their owner sent a fist crashing into my jawline. *Looks like he remembers me, too,* I thought grimly, spitting blood. And then the fist was back for an encore.

I ducked and looped some of the slack of the cord I'd tied around my wrist through Slava's belt. And waited for Marlowe to jerk him over and plant a fist in Æsubrand's face. And kept right on waiting, because nothing happened.

Maybe because Slava's bodyguards had finally gotten a clue that, hey, you know, maybe there's a problem with the boss. A glance at the office showed that three of them had joined the fun. And while that wouldn't normally have mattered, they were probably the only senior guys still upstairs. And Marlowe wasn't having a great night.

Of course, neither was I.

"There's a reason—*oof*—that levitation charms aren't used on people," I gasped, twisting to avoid the fist of doom, and sending us into a spin that had Slava cursing in Russian and trying to bite me. "Not live ones, anyway. Every time—ugh—the aura fluctuates, there's a chance—damn it, listen to me!"

But Æsubrand wasn't. And I didn't think that was likely to change. I didn't have a lot of persuasive ability and he didn't have a lot of respect for humans—or any at all.

But it looked like someone else did.

Slava stopped his attempts to throw both of us into the void long enough to glare at me. "What you say?" he demanded, in heavily accented English.

"I'm saying that every time your aura fluctuates, it stresses the spell," I told him clearly, hoping the asshole trying to kick my head in might overhear. "We have to get down from here, or any moment—"

"Any moment *what*?"

"Plop," I said, indistinctly this time, because I'd just ended up with a mouthful of dirty leather.

I grabbed the damn boot, trying to sling it and its owner against the side of the building. Or the roof, where at least I could shoot the son of a bitch. And it might have worked—if Slava hadn't started thrashing around like a blowfish out of water.

"What the hell is the matter with you?" I demanded, as he almost sent me flying.

"I know this plop," he told me violently. "You think I don't? I have been in this country thirty years! I know this word!"

"Then why are you fighting me?"

"You weigh me down, both of you. Get off!" He punctuated his sentence by elbowing me viciously in the neck.

And then someone started shooting at us.

Of course they did.

I looked up to see Marlowe hanging out of the office window, but he wasn't the one firing. He was the one on his back getting choked by the vamp trying to push him to his doom, while the vamp's two buddies took potshots at us. Only they weren't likely to get any brownie points from the guy they'd just shot in the butt.

"Not me," Slava sputtered. "Shoot them. Shoot *them*!"

But Æsubrand didn't seem to like that idea. Or, rather, he liked it fine where I was concerned, just not for him. Which was easily remedied by jerking Slava around, so that I faced the window full of shooters.

Who promptly drilled me through the shoulder.

It probably would have been through the heart, but Marlowe was giving them hell. The choker's head suddenly exploded, like a watermelon under Gallagher's hammer, and Marlowe snarled and threw the bloody stump at the shooter. The result was another miss, but then a backup squad muscled in the door and I decided that maybe it was time to return a favor.

I pulled the gun I'd taken off the mage and drilled one of the guards right between the eyes.

But not with a bullet.

At least, not the normal kind.

A single bullet won't kill a vamp, even a baby, but they do seriously piss them off. So I'd expected him to lose interest in Marlowe and start firing at us. Which is why I'd jerked us back around so that Æsubrand was facing him.

I had not expected him to turn a weird, all-over white and freeze in place.

Literally, I realized a second later, when Marlowe slammed the butt of a rifle up against the guy's head and he shattered into a few dozen pieces. Several of which tumbled out the window and smashed against the concrete below. And Marlowe's head jerked up.

"Where did you get *that*?" he demanded, looking envious, even while getting hit over the head with a chair.

"Off the mage," I yelled back, staring at my new toy in disbelief.

And then Æsubrand tried to kick it out of my hand.

He didn't succeed, but only because I was gripping it with the fervor of a saint holding a sacred relic. But the blow still hurt like a bitch, turning my whole hand numb. I didn't get a chance to retaliate, however, because the wind, which had been unusually calm, suddenly decided to pick up.

And why didn't I think that was a coincidence?

Maybe because I'd seen what Æsubrand could do with the elements.

Most fey were good with one, maybe two. But as far as I could tell, he was good with all of them. His mixed heritage could have been the reason, with two great houses of the Light Fey melded into one. Or maybe he was just talented that way. But I didn't think it spelled good news for me.

And then I knew it didn't when what sounded like a

freight train came whistling through the space between buildings, gaining momentum on the way.

I started frantically trying to shoot him with my numb hand, since I needed to hold on with my good one. Which would have worked better if he hadn't taken that moment to start kicking me in the head again. It became a race to see if he could kick me off before I could line up a shot I couldn't feel and take him out.

I lost.

My neck snapped back, making me wonder if it was broken. And then making me wonder some more as it flopped about randomly when he lashed out again and I went flying. For a second, until the cord jerked me up and pulled Slava's pants down and we met in the middle, with me hanging off my possibly dislocated wrist from the belt of a pair of trousers that had slid down his chubby legs to puddle around his flailing feet.

And this time I didn't have a convenient vampire to hide behind. This time I didn't have anything but a limb that I had grown quite attached to left vulnerable and exposed and useless. And a body being slung around like a newspaper caught in a storm as the two conflicting air streams met and mixed and created a miniature cyclone outside Slava's ballroom.

And a gun I still couldn't feel.

Which was going to have to do, I decided, as Æsubrand said something that sounded like a curse and raised a heel. And I managed to get the weapon pointed more or less in his direction. And fired.

It worked. Sort of. Or it would have, if Æsubrand hadn't dodged at the last second, so that the shot intended for him hit—

Well, crap.

I scowled, Æsubrand cursed, and Slava went white and cold and frosty.

And then the storm hit us, with a force like a closed fist. And when I say "us," I mean Marlowe, too, who finally managed to grab Æsubrand when we slammed back against the building. Just in time to get dragged out the window when an updraft hit.

On the plus side, getting pounded in the face a couple dozen times by a ticked-off master vamp seemed to be messing up Æsubrand's control over the weather. On the negative, that made our wild ride even wilder, with nobody steering. Except fate, the evil bitch, who decided to toss us up, up, up and over. And onto the building's flat roof.

Where a bunch of vamps were pouring out of a rooftop door and running straight at us.

"Oh, come *on*!" I screamed, because they weren't Marlowe's. And they didn't look too happy at having the boss turned into an icy-pop. Or at being blown back against the door by a pissed-off fey prince.

But that would have actually improved our odds—if a shiny black helicopter hadn't chosen that moment to loom up over the building. Slava's ride, I assumed, only it seemed that the guys on board had been brought up to speed by somebody. Because, instead of landing, they started trying to maneuver so that the vamps inside could level machine guns on us.

And that was enough to get even the dynamic duo's attention. They stopped battling each other long enough to stare, openmouthed, at this new threat. "Are they idiots?" Marlowe asked. "If they hit Slava, he dies!"

Æsubrand's bloody face whipped around. "He is not dead now?"

"No. Vampire flesh does not behave the same way as human—"

"But he is frozen!"

"He can be thawed," Marlowe said, wiping his bloody face. "As long as he doesn't end up in pieces before then."

"That would not be a risk had someone not shot him!"

"I wasn't trying to shoot him; I was trying to shoot you!" I told Æsubrand furiously.

"Then you have exceedingly poor aim."

"You dodged!"

He looked at me like I was slow. "And you expected me to stand still?"

"I didn't expect you to be here at all! What the *hell*—"

Æsubrand didn't get a chance to answer, assuming he'd been planning on it, because the helicopter opened fire. For about a second. A burst sparked off concrete, but came nowhere near us, thanks to the wind that smacked the copter like a giant fist, picking it up and throwing it through the air. Straight at the water tower.

The wooden relic was old enough to be considered an antique, constructed at the same time the building was. It didn't look like it had ever been updated—no one saw it from the street and it satisfied the ordinance requiring buildings to have an independent source of water. Only this one was about to be in violation, I thought, as the copter smashed into the tower, and the tower fell over and smashed into the ground, and a huge wave of water spilled out and smashed into Slava's vamps, who had gotten back to their feet only to be washed off them again.

And I decided to keep them that way. I'd finally managed to wrestle my wrist free, allowing me to actually aim two-handed as I raised the mage's gun. And fired.

But not at them.

There were too many of them and they were too spread out, and anyway, there was a better choice. Like the cresting wave that was breaking over them in a roar and a rush. And that was going to be breaking over them for a while—like until someone chipped them out. Because what I was suddenly looking at was a giant frozen wave with little vamp parts sticking out of it.

It looked like a bizarre modernist sculpture: a fusion of the tower and the huge splash of liquid, with the still-burning helicopter tacked on at one side. Even the fire had frozen, the water vapor congealing around it, giving me the extremely odd sight of flames dancing behind the ice for a moment. Before lack of oxygen snuffed them out, leaving black smoke trapped in their place.

Okay, I thought dizzily, that went better than expected.

Or maybe not. Because when I spun and tried to shoot Æsubrand, nothing happened. Except that his battered face acquired an evil smile and Marlowe's acquired a dark scowl and then they were at it again, falling to the concrete in a snarling pile of thrashing limbs.

Marlowe must have been too depleted for his super-duper master power to be available, but there was nothing wrong with his brain. And he'd figured out the same thing I had on that wild ride with Slava—Æsubrand's power didn't work so well up close, because it caught him, too.

And speaking of Slava—

Where the hell was Slava?

In the few seconds my attention had been diverted, he'd disappeared. Which was stupid; it wasn't like he could just get up and walk off. Except that that was exactly what he had done.

Sort of.

After a couple seconds of panicked looking around, I finally spied him. A frozen, pantsless vampire drifting out over the void between buildings, like a balloon a kid had just let go of. One that was getting farther away by the second.

But that wasn't yet quite far enough.

I stuck the empty gun in my waistband, hiked up my skirt and ran, straight for the roof's edge. I heard Marlowe yell something, but it was lost in the massive gust of wind that was rushing up behind me, trying to beat me to my target, to send him skittering out into the void ahead of me. But either Æsubrand was tiring or I was getting my second wind, because for once, my luck had turned. The gust hit me at almost the same moment that my feet ran out of roof, and actually worked in my favor, propelling me up and out farther and faster than I could possibly have hoped for on my own, almost making me overreach my target.

But not quite.

My fingers grabbed the frosty, slippery surface, and my arms and legs wrapped around it, and my head tucked low, and then Slava and I shot ahead, like an odd-shaped bullet barreling through the Manhattan sky.

It was a mad rush, surfing the crest of a wave of wind across the city. No, it was more than mad; it was breathtaking and death-defying and so stupid it made my head hurt. But it was hard to care with the wind whistling past my ears and the city streaming by below and Slava's building fast retreating into the distance.

I clutched him harder, little half-crazed gasps of something I finally recognized as laughter slipping out from between my lips, because, crazy or not, *it was working*.

At least it was until the charm suddenly gave out.

It took me a second to realize what had happened, because I'd assumed that the freezing process would have stabilized it. And maybe it had. Maybe it had lasted longer than it should have on a body, although that was cold comfort considering that in a second we had gone from tearing across the sky to tearing toward the ground.

Battery Park was coming up, the greenery a dark swath against the brighter buildings, with the city lights wavering in black water beyond. But it didn't look like we were going to make it that far. And even if we did, hitting the ocean from this height and speed would be virtually the same as hitting concrete.

I tried to think, in the few seconds I had left, to remember all those rules about what to do if falling from a height. But the thing about those rules is, they were made by someone safely on the ground. And it's a little hard to take them seriously when your eyes are tearing up and the wind is roaring in your ears and the ground is rushing up at you at a rate that is clearly not survivable unless you suddenly grow wings. And while I have a fair number of skills to call on in an emergency, I don't number flying among them.

Fortunately, someone else did.

Slava and I were heading straight for a hard ribbon of sidewalk snaking through the park when something caught me. For a second I thought the charm had suddenly reengaged, until the force of being jerked skyward again almost bisected me, and caused me to lose my grip on the frozen bullet. Which continued on our former trajectory, plowing through the air and then—

"No!" I yelled, but it was too late. Slava hit the ground at something like eighty miles an hour, with a sound like

a gun going off. And he didn't shatter like the other vamp so much as disintegrate. Some larger pieces hit the ground here and there, but a good third of the body went up in a cloud of sparkling, icy particles that melted on the hot August breeze, shimmering away into nothingness as I watched.

I cursed silently, too out of breath for anything else, but someone heard.

"You're welcome," a rich voice said behind me.

My feet gently touched down on springy grass a moment later, and I whirled drunkenly around to see Slava's floor show standing in front of me. He looked a little different, with those huge wings outspread, blocking half the sky. Until they folded up against his back again, somehow managing not to tangle in the long black hair.

The eyes were the same color, darker than mine, to the point that they didn't seem to have a pupil as they regarded me quizzically. "For such a small creature, you cause a lot of trouble."

"So people ... keep telling me," I said, dizzy and weaponless, and wondering what this new hell was.

But hell wasn't looking particularly threatening. If anything, hell looked vaguely amused. "Those people would be correct. But you are, if you'll forgive me, playing a tad outside your league."

"And what league ... would that be?"

But he just shook his head. "This is more dangerous than you can handle, dhampir."

"I can handle a lot."

"And that goes for your people, as well." He smiled at me gently. "Tell them to leave it to us."

"Who is us?" I yelled—at no one. Because he was suddenly airborne again, his massive wings beating the night hard enough to knock me down. And by the time I got back to my—very shaky—feet, he was gone.

Leaving me with a dead vamp, a bunch of bruises and no answers.

Chapter Twenty-four

"Okay, very funny. Now let me in!"

Nothing. I might as well have been talking to the brick wall instead of the speaker set into it. And it did not make me happy.

It was raining, Verrell's omelet was long gone, and I had a dead vampire in my trunk. And considering that the damned Senate were the ones who had wanted him so freaking bad, the least they could do was open the door. I pushed the button again, a long, sustained buzz that I really hoped gave somebody in there a headache, but the result was the same.

Great.

I got out, leaving my car blocking the entrance to the garage, and skirted the building. The East Coast Office of the North American Vampire Senate, Central Manhattan Branch, aka Central, was located in a mansion built around the turn of the century by some robber baron with more cash than taste. Improvements had been made in the years since, but most of them had involved privacy. Which was why, despite the glass inserts in the ornate mahogany doors, I saw only my own face staring back at me: pale, bruised skin, mascara that had run *everywhere*, and rain dripping off the end of my nose.

It was spotting my new leather jacket.

Goddamn it.

I should have left the jacket in my car, but I'd needed it for modesty's sake, since Marlowe's magical fabric hadn't proven so magical after all. Of course, it might have been fine if it hadn't started raining halfway through the long hike back to Slava's. Which I'd chosen over explaining to a cabbie why I was wandering around Manhattan looking like a war victim.

So in addition to being bruised and bloody and barefoot, I was close to indecent by the time I slogged ten blocks in a downpour.

And found Slava's all but deserted.

The guests had fled, Æsubrand had taken off immediately after I had, and Marlowe and his senior vamps had taken off after him. The younger ops had been left to pacify the human authorities, who were out in force by the time I returned, and to chisel out the ice cubes upstairs, who were being carted away for interrogation on the off chance that they knew anything. And to deal with me.

Only they hadn't seemed to know how to deal with me. They hadn't said anything as one of them brought my car around, and another gave me his phone—because mine was in my purse and my purse was God-knew-where—probably so the boss could call and cuss me out later. And then a third handed me a couple of trash bags, because Marlowe wanted a delivery.

Oh yes, he did.

I'd stared at the vamp and he'd had the grace to look embarrassed, because we both knew what this was. Okay, yes, some top-notch necromancers, like the kind the Senate had on call, could occasionally extract information from a recently dead vamp brain. But "recent" did not equal the hour and a half Slava had been out of commission by the time I dragged him back. The necromancers who had prowled the battlefields in the bad old days, searching for important corpses to brain-loot, had known they had only minutes at best. And those corpses hadn't been frozen, broken into chunks and half vaporized.

So, yeah, I was going with the revenge theory. But I'd taken the damned bags anyway, because I doubted I'd get paid for tonight—and I was *so* getting paid for tonight—if I didn't. And because it was SOP to clean up your own mess, especially when it involved a bunch of vamp parts littering a popular tourist area. And now all I wanted was to drop them off and have this nightmare of an evening finally be over.

Only I couldn't if nobody ever let me in.

I pulled out my phone and stabbed in Marlowe's number, even though it was already programmed, just for the satisfaction. But I may as well have saved myself the trouble. I wiped the rain off the phone's little face and the mystery was solved: no bars.

I shook it, even though that never helps.

It didn't this time, either.

"You're going to make me do it, aren't you?" I demanded.

Apparently, it was.

I gave in and performed the traditional dance to the cell phone gods, holding it up, turning it around, doing the hokey pokey and restraining a strong impulse to smash it against the wall. And nada. Unless you want to count a sad little blip, which I assumed was the electronic version of the finger.

I shoved the useless thing back into my pocket and looked up at the discreet camera hidden inside some elaborate stonework, knowing that someone was getting a belly laugh at my expense. I didn't bother to scowl back. The problem with being five feet two, dimpled and female is that no matter what your reputation, most people are going to underestimate you.

Even people who ought to know better.

I sloshed back to my car and got in.

There were advantages, I reflected as I backed up, to driving a piece of crap. Like you didn't have to worry about leaving coffee rings on the dash or getting mud on the carpet, and finding the occasional fossilized French fry was more a source of wonder than a reason to freak out. You also didn't let the thought of a few new dents bother you. Like when you put it in drive and floored it, spraying water and mud while gunning straight for the lousy security door that nobody had ever bothered to replace. Because who would be crazy enough to break in to a mansion full of vampires?

Guess they found out, I thought, grinning as my ancient Firebird tore through the flimsy wooden shell over the entrance and flew down a corridor, burning rubber straight into the well-maintained interior.

Which for some reason smelled like ass.

I skidded to a halt beside some beautiful old exposed brickwork. As always, the place looked more like the nineteenth-century carriage house it had once been than a parking garage, with dark wooden beams and original tack on the walls. Unlike always, it smelled like the horses were still in residence.

Rotting, diseased horses, I thought, wrinkling my nose as I got out.

The lights were flickering, like the storm was causing electrical problems. But not enough that I couldn't see that the damage was minimal. And hey, the bumper had been lumpy anyway. I went around and popped the trunk.

And dear *God*.

It looked like I owed the horses an apology, because I had found the stink and the stink was me. Or, at least my passenger, who had still been more or less frozen when I picked him up, but no more. Slava was sloshing around in his little Baggies, one pale blue eye staring through the film like a goldfish being carted home from the store. And reeking like a three-day-old corpse left out in the sun.

I swallowed, suddenly less concerned about dinner. It looked like my mad dash had ruptured a bag, and something absolutely foul was leaking out. And yeah, vamps decay faster than humans, having a head start on the whole dead thing. But *damn*.

And now I was going to have to drag him all the way upstairs.

I looked up, hoping for some outraged staff coming to bitch at me about the door, fully intending to pawn Mr. Slushy off on them. But either they were really in a mood or they'd been warned about what I had in the trunk, because no dice. I grumbled something uncomplimentary about their ancestors and leaned in to grab bag #1.

And was grabbed back by bag #2.

For a second, I just stood there, years of experience no match for the sight of a half-liquefied arm trying to choke me to death. But I snapped out of it before it snapped me, and I grasped the slimy surface—only to have the remaining skin slough off like a molting snake. I choked down nausea and staggered back, tearing at veins and sinew and protruding bone, while cold, gelatinous fingers clawed at me.

I couldn't seem to get a grip on the slimy flesh, so I pulled a knife from my jacket and sawed through the wrist, causing the hideous thing to spasm away from my neck. It dropped like a bloody spider onto the ground, or maybe a hand in a fingerless glove. Because the fleshy tips had come away, leaving only the bare bones sticking out.

Which I suppose is why it made a clicking noise on the concrete when it suddenly lunged at me again.

I pulled the mage's .45, which I'd reloaded in the car because it isn't paranoia when shit like this happens *all the freaking time.* And nailed it straight through palm. And then I shot it again. And again. And then one more time because *gah!*

I didn't stop until it was a bunch of tiny, unconnected pieces twitching uselessly on the floor and I was panting and trembling and seriously revolted.

And then I noticed that my hands were on fire.

Not literally, but it sure as hell felt that way, and it wasn't my crazed imagination. Angry pinkish red blisters were rising from my skin as I watched. And I didn't need to feel my neck to know that the same thing was happening there, like acid had splattered me wherever that thing had touched.

And not just me. The floor underneath the remains of the hand was blackening, while a nauseating yellow fluid seeped from the flesh and boiled into the air, adding to the stink. And to the whole skin-tightening horror thing we had going on in here.

And that was before my trunk started to spew out the rest of bag #2 in gory chunks.

One got caught in an oil stain from somebody's car and writhed around, like an eel in water—except that eels don't usually set oil on fire. But others were making more headway, leaving blackened, bloody trails on the ground as they wriggled and clawed and slimed in my direction. *And okay,* I thought, backing the hell up, money was a good and fine thing, but on the whole, I really thought the Senate could have this one.

I turned around and started for the ramp—and the door and the rain-soaked street, which, yeah, was looking pretty good right about now.

Only I wasn't going to be seeing it anytime soon, as I discovered when I started up the ramp. And smacked straight into something I couldn't see, but that packed a wallop, sending me rolling back down the incline again, smoking and swearing. And looking up to see an imprint of my body at the impact point, weirdly inverted face, flailing limbs and all, etched on what appeared to be thin air.

It wasn't. The glowing bluish me faded in seconds, leaving only a ghostly outline flickering in the ominous lighting. But the reason for it remained: someone had turned on the Senate's wards, which probably explained why the lights were messed up and why my phone hadn't worked. Wards as big as the Senate's played havoc with electrical devices.

They also kept things out really effectively.

Like '89 Firebirds, for instance.

So either someone had just raised them, coincidentally right after I arrived, or someone had dropped them to let me through and then raised them again right after. And for some reason, neither of those options was making me feel all that great. And that was before somebody screamed, a high, ear-shattering sound that sent me back to one knee before I'd finished getting to my feet.

I looked around, dizzy and disoriented, trying to figure out the direction. But it was a little hard when all I could see was a slurry of bricks and cars and impossible horrors all sliding together in a gut-wrenching stream of what-the-hell. And then whoever-it-was did it again.

From inside my head.

"Shut up!" I yelled, smacking my blistered hand down on the floor, hoping the pain would help clear my messed-up brain. It didn't, but something else happened, although I wasn't sure it was an improvement.

Because suddenly I was hearing voices.

"Wha—who? Is someone there? Who is that? Who is THAT?"

"Stop. Screaming," I grated out, because the voice had almost been as loud as the initial shriek.

"Whoisthatyoutellmerightnow!"

"Augggh!" I replied, because a pinkish blur had taken that moment to come soaring at me through the air.

I managed to put a bullet in it, and it flew back, squelching against something out of sight. Which didn't make me feel much better, because the other things had figured out that they could jump, too—I guess by muscle contraction, although I really wasn't into analyzing it right then. I was into not letting them get on me, which meant shooting them out of the air while scooting backward through a room that was still fun-housing around me.

And while a hysterical voice demanded that I save its ass.

"Would you *shut up* until I save mine?" I hissed, and it abruptly cut off.

With the reduction in sound came an easing of the carnival ride in my brain, allowing me to scramble behind a concrete barrier. I crouched there, eyeing the approaching hoard of vamp parts in disbelief and trying to slam home a new clip. It was the second of only two I'd had in my emergency kit, because I don't use a .45 that much.

Or at all, if I couldn't get this one in, which was taking forever because of the blisters.

And maybe because a random bit of Slava had just leapt off the floor and *smacked* against the barrier. And then another and another, splattering the other side like acid freaking rain. Until one missed, flying over my head and taking out the windshield on a BMW.

I stared at the cracks spidering across the supposedly

shatterproof glass. And decided I could really live without finding out what that felt like. I slammed the clip home and *moved*.

Tap, tap, tap.

I swear, it felt exactly like a finger hitting the inside of my skull. I had a sudden vivid image of that annoying paper clip guy that Microsoft created to torment people. *It looks like you're having a nervous breakdown. Would you like some help?* I thought wildly, and flung myself behind a car.

"What? What did you say?" The voice was back.

I ignored it, being kind of busy not dying. It was like the damned things knew where I was. I was doing everything right—keeping low, using the cars as cover—but wherever I went, they took out windows, dented doors and sent the smell of molten rubber into the air when they smacked into tires.

It was like being in the world's grossest shooting gallery.

It was also impossible.

Leaving aside that no vampire could still be alive after that kind of damage, there was the fact that even magical creatures have physical rules. Whacked-out physical rules, but still. And without some kind of sensory organs, there was simply no way for them to—

Tap, tap, tap.

Is this thing on? I thought irrelevantly.

"Stop it! Stop it right now! Oh my God, this is typical. This is so— They finally send someone after me and she's insane."

"Only part of the time," I said, because for some reason, talking to myself didn't seem all that strange right now.

There was a sudden silence. And then the floodgates broke. *"Dory? Dorina? Oh God, oh my God, is that you?"*

"Yes, and I'm kind of busy—"

"Don't give me that! You come get me, do you hear me? Youcomegetmerightnow—"

"Radu?" I cocked my head, because that particular brand of shrill entitlement belonged to only one guy.

"OF COURSE IT'S ME! Who else has been scream-
ing for help for the last twenty minutes? Where the hell
have you been?"

"Twenty minutes?" I repeated, in disbelief. Because
whatever else could be said about the Senate, it reacted
smartly in a crisis. *"Who did you call?"*

"Anybody! Everybody! What, do you think I'm going
to be picky when I'm facing THAT?"

And suddenly I was getting not just sounds in my
head but visuals, too. There was a stomach-churning second of disorientation as my head stayed completely still
and yet also whipped around, and then I was staring at a
glass wall in what looked like a lab. And on the other
side—

"What the hell are those?" I demanded, staring through
Radu's eyes at a bunch of . . . well, they were vampires. I
knew this because I'd seen them less than two hours ago,
frozen on top of a building. Which was why it was a little
odd to find them currently up and mobile and scratching
at the glass, including one still half encased in ice—

"WHAT DO THEY LOOK LIKE?"

I knew what they looked like, but that wasn't possible,
that was just crazy, because vampires didn't—

Something dropped onto my back and I screamed and
wrenched my jacket off, throwing it as far as I could and
blasting the shit out of it at the same time. I stood there,
panting, my eyes flicking around the room for the next
target, and decided that maybe I could cut Radu a little
slack. Because vampires didn't form themselves into fleshy
grenades and fly around, eith—

I stopped, having caught sight of the bag I'd dropped
when the arm of doom grabbed me. It had somehow remained intact, maybe because most of the parts with the
muscle were in the other one. But the face was still pressed
against the plastic, and the staring blue eye was now . . .

Staring at me.

Son of a bitch.

"Hello? Hello? What's happening? Why aren't you
talking? Are you coming to get me OUT?"

"Give me a sec," I said, trying to line up a shot through

a cracked windshield. It would have been easy—except that the air in front of me was suddenly full of flying flesh. It looked like a hurricane had hit a butcher shop, which freaked me out less than the fact that *it knew*.

"I DON'T HAVE A SEC!"

"Where are you?" I asked, waiting for an opening while a hail of bloody rain pitted the car.

"Where else? The morgue in the basement."

"And that is how far from the carriage house?"

"I don't know! I never come in that way!"

"Then look it up," I gritted out, as something sizzled against the wall behind me.

"My computer is outside. Just ask one of your crew!"

I didn't say anything.

"You . . . you do have a crew . . . don't you?"

"Not exactly."

"Not exactly? NOT EXACTLY? What do you mean, not—"

The rest of his diatribe was lost in the sound of a .45 obliterating an eyeball. And as soon as it did, all the little things fell to the ground, twitching aimlessly. And then finally went still.

Okay, I thought. *All right.* It looked like all those video games had had the goods, after all.

So, yeah. Easy.

I swallowed. *"Radu. Tell me what level you're on."*

"I don't . . . It's . . . it's the next to lowest. I think . . . Yes, it should be fourteen on the elevator." An ominous crack echoed through whatever crazy connection he'd been able to make. *"Dory."* His voice had suddenly gotten very small. *"Hurry."*

"I'm coming, 'Du. Just . . . sit tight. I'm coming."

Chapter Twenty-five

Since I had exactly one gun to my name and was almost out of ammo for that, my first stop was the car and the battered toolbox on the floor in the back. It contained emergency supplies, including a couple nice ten-inch knives that I pocketed and an even nicer .44 Magnum that I didn't. Because I was hemorrhaging weapons lately, and had had to press it into service just in time for Slava's guys to take it away.

I took the box of .44 ammo anyway, just in case I ran across a usable weapon. But even assuming I did, I wasn't going to make it to 'Du with that alone. I needed more weapons, a *lot* more ammo and some dirty tricks.

Fortunately, I was in the right place for all three.

"*'Du. Do you know where the nearest weapons cache is?*" I asked, picking up my once expensive leather jacket, which now resembled a target at a shooting gallery. But I didn't have a choice; thanks to Marlowe's idea of evening wear, I had nothing else to hold all the—

I suddenly realized that Radu hadn't responded.

"*'Du?*"

Nothing.

I felt a cold hand clench in my chest when he didn't answer, when I didn't even get a sense of him in my head. But that didn't have to mean anything. My mental abilities weren't exactly reliable. I was like a radio that could usually only receive, and that didn't even work half the time.

So 'Du might be fine. *No, he* was *fine,* I told myself

fiercely. He was a damned second-level master and a Basarab. He'd spent five hundred years outfighting, outsmarting and just plain outlasting the hell out of everybody. He would hold out.

Now I just had to get to him.

Considering the Senate's level of paranoia, there were probably multiple weapons caches tucked around, though they'd neglected to share their location with me. But when I'd shown up to join the posse tonight, I'd seen a couple of Marlowe's boys coming out of a hall by the main reception desk, still buckling on holsters. It didn't necessarily mean anything, but it was the only clue I had. So I headed for the lobby, hoping I was right and that the guys on duty hadn't emptied it already.

And . . . they hadn't, I thought, coming to a halt just outside the door.

Or if they had, it hadn't done them any good.

The tasteful gray marble columns, impressive onyx desk, and cheerful old-world scenes that usually greeted visitors weren't looking so cheerful anymore. Not covered in vast slashes and strokes and dribbles like a modernist painting. Blood sprayed the walls, where weapons' fire had already marred the soft blue paint, beaded on the surface of an antique table and spattered the petals of an ornamental arrangement.

It wasn't so much a problem on the floor, however.

Since most of it was missing.

I approached the blackened, jagged hole of what had once been an inlaid marble star with caution, since the sides were still smoking. And looked down into the next floor. And the next. And the one after that. Something had just carved a Volkswagen-sized hole through four stories and was working on a fifth.

And there was no need to wonder what that something was: the sickly neon green puddle at the bottom was sending up fumes that caused me to jerk my head back abruptly, eyes watering and throat seizing up. *Somebody just used a weapons-grade potion and you stick your head in the fumes? Great, Dory. Freaking great.*

I backed off fast, my eyes flicking around, in case

somebody was planning to capitalize on my stupidity. But I didn't see anyone. Just a blackened chandelier overhead, crystals chiming softly in the air-conditioning, scattered papers underfoot and someone's spilled tea.

And a guy nailed to the wall by four huge daggers.

I'd rounded the reception desk and almost come nose to nose with him before I shied back, gun up and heart missing a beat. He was behind a short wall separating the desk from the rest of the room, and was facing the main doors. Like some macabre sort of greeter.

I stared at him for a second, unsure if my blurry eyes and the crazy lights were playing tricks. And they were, sort of. Because the lower body wasn't in shadow as I'd first thought. It wasn't there at all, unless you counted the snakelike spine glistening palely against the darker wall.

And curling up and down like its owner was still alive.

After a moment, I swallowed and started to edge around, only to have a spear of light fall over the face. And I got a second shock. Because he looked horribly familiar.

The head was down, with the chin resting on the breast, so I couldn't see the face. But the hair was dark and about the right length. And so were the weight and the height, as far as I could estimate, considering the damage, and—

And suddenly I couldn't breathe because I thought it was 'Du.

I took another few steps forward, and I still did. Even when I gently cupped one cheek, to avoid the dark blood that had dripped down covering the chin. And pulled the face up, into the light. And felt my spine turn to water.

Because it wasn't him.

The features were handsome, but lacked 'Du's hint of the exotic. And the hair was faintly curly instead of his shining waterfall. And the clothes, now that I saw them up close, were wrong: a dark suit, well made but not up to the family's exacting standards. I licked my lips, feeling my heart rate back off the danger zone.

Until the head suddenly moved in my hand.

And the eyes—cold and dark and dead—fixed on me.

I froze, because there was no life in them, no spark, much less the glow of a vampire in distress. But there was cold, calculating intelligence, nonetheless. Not in them so much as behind them. Like someone was using the dead man's face for a mask.

And there was only one creature I knew who could do that.

Necromancer, I thought, staring at him through his proxy's eyes. Which made sense, given what Radu was facing downstairs. But it still seemed impossible.

Technically, a dead body was a dead body. And necromancers could exert control over any that wasn't already in control of itself—like a vampire—and sometimes even then. That was why they'd once been killed on sight, and why any with serious power often still were, despite the Senate's claims to the contrary. Lower-level vamps could be taken over by a powerful necromancer and used as spies against their own kind. It had happened often enough in the bad old days, if rumor was to be believed.

But this wasn't a lower-level vamp. He wouldn't have been on the desk—considered the first line of defense—if he was. So what the hell?

I didn't get an answer—unless you counted the eyes suddenly narrowing, and the mouth screwing up. I jerked to the side, hard enough to wrench something. But it ensured that the spit intended for my face hit my shoulder instead, splattering against the heavy leather with an acidic hiss. And then I was out of range, rolling and flipping and putting three bullets through the evil thing's eyes.

Which didn't stop it from laughing.

I snatched off the jacket, breathing hard and cursing. And watched the leather bubble and burn and then disintegrate into a baseball-sized hole. I pulled a knife and ripped off the sleeve, wishing I had the ammo to spare to obliterate that horrible grin.

But I didn't, because I'd just announced my presence to everyone here. Or if I hadn't, that thing probably had.

Was that why he'd been left there? Some kind of early-warning system, a CCTV for the magically inclined?

I didn't know, but I didn't intend to wait around and find out.

I pushed on, navigating around puddles of still-sticky blood in case any of them might burn my feet off. But it was impossible to miss the stuff completely. It had even run into the grout between the tiles in the elevator alcove, placing a red grid on the floor. Hell, even the potted plants were splattered with it.

Which was kind of disturbing, since they also appeared to be moving.

Now what? I thought, gripping my gun tighter. But I didn't retreat because I couldn't. The damned plants were framing the hall running between the reception area and the elevators. And of course it was the one I needed. So whoever or whatever was back there was about to get—

"Aughhhh!"

I'd jerked on a quivering frond, only to have it jerk back. And scream. And then go running wildly down the corridor away from me, shedding bits of leaves and moss and making strange huffing shrieks. Right up until it ran out of hallway.

It ricocheted around for a second, as if trying to find a branching corridor that wasn't there. And then it seemed to go a little mad, turning around and coming back again. Which was less of a concern than the fact that it appeared to be sprouting hand grenades like some weird sort of fruit.

One of which fell off and went bouncing along the baseboard.

I didn't wait to see if the pin was still in it or not. I stumbled back a few steps and then turned and ran, right back the way I'd come, across the lobby and through a corridor and down a flight of stairs, slamming the garage door behind me. Only to have frantic fists beat a staccato hail on it a second later and someone start screaming bloody murder.

I hesitated a second, but I thought the screams

sounded a little familiar. And even if I was wrong, whoever it was didn't seem interested in attacking me so much as in getting the hell out of Dodge. I jerked open the door and something flew through, just a green blur against the dim garage, right up until it hit the bottom of the incline.

At which point it dropped like a stone, screeching and flailing around like some kind of panicked banshee.

A muffled *boom* came from the other side of the door and I waited a few heartbeats, holding my breath. But there were no other sounds, like running footsteps coming this way. It looked like whatever was downstairs was either deaf or was waiting for me to come to it. Which would have been fine if that hadn't been exactly what I was about to do.

But at least it gave me some options.

I peeled myself off the wall and went to see what the blubbering thing was doing.

It was blubbering. And writhing. And sizzling slightly because it had just run into the wards at top speed.

It also wasn't an it so much as a he, and a familiar he at that.

I bent over and jerked him up, and this time he didn't try to run or even respond, except to continue a litany of "I don't know, I don't know, I don't know, I don't *know, know, know, know, know —*" until I slapped him.

That shut him up. For about a second. And then he started quivering all over and screeching, and throwing bits of himself at the ward, tearing off leaves and fronds of what looked like half a dozen different plants, pieces of which had been stuck into and taped around a familiar-looking pair of assless pants.

"Ray!" I said sharply, only to be ignored. "Ray!"

He just stared at me out of a blackened face, like some kind of whacked-out commando who'd failed camouflage school. His blue eyes were wide and glazed; his black hair was sweaty and sticking up everywhere; and he was drooling slightly. He looked completely out of it, and that really wasn't going to work right now.

So I slapped him again.

Only to have him promptly slap me back.

After which followed a bitch-slapping fest that I won by virtue of kneeing him in the gonads.

"Oh. Oh God. Oh God, oh God, oh God, oh God, oh God!"

"Get up!" I told him impatiently, because I hadn't hit him that hard.

But he just continued to moan and roll around, to the point that I seriously contemplated leaving him there. But Ray had been stuck here for a couple weeks while the Senate pumped him for information, and there was a good chance he knew more about this place than I did. He could hardly know less.

So I jerked him up again.

And was rewarded by a slightly more sane, if entirely infuriated glare. "The fuck was *that*?" he screeched.

"That was to get your attention. I need—"

"You hit me in the *nuts*!"

"And I may do it again if you don't—"

"You don't just go around hitting guys in the nuts!"

"Ray—"

"You just don't, okay? That is not cool. That is not on. That is not—"

"Ray!"

"—ever, ever—*God*! There's got to be some damned limits—"

So I did it again.

"*THE FUCK?*"

"Ray. Get a grip—"

"*I have a grip!* I have a damned fine grip! If I didn't, I'd be dead already, and I don't know why I'm not and it's no thanks to you and *where the hell have you been?*"

"That's what I'm trying—"

"We have to have a talk," he told me, his voice trembling slightly. "About your responsibilities as a master."

"I am not your master."

"One of which is protection, okay? Which I haven't been seeing too goddamn much of!" He took off his bushy hat and threw it at the floor. For a second he just looked at it, a crumpled mass of leaves and Scotch tape sliming about in an oil slick, and then his face crumpled, too. And he grabbed me in a bear hug that threatened my ribs. "Oh God," he said brokenly. "I didn't think you'd ever get here!"

I just stood there a second, completely nonplussed. Of all the crazy things that had happened today, I thought this might actually top the list. I had a master vampire sobbing in my arms and no idea what to do about it.

Except for the obvious.

"Ray?" I told him, stroking his dirty, disheveled hair.

"Hmm?"

"I know you're upset—"

He nodded into my neck.

"—and you've probably been through a lot today—"

He nodded harder.

"But right now I need you to do me a favor."

He looked up. "What?"

I clenched a fist in his mane and jerked his head back. "Man the hell up!"

"Oh, that's nice!" he said, wrenching away. "That's just great! Do you have any idea what I've been through?"

"No, and I don't care."

"You *suck* as a master!"

"I am not your master!" I said, pulling a rifle sling over his head and checking out the gun attached to it. Which I supposed he'd been using for a club, since it contained no actual bullets. "Where's the ammo?"

"Like I know. I got it off a dead aide," he said, talking about one of the Senate's human employees. "But I couldn't stay to frisk him 'cause there was more of those things coming—"

"What are they? Where are the Senate's people?"

"*They're* the Senate's people! Don't you get it?" He glanced around fearfully. "It's like *Night of the Living Dead* around here, *except they aren't living.*"

"Just tell me what you know," I said, and started stuffing my pockets with grenades. And cut my finger on a freaking *cleaver* he had wedged up in there.

"I don't know anything, okay? I just—" He stopped

and took a deep breath, I guess for effect. Or maybe because in times of stress, old habits resurface. "I was in the break room, trying to make myself a damned cup of coffee. 'Cause Marlowe had to do something tonight and didn't have time to yell at—excuse me, interrogate—me some more until tomorrow. But they wouldn't let me go, not even back to your place to get a change of clothes, assuming that stupid driver ever brought back my luggage. Even with my shirttail out, it's getting a little drafty in—"

"Ray."

"Yeah. So they just left me here. And I was gonna make some coffee and then do a little Web surfing, maybe watch some TV. But I'm down in the kitchen and I hear this commotion outside in the hall. So I open the door and there's one of the guards getting slammed against the wall by this guy. And the guy was like—he was messed up. Blood and stuff everywhere, all oozing and holes and—and he was dead, okay? Not our kind of dead, either, but DEAD dead. And soon the guard was, too—"

"And then he came after you?"

"No, then *they* came after me. The guard—he gets up, staked, brains splattered all over the wall and everything, but he freaking *gets up*, and then they see me and they're *fast*. But I got the door shut and I know this place like the back of my hand, right? So I managed to—hey, what are you doing?"

"I'm going to need some help," I said, grabbing his arm and dragging him back toward the door.

"What?" His eyes bugged out. "Are you crazy? I'm not going back in there!"

"I'll protect you."

"Yeah, right!" He jerked back. "You got a rifle with no bullets, a handgun and some grenades. And let me tell you something about the grenades—"

"They don't work too well in close quarters."

"They don't work at all!" he said, pulling back as hard as he could—which was pretty damned hard. "Not against those things. They just keep coming! And then you've got pieces and blood and ooze and—aughh!"

I'd dragged him to the door and kicked it open, in preparation for shoving him through, but he'd grabbed one of the nearby wooden support beams and was holding on for all he was worth. "No! No, no, no! I'm not—"

"Listen to me! I just need your help for a minute. Then you can hide while I go get Radu."

"Radu?"

"He's trapped in the basement. That's why I need to get down there. Then I can—"

"Do nothing," Ray said savagely. "'Cause then you'll be trapped, too, in a basement full of—what the hell. Why don't we call 'em what they are? They're freaking zombies! *Vampire zombies*, which doesn't even make sense—I mean, who *does* that?"

"A necromancer. A powerful one."

"No. Uh-uh. They try to co-opt babies when they can, or they used to anyway, but this is different."

"Because the guys in there are masters?"

"Because the guys in there are *dead*! I told you, DEAD dead. And you know how fast our bodies decay. We make terrible zombies! Everybody knows that. We're falling apart within hours."

I blinked, because something had finally made sense. "Yeah. But what if someone doesn't need hours, or at least not many of them? You're also a lot stronger, and faster, than a human."

"But zombies take a lot of power to create, like a LOT of power. You gonna throw that away for a couple hours?"

"If the prize is big enough." I just didn't know what the prize was supposed to be. This was a working base, not a treasure house. And even if it had been . . . the Senate practically defined revenge. What was here that was worth that kind of risk?

"Look, whatever, okay?" Ray said. "Point is, there's a ton of them down there. You'll never even get to Radu, and if you do, you'll never get—"

"There's also a portal," I told him.

He stopped struggling. "What?"

"You're the portal king. You must know about it."

"Know about—wait. What?"

"The Senate's portal—"

His eyes widened. "The big boy is *here*?"

"What big boy?"

"What big boy?" Ray stared at me like I was slow. "It's only the biggest damned portal in existence! Connects to I don't even know how many lines! And you're telling me that it's been here *all the time*?"

"I don't know about—"

"Wait. That can't be right." His eyes narrowed. "They'd need a ley line sink for something like that, and they don't got one here. That's why everybody always assumed it was at the consul's place upstate."

"Which it probably is!" I said, exasperated. "I didn't say they had *that* portal, I said they had *a* portal. It connects Central to the consul's residence in case of an emergency." And if ever anything had qualified . . .

"But—" He looked outraged. "Those slimy sons of bitches! They told me they didn't have one here! Said it was for security reasons!"

I gave him a look, and dragged him off the pillar. "Would *you* tell you it was here?"

Ray thought for a second. "Okay, point." He looked at me and his demeanor became more businesslike, as if talking about something he understood had calmed him. "But that don't matter, 'cause you're not gonna get to it."

"I will once I get to a weapons locker."

He shook his head. "That won't do any good. They're behind wards."

"What kind?"

"The kind that shocked the crap outta me when I tried to break in. They need a guard's touch to open. And there ain't any more guards. Or if there are, they're being real quiet. I hadn't heard anyone for maybe fifteen minutes when you—*why are you still dragging me in there?*"

"I have an idea."

"Oh, great." He looked heavenward. "She has an idea. Have you been listening? They'll *kill* us!"

"Not if we kill them—" I began, only to cut off when a sudden rushing noise filled the air. And Ray grabbed my gun and went ballistic on something on the wall over our heads.

"Die! Die! Die!" he screamed, emptying the clip and causing spent shells to rain down all around us. And okay, maybe I'd been wrong about the calm thing. Because he was just standing there, trembling and panting and staring—

At the air-conditioning vent that he'd just shot the crap out of.

"—first." I took my smoking gun out of his limp fingers and patted him on the back. "See? That's the spirit."

Chapter Twenty-six

"Oh, good. That's ... Yes," Ray said, slumping against the wall as the shield protecting the cabinet dropped.

I felt a little light-headed, too, because there were actual weapons in the weapons case. Not a lot—somebody had been here before us—but anything was better than we had. "Get rid of it," I told Ray, passing over the loathsome thing we'd used as a key.

"You're inhuman," he told me. And snatched it.

And as soon as he was out of sight around the corner, I let my head fall onto the cool, shiny metal of the cabinet for just a second. I could still vaguely feel it squirming in my palm, like its body was doing on the lobby wall. I tried to tell myself that the guard who had provided the handprint—and the hand—we'd needed would have approved. The creature that had taken him over wasn't him, and if he'd been here, he'd have wanted us to do what was necessary to avenge him.

I knew vamps well enough to know that, even if I hadn't known him.

But my brain kept wondering who he'd been. Or if I'd met him before. Or about how I'd feel if someone had just sawed off part of Louis-Cesare in order to fool a stupid—

I shuddered in visceral horror all over, hard.

And looked up to see Ray staring at me.

He didn't say anything and neither did I. I just licked my lips and went back to work, because weakness right now was not fucking okay. I started searching through the cabinet looking for something better than the damned .22—why the hell did they even have a .22?—that someone else had rejected. Someone else who was probably dead, because whatever they had picked hadn't been good enough.

And that went double for what they'd left. I grabbed a couple clips for the .45, shoving them in my pockets. And then just stood there, lusting after my favorite shotgun—a sweet, double-barreled 10-gauge loaded with three-and-a-half-inch shells. Every time I pulled the trigger, it was the equivalent to four blasts from a standard 12-gauge or a nine-second burst from a submachine gun.

It was glorious.

Only for this, I would have liked two. Or three, in case I ended up breaking one over something's head. What I found instead was a sad little .410, all alone in the back, because nobody hunted zombies—much less freaking vampire zombies—with a rabbit gun.

Nobody except me, since there was no alternative and I was out of time.

I flung it over my shoulder, grabbed all the ammo that would fit it and turned to Ray. He'd given me the layout of the lower floors, and helped distract the guy we'd used for a key long enough for me to do what had been necessary. If I got out of here, I owed him a lot.

"Keep your head down," I told him. "I'll send help as soon as I'm out."

He just stared at me. I didn't have time to figure out what his problem was, so I just clapped him on the shoulder. And took off for the bank of elevators.

They were to the left of the reception desk, in a little alcove of their own, but still plenty close enough to the main room for my purposes. In fact, things were looking about as good as they could under the circumstances, until I caught sight of one of the elevator panels. I got out and checked the other elevator, but it was the same story.

Son of a bitch.

"What the fuck are you doing?" Ray demanded, sticking his head in the door.

"There's only twelve lower levels," I told him.

"What?"

"There's only twelve, but Radu said he was on fourteen." I looked up. "Why would he say that?"

"Who the hell cares?" Ray looked at me like I was crazy. "You can't use the elevator—are you nuts?"

"Why not?"

"Why not?" The lights flickered, and he waved his arms. "That's why not! What if you get stuck between levels? What if they hear you coming? What if—"

"They're supposed to hear me coming."

"What?"

"This is just a diversion," I told him, looking at the main lobby. And at the gory creature that was still stuck to the wall. "To draw some of the vamps away from the stairs."

"And how does that help? You'll still have—"

"And to blow a bunch of them up. I've rigged a trip wire across the door. They fight their way into the elevator, and our odds will get a whole lot better."

Ray's forehead wrinkled as he stared down at the complete absence of any such wire. "But I don't see—"

I clapped a hand over his mouth, turned him around and pointed him at the damned vamp. Who was now blind, and missing a hand, but not deaf. "They'll hear the elevator, assume I'm crazy enough to come down that way, and get themselves blown up."

Ray wrenched out of my grip and turned around to stare at me. And then at the elevator. And then at me again. And then he started shaking his head and gesturing and mouthing something I didn't even try to interpret because I could guess pretty well.

"Meanwhile, I'll run down the stairs *on the other side of the building* and get 'Du," I told him. "Do you get it now?"

"Yeah. Yeah, I get it," he said savagely, as the elevator doors started to close. With me inside, because regardless of what I'd just told Ray, I didn't have the ammo or the firepower to fight my way down twelve floors of vamps. The idea was just to make them think I did, and buy me some time for what I really hoped would be a quick trip.

And yes, Ray had a point. This was insane and stupid and a whole list of other things, but it was also the only plan that might work. Only it didn't look like he thought so.

He stared at me for half a second, looking mad as hell for some reason I didn't particularly get. And then he apparently went crazy, too. Because he turned sideways and slipped through the narrow crack, right before the doors shut. Leaving me with nothing to do but glare, because I was holding down the twelfth-floor button and the close-door button at the same time and didn't have a hand free to slap him.

It was an old trick that worked for a lot of elevators to take you straight to your floor regardless of who else might have mashed a button. In other words, it was the express route down. Not that I expected to make it the whole way, but even half would improve our odds a lot.

At least, it would if there hadn't been any senior masters on duty tonight. I was assuming that was the case because of the speed of the takeover. It looked like the necromancer had used Slava's boys as a kind of Trojan horse, and they couldn't have gotten here more than half an hour before I did. And Radu had been in distress ten minutes after that.

That didn't say senior master to me.

At least, I really hoped not, or this was going to be a very short trip.

Of course, it might be anyway.

An arm suddenly punched through the door panel when we were on level six, only to get withdrawn, missing a good deal of flesh, when we hit seven. Where several more tried to widen the gap, but I kept my finger on the button and Ray grabbed my .45 and shoved it through the hole and just kept on firing. I don't think he could see what he was aiming at, but it didn't matter; it kept them back from the door, which was all we needed.

Or more or less kept them back. By level eight, the door was dented all over as fists and feet caved in the heavy metal, and by nine it was buckling and by ten there were faces staring at us through gaps big enough to drive body parts through and by eleven enough of those parts had been wedged inside that the elevator shuddered to a halt. I could still hear the gears grinding, trying to take us down, but nothing was happening, and that wasn't good.

"You have a plan for this, right?" Ray said, not looking at me because he was too busy hacking at body parts with his cleaver. Which wasn't working so well, because the acid had mostly eaten through the blade.

"Get out of the way!" I told him, hitting the button to go back up.

The sudden reversal, along with a few blasts from the shotgun to clear the door, worked to get us going again. But in the wrong direction. And some of our newfound friends thought we were leaving too soon, because now the floor was starting to dimple, too, as fists and feet hammered at it from underneath.

"How are they holding on?" Ray yelled, firing his rifle as we shot back up, because he'd already emptied my .45.

"Vampires!" I said, knocking him out of the way and grabbing two grenades. I tossed them out the shredded door on level ten, went up to nine, hit stop and waited.

"What the—" Ray began, but I cut him off.

"How many upper-level masters were here?"

"What—I—" His head jerked up as somebody landed on the roof. And somebody else stared at us through the slashes in the door, just two dead eyes that didn't glow anymore in a darkened corridor.

"Ray!" My voice snapped his attention back to me.

"I dunno. I dunno. Not many. Most are at the games; everybody with enough clout traded shifts and got off."

"Good," I said, as an explosion from the floor below rocked the elevator around us.

But it still worked when I hit the button to go back to level ten, the doors opening onto a smoking war zone of twisted metal and acid-etched walls, and blown-apart bodies that were still moving. Like the intact ones tearing through the elevator floor behind us. And the ceiling above us.

"Now what?" Ray demanded, as I grabbed two of our last three grenades, pulled the pins and tossed them into the elevator as we left it, right after I hit the button for eleven.

The doors closed, the elevator of doom plunged, and we ran flat out. Down the dark hall and into a now deserted stairway, since most of the bad guys on this level were currently grease marks on the walls. Most but not all.

I slit the throat of one right outside the door, bisecting it in passing all the way to the bone. Had to shoot another at the bend of the stairs, because he was leaking acid and I couldn't get too close, and the sound drew the attention of three vamps in the corridor at eleven. Who turned and started tearing our way, just as the elevator exploded behind them. They ended the journey in pieces, landing against the hall door with meaty thuds and a wash of red against the small square window.

Ray stared at it as we ran down the last flight, maybe because the vamps' body parts were already thumping against the metal kickplate. And then at me as I paused to reload outside the door to level twelve. But he didn't say anything, just reloaded his own gun with slightly shaking hands, his eyes flicking back and forth between the stairs behind us and the door ahead.

And then I kicked it in and we were through.

Into nothing.

Nothing weird, anyway. Just an empty, quiet corridor, fresh and clean and smelling faintly of some kind of pine cleaner, odd only because nothing was. There were no homicidal body parts, no corpses, no gore.

And no Radu.

I kicked open doors on one side of the hall while Ray took the other. But all we found was a few offices, a couple of holding cells and what looked like an interrogation room complete with two-way mirror. It was coldly clinical, completely unlike the baroque facade upstairs or the luxury guest and meeting spaces on the upper floors.

I guess nobody made it down here who needed to be impressed.

"Okay, okay, okay," Ray said, looking around the empty interrogation room. "Okay. He isn't here. *So where the hell is he?*"

"Level fourteen."

"There is no level fourteen!"

"There has to be. There's no lab on this floor."

"But you saw—"

"If it's a restricted level, they may not have put it on the elevator pad. That doesn't mean it's not here. We probably need a key for an override."

"Which we don't ha—"

I clapped a hand over his mouth as the door was kicked open. It was the one to the other half of the room, where a conference-type table sat surrounded by chairs and harsh lights. We watched through the mirror as a couple of long-haired corpses came in.

A lot of the older vamps have long hair, because they like it or because it tended to be the norm in earlier centuries or because human fads can bite them. But most of them keep it closely confined, not straggling in bloody clumps over acid-pitted faces. The one closest slowly turned his head in our direction, and I saw that half his cheek was gone, leaving just a raw, red cavity that looked like it was getting bigger as I watched.

And how the hell did *that* work? If the acid ate through them, too, why were they even mobile? Why weren't they a bunch of blackened bones on the floor?

And then I noticed: the one who looked the worst was one I knew. Not personally, but I'd seen him on guard duty a time or two when I came to get paid. But the other—well, judging by the tux, I had to assume he was one of Slava's guys.

And he looked a little different.

A good bit of his once expensive tux had been eaten away, giving him the look of a yearlong castaway on some desert island. But the skin underneath, other than being corpse white, was fine. And while he had some blood on him, I didn't see any obvious wounds, meaning it probably wasn't his.

So Slava's boys weren't harmed by whatever corrosive was flowing through their veins, but everybody else was. And that didn't spell coincidence to me. That spelled forethought and planning and deliberation and—

And setup.

My eyes widened as the implication hit. We'd just been played. Again.

But not by Slava, who had been as toxic as the rest of them. And who didn't have the skills for messing around with vamp DNA. So by the necromancer, obviously, and whoever he was working with, which I was suddenly having a hard time believing was just a group of smugglers.

But there was no time to work it out now, not with the tux reaching for the doorknob.

I shoved Ray at the hallway door, shot out the window and dropped our last grenade. Then I went pelting out after him, only to find him looking from the smoking elevator shaft to a horde of vamps coming down the stairs. And apparently deciding on the latter, because he yelled and started to charge like a crazy man before I grabbed his collar and threw him the other way.

"What good is that going to do?" he yelled. "It won't go up!"

"Good. Because we're going down," I said. And pushed him into the elevator shaft.

The grenade went off as we dropped, rattling the walls around us and sending a billow of smoke into the air over our heads. Which probably would have bothered me more except that I'd guessed right. The shaft didn't stop at level twelve.

And while that was great as far as the plan was concerned, a two-story drop isn't fun even when you're at your best, which I definitely wasn't. And even when you don't land in a mass of twisted metal from the elevator you just blew to smithereens. And even when you don't look up and find a bunch of bloody vampires glaring down at you from the doorway you just jumped out of. Although they worried me less at the moment than the smoking remains of the elevator on the floor above them, which was sparking and swaying and looking like it was about to—

"Fuuuuck!" Ray said, summing things up. Right before he started shooting at the vamps and I got to my feet, fell down, got up and started wrestling the doors open to level fourteen. There was a stabbing pain in my left calf, my ankle kept trying to collapse on the other leg, and then a vamp jumped down.

Right on top of me.

He was riddled with damage from Ray's bullets or shrapnel or whatever fighting had taken place before I got here. Or maybe all three. He was less a vampire at this point than a bunch of holes in the vague shape of a vampire, which didn't stop him from sinking his teeth into my shoulder.

I grunted in pain, because it hurt like a bitch. And worse, that's not an easy hold to break. The feeding instinct takes over as soon as they latch on, and the blood they drain gives them extra strength even as it weakens their victim.

Only that wasn't happening this time.

The vamp raised his head after barely a second, looking vaguely puzzled, like I didn't taste so good. Or like his body couldn't process what he was sucking out of me when he was no longer, in any sense of the term, alive. He just didn't know it yet.

I helped him out with that, slinging him against the concrete wall of the shaft, and then getting splattered with vamp parts when I shot him at point-blank range. I realized a bare second later that he wasn't one of Slava's, and that the splatter oozing down my face and cleavage wasn't burning me to a cinder. But I screamed anyway, because I felt like it, and because it wasn't like everybody didn't already know where we were.

And all of them were probably going to be here any second.

I grabbed Ray's arm. "Come on!"

And he tried. But he'd run out of ammo, and in the split second it took him to slam in a new clip, three more vamps dropped down the shaft, like dark bullets. They landed in a V formation, and the one in front grabbed Ray's other arm and jerked back, stretched him between us.

Everybody froze.

Chapter Twenty-seven

Ray watched me with big eyes, but didn't say anything. *I finally found out what it takes to shut him up,* I thought. And then I raised my gun an inch so it was aimed directly between his captor's eyes.

"Stop three with one weapon?" the vamp asked. "That would be impressive."

"Like your brains when I splatter them all over the wall."

I'd suspected I wasn't actually talking to the guy I was facing, who was looking a little, I don't know, *dead*, for an animated conversation. But I was sure of it when he grinned. "Not mine, dhampir. You forget—I am not there. You won't clip me this time."

"This time? Do I know you?" Because I didn't know many necromancers. And only one powerful enough to pull off something like this. But he was supposed to be as dead as the vamp I was facing, burnt to a crisp in a raging fire.

Or, you know, not.

It didn't look like I was going to get confirmation, though. Because the necromancer just shook his puppet's head. And the other two vamps did the same thing at the same time, like they were on a string.

So not really three pairs of eyes, then.

"No, no, none of that," he tut-tutted. "Not that I expect you to get out of this, but you have proven to be ... resilient. I think I shall save my explanations."

"Well, that's going to make this pretty boring."

He grinned wider. "I do not think you will find it so."

And yeah. Guy had the creepy-comments part of the villain thing down pat.

"But I did wish to thank you for letting us know where your uncle is hiding. He has proven elusive."

I didn't say anything, but that kind of clinched it. A decent number of people knew I was a dhampir, but damned few realized who my father was. Much less my uncle.

One did, though. One old, powerful necromancer did. Because he'd last attacked me at Radu's estate.

"He's like that," I said evenly.

"But now, I am afraid, our little game is over."

"Might want to do a recount," I told him. And dropped Ray's hand.

"W-what are you doing?" Ray demanded as he was abruptly jerked against the vamp.

"Sorry." I grabbed something out of my pocket. "But you know too much. I can't let them have you."

"Bullshit!" He stared at me, hurt and bewildered and mad as hell. "What are you—auggghh!"

He broke off in a genuinely terrified scream as I pulled my hand out of my pocket and threw something on the floor. Because I guess he didn't know I was out of grenades, any more than the vamps did. They dove, scrabbling around in the trash, and I raised my gun—at the ceiling. And shot out the last support cable on the elevator.

There was no time to get out, no time to do anything but grab Ray, who was looking at me like I'd gone crazy. And jerk him back into the one safe place as the whole burnt-out, messed-up, bloody elevator car came crashing down around us like a ton of bricks—or two tons, since that's what the thing weighed. The remaining part of the floor crushed the three puppets, even as the hole left Ray and me standing in the middle of a smoking ruin.

Staring at each other.

"What the hell did you throw?" Ray demanded after a moment.

"A spent cartridge."

He just looked at me some more.

And then the bell dinged and the part of the doors that was still intact slid open.

On a bunch of very pissed-off vampires.

"It's out of service," Ray snarled, and blew one of their heads off.

He jumped out, but I was still in the hole, thanks to the shaft extending below door level.

Which made it hard to see faces but put me on a line with everyone's legs. So that was what I targeted, shattering the kneecaps of every vamp I could see. And while normal vamps, much less masters, could have healed an injury like that on the run, these weren't normal vamps anymore.

And they weren't healing.

The horror-movie looks should have already clued me in on that, if my brain hadn't been occupied with freaking out. They looked like they did because their bodies, once damaged, stayed that way. Which was the first piece of halfway good news I'd had, and which explained why they went down like ducks in a macabre shooting gallery.

And why I started to think we just might have a shot at this.

Until Ray screamed again. It wasn't his usual panicked yelp, which I'd sort of gotten used to by this point. It was a full-on agonized shriek, maybe because two vamps had grabbed him and were doing their best to tear him apart.

I put a bullet in one vamp's head, discovered that was the last in the .45 and pulled the shotgun. And found that it was empty, too. So I jumped up, grabbed a knife and drove it into the vamp's shoulder.

Who didn't so much let go as have Ray wrench away with the hand and arm still gripping him. A punch in the solar plexus had the vamp doubling over, an uppercut had him straightening up again and then a boot to the stomach had him flying back into several others. And then we were stumbling through a heavy steel door because there was nowhere else to go, and barring it behind us.

Ray collapsed to the floor, screeching, and I beat the damned arm off him with the barrel of my now useless weapon. And then looked around for something to trap the gory thing with. And saw a row of familiar-looking steel cabinets lining one wall.

How appropriate, I thought, pulling a drawer open and tossing the hideous thing inside. I slammed it shut and didn't even hear it rattling around. Not too surprising— the front panel had to be a foot thick.

Nobody knew better than the Senate that "dead" is a malleable term.

"We're in the morgue," Ray said faintly, looking at the row of coolers with glazed eyes.

"Yeah."

"Fitting," he said, and tried to say something else, but got a mouthful of blood bubbles instead.

I jerked open his shirt, and yeah, he was messed up. Maybe because the damned vamp had bled all over him, and he'd been one of Slava's boys, so the result was akin to having an acid bath. Or because he'd landed badly, tearing his leg open on something that had left a wound ten inches long.

He'd managed to close it, vampire healing being what it was. But he couldn't replace the blood he'd lost, and he'd lost a lot. And now somebody was trying to cave in the door behind us and finish the job.

I ignored them and knelt beside him, having no time for my usual squeamishness. And shoved my arm under his nose. Not that it did any good, other than to have him give me another weird look, confused and hopeful and wary and shocked, all rolled into one. It made him look constipated.

"What are you waiting for?" I demanded.

"I—what?"

"Feed, damn it!"

He stared at my arm; he stared up at me. He didn't move. "Why are you doing this?"

"I lost one partner this week. That's my quota."

"Partner?"

"Well, you said it. I make a lousy master."

Ray just looked at me for another moment, and the constipated look got worse. And then his fingers closed over my forearm, slowly, delicately. "Yeah, well. I may have to rethink that," he said, and began to pull.

He wasn't biting, just pulling blood molecules directly through the skin. But I had to swallow and look away, not to show how much I really, really hated this. But I guess I didn't do so great, because Ray started talking again. Only this time I didn't mind so much.

"So I guess this makes me your sidekick, right?" he asked. "Like I could be . . ."

"Robin?"

He scowled. "I ain't no Robin."

"What's wrong with Robin?"

"What's wrong?" Ray rolled his eyes. "Two words: green Speedo. And he was lame. Batman was always having to save his ass."

I didn't say anything.

"Hey, I was doing okay before you showed up. All right?"

I decided not to comment on that, mainly because I hadn't been doing any better. "So Robin's out."

"Yeah, yeah. Anyway, I always figured I'd be more like . . . Q."

"Q?"

"From James Bond. You know."

I looked at him. "But Q had stuff."

"I got stuff."

"Yeah, but Q had *cool* stuff."

Ray scowled. "I got cool stuff," he told me. "But we shouldn't need it. This is Central! There's got to be a crap ton of defenses built in."

"Yeah," I said, glancing around. But I didn't see anything that looked particularly helpful. Just a few exam tables, some dirty footprints and the rows of coolers built into the wall.

One of which appeared to be vibrating.

And it wasn't the one I'd thrown the arm into.

Great.

"Oh, crap," Ray said, staring at it. Looking like a guy

who had just about reached tilt and couldn't take one more piece of bad news. I didn't feel any different, especially when I stood up and wove a little on my feet from light-headedness. But better to deal with whatever it was now, while it was trapped, than have it pop out in the middle of the coming fight.

I grabbed Ray's rifle and sidled up alongside him, trying not to think of some of the things the Senate could have on ice. Or that Ray had all of three bullets left—our last. Or that neither of us was exactly in shape for hand-to-hand right now.

I just nodded at him, gripped the pull, took a deep breath.

And yanked open the drawer.

Only to have something jump out at me, so blindingly fast that I couldn't even see it clearly. Something that grabbed the gun, jerked up the barrel and caused the shot I managed to get off to hit the ceiling. Something with a fan of dark hair, a porcelain fist, and a flash of turquoise eyes—

And lashes longer than mine, I thought, relief making me weak-kneed. "Radu!"

"Don't be ridiculous," he told Ray. "*I'm* Q."

I slumped against the side of the coolers. "You could have told me where you'd be!"

"Well, I didn't know, did I?" he asked, releasing the gun so he could climb out. "I had to improvise."

"So you put yourself in the *morgue*?"

"Zombies are stupid, Dory."

"But the necromancer controlling them isn't!"

"But even the best of necromancers can't control more than two or three puppets at a time. Or see through everyone's eyes. And whatever you were doing was keeping his attention nicely," Radu explained.

"Glad I could help."

Radu nodded regally. "The only inconvenience was that, once in, I couldn't contact you or any vampire in the area might have felt it. But I knew you'd find me." He gave me a stern look. "Although I must say, you took your time."

"You're welcome," Ray said sourly.

Radu glanced at him. "Why is he here?"

"He's my team."

The door shook as something all but buckled it from the other side. "And what is that?"

"The bad guys."

Radu put his hands on his impeccably tailored hips. "What kind of a rescue is this?"

"A do-it-yourself kind," I told him, my eyes lighting on a couple of fire extinguishers. "Where's the portal?"

"On the floor below, of course."

"Of course. And how do we get there?"

"There's a ramp at the end of the hall. But it won't do any good, I'm afraid."

"Why not?"

"Well, really, Dory." Radu looked at me impatiently. "If it were that easy, I'd have simply managed things myself, wouldn't I?"

"I dunno. Might have messed up your manicure," Ray muttered.

Radu ignored him.

"What's wrong with the portal?" I asked, dragging the fire extinguishers off the wall. And blessing the vamp paranoia about fire, because they were huge.

"There's nothing wrong with it. I just don't know the password."

I stopped, halfway to the door. "What?"

"*Shit,*" Ray said violently.

"What password?" I demanded.

"Well, for the shield, of course," Radu told me.

"Stop saying that. There's no 'of course' when I don't know shit about this place! And what shield?"

"The one designed to keep anyone from using the portal to gain unauthorized entry, of—" He broke off at my look. "Well, didn't you expect the Senate to have something? Considering how many enemies—"

"I expected you to know how to turn it off!"

"Well, I would, if I usually worked here. But I don't and the passwords are changed on a weekly basis. And, of course, I always have escorts—"

"Stop saying that!"

"Well, I'm sorry—"

"Save the apologies," I snarled. "You have to remember!"

"Well, I can't—"

"You have to! You were there when they said it!"

"Dory. One has staff so that one does not *have* to remember."

"Goddamn it, Radu, that's not good enough!"

"Well, just shoot me then!"

"I don't have any bullets!"

Only that wasn't actually true, I realized a second later. I had bullets; I had a whole box of them for a .44 Magnum. I just didn't have the Magnum.

But I did have the .410.

I grabbed it and pulled out the box of ammo, shoving loose bullets into my coat pockets and one into the autoloader of the gun. And yes, it fit. But that wasn't necessarily good news.

The problem was that Magnum bullets pack a whale of a punch, and not just on whatever they hit. They also put tremendous pressure on the barrel of the gun firing them. Including more than was recommended for a .410.

Like, *far* more.

Don't try this at home, boys and girls, I thought, and filled the autoloader with another three shells, which was as many as it would take. And wasn't that going to be fun?

"Shit, shit, shit." That was Ray again, only he was looking at the gun this time. Like he thought this was crazy, too.

"Can you hack it?" I asked him, as the pounding increased to a crescendo.

"I don't know. I don't know." He shook his head. "Somebody else's, sure, given enough time, but—"

"You're not going to have a lot of time," I warned him.

"How much are we talking about?"

I checked my ammo. "Two, maybe three minutes."

"What?"

I grabbed his shoulders. "You're the best. You said so. You've hacked portals all over this city—"

"But not the Senate's!"

"You've hacked some of the Senate's."

"But not the gateways!"

"Ray." I looked at him seriously. "We are not getting back upstairs, okay? I'm just laying it out there. We go through the portal, or we don't go at all."

"But you—you're good—"

"I'm not that good."

"But best-case scenario—"

"We die on a higher floor, that's all. There's just too many of them."

He stared at me.

"You can do this."

"I—you don't understand," he whispered. "I'm a screwup. I've always been a . . . I *can't*—"

"Yes, you can. You can and Radu's going to help you." I looked at him. "Aren't you?"

And it was a testament to how fucked we were that even Radu was looking serious. He nodded soberly. "I know the old passwords, and the kind of things they use. I can . . . guess . . . at this one."

"He can guess," Ray said faintly, as I pulled them over to the door.

And looked at Radu. "When you get through, tell them that I think we're dealing with Jonathan. Tell Louis-Cesare." Because he and the necromancer had a past, and he needed to know.

"You can tell them," Radu said quietly.

"Yeah, well. Don't wait for me. If you get the portal open and I'm not close enough—"

Ray said something really foul.

"I don't have time to argue," I told them, my head pounding so hard the room was pulsing in and out. "Just remember, all right?"

Radu nodded, Ray glared and I licked my lips.

And then I threw open the door.

The corridor was packed with vamps, but only two fell in—the ones who had been trying to batter down the door, presumably. And got heavy extinguishers shoved into their stomachs for their trouble. "Hold these," I told them, while Radu shoved them viciously toward the hall. They staggered backward and I pulled the peashooter. Which made a hell of a bigger bang with Magnum bullets in it.

Especially since I'd aimed for the extinguishers.

The cylinders exploded like white bombs, more spectacularly than I could have hoped for. Instantly, the entire corridor disappeared under the dense cloud of icy vapor, thick as a blizzard and bitterly cold. It boiled up everywhere, freezing the sweat in my hair and the rivulets coursing down my back, and frosting my eyelashes. But not before I glimpsed another bunch of vamps jumping down the elevator shaft.

It looks like the necromancer has lost his sense of humor, I thought.

And then somebody took my hand and jerked me in the opposite direction.

I knew we were moving lightning quick—Radu had grabbed Ray and me and he wasn't wasting any time. But it suddenly didn't feel that way. I'd had this happen occasionally in battle, when time seemed to invert itself, and the crazier everything got, the slower it seemed to go. I felt the ice crystals in my half-frozen hair hit my cheek softly as I turned my head. Saw a bunch of dark figures erupt out of the mist right behind us. Felt bullets tear through the air, so close one brushed the tiny hairs on my temple, a smooth, slick caress.

And then we hit the ramp and things sped up again.

I twisted out of Radu's grip. "Go! Go!" And pushed him and Ray toward the swirl of color I couldn't see because the corridor bent maybe ten yards behind me. And then I was slamming into position behind the wall.

Three vamps followed us around the corner, outpacing the rest by a large margin, like they just appeared out of thin air. My first bullets exploded the first one's head before Radu and Ray could get away, spattering them with a fine spray of mist, blood and snow. And thankfully it was one of ours, because nobody started disintegrating.

Then I took out the second, slammed the third's chin back with the barrel while I reloaded, and then blew half his chest away in the blast.

It didn't kill him, but it slowed him down enough that I was able to get a knife across his throat, sending the head lolling uselessly about on the neck. And him stumbling blindly back around the corner. And into three of his friends.

That would have been enough to make a human slow down or possibly rethink his approach altogether, but zombies don't think. They only obey, like the ones in the elevator shaft had. And the necromancer was pissed.

But I didn't have time to think about how screwed we were. I didn't have time to think about anything except loading and firing, so fast my fingers were a blur, so fast I could barely aim. So fast that, despite the distance, some shots went wild, hitting shoulders or torsos or legs instead of heads. Which slowed them down but didn't stop them because *zombies*.

And the necromancer wasn't stupid; he was keeping the ones with guns in the back so I couldn't steal any off the bodies. Not that I had the ammo for them if I did. A few shots and they'd be as worthless to me as rocks.

But there was one advantage, because it looked like Radu had been right. The necromancer couldn't control more than two or three at a time on anything other than autopilot. At least, those were the numbers that kept rushing my position, using vampire speed against me, while the others just kept coming, pushing steadily forward, getting into position to be of use to the master.

And they were doing a damn good job of it.

In less than a minute, I had to fall back to the first bend in the ramp, shooting another rush as I went, which hit the fairly steep incline and rolled down toward me, one of them still moving and trying to attack even as I pulled back, tripping over spent shells and trying to reload while walking backward. I somehow made it without falling on my ass, but it didn't help much. Because the ramp was shorter than the corridor, and every step they took meant that the next rush was faster.

The main group was going to be here any second, and that would be it, but I couldn't worry about it now. All I could keep doing was loading and firing. And trying to breathe through a fog of gunpowder and CO_2 and bloody mist, and trying to hear past shots echoing off the walls and the ringing in my ears, and trying to reload a gun that had grown so hot it was burning my fingers because the barrel wasn't meant to take this kind of pressure.

And then, suddenly, that wasn't a problem anymore.

I'd just shot two vamps through the head with one bullet, which had stopped that particular rush. But that piece of luck seemed to have bottomed out my supply. Because a vamp I hadn't seen came out of nowhere and grabbed the gun, moving in a blur I didn't understand until I looked up—

And *shit*.

One of Marlowe's senior masters, one I'd nicknamed Frick because he and his partner, Frack, had never bothered to introduce themselves, must have been sent along with the newbies. Because he tore the gun from my hands in a blinding motion and then I guess he slammed me in the head with it. All I knew was that I hit the wall, pain flashing through my skull. And for a second, all I could see was the corridor whirling around me—

And an image of Frick turning my own gun on me.

I dove for the nearest cover—another zombie—even knowing I wouldn't make it. Or that if I did, it wouldn't matter. Because a Magnum shell could tear through a couple of bodies, maybe more, especially at point-blank range, which is what this was—

Until the gun blew up in his face.

There was a blinding flash of light and a crack so loud that it even tore through the ringing in my ears, so loud that for a minute there I thought it had been a bullet. But the bullet had ended up lodged in the overheated, overstressed barrel, which it had solved by splitting it right down the middle.

Flaming fragments flew out everywhere, like a small bomb, setting the nearby vamps aflame. Frick was hit the worst, with what would have been flash burns on a human setting his whole arm alight. But he was a master, so he just kept coming, ripping the vamp I was using as a shield to pieces even as the flames spread up his torso and engulfed his head, those dead, burning eyes still staring into mine, while the maniac controlling them laughed and laughed—

And then someone was grabbing me around the waist—from behind—and time did the slo-mo thing again. Only I could hardly tell the difference, because it was Radu who had grabbed me, and he wasn't wasting time. Frick lunged for us both, Radu jerked me violently backward, and something blue and shimmery reached out and caught us like a fist.

And then we were gone.

Chapter Twenty-eight

The people were clustered together in a little knot far below, in the center of the cavernous space. It wasn't a storehouse like some of the others. There were large pieces of rusting machinery hunched in the shadows, like sleeping giants, visible against the starlight filtering in from a gap in the roof. The faint light also glinted off the crossbeams cutting through the air just below, like the one on which I was balanced.

A factory, then. But one long abandoned and unused, with no slick smell of oil or harsh tang of gasoline. Just dust and rust and rot. And a bright thread of life running through it from the grasses pushing up through the cracked concrete floor.

It was not echoed in most of the people, despite the fact that all of them were on their feet and some were quite animated.

If that had been true for all, they could have met mentally and saved themselves the danger of an assembly. But there were humans in the mix, hotter, brighter lights next to the cool colors of the vampires. And, to my surprise, even a few fey, burning like candles against the dark. And most humans and some fey are mind-blind, requiring a face-to-face meeting.

They did not appear to be enjoying it.

The air shimmered around them in wildly fluctuating colors, nervous purple, angry red, and the sickly yellow-green of fear, blending into a cloud the hue of a bruise that stank of suspicion, recriminations, panic. No, it was less like a bruise than a gathering storm, with the sparks like threads of lightning in the heavy atmosphere.

And then someone chuckled.

"You think this is a joke?" one of the vamps lashed out at another. He was a large man, swarthy, with hard black eyes and an off-center nose he hadn't bothered to try to conceal. He was dressed in jeans, a generic polo and a Windbreaker, the cheapness of the outfit belied by the expensive watch on one hairy wrist. He was one of the more powerful of the assembled vampires, third-level easily, perhaps a weak second. And he was angry.

"Yeah," another vamp said, crushing a cigarette under his heel. "Yeah, that's exactly what I think it is." He was smaller, slimmer, fairer, and dressed so well as to look almost foppish next to the larger man. But he was also the only one who rivaled him in power.

"Then share the gag. The rest of us could use a laugh!"

"It's the almighty Senate and their holier-than-thou lectures on the rules. Rules they don't bother to follow when it's easier to slit our gullets and dump us in a portal!"

"And that's what you call funny?" one of the other vamps demanded. His power swirled around him in a dark blue haze, but was shot through with streaks of the larger vampire's crimson. A senior servant, then.

"It's called irony, genius. Look it up."

"If it was the Senate," one of the fey said mildly, her light, lilting voice at odds with the vamps' harsh tones.

"And what is that supposed to mean?" the first vamp demanded.

"I think you know. That it could be one of us."

"Bullshit!"

"No, not 'bullshit,' " she said, making the ugly word almost musical. "We are competitors. A major force has been removed. Someone must fill that gap."

"I agree," said another vamp. Short, blond, innocuous-looking. And dressed like the teenager he was pretending to be. "Why should the Senate resort to murder when they can have a big trial, show how powerful they are? It's not like they ever pass up the chance."

"It isn't one of us," the first vamp said impatiently.

"You so sure of that?"

"Sure enough to invite you all to meet. If I thought one of you was some kinda modern-day Jack the Ripper—"

"Naw, he's on the Senate," someone said. And this time a few in the group gave genuine, if nervous, laughs.

"—would I have got you together? So you could kill me easier?"

"You might if you knew you were safe," one of the humans pointed out. A small, dark man, he matched the two others he'd brought with him closely enough that they were likely related. They were also all enveloped in a grayish tan smog, a muddle of colors for the muddle of different magical devices they were using, each of which had probably originated from a different source. It swirled around them like a borrowed cloak, not theirs, but serviceable enough.

Which probably explained why no one had yet tried to drain them.

"And exactly how would I know that?" the big vamp demanded.

"If the one killing everybody was you."

His servant's power flared, going from navy to cerulean in an instant. But just as fast, the crimson streaks of his master's power brightened, and then tightened around his like a clenched fist. The servant went pale and backed down, and the master glared at the mage.

"Shut it!" Arrogant humans were not popular, even when tempers were not running high.

But the human did not shut it. "No, I don't think I will," he said pleasantly. "And you should know that I've taken precautions. If I were to suffer some . . . unfortunate accident . . . on the way home, you would not outlast the week."

Unlike his servant, the vamp didn't noticeably react, other than to roll his eyes. Nor did his power even flare. He'd expected the accusation.

"Right. Sure." He flung out a hand. "I'm guilty as all hell. Only—if I got the resources to kill off fifty guys—fifty fucking good guys— in a couple days, why haven't I taken over by now? Why am I even talking to you? I should be *sitting at home, with a glass in my hand and a smirk on my face, waiting for my supermen to come tell me they plucked off another bunch of the competition. But do you see me at home? Do you see a drink in my hand?"*

"Then why did you ask us here?" the second vamp demanded. "I almost didn't come."

"But you did. Why?"

"Because we got a problem."

"And that's why I called you here. 'Cause I noticed something about those deaths. Not a single one was somebody into narcotics or magic or weapons or ordinary shit. No. They were all in our line of work. So I wanna know"—his glance went around the small circle—"which one of you losers brought in something he shouldn't have?"

The room exploded for a moment in violent outbursts of color and sound and recriminations. But I was no longer listening. I was watching one of the fey.

Occasionally, a tendril of someone's power would rub up against that of another's and spark in the air, like the words their masters were exchanging. One of the tendrils curling off a male fey rose a little higher than the rest, like a twist of smoke escaping from a fire, if smoke glowed from the inside. It could have been random, but I didn't think so. I stepped back, back, back, as it rose, silent, ominous, searching.

It did not find me.

But something else did.

"You do not listen very well."

The words were mild, unthreatening. But they were also something else that wasn't. They were in my head.

I spun away, kicked out and somersaulted backward, barely missing the searching tendril in the process. But barely is good enough. And landing steadily on the pitted metal beam was better, knife in hand and coming up—

And slicing only air.

I looked around, confused, because someone had *been there. And still was, for the next instant, the knife was plucked from my grasp—from behind. I spun again, and this time, I saw . . .*

Something new.

That was rare enough to make me pause, if only for a split second. But that was all it took. The edge of my own knife found its way under my chin, denting the skin over the jugular as it pushed up, forcing my head back with it.

"And I am not in the habit of repeating myself." *A rich masculine voice echoed in my mind as I absorbed the sight of a creature made of light.*

Hovering in midair.

It was why I had not seen him. I had been looking for someone behind me, balanced on the narrow beam as I had been, because people did not walk on air. But then, people did not burn silver bright against the night, either, like a fallen star. It was so intense he may as well have been invisible, because I could not look directly at him. But I did not think it would have helped.

I had never known anything to give off power like that.

"I understand your Senate's interest in these creatures," *he told me.* "But your habit of interfering in my affairs is becoming . . . annoying. It must stop."

I heard the words, but they barely registered. I was too busy trying to retain my balance against the waves of energy rippling over my skin. It felt like a consul. It felt like the end of the world. And then he moved closer and it grabbed me, coiling around me like a vise.

And I Screamed, putting all my power behind it.

The creature fell away, spiraling to the ground like a wounded bird, and I grabbed the beam, barely able to avoid following him. I teetered there for a long moment, breathing harshly, strangely light-headed and terribly weak. I hated feeling weak.

I was also beginning to hate new experiences, but they were becoming . . . fairly . . . normal. . . .

The dizziness in my head was going to reach my limbs soon enough, so I jumped, giving myself time to find the ground my own way. It was farther than I should have risked, but a vampire broke my fall. He didn't complain, being as unconscious as the rest of them.

And as the light being lying crumpled on the floor, not five yards away.

I knew I should leave. I was weak and he was powerful, and I had been lucky enough to catch him off guard. I shouldn't press it.

But the psychic scream would leave him unconscious for a few minutes at least, and I wanted to know . . .

Why he looked like her.

His light hadn't dimmed. It was spangling the weather-beaten walls and splashing the ugly floor with a pure white luminescence. He had landed on his side, huge wings spread out behind him, and I had been wrong. I had thought they were made of light, some projection of his aura, but they were real. Soft but strong under my hands, like the shoulder I finally grasped, and the face I revealed when I tugged him over.

A face with wide-open eyes, and dark irises reflecting my own startled face.

"That was a good trick," *he told me softly.* "Want to see another?"

And he slid into my mind, smooth as glass.

Lightning flashed, thunder boomed, and I sat bolt upright, sucking a harsh gulp of air into screaming lungs. I felt the bolt all the way through my head, a flash of agony across my temples, pain exploding behind my eyes. I didn't know where I was and it was pitch-dark and something was moving off to the side.

I screamed as it brushed my face, a whisper-soft caress that was somehow more ominous than a blow. And then I grabbed it, far slower than my usual speed, but quick enough to—

Capture the delicate sheer from over a window.

I couldn't see the window, couldn't see anything, but the silky fabric was cool with the night breeze, and smelled faintly of a soft drizzle falling somewhere outside. It was safe, it was nothing to worry about. It was just a stupid piece of fabric.

So let go of it, Dory, I told myself, as my clutching fingers stayed stubbornly shut.

I finally pried my fist loose and let the curtain fall back into place. My eyes had adjusted, and I could see a tall rectangle of dark gray with what might have been tree branches outside, whipping in the breeze. I decided to go with that thought, because I didn't think my heart could take another jolt. It was already threatening to slam its way through my ribs as it was.

Where the hell was I? I'd just been at Central with Ray and Radu. Hadn't I? And something had gone wrong, something about vampires and necromancers and . . .

God, my head hurt.

I lowered it into my shaking hands and closed my eyes, but it didn't help. Pieces of reality and the tattered fragments of a dream tumbled around in my mind like trash in a whirlwind, impossible to sort out. Particularly when I was in pain.

A lot of it, I realized, as my thudding pulse sent heated beams flashing back and forth between my ankle and my head, kindly stopping along the way to light up a dozen other hot spots around my body. Like a commuter train of pain. Or like a giant had grabbed me and twisted, trying to pull me apart—and damned near succeeded.

Everything hurt, from the wounds I could remember getting, like the throbbing ache in my calf from the piece of metal I'd fallen onto in the elevator, to the ones I couldn't, like the slick skin on my hands and arms, new and too smooth, like freshly healed burns. Or the pain in my jaw, as if it had been dislocated at some point and then shoved back into place. Or the bullet wound in—

I decided to stop counting.

But maybe that was why I felt so strung out, so unraveled. My cheeks were hot, and when I put a hand up, it came away wet. I rubbed the moisture between my fingers, confused. The pain wasn't *that* bad. And I couldn't remember the last time I'd cried. I couldn't remember. . . .

"Dory?"

My head jerked up, my heart in my throat, but I still couldn't see much. Just velvety darkness, seamless and unbroken, except for a wedge of misty gray seeping in through an opening door. It looked like maybe there was a treeless window in the next room and diffuse beams of moonlight were spilling over.

Just enough to limn the shape of a man.

I couldn't make out features, but I didn't need to. Didn't need the breadth of shoulder or the glimmer of liquid eyes that were all the faint light would show. He stepped beside the bed and the scent was enough, rich, sweet, and completely addictive—

"Butterscotch," I murmured, and reached for him.

"What?"

I didn't answer; I just kept tugging at him with all the strength of an anorexic puppy. But he came anyway, sliding a knee onto the smooth cotton sheets and then lying down next to me. He had on a robe, some silky thing. I pulled it off. I needed warmth and skin and—

Yes.

"You're not supposed to be awake," he told me softly. And then he tried to gather me up. But that wasn't what I wanted.

"No." I pushed at him, ineffectually.

"What is it?"

"Little spoon."

"You are hungry?"

I didn't answer, because he wasn't making sense. I just arranged him the way I wanted, needed. A big, warm, muscle-y pillow that I could drape myself around, like a child with a favorite toy.

A toy with a lot of hair. A mass like silk hit me in the face, making it hard to breathe. I pushed it up and over the soft mound of the pillow, and then snuggled up behind him, pressing my face to a neck that smelled like—

Yes.

Yes.

I took a deep breath, and sighed it out into his ear.

"Ah," he said, a hand covering the one I'd placed on his stomach, as I pulled him back against me. "I see."

I sighed again, my whole body relaxing. The pain, the confusion, all of it releasing, slipping away. Like the room. And then a thought occurred, right on the edge of sleep.

"If I'm not supposed to be awake, why are you here?" I mumbled.

"To be the little spoon."

And okay, that made sense.

I pulled him closer and fell off the cliff. And this time, I didn't dream.

Chapter Twenty-nine

I awoke a second time to sunlight seeping over the bed, which freaked me out until I realized that Louis-Cesare wasn't there. Nobody was. I lay in the middle of an orgy-sized bed without the orgy, or anybody for company except a butterfly flirting with the sheers over the window.

I was hugging a comforter, which was big and plushy, but a lot less satisfying than its owner would have been. And Louis-Cesare was its owner, I thought blearily, gazing around. Because if ever a room had matched the man ...

The walls were cream, topped by an elaborate molding done in little rosettes and curlicues and swags, to match the surround on a fireplace and the thin stripe on the blue Louis-the-something chairs in front of it. It would have been a little too precious, a little too feminine — except for the heavy curtains framing the tall French windows.

They were thick, midnight blue velvet, a huge stretch of it, easily twelve feet long, and not the synthetic stuff, either. Plush and buttery and vaguely medieval, they looked like they should have been gracing a Roman emperor's tent, or some barbaric king's chamber. Like the exposed beams in the ceiling and the rough planks on the floor.

The room reminded me of its owner, all genteel old-world manners on the surface but something more primitive below. I preferred the primitive, but I couldn't deny that the veneer had its charms. Like the view outside the windows, where garlands of fat white roses were nodding in a breeze. Possibly the one stirred up by the yellow butterflies that were feasting on the abundance, so thick in places that they looked like another kind of flower.

It was . . . well, it was stupidly beautiful.

It was also really weird.

Not the view, but the fact that I was looking at it. I'd expected to wake up at the consul's, despite the fact that that would not have been fun for so very many reasons. Like the last time I'd visited, when I'd thought my head was going to explode. The sheer number of vampires—strong, highly ranked ones—buzzing around in there had set my dhampir blood to boiling, and made me feel like a few thousand ants were running across my skin.

Bitey, angry ants.

But we'd been headed there, since as far as I knew, that was the only place Central's portal went. And since I wasn't dead, I assumed we'd made it. So why was I lying in a bed that smelled like Louis-Cesare? In a room that looked like it had been designed for him?

I didn't know, and right then I didn't care. Possibly because I was starving to death. Or maybe for another reason. I sat up and the world went swimmy, a slur of yellow and white and midnight blue that would have been pretty if I hadn't thought that maybe I was going to throw up.

I flopped back against the pillows, wondering what the hell? Because I hadn't been hurt that bad, had I? I couldn't remember anything after being plucked off my feet by Radu, but I didn't think so. And all the parts seemed to be accounted for, which was always a good sign. And while my rash of bruises had acquired another layer, I could live with it. I could live with a lot if the room would *just stop spinning already*.

But there was nothing to do except lie there and admire the view while it did its thing, until it finally got bored and quit. I stayed put a few more minutes, just to make sure, because puking in somebody's bed is not the way to get invited back. But my stomach felt okay all of a sudden. In fact, it was up and ready to rumble—or to yell at me to feed it something already.

I fell out of bed, because it was becoming kind of a habit now. And because the mattress gave me a support to help get me to my feet. And because my stomach was demanding that I follow the fragrance of frying butter that was seeping in from . . . somewhere.

It smelled so good that I was halfway to the door before I realized I was naked.

I grabbed the only thing available — a huge blue brocade robe that had puddled at the foot of the bed and then at my feet once I dragged it on. But it covered the bruises and it smelled better than whatever was coming from downstairs. Which was saying something, considering how hungry I was.

Then I went looking for breakfast.

I didn't meet anybody on the way, which wasn't too surprising. Judging by the view out the window, it was high noon, and the closest thing to hell in the vampire day. Most would be sleeping through it, waiting for nightfall, particularly the younger ones. Some of the masters were undoubtedly up for security's sake, but they must have been patrolling somewhere else, because I didn't see them.

I did see a ton of rooms that didn't look like they were involved in a reno. Not unless the default around here was "palace." There wasn't a half-painted wall or a drop cloth or a half-filled packing box in sight. Just room after room filled with fresh flowers and old paintings and sparkly chandeliers and rugs so luxurious that my bare toes were hardly visible over the nap.

And mirrors. Lots and lots of mirrors, each and every one showing me back an image that didn't belong here, that didn't go with any of the above. So it was kind of a relief to follow my nose down a small access stairwell and into a huge underground kitchen.

Where a couple of vampires were arguing over a stove.

"Eet ees an abomination," Verrell was saying, his entire frame vibrating in indignation.

"You haven't even tried it yet," Ray said, poking at something in a pan. He'd finally acquired some new clothes, I was relieved to see—just jeans, loafers and a bright orange polo, but far better than the jungle man getup. "And anyway, you're one to talk. If there was anything to eat around here, I wouldn't have needed to call my boys to—"

"Nothing to eat?" Verrell gestured around expansively at the long rows of cabinets and the walk-in pantry and the two fridges wedged in between old stone countertops. "Zere is everything!"

"Blood sausage. Tripe. Freaking pâté, man." Ray shook his head.

"And what ees wrong wiz zee pâté?"

"What is wrong? You take a duck, shove corn down its throat until it pukes, and call it cuisine?"

Verrell drew himself up. "You are zee Philistine," he accused, pointing at whatever was in the pan. "And zat ees not food. Zat ees not even—" He caught sight of me standing in the doorway. "Ah, zere, you see? She ees up and nothing is ready!"

Ray looked over his shoulder, and waved a greasy spatula at me. "Ignore him. It's almost done. Get some beer, will ya?"

He nodded at a couple of brown paper grocery bags on the counter, and I moseyed over to have a look. There was beer. Three different kinds. And snacks, most of which I didn't think were long for this world if Verrell's expression was anything to go by. Apparently, Slim Jims did not count as food, either. I tossed a brew at Ray and got one for myself, and sat down at a big wooden table, stomach rumbling.

"I'm introducing Verrell to the wonders of fried egg sandwiches," Ray said, flipping one of the components onto a piece of buttered toast. He slapped some Velveeta and another slice of toast on top and squashed the whole ooey-gooey mess with his spatula in the frying pan for a minute. Then he slid it onto a plate and set the plate in front of me.

I took it a little warily, because I hadn't known that Ray could cook. But it was perfect—the sandwich part crisp and buttery and the yolk just a little runny with the white browned around the edges. I dug in.

"See?" Ray said to Verrell, looking smug.

"She ees starving. Eet ees not a fair test."

"I think I'm gonna crumble some potato chips in the next one," Ray said, eyes narrowing. Verrell squinted back. And then suddenly the brown bags of goodness were gone, the pudgy chef booking it out of the kitchen with one under each arm.

"You're not gonna chase him down?" I asked a little wistfully. Because this was not a one-sandwich morning.

"Relax," Ray told me, and pulled up the edge of a kitchen towel. "I got more."

And sure enough, there was more faux cheese under there—but no potato chips. Too bad. It had sounded kind of intriguing.

Ray lost no time in getting to work on a replacement, and I went back to making room for it. So there wasn't a lot of talking until he slid plate number two under my nose. And sat down opposite me with one of his own.

"So, your guys are here?" I asked, butter dripping down my chin.

Ray saw and grinned. "Yeah. Louis-Cesare said he didn't mind, and they're safer here, at least till I can get things worked out."

"And where is Louis-Cesare?"

Ray rolled his eyes. "Getting his ass chewed, probably."

"Why?"

He looked up, halfway through a bite. "Oh, man."

"Oh, man what?"

"Oh, man, I knew you didn't remember."

"Remember *what*?"

"What happened after we came through the portal." He looked at me in amazement. "You don't, do you?"

No, and I was suddenly thinking that might be best. I didn't usually get a description of one of my blackouts that made me happy. Or, actually, ever.

But Ray was already telling me.

"It was crazy. I was trying to hack the portal and Radu was rapid-fire guessing passwords, and I'm not sure which of us succeeded but I think maybe it was both. Or maybe that thing is just so damned powerful—I mean, did you *see* it on the other end?"

"No."

"Oh, yeah. Well, anyway, it's huge. And when we broke the seal it just flat out *grabbed* us—and not just us, but half the guys in the corridor."

"It took the zombies, too?"

"Oh, yeah. Fire and all. And that damned master, you know, Marlowe's guy?"

Frick. I nodded.

"Well, he just didn't quit. He grabbed hold of you halfway through the portal and then we were tumbling around and Radu was trying to beat him off you but there wasn't time and then all of us shot out the other end. And I mean *shot*, like we must have gone two, three dozen yards, fighting and yelling and rolling and smoking." Ray waved a beer bottle around. "It was crazy!"

"I bet."

"And I hit a wall and almost got my head stove in, and by the time I got back to my feet, people were pouring in from everywhere and you and that master zombie were going at it and your eyes had gone all glowy and you'd ripped his damned *arm* off and were beating him with it—"

"I did not."

"Oh, yeah. You so did. Only it was more the fire that got him in the end. You round-kicked him and he hit the wall and kinda went *poof*, just crumbled—"

"And then that was it?" I asked—hopefully, because Ray's expression was kind of looking like that hadn't been it.

"Oh, hell no. I mean, it might've been, but you didn't stop. You were completely freaking out—just attacking everybody."

I stopped chewing, my appetite suddenly evaporating. "I went dhampir at the *consul's*?"

"Oh yeah. Big-time. It took like a dozen of 'em to

hold you down and I didn't know if even that was going to be enough. You kept throwing them off, and they were hitting the walls and flying into the air and—and you shoulda seen a few of their faces. It was priceless."

Yeah. Priceless.

I got another beer. "But that ended it, right? I mean, when the guards arrived—"

"Oh, the guards weren't doing shit," he said dismissively. "They tried, but the only people getting anywhere were the upper-level masters who saw you chewing up the guards and started lending a hand. Only they were having problems, too. And I think a few people were starting to get worried, 'cause a couple drew weapons. And then Radu started yelling at them, and then Louis-Cesare ran in—"

"Why was he there?"

"I dunno. He said something later about wanting to talk to your father—maybe about Zheng. I don't know. I didn't get a chance to ask him much, 'cause we came in different cars—"

"Came where?"

"Here. The estate he just bought. It's like eight miles from the consul's place, so it wasn't a long—"

"But *why* are we here?"

"If you'll give me a minute, I'll get to that," Ray said. "So he runs in, right? And this is where the crazy part starts, 'cause he begins helping you—"

"Helping me do what?"

"Attack the Senate guards." Ray saw my expression and nodded. "Yeah. Like I said—crazy. And then people really started freaking out, like they were more worried about you two than the damned burning zombies that were still wandering around. And more were spurting out of the portal every minute until finally somebody wised up and shut it down, and then your father showed up—"

"Great." So much for showing him how in control I was these days.

Or for getting rehired.

"And then he did something, I don't know what, but

you passed out. That was about the time the consul came in and ordered you to be taken to Lord Mircea's rooms— I guess he's got a suite there or something—'cause of course they're gonna want to question you about what happened at Central—"

"So why am I here and not there?" I asked, cutting him off. Because I really didn't want any more details.

"'Cause Louis-Cesare told her no."

I'd been halfway through a swallow, and almost choked. And then Verrell was back, clapping me heavily between the shoulder blades. Which would have been great, except the only thing I had stuck in my throat was surprise.

"What?" I finally managed to gasp.

"Yeah." Ray nodded. "That was kind of everyone's take on it."

"Is he *crazy?*" I hissed. "He's in enough trouble—"

Verrell made some kind of French sound, and went to get me some water. "He is Louis-Cesare de Bourbon," he said, with a Gallic shrug.

"He is an idiot! He should have left me there!"

"He should have done no such thing. You were hurt, no?"

"He's going to be hurt more!" The consul was a vindictive bitch, and that was on a good day. And if she'd just had her place trashed courtesy of us and the zombie brigade, it was fair to say that this wasn't a good day. And even if she overlooked that, getting contradicted in her own house—

Goddamn it. Sometimes I thought the damned vamp had some kind of death wish.

Verrell made another of those sounds, the kind that defy translation. But this one sounded amused. "Zey need him."

"They won't always! And if he keeps this up—"

"And he was right. Zee atmosphere, it was driving you mad. Had you woken up zere, you might 'ave gone the crazy again. And 'ow could you rest and sleep and heal in zat place?"

"I'd have managed," I said grimly.

"But why must you? He 'as beeg shoulders," Verrell said, clasping mine, his hands gentle. "And you are so small, so delicate. I cannot believe what zey say—"

"Oh, believe it," Ray said drily.

"I don't need him fighting my battles for me," I said, and shrugged him off.

The small chef looked sad. "But perhaps he needs."

"What?"

He sighed and licked rosy lips. "I nevair say this, but . . . you know about zee *salope, non*?"

"What?"

"Zat witch, zat—*Christine*." His expression looked like he'd just gotten in a side of beef crawling with maggots.

"I take it you didn't like Christine?"

The chef made a fugue of gestures, rolling his eyes, shaking his head, waving his hands. Like he was having a small fit. "Like? Like? *Non!* We do not *like*. She was no good for heem. She use heem. For years and years and—" He made another noise. "But he feel the guilt, you comprehend? He think she need heem. And she let heem think this way, to bind heem to her. But there ces no help. She ees mad. She wants only to harm, and she hurt heem, so much—"

"I don't see what that has to do with me."

"Do you not?" Verrell tilted his head. "But you must. He could not help her, *non*. No matter how much he tried. But you—"

Ray cleared his throat. "Uh, Verrell—"

I stared at the chef. "What are you saying?"

He beamed at me. "You are like her, you know. Pretty and petite and in trouble—"

Ray stood up. "Verrell!"

"—but not evil. He could not help Christine, but you—" Verrell nodded happily as the kitchen spun and the world came apart. "He can save you."

Chapter Thirty

"I don't think they tailored this thing right," Ray said, sliding me a look.

I didn't answer. I was staring out the window of a shiny black car—I hadn't even bothered to notice what kind—that was taking us back to the consul's. Her people had called an hour or so ago, rescinding my reprieve and ordering me back. For that interrogation, I assumed, although I didn't really care.

I didn't care about much right now.

Which was probably why I'd let Louis-Cesare's people dress me up like a French Barbie doll. And because it had been that or wear the damned bathrobe. And because I knew they weren't doing it for me. They were so happy to help their beloved master with his latest hard-luck case that it had been almost pathetic.

Damn, I thought. How bad had Christine had to be for a dhampir to look good?

"You, uh," Ray said, and then he stopped in order to tug on the jacket of his sharp blue pinstripe. Which regardless of what he believed, fit him perfectly. Just like the gray Dior-esque skirted suit I was in, complete with black kid gloves. Because it might be August and hot as hell, but damn it, they matched the outfit.

It shouldn't have surprised me. Of course Louis-Cesare had his own tailor. Of course he did.

"Um, so," Ray said again, as beautiful Adirondack scenery passed outside the heavily tinted windows, looking vaguely spotty because of the veil on my chic little hat.

Screw it. I took it off and tossed it on the seat, ignoring the disapproving look I got from the chauffeur. I'd just trashed the consul's house while half naked and shoeless. I didn't think a missing hat was going to scandalize anybody.

And I didn't care if it did.

"You know, it's like this," Ray said.

"Shut up."

"Yeah, yeah. I know. I should shut up. And I will—"

I laid my aching head back against the seat.

"Just as soon as I point out one thing."

Of course.

"He's a *cook*, all right? I mean, like he knows anything."

"He's a master. And he's been with Louis-Cesare for years."

"So? I'm a master, and I been with Cheung for years. And he never told me shit. And I doubt Louis-Cesare was having heart-to-hearts with the kitchen staff. The guy was probably just talking, you know? Like people do—"

"Like people who said they were going to shut up?"

"Fine. Be that way. But he's stupid about you. And it's not because he wants some kind of redemption for Christine."

"You don't get it. He thinks he killed her."

"He *did* kill her, but only trying to save her. And if he hadn't done anything, she'd have died anyway. Those damned dark mages had almost drained her dry."

"Dark mages she'd have never met if Louis-Cesare hadn't sent her to the guy who sold her to them."

Ray narrowed his eyes. "Are you blaming him? 'Cause he couldn't have known that. That mage was supposed to be legit—"

"I'm not blaming him," I said wearily. "I'm telling you how he thinks."

He'd tried to help Christine, a wandering, sick, clueless witch that his vampires had stumbled across, by seeing that she was nursed back to health. And by then sending her to a supposedly upstanding mage for training and integration into the magical community. She had been born into a human family who viewed magic as being of the devil, and had afterward been raised in a convent, of all things. So she'd had zero help in learning to control her gifts.

He'd done all the right things, but somehow it had all gone to hell anyway. The mage had been desperate for money, and had sold her off to some nefarious types who had promptly drained her of all her magic and most of her life before Louis-Cesare tracked her down. And realized that there was only one way to save her.

But she had been too far gone, and the Change hadn't worked. She'd become a revenant, a mad killing machine who had processed her early religious training into a seething hatred of all vampire-kind. She was completely mad and should have been killed on the spot. In any other family, she would have been.

Just like me.

A lot of vamps viewed dhampirs as basically half-human revenants, and believed the remedy for us both should be the same: a quick stake and a hasty bake in the nearest bonfire, just to be certain we never came back. But Mircea had let me live, just as Louis-Cesare had continued trying to save the unsavable. Just like he was doing now.

Well, at least now I understood his interest in me better. It had never really made sense before. Cinderella finding her prince made a good story, but it rarely happened like that in real life. In real life, we were attracted to people who were like us.

And no two people could be more different than me and Louis-Cesare.

"He's stupid about you," Ray said, glaring at me. "And you're stupid about him. You're both stupid about each other, which would be great if you weren't also really fucking *stupid*—"

"Ray."

" — and can't see it. That's all. That's all I'm saying."

And for once he actually did shut up. Maybe because we were turning into the long, curved driveway and were about to arrive. *And there's one good thing to come out of this whole lousy day,* I thought as I gazed out the window at the consul's marble wedding cake of a house. After last night, the sight of it should have been tying my stomach into knots.

And I didn't feel a thing.

Just like I didn't feel anything about Louis-Cesare. Nothing that I hadn't already dealt with twice over, anyway. Nothing that I hadn't known from the moment I met him, looking like a freaking Armani model who lived in mansions and had a personal tailor and didn't need a low-rent problem showing up and causing him shit on a regular basis. Shit that he dealt with because of some misplaced sense of noblesse oblige that I didn't need and sure as hell didn't want. He was going to get himself killed still trying to make it up to Christine, when it would never be okay because she was dead and gone and it was *over.*

Like any crazy ideas I'd ever had.

Ray said something under his breath that sounded like "stupid," which I ignored since the car had just glided to a halt. Leaving me with nothing left to do but get out, so I did. And walked inside without waiting for him because there was someone I needed to see.

A couple extra atmospheres hit me as soon as I passed through the front doors, but nobody else did, so I guessed I really was invited. It surprised me that there was no welcoming committee, probably armed to the teeth, but maybe they'd expected me to act like a lady and sit in the car until they arrived to open the door. Since they knew me, I couldn't imagine why they had made this assumption, but since I was out, I decided not to waste the free time.

A servant pointed me toward a ballroom that put Slava's to shame, a huge marble and mirror monstrosity that took up at least a third of the bottom floor of the main house. It looked like it could hold a few thousand people without anybody having to rub elbows. Only most of them were missing since it was midday and they wanted to be fresh for the fights tonight.

But not all.

There were a couple dozen vamps doing a Cirque du Soleil impression in and around the four great chandeliers that glittered a couple stories overhead. I was surprised they hadn't removed those, despite the lack of windows, since they looked like they'd probably cost a fortune. And since they seemed to be getting in the way.

Or maybe not. Vamps bounced off walls, somersaulted, hit the floor and sprang back into the air. And shed sparks off each other's swords as they clashed eight, ten, sometimes twelve feet off the floor. And yet somehow they managed not to so much as shiver the crystals on the consul's precious antiques.

It was very impressive.

It was also bullshit. Which was possibly why the guy standing by the far wall had a sardonic expression on his face as he watched his boys go at it. Zheng knew as well as anyone that real fights don't look like they were choreographed by Hollywood. Real fights are ugly, brutal and short.

But he didn't seem too interested in demonstrating that at the moment.

He was leaning against one of the mirrors that was pretending to be a window and didn't bother to straighten up as I approached. But since he also didn't reach for a weapon, I decided not to mind. And it wasn't like he didn't have plenty at hand. A table at his elbow held one of just about every type of blade weapon imaginable, all lined up and shining mirror-bright under the lights.

"Looking good," he told me, checking out the finery. "Although I gotta say, I liked last night's outfit better."

"You saw that?"

"Hard to miss." He nodded toward the far end of the room, where a huge mirrored wall reflected the antics of the acrobats.

"That's where the portal comes out?" I asked, my stomach sinking.

"What were you expecting?"

"I . . . hadn't really thought about it." But if I had, I'd have been hoping for a nice, dark basement or a se-cluded alcove—anything that wasn't front row center. Literally, since graduated rows of seating lined the room on that end. I supposed so the important types could watch the disembowelments in comfort.

Or watch me make a fool of myself up close and per-sonal.

"Not surprised you don't remember," Zheng said, grinning. "You were kinda busy."

"Hope I didn't interrupt anyone's performance."

"Naw, we were on a break," he said, as one of his guys, the albino with the spiky hair, dropped out of nowhere to grab another weapon from the pile. And to give me a hissing scowl before rejoining the fray.

Zheng laughed. "Ignore him. He's still butt hurt about the other night."

"Your boys are looking good," I said, since we were being so polite.

"They better be. They're doing an exhibition tonight, before the big finale."

"That's tonight?"

He tilted his head in acknowledgment. "Guess they thought it would be fitting, having my boys entertain. Seeing as how I'm about to join their precious Senate."

"I'm sure they're thrilled."

White teeth flashed in a tanned face. "I'm sure."

I glimpsed Ray standing by the ballroom doors, peer-ing in, and figured time was up. "I came to say one thing," I told Zheng. "I am not under Louis-Cesare's protection. I fight my own battles."

"That you do."

"You have a problem with me, you come and see me."

"Our problem wasn't with you," he said, glancing at Ray. Who had sidled in the door and was now slinking closer, back to the walls, wide eyes on the lethal perform-ers.

"Or with Ray," I said, sighing. Because somebody had to look out for him.

Zheng noticed the lack of enthusiasm, and grinned
wider. "Lord Cheung said to tell you that he finds Raymond to no longer be of interest."

"Why the sudden change?"

"Ask him. See what you get."

"I already know what I'll get."

Ray put on a sudden burst of speed and grabbed my
hand. "They're waiting. I was sent to get you."

"In a minute."

"No, *now*." He shot a look at Zheng. "And they know
where she is, don't think they don't. They know who she's
talking to. So if you're thinking about payback—"

But Zheng just rolled his eyes. "I think everybody's
agreed. Putting up with you is punishment enough."

"I don't know what the hell you're thinking sometimes,"
Ray hissed, as we followed a couple of helmeted warriors down a highly polished hallway. "After what happened last night, you just run off? Like they're not gonna
care?"

"I needed to talk to Zheng-zi."

"I needed to talk to Zheng-zi," he mimicked. "No, you
did not! You need to stay away from that guy. He's bad
news, okay? The whole family is."

"It's your family."

"Not anymore. And I'm not crying over the loss, all
right?"

I didn't answer because it hadn't been a question. And
because I was busy trying not to fall on my ass. The smart
gray pumps I'd been given to wear had a one-button
strap, fashionable pointed toes, and the red soles of a
famous design house. Unfortunately, they also had four-
inch heels and no traction, although that might not have
been a problem if the consul hadn't been aiming to im-
press.

Not me, obviously, but the senior masters in town for
the challenges obviously rated better. Including floors so
glossy they would have been blinding had any sun been
allowed to penetrate this far. As it was, they were slippery as hell, and falling wasn't an option.

After my unauthorized detour, four guards had been delegated to see to it that I reached my destination. And they weren't wasting time. I had the impression that if I slowed down, the two behind us would just flat out run me down.

And they could probably do it, too. Every one of them was a high-level master, second and third, at a guess. Which was why it was kind of impressive that the consul had persuaded them to wear the Halloween costumes they currently had on.

Of course, I'd heard that persuasion was her specialty.

Or maybe they just enjoyed dressing up like Roman centurions, complete with shiny gold breastplates, matching greaves, and helmets topped by huge red ostrich plumes. And they weren't the only spit-and-polish types in evidence. Pretty much everybody I saw had on some type of special attire, to the point that I decided I owed Louis-Cesare's people an apology.

This was not the kind of place where you wanted to be caught wearing sweats.

"They really went all out, didn't they?" Ray said, looking about in awe at the mirror-like surface of the marble.

Or maybe it was the silk banners framing every door that got his attention, emblazoned with the Senate logo in vibrant red and gold. Or the pairs of guards, rippling with power, who framed the banners. Or the high-arched ceilings, or the floors inlaid with the consul's personal emblem in lapis and coral, or the ancient statues and priceless vases stuck carelessly in niches, like bric-a-brac.

So, yeah. All out.

I couldn't recall being that impressed the last time I was here. But then, I'd been trying not to collapse under the burden of the power that practically permeated the walls. Which wasn't exactly fun at the moment, either, so it was a relief when we finally stopped in front of a door.

Which promptly opened in my face.

"When you said Jonathan, did you mean Waldron?"

I blinked at Marlowe, who had been looking worse every time I saw him and now appeared to have been dragged through a combine backward. He was still in the purloined clothes from last night, despite having had plenty of time to change. In addition to being ill-fitting, they were now dirty and torn and bloody. I stared at a hairy knob of a knee, which was poking through a rip on one trouser leg. He looked like a hobo.

"What?" I asked stupidly.

"The necromancer," he said, and then popped back inside before I could answer. I guess the idea was for me to follow him, which I would have—if there hadn't been two grim-faced soldier types still in front of me.

One of whom was flat out staring me down.

And fingering the pommel of the sword at his side. You know, the sword he looked like he'd like to show me personally just as soon as I gave him the slightest excuse. Like trying to push him out of the way, for instance.

It occurred to me that this level of animosity was a little unusual. Not if we had met somewhere at random—plenty of vamps have taken against me through the years for the terrible crime of existing. And that was without my occasional diplomatic failure. But here. Now. In the consul's home, within a short distance of a bunch of people who would not be happy to see me in pieces.

Not until they'd questioned me, anyway.

Of course, if he'd been among those whose feelings got hurt last night . . .

But no. He'd still have to have his lady's permission to provoke me, since anything else would end with him as target practice for the night. And, of course, she wouldn't give it. She was classier than that.

Sure she was.

He was still staring at me, and I hadn't really noticed before that the helmets had protrusions—nose guards and huge chin guards that obscured most of the face. But his stance was enough to make it clear that he was getting a little intense. Like he might not wait for that provocation. Which would be a shame, since if I was about to take a hit, I'd at least like to deserve it.

"I like your skirt," I told him, smiling gently. And felt the other two guards crowding up behind.

Yeah. This was going to be fun.

Or maybe not.

"Hey! Hell*ooo*?" Ray said loudly, squeezing between two masters, either one of whom could have squashed him like a bug. "We're here already. Where the hell's your manners? Let the lady through."

And weirdly enough, they did. Maybe because Ray had just alerted the whole hallway to the fact that there might be a problem. Or maybe because no one wanted the ignominy of attacking a guy three or four ranks below them. That didn't exactly add to a person's rep, not to mention that I would then have been within my rights to demand reparations for any harm done to my servant.

And I wouldn't be asking for cash.

Upper-level vampire customs were pretty intricate, but Ray seemed to have them down cold. Either that, or he'd gotten lucky. But, hey, I'd take it.

"That was pretty slick," I told him, as we passed down the hall, unimpeded.

"Don't talk to me," he whispered savagely.

"Sorry. I just wanted to say—"

"Nothing. Don't say anything."

I brushed his shoulder, and got the stare of death. "You had a fuzzy."

"God, just —I can't take you anywhere."

And then we were through.

Chapter Thirty-one

As interrogation rooms went, it wasn't bad. It looked a lot like the house I'd just left, but instead of French country, it was English library. Or maybe French library, since the carpets were Aubusson and the paintings were lacking hunting parties or dogs.

I plopped down in a big red leather chair, since it was the only one left. Ray appropriated the matching hassock. That left us facing the interrogation squad, who had arrayed themselves in front of the fire.

Mircea was sitting the closest, and looking as perfectly pulled together as always, or maybe that was just compared to Marlowe. Radu, on the other hand, was looking like nothing had ever happened. He had changed into a frothy confection of a shirt and champagne knee pants, the latter reflecting the flames that someone had stoked up, because this place was always cold. For once, he matched the room, while Mircea's dark, modern suit looked like an anachronism.

Louis-Cesare wasn't in sight, and for some reason—some stupid, stupid reason—I felt my stomach fall a little. And then he came through a side door with a tray of coffee, looking edible in a pale blue shirt and fawn trousers. And, suddenly I remembered all the reasons I had for not wanting to see him.

Sometimes I don't make sense, even to me.

But it wasn't really an issue right then, because Marlowe had no intention of allowing time for small talk.

"May we begin?" he said crisply, and threw something at me.

I flinched, but it stopped in midair, a little flash of light that resolved itself into the rotating head of a man. It wasn't a flat, computer-like image, but solid and 3-D, like one of Madame Tussaud's pieces had suddenly come to life. It was creepy as hell.

Of course, considering the subject, that was a given.

The pale gray eyes, white-blond hair and manic expression would have been disturbing enough—Jonathan didn't even try to look sane. But it wouldn't have mattered. The guy could have been the friendliest-looking on the planet, and the memory of the last time I'd seen him, and of his face as he pushed his fingers and then his whole hand into Louis-Cesare's side, would have been enough to send a bad taste flooding my mouth.

It didn't seem to be making Marlowe too happy, either. His previous neutral expression had slipped into a sneer of distaste. "Is this the man you meant?"

"I—yes."

"How certain are you?"

"He didn't name himself, but I don't know a lot of necromancers. And I've only ever wounded one."

"Wounded?"

"He said I clipped him."

"Well, I thought you did more than that," Radu said, sounding aggrieved. "The bastard was supposed to be dead months ago!"

"He is not so easy to kill," Louis-Cesare said quietly.

He was watching the revolving head entirely without expression. As if he wasn't looking at the face of the man who had kept him prisoner for months, taking him to the edge of death night after night, in order to drain him of every last bit of magical energy. And then feeding him up, coaxing him around, relying on Louis-Cesare's abilities as a powerful first-level master to bring him back from the brink.

But only so he could do it again. And again. And again.

And yet Louis-Cesare just stood there, as calmly as if we were discussing the weather. I didn't think I could do that, if I were him. In fact, I wasn't feeling so calm anyway. I had a real, deep-seated desire to grab that smug, revolving face, to sink my fingers into that pasty flesh, to squash it between my hands and watch it explode like a—

I suddenly noticed that everyone was looking at me strangely. But nobody said anything. I sat back in my chair and folded my hands.

"If that is all she has for identification, he may well be," Marlowe told Radu sourly, after a moment. "It's damned little to go on."

"He wasn't in a talkative mood," I said, keeping my voice calm. "But he knew Radu was my uncle. And not many people do."

"And it is a favorite device of his," Louis-Cesare added, "to feign death. To take on a new name and begin again, throwing off his pursuers. He is Waldron this century; when I knew him, he was VanLeke."

"This century?"

"He was born, as far as we can ascertain, sometime in the Middle Ages," Marlowe said shortly.

I blinked, thinking I'd heard him wrong. "What?"

Louis-Cesare nodded. "I do not know the exact year, and am not certain that he does. But he mentioned once, while I was his prisoner, that he remembered his father taking him to Cordoba when Spain was still under Muslim rule."

"But . . . that would make him what? Five, six hundred years old?"

"At least, yes," he said, his voice steady. As was his hand when he handed me a cup of coffee. "I would say older. I did not get the impression that the Reconquista was threatening the city at the time. He and his father had fled there specifically because it was quiet."

"Cordoba was retaken in 1236," Mircea said. "Meaning he could be eight hundred or more, assuming he was telling the truth."

"He had no reason to lie to me," Louis-Cesare said.

"At the time, he did not believe I would ever leave his hands again."

Everyone went silent for a moment, out of respect for what he'd been through. Everyone except me. I wasn't interested in mourning what had happened. I was interested in making sure it didn't happen again.

And it could, if one damned necromancer was still alive. Louis-Cesare had fallen into Jonathan's hands because he'd traded himself for Christine, to be drained in her place. And Jonathan had never forgotten his source of unlimited power or ceased trying to get him back.

"I don't understand," I said harshly. "I know it's possible to extend life with magic, but *that* much?"

"It can be done," Marlowe said grimly.

"Then why doesn't everyone do it?"

"Because not everyone wishes to go mad!" He made a savage gesture, and the disembodied head disappeared.

He was looking a little tense, so I looked to the others for an explanation. Which Radu was happy to provide. 'Du loved to lecture.

"Magical humans are symbiotic creatures," he told me pleasantly, crossing one silk-hosed leg over the other and sipping at his coffee. "Unlike vampires, or normal humans, they derive energy from two different sources. In effect, they are human talismans, feeding from the natural magical energy of the world as well as from food."

"I thought they made magic."

"It would be more accurate to say that they process it, transforming it from its natural, wild form into something they can use. Some of them are better at that than others, of course, and those who are tend to live longer. They can rely more on their magic as their human bodies begin to fade. It's quite fascinating, really."

"The stronger the mage, the longer the life," Ray said, quoting an old saying. Which was a mistake, because it reminded Marlowe that he was there.

"You. Out," he said, hiking a thumb over his shoulder.

"Why? I was there—"

"And you gave your statement last night. I don't know what the hell you're even doing here."

"Supporting my master."

"Supporting—she is *not* your master!"

"Yeah, well. We're in negotiations."

And suddenly something shifted behind Marlowe's eyes. The rich brown went dark and flat and dead, and I put a hand on Ray's arm because he did not need to make a wrong move right now. Not that I thought it was too likely. He'd frozen in place, the bones in his wrist going completely rigid. It was like I was gripping a statue.

Until Marlowe said: "Get. Out."

Ray got out.

Sometimes he could be smart.

There was a momentary lull while coffee cups were refilled and Marlowe presumably choked down his desire to kill everyone in sight.

"If it's something that they can do naturally, then why does it drive them mad?" I finally asked.

"There is nothing natural about what Jonathan does," Louis-Cesare said.

But Radu shook his head. "A mage consuming someone else's magic is no more unnatural than a human taking drugs. The problem is the amount."

"Jonathan is overdosing?" I guessed.

"In a way, yes. But he doesn't really have a choice at this point. It is possible to extend a mage's life, but it requires a great deal of energy. And as the years pass, the amount needed grows, as their human side breaks down and they become more and more dependent on magic to survive. Considering his age, it is safe to say that Jonathan receives all or almost all of his life energy from magic, and his body cannot possibly produce so much on its own."

"But it's still just magic."

"Yes, but it isn't *his*, you see. And mages are supposed to feed off a mix of food and magical sources. When they start feeding their bodies *only* magic, it throws off that balance. And when they begin feeding them multiple different *types* of magic, since it is not usually possible to obtain as much as they require from a single source, and when some of those types are not even human . . ."

"They short-circuit their brains."

"Something like that. It's very much like a human taking too many drugs, and mixing them in ways they weren't designed to be mixed. It rarely ends well."

"None of which is the point," Marlowe said severely.

"The point is, where is he getting it?" Mircea said.

Marlowe nodded. "He is hemorrhaging magic every moment, simply by existing. Not to mention any spells he may do, and if he was the one behind last night's fiasco—" He threw up his hands. "Even were he on the premises—"

"He wasn't," I replied. "At least, that's what he said."

"He was likely telling you the truth. He is not one to risk his own neck," Louis-Cesare said bitterly.

"Which means he was having to project over a distance," Marlowe said. "Which requires even more energy. Someone, somewhere, is feeding him a great deal of power. A very great deal."

"Which may well be why we haven't heard from him," Radu pointed out. "He doesn't need Louis-Cesare if he is being fed, so to speak, by someone else."

"But why?" I asked. "What does a smuggling ring need with an ancient, crazy necromancer?"

"This isn't about a smuggling ring!" Marlowe snapped.

Mircea agreed. "Smugglers work best in secret, trying to hide their tracks and avoid the authorities. They rarely provoke them, and certainly not in such ways."

"Then who does?" I asked.

"Someone who wants to make them look bad."

"What?"

Marlowe nodded. "That could be one point of this whole fiasco—making us look like fools. We finally persuade the senates into an alliance for the war—an alliance, I might add, that is paper-thin and hanging by a thread—"

"You think this is about the war?"

"What else? If someone wanted to make us look weak, they could hardly do better than to kill our agents at will, to attack us in our own base—"

"We think that's why they—whoever they are—

needed Jonathan," Radu explained. "To attack Central. There's not too many ways in there, you know."

"And then there's the matter of what they did when they broke in," Marlowe said, and threw something else into the air.

This image was flat, black and white and grainy. A security camera feed, I supposed. It hovered in the air like the other, only it was transparent enough that I could see Radu blinking at me from the other side. I shifted in the chair slightly, putting the wall as a backdrop, and saw the main doors at Central. Frick was being buzzed through at the head of the group of Slava's boys, who filed into the lobby and—

"What are they doing?" I asked, stunned.

"Slitting their throats," Marlowe said, as the group did exactly that, almost in unison.

And, as anyone would, the vamps at the desk ran forward to try to stop the slaughter—and ended up being part of it. Frick threw something on the ground, sending a wash of smoke into the air that obliterated the camera feed for a moment. And when it cleared, the guards were gone and the gaping hole I had found when I arrived was in their place.

It looked like a pit out of hell, the edges still smoking and on fire. Which didn't stop Jonathan's zombies from jumping down into it in orderly rows. They were completely fearless, completely without hesitation, despite the fire and vamp flammability and the resistance they were about to meet. I watched them, mesmerized, the hair standing up on my arms, the eerie quiet making it all the more disturbing.

"They bypassed the main defenses by going through the floor," Mircea told me. "And then proceeded to kill everyone they came across. The acid compound in their veins made it easy."

I nodded. The fight with Slava had given me a heads-up—I had known to stay out of range. But the vamps at Central hadn't. And even if they won a fight, the tainted blood that sprayed all over them would begin eating them alive, slowing them down, and then the next group they met, when they were already confused and weakened and in pain—

I shuddered. And apparently I wasn't the only one.

"Turn it off," Radu rasped.

"She needs to see—"

"She's seen! Turn it off!"

The staticky horror blipped out, like an old-fashioned TV signal, and Radu got up and went to the bar. Which is how I ended up with a glass of very fine port.

It didn't help much.

"They killed every single person there?" I asked. "I thought maybe someone . . . was hiding. . . ."

"No," Louis-Cesare said. "Only Radu and Ray survived, thanks to you. Those creatures killed everyone else."

There was a short silence. Very short, because Marlowe wasn't in the mood for introspection. Marlowe was in the mood for blood.

"But that is all they did!" he rasped. "They didn't even bother to turn off the damned cameras! We've watched the whole event now, several times, and there was no copying of files, no attempt to access the vault, no prisoners liberated. They came in, they killed everyone, the end."

"Why?" I asked, bewildered. "And how do you get a whole group of people to die for you? Especially like *that*?"

"We believe they were likely already dead when they arrived," Mircea said quietly. "And that the throat slitting was merely a diversion. As to the why . . . It is possible that the idea was to give everyone a reason to question whether the alliance should stand. And, if it does, under what leadership."

It took me a moment to process that. "You're saying this could be someone on *our* side?"

"It is possible. There were a number of consuls who wished to lead the alliance. They were less than pleased to have ours put in charge. And if she is made to look weak enough . . ."

"But the other side in the war has even more reason

to oppose our union," Marlowe pointed out. "If they've found out about it, they'd want to crush it quickly, before it gained us an advantage. Not to mention—"

"No," Mircea said stubbornly. "This is a vampire plot."

"We don't know that!"

"It's too intricate for anything else."

"But . . . wait," I said, my head starting to hurt again. Which was what usually happened when politics were brought up. "Jonathan is with the Black Circle. He's a dark mage."

"And we are fighting the Black Circle."

"Yes, but . . . the Black Circle has always been involved in the slave trade with Faerie. And wasn't that the assumption we were going on—that someone is trying to control the smuggling trade now that Geminus is out of the picture? Why not them? It would be a lot easier to bring things through for the war if they controlled most of the portals."

"Yes, but Dory," Radu said gently, "it's a question of ability, not of desire."

"Come again?"

"The Black Circle can't manage the sort of communications shutdown we saw last night," Marlowe said bluntly. "No mage can."

Mircea nodded. "Telephones, computers, that sort of thing—yes. Merely activating the more powerful wards would take care of that. And if not, there are spells. But no spell can shut down a vampire's ability to communicate with other vampires."

"No spell you know of."

"No spell at all," Marlowe said flatly. "There are limits to magic, as with everything else, and we know what those limits are. We have lived with the mages—and fought them—for centuries. We know what they can do and what they can't, and they cannot do what Radu described last night!"

'Du nodded. "I don't pretend to be all that powerful, but I *am* second-level. And I was, er, motivated. Yet I could not reach anyone."

"You reached me."

"Yes, once you came inside the sphere of whatever influence was being exerted. But not before that. You didn't hear me outside."

"No."

"And yet, believe me, I was screaming my head off."

"That bring us to the question," Marlowe said grimly. "Who the hell is working with Jonathan?"

"A senior master?" Radu offered, looking at his brother.

"It would have to be someone more powerful than Radu in order to block him," Mircea agreed. "Someone with significant mental abilities."

But Marlowe didn't seem to like that idea. "There are only a handful of masters in the world capable of that kind of demonstration."

"That we know of—"

"And I do not relish approaching them and accusing them of treason! Not at any time, but particularly not now."

"It would not serve to strengthen the alliance," Mircea said drily.

"That's why you wanted Ray gone," I said, catching up. "You're worried about Cheung."

"Not Lord Cheung himself, no. His gifts lie in other areas. But his lady—"

"I thought he and Ming de didn't get along," Radu said, talking about the head of the East Asian Court.

"That is the story," Mircea said wryly. "But it could have been manufactured. And Ming-de is a powerful mentalist. I was selected to go to her court as our ambassador over a dispute some years ago, because she had managed to influence everyone else we had sent."

"Ray isn't a spy," I told them. "Cheung has been trying to kill him!"

"And perhaps now he is trying to use him."

"Then why did he want him back? Ray said Cheung wanted him to help bring in something big. But Zheng just told me that they don't need him anymore."

"It could be unrelated," Marlowe said. "Unlike Lord Mircea, I am not convinced that this is part of our problem. Cheung might have been planning to bring in a shipment at one time, but is now attempting to distance himself from the smuggling issue."

"Why? What changed?"

"What changed is that more smugglers have been turning up dead. My men have been trying to question them, but finding only houses full of corpses."

"Someone is tidying up loose ends," Louis-Cesare said.

"But that someone doesn't have to be a vampire," Marlowe pointed out.

"What's the alternative?" Radu asked. "There's just not that many creatures who—"

"Æsubrand," I cut in. "He was there. At Slava's."

"Yes, but he's fey," Radu protested.

"So?"

"The fey are known for their abilities with the natural world, not with the mind."

"Caedmon has mental abilities."

"Yes, well. That's Caedmon," Radu said sardonically. "We are talking about—"

"His nephew, who could have inherited all sorts of—"

"Could have does not mean did."

"He's *fey*. It's possible."

"Don't let your animosity for the creature cloud your judgment," Mircea told me. "It's possible that he was there for an entirely unconnected reason."

"Such as?"

"Such as the fact that the fey are vindictive little shits," Marlowe said impatiently. "Slava was rumored to import fey slaves—"

"Something he's been doing for years, and nobody has seemed to care."

"—and then there's the weapon you found last night, which had fey magic written all over it. Or so it appeared."

"You didn't examine it?"

"I might have, had you managed to bring the thing back!"

"Or you might have asked Æsubrand about it, had you caught him," Louis-Cesare murmured blandly, handing Marlowe another cup of coffee. And getting a blistering glare in return.

"Wasn't it at Central?" I asked.

"No," Marlowe said shortly. "Of course, considering the amount of acid leaking about the place, it could have melted into a puddle before we got there. But we didn't find any stray .45s inundated with a fey spell."

I shook my head. "I think it was just a regular gun. I used standard ammo in it without a problem. It seemed to be the bullets that—"

"Yes, but since we don't have it, we can't know for sure, can we?" Marlowe asked sweetly.

One of these days, I swore to God . . .

"So you think it was some rare fey thing we're not supposed to have?" I asked, gritting my teeth. "Because we're talking about bullets here, not some rune or—"

"I have no bloody idea! I was merely pointing out that Æsubrand could have had a reason for being there that had nothing to do with us. And indeed, that was likely the case, since he was attacking Slava, not helping him!"

And okay, he did have a point there.

"But it doesn't matter because he isn't the one we want!"

I blinked. "Then who is?"

"Oh, no, not again." Radu sighed, and got up to get himself another drink.

"What?" I asked.

"Have you forgotten?" Marlowe asked. "The Irin."

"Now who is letting prejudices cloud judgment?" Mircea murmured.

"But what possible interest would a demon have in human smuggling?" I demanded.

"For the last time, this isn't about smuggling!" Marlowe snapped. "And if that creature's performance at Slava's was anything to go on, he is perfectly capable of causing the kind of mental disruption—"

"To what end?" Mircea broke in. "The demon lords—"

"Have every reason to keep us disunited. The stronger we are, the more restrictions we place on them. They didn't like our alliance with the mages, and I doubt they enjoy seeing a strong, united vampire coalition any better!"

"And to that noble end, they send one operative?" Mircea asked drily, looking like a man who had discussed this about all he wanted to.

"They sent an *Irin*, and you know what they—"

"Um," I said, and stopped.

Everyone turned to look at me. I sighed. I'd been hoping to keep that particular piece of less-than-stellar work out of this, but I should have known. It just wasn't how my luck was going.

"He helped me at Slava's," I admitted.

"What are you talking about?" Marlowe demanded.

"The charm broke," I said bluntly. Because how I phrased it wasn't going to make a difference.

"We knew it was likely to do that."

"Yes . . . but not twenty stories up."

"*Twenty*—" Mircea broke off, but his expression said volumes. I was *never* getting rehired.

So I might as well come clean. "I'd be dead now, but he caught me," I told them. "And if he was working against us, why bother to do that?"

"To ensure that you returned to Central with Slava's corpse," Marlowe said, glaring at me. I don't know why. For messing up, for poking holes in his pet theory, or just because he felt like it.

I glared back for the last reason. "Yeah, except Slava wasn't needed. His boys were doing a pretty good job of trashing the place all on their own."

"And yet, you were let in—"

"—to lead them to 'Du. The question should be why did they want him?"

We all turned to look at Radu. "Well, I don't know," he said crossly.

"We've been through this," Marlowe said savagely. "We've been through all of this, over and over, and none of it gets us anywhere! Radu knows entirely too much about too many things to even begin to guess—assuming it was his knowledge they were after in the first place."

"Well, what else would they want him for?" I asked.

"Thank you very much," Radu told me.

Marlowe said a bad word. "We can speculate all bloody night and get nowhere! There are too many suspects and too many possible motives. We don't need guesses; we need to *know*. And there is only one way to do that."

And suddenly everyone was looking at me again.

Shit.

Chapter Thirty-two

"You want me to go back under, don't you?" I asked. "To see if I remember anything else."

It was kind of obvious. It wasn't like I got invited to these high-level meetings often. I should have known they were leading up to something.

But Mircea surprised me. "Not . . . precisely."

He and Louis-Cesare exchanged a glance, and for some reason, it almost looked like Louis-Cesare was the aggressor. His lips tightened, his brows lowered, and he looked . . . well, he looked pissed. Which was not an expression Mircea was accustomed to getting from many people.

Even weirder, he didn't object. He just sat there and took it, without saying anything, at least not audibly, and without glaring back. It was bizarre.

But not as much so as when he broke the eye contact to look at me. And his expression then . . . I'd never seen that expression. Not from Mircea. It was . . . raw. Pained. Almost . . . afraid.

Why would Mircea look afraid. Of me?

"There is something your father has to tell you," Louis-Cesare said forcefully.

Mircea didn't say anything.

"We discussed this," Louis-Cesare prompted after a moment.

"Discussed me?" I asked. "When?"

"After your . . . after the events in the garden," Louis-Cesare explained. "I was . . . confused."

"About what?" I asked harshly. My little descents into madness weren't my favorite subject. "You'd seen it before."

"Yes, but you had not. And you were afraid—"

"I was not."

He just looked at me.

I looked back. I wanted another topic. "If you want me to try to go back to the wharf, to see if I remember anything else—"

"Yes, but not yet," Mircea said, finally speaking.

"Why? I'm willing to take the risk." I hadn't enjoyed the last trip, but Marlowe was right. We needed facts and we needed them now.

"I . . . am not sure you are." Mircea got up and went to the bar, but then didn't fix himself anything. He just turned around, his hands on the polished wood behind him, his face expressionless. And looked at me. "I am not sure that you know what the risk is."

I glanced at the others, but didn't get any help. Everyone else was looking at Mircea. Everyone but Louis-Cesare. He was looking at me, but he didn't say anything.

Obviously, this was Mircea's story to tell.

And he told it.

"Do you remember when we met for the first time?"

I just stared at him. It was pretty unforgettable. I'd tried to stab him, mistaking him for his brother—the man who had ordered my mother's execution.

Mircea had fled the country after becoming a vampire, horrified at his transformation and afraid that he would hurt the ones he loved—including her. He hadn't known she was pregnant at the time he left, and found out only when he returned—and saw an unmistakable resemblance in the features of the child trying to gut him. He had gotten the story out of me—what little I knew. That she had gone to ask for help from the local lord, who was the brother of her missing husband.

And been brutally murdered for her trouble.

"Of course you do," Mircea said, looking at me. "It was a stupid question."

He started to pace. If I hadn't known better, I'd have

said he was stalling, nervous. But Mircea didn't get nervous. Or if he did, he never showed it.

"I took you to Italy," he said, staring out the window. "I didn't know what else to do. Vlad knew it was only a matter of time before I discovered his treachery, and he intended to kill me before I could kill him. If I had had a master, a family, to rely on, that would not have been a problem. But I did not."

I nodded. Mircea had been cursed with vampirism, not made through a vampire's bite, and therefore had been on his own from day one. I often wondered if that was what had made him as chary as he was, as loath to trust anyone. Maybe he'd never had a chance to get in the habit.

"I don't remember Italy," I told him.

"No. You wouldn't." Mircea had wiped my mind of all things related to Vlad, so that I wouldn't go back and try to finish the job. And for some reason, it had taken a ton of other memories as well.

"I do," Radu said suddenly. "We had a lovely villa. Not that I was there then, of course, but later . . ." He trailed off as everyone looked at him. "Er, I . . . I think I shall go get some fresh coffee. Kit?"

"I don't want coffee," Marlowe said shortly.

"Yes, but I could use the help."

"Get a servant to help you."

"Kit—"

"Don't bother," I told Radu. "He's probably got the room bugged, anyway."

Marlowe didn't bother to deny it.

"Why are you telling me this?" I asked Mircea.

"It is . . . somewhat relevant to our current situation. But if you would prefer privacy—"

He looked almost hopeful.

"I would prefer to know what you're talking about."

Mircea never talked about the past—or almost never. I was getting what I could, while I could.

Before he changed his mind.

"Very well. We went to Italy," he said, and then he stopped. But this time it was apparently just to gather his thoughts, because he continued a moment later. "We didn't have a villa," he told me. "Or a palazzo, as we were in Venice at the time. I had had to leave Wallachia with very little money, and much of that had been spent in the years before we met. But I made a tenuous living as a gambler—"

"A *gambler*?"

An eyebrow arched. "That surprises you?"

"No," I said slowly. I could see it, strangely enough. Mircea always sounded like the voice of reason, a sea of calm in comparison to Marlowe's tempest. But he took chances when he needed to. He just didn't gamble on the small stuff.

"I discovered that it is easy, when you're a vampire," he said wryly. "Although I did not make as much as I would have liked. Venice was not so large in those days and word spread when someone never lost."

"But we did okay," I guessed.

"Financially, yes. But there were . . . problems."

"What kind of problems?"

"The usual. I was a foreigner, and although Venice was a port city, there was a certain amount of prejudice in the human community. And among the vampires, there were always those wishing to add a lone, masterless vampire to their fold, if they thought he might be of use, whether he wished it or not. And then there was the difficulty of monitoring the situation back home from a distance, and health concerns with my old tutor, who was with me, and all of the things about my still relatively new condition that I had yet to figure out, and—" He looked up. "And then there was you."

"What about me?"

"You were manageable, at first. Hostile at times, and suspicious, isolated in a new city where you did not speak the language, and resentful of the clothing I made you wear and the manners Horatiu was attempting to instill."

"Like eating with a fork."

"They were not common at the time, thankfully. Although you were no better with spoons, preferring to merely tip the bowl up and drink from it."

"You had a little barbarian on your hands," I said, embarrassed. Although I wasn't exactly polished today.

"It was understandable. You had lived on your own, survived on your own, for years. It was not your manners that concerned me."

"It was that I was dhampir."

He was silent for a moment. "No," he finally told me. "It was that you were dying."

I blinked at him. "What?"

"I did not understand the problem, at first," he said quietly, sitting on the hassock Ray had vacated. "I barely knew what a vampire was in those days, much less a dhampir. But something was clearly wrong. You were not eating. You were not sleeping. I woke more than once to find you missing, and had to scour the city for you. One time I found you, unconscious, surrounded by wild dogs. Had I arrived a few moments later—"

"I was sick?" I asked, confused. Because I was never sick.

"No. Or, rather, not in a human way."

He got up again, as if he couldn't stay seated, and then sat down again, as if he didn't find anything helpful in pacing. "I finally came to realize that the two sides of your nature were out of balance, and competing with each other. Your vampire half was growing in power as quickly as mine had, like one who was on the fast track to becoming a master. But your human side . . . was human. It was becoming swamped by the other half of you, subsumed, undermined. And, I was very much afraid, would soon be completely overcome."

"Why not let it be?" I said harshly. God knew, I'd tried, more than once.

But he was shaking his head. "You are not vampire, Dorina. You are not human. You are both and neither. Just as the mages go mad trying to feed from only part of their nature, you cannot exist without your vampire half. And it cannot exist without you. You need each other. But you were also killing each other. Or, to be more precise, it was killing you. Not intentionally, but that did not matter. It was growing too strong, too fast, and you could not keep up."

"But obviously, I did."

Mircea got up again. I felt like yelling at him to make up his damned mind, because the constant movement wasn't doing my nerves any good. But I didn't. He didn't look like he was having fun with this, either.

"I tried to find help," he told me. "But there was no one to help. No one who knew enough about dhampirs to tell me anything. Everywhere I went, the message was the same: she will not live. They never live. Do her a kindness and end her life, before the process drives her mad—and she ends the lives of everyone around her!"

His eyes flashed amber bright, as they usually did only when his power was surging, and his face stuck on a snarl. He looked angry, suddenly, furious, as I'd rarely seen him. I didn't envy whoever it was who had told him that.

I didn't say anything, but he turned on me anyway. "But you were *Mine*. My child. And I would not give you up."

"What did you do?"

"I saved you. In the only way I knew how. You needed time. Time for your human half to mature, to catch up with your vampire side. But as things were, you would not have that time, would never get that chance."

"Mircea. What did you *do*?"

He licked his lips, and then he came out with it. And it was nothing I'd ever expected and everything I'd always known. "I . . . separated you. Not physically, of course, the twin halves of your nature share a body. But mentally. I used my growing abilities with the mind to . . . put a barrier between the two parts of your nature, of your consciousness. So that you were not awake, not aware, at the same time. So that you did not interfere with each other's development."

I stared at him, but he didn't pause. Didn't give me time to absorb it. As if he was afraid that if he stopped talking, he wouldn't start again.

"And then I erased the parts of your memory that were flawed. Where cracks had started to form because of your shared consciousness. At first, I thought that you would lose only a few months, the worst ones, when you had begun to deteriorate so quickly. But once I began, I realized that the mind is not so simple. That memories are not so simple. They are connected in strange ways, intertwined because of a myriad of things—a smell, a sound, a taste. I had to take out an entire month of your memories from when you were a child, because the sound of a ship's bell, ringing outside during one of your fits, had had the same tone as a church bell in the city you had been passing through at the time. . . ."

"You told me that you erased my memories because of Vlad," I said numbly. "You told me—"

"Yes, and that was not a lie. But removing your interest in gaining revenge on my brother was a relatively minor thing. It did not require erasing years of your memory. But gaining you an element of peace, of breathing space, did."

"Why didn't you tell me? Why did you *never* tell me?"

"I thought of doing so, countless times—"

"Then why didn't you?" I asked, incredulous. "You didn't think I deserved to know?"

"Of course you deserved to know! Some of the memories I had had to remove were of your mother. I would never have deprived you of those! Never—"

He turned away.

"I was afraid," he told me, after a moment. "I was . . . this wasn't something I was taught how to do. I did not have a master whose advice I could ask. I had done what I had done out of desperation, and it had worked. But for how long remained in question. And the mind is resourceful. The more information it has, the easier it can build bridges around and between damaged areas. The faster it can put the pieces back together. The whole idea was to give you time—"

"But I've had time. I've had *five hundred years*. Didn't you think—"

"Yes! I thought. A thousand times, I thought. But you were alive. You were sane. Not entirely happy, perhaps, but better by far than the vast majority of dhampirs who have ever lived. I was mortally afraid to do anything to upset that balance. But then you managed to find a way to do it yourself."

It took me a moment to understand what he had just said, because my mind—what was left of it—was still reeling. "Fey wine."

He nodded.

I licked my lips. "Claire thinks . . . She said it was like shutting a valve on an engine, and letting pressure build up."

"An apt analogy. And one I realized too late. It was not until after the events on the wharf, when I went into your mind to retrieve your memories, that I understood . . . and the cracks are too wide, too large, for me to repair. I do not know how much longer the dam I put in place would have lasted, but . . . it is crumbling now."

"Crumbling?" I had been staring at my hands, but now I looked up.

"But you did it once," Radu interrupted. "Surely—"

"She was a child then, Radu! She is one no longer, and she is powerful."

"Well, yes, but so are any number of others, and you've never had any difficulty with—"

"Radu." That was Kit.

"Yes, well. Still."

"Dorina has inherited my abilities, to an extent," Mircea said, meeting my eyes, and then looking away. "I do not know to what extent, for they have never been given proper expression. That requires a whole mind, something she has never had."

"That's why I never . . . I didn't gain anything . . ." I said, thinking of the master powers that all vampires acquired, if they lived long enough. Some more than one. But I had never developed any of them.

"Yes. That is why, when cracks appeared in the separation between the two parts of you, you began to be able to mind-speak. You could not do it with your vampire half isolated, since it is that part of you which carries the ability."

I was silent for a moment, but it was useless. I couldn't even begin to process it all, or even to form the right questions. Except for one. "Why are you telling me this now?"

Mircea didn't say anything, but Marlowe spoke up. "You think this is why she can't remember what happened after being attacked, don't you? That she slipped into her vampire nature. That it's that part of her that holds the memories we need."

Mircea nodded. And then he looked at me. "I do not wish to do this. I cannot repair the damage to the partition I put in place, but I can keep from causing more."

"And this will cause damage?"

"I do not know. Neither does anyone I have asked. But even if not, there is the other part of you ..." His eyes met mine, and they were grave. "And I do not think you want to meet this part."

"Why?" Louis-Cesare asked. "I have met her. She is Dory—"

"She is Dorina," Mircea corrected sharply. "She does not use the diminutive. Ever. And she is dangerous."

"What first-level master is not?"

"First?" Marlowe said sharply.

"My contact with ... Dorina ... has been limited," Mircea said. "She does not trust me. I am what she preys upon. But yes. That would be my estimate of her power."

"A mad first-level master," I murmured. "Haven't we been here before?"

"No." That was Louis-Cesare.

"Yes. I suppose I have more in common with Christine than I thought."

"You are nothing like Christine!"

"Funny. That's not what my victims say."

"What victims?"

"Or, I guess I should say, Dorina's victims. She piles up quite the body count."

"As do we all, when need be. If you had not 'piled up' the bodies last night, my Sire would be dead. You are efficient at killing; but that is not in itself an evil. Or else every nation on earth with an army is evil. Every police officer who has killed in the line of duty—"

"Police kill to protect!"

"And how do you know that she—that you—do not?"

"Stop calling me that! I am not her! I don't kill for sport."

"And again I ask, why do you believe she does? When have you seen her—"

"I don't see her! I've never . . . almost never . . . seen her."

"Then how do you know?" he persisted. "You wake up surrounded by bodies, but you were not awake when they were attacked. You do not know what the provocation may have been. Only that they are dead. Had Dorina suddenly woken in Central last night, after you went in, might she not have thought—"

"That's not the same! I had no choice!"

"And perhaps neither did she. We won't know until we speak with her—"

"I'm not going to speak with her!"

"Then I will," Louis-Cesare said simply.

"What?"

"I have done it before. I have spoken with her once, perhaps twice—"

"When—?"

"The last time was in your garden, two nights ago. I made a mistake, and she was . . . displeased. . . ."

"She wanted to attack those fey," I said, remembering. "Wanted to . . . to find out if she could beat them."

"And who would not? Many of our people, given the chance, would like such an experience. So little is known of them . . . a new enemy, whose abilities are not entirely, or even mostly, understood. Whose skill set may equal our own, and whose lives are long enough to have been—"

He stopped, probably because everyone was staring at him.

"I did not say I intend to do it."

"That would be best," Mircea said, drily. Then he looked at me. "It is your choice. We need the information, and it is possible that Dorina may have it. But I will not force the issue."

Marlowe started to erupt, and Mircea's voice sharpened. "It is your decision. Your risk. It can be no other."

Radu cleared his throat. "There is, well, one thing," he said, diffidently.

Mircea looked at him.

"I . . . have never met Dorina. She does not know me, doesn't have any reason to trust me. And without trust, an anchor is useless."

Louis-Cesare looked at me. "I will go," he said simply. "I will be your anchor, if you will permit it."

And then everyone looked at me.

Again.

Chapter Thirty-three

I stayed in the chair. Mircea settled back on the hassock, facing me. I don't know quite what I'd been expecting; probably something like last time, just falling off the world with no warning and no transition. But it didn't work quite like that. I pulled my feet back to give him room, and then looked up.

And found his normally dark brown eyes blown completely black.

It threw me for a second, because the usual color change that comes with his power goes in the opposite direction—to bright, light-filled amber. But now it was more like looking into two inky pools. Except even ink reflects some light off the surface and his eyes weren't doing that. It looked disturbingly as if they weren't even there anymore, just dark, dark nothingness behind his lashes, like the fog boiling over the memory cliff in my mind.

And then all up around me, as if the room had caught fire.

And then closing over my head as he caught my wrists, to keep me from standing up in alarm.

And then gushing out in front of me as I walked through it and out the other side.

I stumbled slightly, having to adjust to suddenly finding myself standing instead of sitting, and to being on a dark wharf instead of in a cozy library. But it only took a second, and then I was looking at the same scene as before. Except for the fog.

Instead of evaporating, it ruffled out over the ground, swirling around me and then surging outward, until the whole scene was covered with it, waist-high. Tendrils reached even higher, as if grasping at the dark, cloud-filled sky, the intermittant stars, and the yachts bobbing at anchor. Or at the pier, sitting quiet and blood-free.

Obviously, the fun hadn't started yet.

"Looks like we're early," I said—to nobody. Because when I turned around, Louis-Cesare wasn't there.

But something else was.

I blinked stupidly at it. And okay. Maybe I'd been a little hasty with that same-scene comment.

Because that? Wasn't the same at all.

I was looking at a huge expanse of gray stone, smooth in places as if wind and rain had scoured the corners, and sharp in others where centuries-old chisel marks remained visible. It looked like a thousand walls I'd seen, edging roads or circling towns or doing wall-type things all over Europe. None of which had included slicing through the middle of an SUV on one end and a yacht on the other.

But that's what this one was doing, bisecting the harbor from parking lot to waterline and beyond. I stared upward, feeling dizzy because the top stones were maybe fifty feet high. *I separated you,* Mircea had said.

Yeah. That was one way of putting it.

Goddamn, no wonder I was crazy.

But amazingly enough, the size wasn't the strangest thing about the wall-that-shouldn't-be-there. Neither was the gaping gully in the middle that looked like someone had driven a giant-sized bus through it. Or the jagged bits that had burst out ahead of the explosion, the interiors of which failed entirely to be gray and rocky and stone-like, opting instead for pink and pulsing and ... alive.

No, what had my skin tightening all over my body was the strands of something viscous and gooey and glistening that had burst outward with the wall, leaving a forest of vine-like pinkish filaments behind. Some were lying warped and twisted in the rubble, impossibly damaged.

Others had looped back onto the nearest stone, attaching themselves to it and then sinking inside, only to jumble up underneath with nowhere to go, like varicose veins.

Except for a few. They had neither died nor found a new foothold, but they were also unable to bridge the large gap in the wall. As a result, they were just waving about in the air like horrible seaweed in a nonexistent current.

Or like clutching hands, I thought, stumbling back a step.

And straight into someone's arms.

"It's all right," Louis-Cesare told me, grabbing my arms preemptively.

"All right?" I shook him off, and took a step backward. Because no way was anything about this all right.

"It will be." He looked past me for a moment, at the wall, but didn't seem as horror-struck as I was. Maybe he'd been warned ahead of time; he'd said that he and Mircea had talked. Or maybe it wasn't quite the same when it wasn't your insanity on display.

Bizarre, whacked-out, really gross display. I wrapped my arms around me, and told myself that the cold I was feeling was just the fog. Or my imagination, which seemed to be healthy enough.

Glad something was.

"Where were you?" I demanded, harsher than I'd planned.

He looked back at me. *"Quoi?"*

"You weren't here. When I arrived," I added, because he was staring at me blankly.

"We left at the same time."

"Well, we didn't arrive at the same time! I've been here for five minutes." Maybe more. It felt like I'd been staring at that wall for a while.

Louis-Cesare didn't seem to like that response. "You are sure?"

"Well, it's not like I have a watch!" I said, only to have one appear on my arm.

It was gold, with a little mother-of-pearl face, and it

wasn't mine. It sort of reminded me of one Claire owned, but didn't wear anymore because the whole transformation thing was tough on jewelry. But that didn't explain what it was doing here.

"What the—" I began.

"It is your mind. You can have what you like," Louis-Cesare informed me. Which was great, except that what I'd like right now was a door out of here.

"Is there a way for us to speed this up?" I asked tightly.

He didn't answer for a moment. His head was tilted to the side and he had a distracted look, like he was trying to talk and listen to the TV at the same time. "Your father says he is having . . . difficulties," he finally told me.

"What kind of difficulties?"

"Maintaining the connection. He says we need to hurry."

"That's what I just said," I pointed out. "How do I fast-forward this thing?"

"I . . . he . . . is not sure. He was trying to put you in at the time of the blackout that you experienced earlier. But as an observer. You should have been able to see and report back, without having to experience everything again. Or talk to anyone."

"Sounds good," I said fervently.

"Yes, but it did not work. He does not know why."

"That's . . . reassuring."

"It is not, in fact," he said, staring upward. And not looking happy. He was glowering at the sky as if Mircea was up there somewhere and could see him. I didn't say anything because I kind of hoped he was right.

Unfortunately, that gave me no one to talk to, and my eyes got bored. And started meandering around. And they seemed fascinated by the sickly pinkish light coming from the gash that was flooding the dark landscape like a searchlight.

I don't know why. It's not like they could see anything. It was bright enough, but just like a real searchlight, it didn't work so well in fog. Except to highlight strange bumps and coils and glimmers in the mist, sending Rorschach-like monsters rearing silently on every side.

I suddenly got a severe case of goose bumps, and jerked my head around, sure that I'd just glimpsed—

Nothing.

The only thing behind me was a long shadow of a streetlight, flickering in and out of sight in the churning mist.

I stared at it for a moment anyway, even after I'd identified it, because I suddenly found that I didn't want to look around anymore. Didn't want to see something more substantial than a shadow. Didn't want to know what might have come through that gap.

Because something sure had. And given what the wall probably stood for in my not-so-original brain, it wasn't hard to guess what. And even though that was kind of the point of this expedition, now that it came down to it, I found that I wasn't so keen on meeting that other part of me. That baleful, warped, diseased part that I'd done my best to ignore and avoid and generally suppress the hell out of all these years.

And I was pretty okay with maintaining the status quo.

But my brain, my so-messed-up yet so-helpful brain, had other ideas. It kept showing me glimmers of something slouching through the mist, flickering at the very edges of my vision but staying low to the ground. Hiding. Taking cover, but still visible in glimpses, like the light post's shadow. Hunched and misshapen glimpses that watched me with terrible, demon red eyes.

I couldn't see it very well, since I couldn't seem to force my eyes to focus. Or my head to turn; it suddenly seemed to like this patch of ground just fine, thank you. But what I could see didn't look human.

Of course it doesn't, I thought, feeling sweat drench the body we shared, and my skin start to ruffle. I wanted to scream and flinch and gyrate like someone who had had a horrible insect land on her arm. Only this insect wouldn't come off because this insect was *me*, was part of me, was crawling through the mist like it usually crawled beneath my skin. Always stalking, never leaving, never letting me just live, just *be*, like a normal person because I *wasn't a normal person* and thanks to it I never would be and I hated, *hated*, HATED—

"Augghh!"

I threw out an arm when something reached for me out of the fog, sending it staggering back.

And then belatedly recognized Louis-Cesare.

"Are you . . . all right?" he asked me warily.

"Of course I'm all right," I snapped, staring around, angry because I wasn't. Not enough, anyway. I could feel it, a warm, red tide simmering away somewhere in the back of my mind—or what was left of it. But it couldn't reach me, couldn't help, couldn't even get close.

Because there was something in the way.

Something that was chilling my flesh and making my breath come faster.

Something that felt a lot like fear.

And I couldn't afford that. Anger was heat and light and split-second, adrenaline-fueled timing. But fear was not. Fear was cold and dark and debilitating and paralyzing. People who were too angry in fights sometimes lost, but people who were too afraid always did. Curling up into a ball instead of attacking, begging for their lives instead of fighting for them.

And I wouldn't go down like that. I wouldn't lie down and just be absorbed by this . . . this thing. Just like I hadn't centuries ago.

I wouldn't let it win.

I'll die first, I whispered viciously, too low even for a vampire's ears. *I'll die and I'll take you with me.*

Louis-Cesare had glanced around again. But now he was back to looking at me. "I am not," he told me flatly.

"What?"

"I am not all right. There is something wrong here."

A laugh burst out of me before I could stop it, high and a little crazed. "You *think*?"

He frowned. "Yes, I think. I also think that I am taking you out."

"You know what's at stake."

"I also know what is at stake for you."

"How?" I demanded, bewildered. "*I* don't even know."

And I didn't. I didn't know what would happen if—when—I and my other half had a long-overdue reunion. Didn't know what would change.

Maybe nothing. Maybe it would just be a repeat of that whole scene in the garden—scary for a few minutes, because yes, yes, I could admit now that Louis-Cesare had been right, I'd been scared to death that night. But I hadn't died, hadn't changed, hadn't gone any more crazy—not that I'd noticed.

But then, I wouldn't, would I?

Of course, that had been all of a few seconds, and this was likely to be a lot longer, but the idea was the same. If the other hadn't hurt me, maybe this wouldn't, either. Maybe I was getting all worked up about it for absolutely nothing.

Only it didn't feel like nothing.

It felt like whatever was out there, whatever was stalking me through the mist, was malevolent. Hateful. Fearful. Like it didn't like me any more than I liked it. Like it would like to remove me, kill me even.

Like it wasn't any more comfortable with me inside *its* skin than the reverse.

And that wasn't so surprising, was it? How many times had I thought, *If only it would just die*? If only it wasn't there anymore, maybe I would be okay. Maybe in time I could learn to be normal, or could learn to fake it well enough for a regular life. *My* life, instead of the bastardized time-share we had going on.

Would it be so strange if it had thought the same?

"Dory!"

I jumped, and looked back around at Louis-Cesare, who was now a few yards off to the left. He'd either moved or I had, unconsciously following currents in the fog. And wasn't that just a great thought to have right now?

"What?"

"I called your name several times; you did not answer."

"I was . . . distracted." And then I got a good look at his face. "What's wrong *now*?"

"I don't know why, but . . . I am having difficulty communicating with your father."

I glanced around. "No shit."

"What?"

I licked my lips and looked back at him. "Remember what Mircea said. I inherited his mental abilities, but they're carried on her . . . on her side of the brain, so to speak. They're under her control, not mine."

"But what does that have to do—"

"Just that if she wanted to block him . . ."

"You believe she is more powerful than your *father*?"

"Not . . . necessarily," I said, not feeling real sure about that. "But they're almost the same age, and he's had to divide his time between a lot of different things over the years. Had to wear a lot of hats. She hasn't. She could specialize—"

"But even so—"

"—and it's *her* brain. She knows it better than he does. She has to."

"She—" Louis-Cesare stopped. "Why are we speaking of her as a separate person? There is no *she*. There is only *you*."

"Sure about that?" I said, glancing around again.

"Yes! She is . . . you are . . . the same. In either form. You are—" He broke off, as if trying to put the impossible into words. And seemed to be having some trouble with it.

Join the club, I thought grimly. It was my head and I didn't know what the hell was going on. And why did I think I wasn't going to like it when I figured it out?

"Dorina . . . she is you as you would have been, had you been born fully vampire," he finally said. "Therefore there are . . . variations . . . in approach, in the way you think, react, fight—"

"So, virtually identical, then."

He frowned at me. "In essence, yes. In your sense of honor, your humor, your innate goodness—"

I laughed.

He frowned more. "It is true. In all the ways that matter, you are the same."

Yeah. That was what I was afraid of.

"Now, please. Stay close while I attempt to contact your father again."

"Okeydokey."

I wasn't going anywhere. But the thing was, I didn't think I had to. I had the definite feeling that whatever was out there was coming for me.

And I guessed it shouldn't have been a surprise.

I'd never thought about it before, but maybe I cramped her style, too. Maybe she resented being woken up in the middle of a nice rampage by someone too horrified to finish the job. Maybe she hated my weakness, my humanness, as much as I hated her vampire-ness, her viciousness. Maybe instead of a crawling bug, she viewed me as a more insidious kind—a leech, taking her strength, her energy, her prowess and squandering them. Living a life no master vampire would have considered for so much as a moment, with no family, no servants, no *respect*.

Yeah. That probably galled.

If there was one constant in vampire society, one thing that defined it more than any other, it was hierarchy. Everybody knew their place and they damned well stayed in it. Unless they were prepared to fight—possibly to the death—for a higher one.

Some people thought it was worth the risk, because status decided everything, from who you served to who served you. From who would consider you for an alliance to who would—or would not—marry you. From where you could live to what jobs you could get to who went through a freaking door first. Status was everything.

But dhampirs didn't have status.

Dhampirs weren't even on the scale.

I wondered how she'd felt about that. How she'd liked having even baby vampires look down on us, watching them insult us, denigrate us, relegate us to back doors and servants' entrances "like the rest of the trash." How she'd felt knowing that we—that *she*—were perfectly capable of destroying the lot of them.

And how long had it been before that resentment had bubbled over, from hatred of them to hatred of me? The cowardly, weak, *human* part of her that played by the rules others had set and scavenged around the edges of vampire society for whatever crumbs it would toss her, like a diseased dog? No wonder she went berserk from time to time, killing everything in sight out of sheer rage that she couldn't kill the one she really wanted to.

Me.

Only she could now, couldn't she? I took another look at that ruined wall or synapse tangle or whatever the hell it was, and realized intellectually what my crawling skin had known from the first glance. The fey wine had let a tiger out of the cage.

And it was hungry.

Chapter Thirty-four

All things considered, it really wasn't much of a surprise when Louis-Cesare suddenly looked up, his face puzzled. "There is some—" he began, and stopped.

For a second, he looked like an old-fashioned TV signal going on the fritz. All the color drained out of his body and it blurred into jagged lines for a moment. And then he simply winked out.

It was almost a relief.

She'd taken enough from me, through the years. Family, friends, *sanity*. Any chance of belonging anywhere.

She wasn't going to take him, too.

"He's not like us," I whispered, into the rolling fog. "He's honest and stubborn and stupidly brave. And he thinks we're the same. But we know better. Don't we ... *sister*?"

There was no response.

What a surprise.

I glanced at the wharf. I'd seen it as it was now, lying pristine and clean, waiting under the moonlight for the scene that was about to unfold. Louis-Cesare had seen it afterward, smeared with blood and ash and what remained of my onetime partner. What we needed was what had happened in the middle, and only one person I knew of had it.

I melted into the fog, circling around toward the wall's bloody gash.

And the memories that lay on the other side.

There was no other choice. I didn't know how to leave,

and it wouldn't have done any good if I had. Leaving would only postpone the inevitable. I was going to have to face her, sooner or later, on her turf or mine. Because I didn't think that wall was going back together again. I didn't know how to repair it, and Mircea had already said that he couldn't do it, not at her power level.

Which meant that he'd already bought me as much time as he could.

And somehow, looking at the sheer size of the thing, of the freaking fortress he'd had to build to imprison her, I felt my anger at him evaporating. I might resent him for not telling me, for not giving me the choice, but for once, I understood. He'd said he'd been worried that telling me might weaken the separation, and that he wouldn't be able to compensate. I didn't doubt it.

I didn't know how he'd built the damned thing at all.

I glanced up at the walls for a split second as I slipped into the gap. I couldn't spare more than that, not and keep an eye out for ambush. But I didn't need to. The size of them, the sheer weight, rose up around me, more massive even than I'd realized, towering over my head like cliffs and disappearing into the distance like a ravine.

There was no end in sight, the mist hiding everything more than ten, twelve yards ahead. But it didn't matter. The cost in power, the only real coin of the vampire world, for what I *could* see must have been ...

God. It must have been staggering.

No way had he done it all at once. Mircea had been on the fast track to master status, fueled by intelligence, ambition and sheer, unrestrained rage at a life that had been anything but fair. But no new master had done this, either.

Or even an old one. Not all at once. It must have taken years—centuries—of pouring strength into me. Of pushing back the power of a creature only a few decades younger than he, a trivial amount in vampire terms. Of constantly monitoring and adding to the protection he had built up, stone by stone, inch by inch, always knowing that one mistake might free her.

And destroy me.

The fog was thicker here, trapped between the sides of the rift, puddling in the middle to the point that it was almost exactly at eye level. Tendrils brushed my cheeks and curled around my face, making it hard to see, and the muffling quality wasn't helping my hearing, either. But I was finding it hard to concentrate on the danger.

I was too busy concentrating on something else.

Why had he done this? It made no sense. No master vampire wasted that kind of power, particularly not when young and vulnerable. He'd said it, and I had no reason to doubt him: other vampires had been trying to add him to their collections. And why not? Such mental gifts were rare. Coupled with his looks and charm and name . . . he would have made an ornament to any court. It must have been a constant struggle to stay independent, to remain outside their grasp, to maintain a sense of self instead of being subsumed into someone else's ambitions, someone else's needs.

So why waste power that he needed so badly?

Why waste it on *me*?

"Dory!"

I heard something through the mist, but it was faint, like a distant echo. Or possibly not there at all. The ravine trapped sound, diverted it, made it seem like it was coming from every direction at once. And the mist was getting thicker, almost like it was pushing back at me, trying to close my path.

"Stop fighting me!"

The voice came again, but it didn't make sense.

"I'm not fighting you," I murmured. And I wasn't. I wasn't doing anything, my mind reeling with fear and confusion and . . . and something else.

Something impossible.

But there was no other explanation. I had been a child, and one rapidly approaching insanity at that. I couldn't have helped him. I couldn't have been anything but a drain. He should have left me, should have done what any other master would have and cut me loose. Or followed the advice of those so-called specialists and humanely put me down before I tipped over the edge entirely.

But he hadn't.

And try as I might, I could come up with only one explanation for that.

I ran a hand over the smooth, fleshy texture of the wall. It was already healing the damage, even if it couldn't close the gap. And somehow, it didn't seem so horrible anymore. Didn't seem horrible at all, in fact.

Slick and warm, it felt like what it was: a healing scar. Not that I had a lot of experience with those. Dhampirs didn't scar, for the same reason that we couldn't get tattoos or piercings or so many other things. Our healing abilities wiped them away, erasing them off our skin in a matter of days or weeks, as if they'd never existed at all. Leaving only fresh, new skin behind.

But the mind didn't heal like that. The skin might forget, but the mind ... remembered. To the point that sometimes it felt like my head was full of scars. Others couldn't see them, but I could.

And every time I got too close to someone, I tripped over one.

The fog was thicker now, cloying, choking. Not mist anymore, not even really like gas. More like waterlogged sheets slapping me wetly across the face, as if I were trying to push through a field of soggy laundry. And serving as the perfect backdrop for dozens of images.

They appeared out of the fog, just the barest of flickers at first, and then more and more, crowding around on all sides. Most were unfamiliar, although it was hard to tell. They looked like flashes of old silent movies projected onto sheets that were blowing erratically in the wind. I saw a glimpse of a ballroom, of huge gowns spinning against flashing mirrors; I saw burnt tree limbs silhouetted against a ridge littered with bodies; I saw faces, so many faces.

And then I saw something I didn't recognize at all, but that drew me forward like a hand. It wasn't the most dramatic scene. It was actually one of the more plebeian. Just a room with stucco walls and flaking paint, and a large window open to the night.

Dusty beams of moonlight cascaded onto a dustier wooden floor, which was obscured by little in the way of furniture. Just a few plain benches around an elaborately carved table, its shiny dark wood and corkscrew legs making it look like it belonged in another room. Or maybe another house.

An easel was set up beside the table and a candle, flickering in the breeze from the window, sat on top of it. The stuttering light looked impossibly bright and warm against the cool blue tones of the room, shedding a golden halo over the floor and part of the table. And lighting up the corner—

—of a canvas.

It was set up in the usual place, looking out onto the canal and the dark water shining below. I never knew why; it wasn't much of a view. Just the shuttered windows of the house opposite and the still, silent boats drawn up outside, tied to listing poles for the night. Because who needed transport at this hour?

Maybe the fine ladies and gentlemen populating the palazzos and bars and brothels, but not around here. This was a working-class neighborhood, filled with men who would be up at dawn, lading and unlading ships or working on construction crews. The women would be going to the markets to haggle over fish or to buy the spices to brighten up a stew for their men's dinner. And the children, the children would be everywhere.

Ragged and dirty and shoeless—and lice-ridden, according to Horatiu, my tutor. He was mostly wrong about that, although I didn't tell him so. And anyway, they were happy, laughing and chatting and staging mock stick battles on the bridges, like their fathers would do more seriously on feast days.

They were amazing, those children, running right along the very edge of the canals, yet never falling in. I could do that, too. And leap from boat to boat, crossing the water without ever needing a bridge, following them on their crazy, circuitous route around the city, laughing at foreigners and giving them bad directions and picking their pockets when they weren't looking.

And using the coins obtained to buy food from the vendors, who knew where we got the money and didn't care. And, oh, the food. I had never known anything like it. Veal liver fried in grape-seed oil and served on little sticks. Stuffed baby squid swimming in fish broth. Huge dishes of steamy polenta with fried fish and eggplant.

And then there were the sweets—oh, the sweets!—unlike anything I'd ever known. The Roma who had raised me before I found my father had made sure I ate, but food to them was mostly tough black bread and vegetable stew, with the occasional scrap of salted pork. But sweets . . . those were rare in camp, and they did not go to me.

Father had bought me my first sweet shortly after we "landed," setting foot on this strangest of cities but not really on land, for it floated. Or so it seemed to me at the time. An impossible, magical place, and even the overcast, rainy day didn't dim my spirits, or the brilliant colors of the waterside market we waded through.

I'd never seen so many people, all in one place, all at once. Rough sailors smelling of fish oil and sweaty workmen covered in plaster dust rubbed shoulders with pretty young slave girls following their mistresses about with baskets, slick con men doing sleight-of-hand tricks for credulous farmers, orphan boys in bright tunics shaking poor boxes, and old grandmas bent double, palms outstretched for coins. Not to mention the painted women in the doorways, with their hair done up in ringlets and their arms jingling with bracelets, calling out offers to passing men. And making rude gestures at the ones who refused.

Father pulled me away from one of them, saying something sharp to her in a language I didn't understand. I didn't care; I hadn't been interested in her anyway, but in the vendor beside her. He was selling platters piled high with sweetened rice cakes, honey fritters topped with gingered almonds, clusters of nuts boiled with honey, and what the Venetians called calisconi—*wonderful marzipan-filled raviolis that melted on the tongue. I hadn't known what any of it was then, but the smell—*

Oh.

The smell.

I had stood, transfixed, the pack of clothes I was carrying hitting the ground unnoticed. Horatiu began to scold me for it, but Father shushed him. And bought me one of everything. And then thoroughly scandalized Horatiu by letting me eat them in the street.

"Like she was some common child!" the old man huffed, his gray hair wafting about in a sudden breeze.

"We're all common now," Mircea told him from inside his hood, a gloved hand smoothing down my short dark hair.

"Speak for yourself." Horatiu sniffed, and went to find us lodgings, while I ate and ate and ate.

I think they thought I would get full, sooner or later. I never did. There had been too many nights after I left the Roma, filled with clawing hunger; too many days of stumbling weakness; too many beatings for theft.

I hadn't minded the beatings so much, but they usually took the food back, too.

But nobody beat me now, and there was always food. Father came back from the bars with bright coins jangling in his purse. And Horatiu went to the markets in the morning and brought home sea bass and shellfish, ducks and chickens, wine and oil, fruit and bread. But not so much the meats, like beef and pork, that the Venetians imported on their ships from our homeland, which were too expensive.

And no sweets.

But that was all right.

These days I got my own.

"Do you like it?" Mircea asked, stepping back from the canvas.

He must have been working on it for a while, judging by the sheet he'd wrapped around his waist, like the aprons the old women wore. And for the same reason— his clothes had to stay nice. He couldn't part the wealthy tourists from their coins if he looked like he needed the money.

And he always made a mess. He said it was the sign of a great artist. I thought he must be the greatest of all then, *because his hands were spotted a rainbow of colors. Like the sheet and the hair flowing over his shoulders and the skin of his chest, because he'd gone shirtless.*

He saw me looking at his multicolored freckles and raised an eyebrow, daring me to say anything. I was going to anyway—I always did—but then he stepped to the side. Showing me the canvas.

And I had to bite back one of the words the street kids had taught me.

Because it was a portrait, and the portrait was of me. That wasn't the surprise—Mircea had painted me before. But that had been a normal painting and this ... well, it just wasn't.

Normal paintings had people stiff-backed and posed and all dressed up. He'd done one of those of me last year, sitting primly in a chair, my ankles crossed, my nicest dress spread out around me. That was what paintings were, or else they were fruit or flowers painted on the walls, like I'd seen in some of the unfinished palazzos I'd poked through.

But this wasn't any of those things.

It was me and some of the neighbor children, crouched below street level, at the base of a bridge, our bare toes gripping the barnacled rocks like the ones I'd seen on a street performer's monkey, somehow staying steady while we stuffed our faces with ill-gotten goods. My eyes were shining, my hair was in my face, and a smudge of dirt or mud was on my cheek. More mud soaked the edge of my tattered skirts, the ones of the too short dress I'd grown out of. But that I kept for when Horatiu napped in the sun after lunch and I slipped out for dessert.

"Well?" Mircea asked, cocking an eyebrow at me.

"I like the water," I said defiantly.

It actually was nice. He'd somehow managed to catch the ripples of our reflections without painting them exactly, by just throwing little splashes of color in between the waves. For some reason, it looked more real that way.

"Thank you," he said sardonically.

He started washing out his brushes. They were the regular kind and hadn't cost very much. Not like the minerals he crushed to make some of the paints. But he was always very careful with them.

"Nothing else to say?" He prompted finally.

"You're not supposed to be awake in daytime."

"Oh, I see. This is about what I am not supposed to do."

For a moment there was nothing but the small ping, ping, ping *of the brush against the side of a water-filled bowl. It was making it hard to concentrate, to come up with a good story.*

And it already wasn't easy. I knew I wasn't supposed to be running around with street kids. Horatiu would ... well, he might have that heart attack he was always threatening if he knew. Mircea didn't talk about the family much, but it seemed important for Horatiu that I knew who I was. And that I acted like a lady.

I didn't know why. Like Mircea said, we weren't that anymore, and it was fine with me. I didn't want to be a lady and wear too many layers and learn proper Italian. I wanted to wear comfortable clothes and run around barefoot and make boats out of sticks and bits of cloth and race them on the canals.

And eat sweet things.

Mircea put the brushes on the windowsill to dry. "There is a reason the rules exist."

"I can take care of myself."

"Against gangs of cutpurses and thugs, I've no doubt." Clink, clink, clink. "You know they are not what concern me."

I sighed. Because we'd had this conversation before. We'd had it a lot.

Sometimes I thought Mircea worried about vampires more than I did.

It was both the best and the worst thing about Venice. Being a port—being THE port—meant that the city wasn't under any one court. It couldn't be; there was too much wealth, and therefore power, flowing through it for any one family to be allowed to dominate. It had been named a free territory, meaning that any vampire could come here, regardless of family connection.

Or lack thereof, in our case.

And because any vampire could come, many did. But I wasn't a fool; I stayed away from the parts of town they patronized. Not that they were usually active when I ventured out anyway.

"How many Others go out at noon?" I demanded, using our code word for the rest of his kind.

Mircea didn't say anything for a long moment. He put away the painting things and then settled beside me on the bench. The breeze blowing through the opening was cool, but he was warm. His hand was still polka-dotted when he put it around my shoulder, drawing me in. But it was warm, too.

It always threw me. They weren't supposed to be warm. Someone had told me that. . . . I couldn't remember who. Some of the Roma maybe. But they'd been wrong.

They'd been wrong about a lot of things.

I put my head on his shoulder and looked at the painting. I decided I liked it. It wasn't a proper painting, but then, I wasn't all that proper, either.

And I did like the water.

Mircea's hand moved up to my head, smoothing down the curls there. They were everywhere, now that he'd made me grow it out. "I know it is lonely for you here," he told me. "I can only promise that we will not be here forever."

I put my chin on his chest and looked up at him. This was the first I'd heard of it. "Where will we go?"

"That is yet to be determined. But I will not always be weak. And every time I gain in power, my bargaining position improves."

"To do what?"

"Many things. Someday, I will be able to make servants—"

I groaned in mock horror. "Not more Horatius!"

He smiled. "There is only one Horatiu. But there will be people who can help us. Give us the means to go away."

"But I like it here."

"You will like other places, as well. Beautiful places. Safe places."

"Places with sweets?"

Mircea laughed. "Yes. Yes, many sweets, which you may eat until you don't have a tooth left in your head!"

"I don't think I would look very good with no teeth."

Mircea kissed the side of my head. "You will always be beautiful. And you will always be safe. I swear it."

I frowned, because his tone had been weird when he said that last. "Why wouldn't we be? What can hurt—"

The scene suddenly froze, exactly like a movie somebody had paused. I blinked, coming back to myself but waiting for it to continue. Only it didn't.

"Start!" I told it stupidly, wiping away even stupider tears.

I didn't know why I was crying. I didn't know this scene—not any of it. Not the room, not the painting, not the sights and sounds and smells of a city that, as far as I was concerned, I'd visited for the first time several hundred years later. And hadn't been all that impressed by.

I hadn't walked through that marketplace or run past those canals. I hadn't looked for that house, to see if it still stood, or searched for that bridge. Or eaten the sweets that I'd seemed so obsessed with.

Because I hadn't remembered any of it.

"Start!" I yelled, furious and desperate. But it didn't. The little girl remained looking up at her father, loose-limbed and comfortable in his grasp, brown curls falling over a plain white shift, naked toes peeking out from under the hem, black eyes mischievous and adoring and—

And when the hell had I looked like that? I'd never fucking looked like that! Only I had.

I had and I'd lost it, I realized, as something sliced across the scene. Like talons through a movie screen, it shredded the delicate image, cutting it to pieces. Like the memories she'd stolen from me. Like everything she'd ever touched.

Bring it, bitch, I thought savagely, right before a crushing blow sent me flying.

Chapter Thirty-five

I hit the ground on my back outside the rift, skidded, flipped—and was hit again before I even got back to my feet. And again. And again. I snarled and grabbed for a dark shadow darting to the left, but clutched only air.

I wasn't sure if I'd missed or if there hadn't been anything there in the first place. I couldn't tell because the fog was getting worse. It was head-high out here now, too, with only puzzle pieces of the harbor visible behind filmy veils. Everything else was billowing clouds lit up by the searchlight illumination of the rift, with the fog giving the beams a nearly solid appearance.

Like the heavy-booted foot slashing out at me.

It would have cracked my jaw, judging by the explosion of air that hit my face as it passed by, but I'd dodged back just in time. Only to have my feet swept out from under me a second later, dumping me on the ground again. And into the middle of a barrage that seemed to come from everywhere at once.

It was a relentless, impossible-to-meet pounding, that had me rolling around the path and still only half avoiding the blows. And reminding me of a small fact that I'd forgotten—I had never been the stronger. Saner, yes, maybe. Most of the time. But our strength . . . that had always come from her.

It was why the temporary block that the fey wine had created had cost me so much in battle. I'd still been better than average—I didn't owe everything to her. But the split-second reactions, the knife-edge balance, the sheer power of berserker rage . . . those I had lost.

But obviously she hasn't, I thought, as that boot came down by my right ear, hard enough to crack concrete.

Rolling to the left, I lashed out at the same time, and landed a punch that—finally—connected. But she melted into the mist before I could follow up, just a shadow among shadows, no more solid than any other. I jumped back to my feet and whirled around, trying to watch every direction at once. It would have helped if I'd been able to concentrate, but I couldn't. Because a big, fat realization had just hit me, harder than her fists.

I wasn't getting out of this.

I wasn't even if she didn't manage to kill me. I wasn't even if I somehow managed to get back without a guide. I wasn't because Marlowe had been in that room.

He'd heard every word that was said before I went in—or under or whatever the hell Mircea had done to get me here. And he'd undoubtedly been given a play-by-play of everything that had happened since. His natural nosiness would have insisted on that much, even without the paranoia of current events to help it along.

But even if not, even if Mircea had realized the implication of that shattered wall and avoided questions, it didn't matter. Marlowe wasn't stupid. He was likely figuring it out right about now. And as soon as he did . . .

As soon as he did, I was dead.

Until now, I'd just been a dhampir. Longer-lived than most, maybe, and a little saner, but a dhampir nonetheless. And as much as the Senate hated my kind, I'd been tolerated because Mircea was who he was. And because I was who I was: strong enough to be useful at times, and weak enough to be controlled.

But Dorina . . . Dorina wasn't weak. And Dorina wouldn't be controlled, easily or otherwise. Dorina was a crazy first-level master with five centuries of experience under her belt and a hard-on for killing vampires.

And now she was out.

Just like Christine.

And we know what happened to her, don't we? I thought grimly.

I didn't get an answer, except for a flurry of blows that came out of nowhere. Including one I thought I'd dodged that clipped me across the mouth, sending a spray of droplets flying. And surprise—it was possible to bleed in here.

Too bad I seemed to be the only one doing it.

"Dorina!"

The voice came again, closer this time, and it must have startled her as much as me. Because there was a half-second lull in the pounding. And I said screw it and used the only advantage I had, and imagined a .44 Magnum into my hand.

It worked great—the hard, cold steel materializing in my palm with no trouble at all.

For about a second—until someone else imagined it right out again.

Fuck!

And before I could come up with any more bright ideas, that damned boot was back, stabbing down all around me. Which wouldn't have been as much of a problem if there had been any cover out here. But there wasn't, except for one of the streetlights. And then not even that after the boot lashed out again, and hit the lamppost.

Or, more accurately, destroyed the lamppost. The metal groaned and bent double, heading for me like a toppling tree. I leapt back to miss it—

And managed to miss the ground instead.

Someone tackled me halfway through the fall, but instead of hitting dirt, we didn't hit anything, with me clawing and fighting and struggling against the arms around me until I heard Louis-Cesare's voice. And then still struggling because we were still falling, even though there was nothing to fall off *of*, except the side of the wharf that we were nowhere near. And anyway, that would have been a drop of a yard or two, not the several floors it felt like we'd plunged when—

Whummmp.

I landed on top of something hard, cold and wood-like, and Louis-Cesare landed on top of me. It wasn't as bad as it could have been, because I think he was trying to miss. But I still ended up with my chin striking down and my eyes crossing and nothing making sense.

And then they uncrossed and it still didn't.

"What the—"

"I brought you into my memories," he told me, a little hysterically, and then he pulled me to my feet. And into the thick of a crowd.

A really unruly one. People were running and slipping and sliding on icy wood, and before I could ask Louis-Cesare what he meant, a guy in a full-length fur coat smashed into me. And my breath—what little was left of it—went out in a whoosh. And then condensed into a cloud in front of my face.

Wherever we were, it was freezing.

"You did what?" I finally managed to gasp, after being towed through what had to be a couple hundred people.

"Mircea sent me back in to get you out," Louis-Cesare told me rapidly. "But it was not working and there was no time and you were—" He stared back at me, jaw clenched. "I had to do something."

"So you pulled me into your *mind*?"

"No. I do not have your father's skill."

"Then what—"

I cut off because the crowd had suddenly gone nuts. We were on the deck of some kind of ship—a big one—surrounded by heavily muffled people in old-timey outfits. Who appeared to be having a collective fit. Because a bunch of them screamed, and a bunch more came stampeding from the opposite direction, threatening to run us down.

Louis-Cesare pulled me into a stairwell before they managed it, and I grabbed him. "What did you *do*?"

"I needed to get you away from that wharf, but I do not know your mind," he explained rapidly. "I did not know where to go. I needed something more familiar ... and there was only one thing available."

For a second, I didn't know what he was talking about. And then I remembered the metaphysical accident a couple months ago. And the fallout that had left me in possession of a piece of Louis-Cesare's consciousness.

It was easy to forget, because it had remained where it had settled, in a hard little lump in a corner of my brain that I avoided like the plague. I didn't poke at it, didn't bother it. And for the most part, vice versa was true. Every once in a while I got a flash of something—people I'd never met, places I'd never been—but I blinked them away and forgot it. Because it wasn't my business, and because I didn't need anything drawing me closer to him than I already was.

But it looked like I was about to get the tour anyway.

"So we're inside a piece of your mind, inside my mind?" I asked, feeling like my head was about to explode.

Which was possibly the case.

He nodded, looking around at the crowd.

"Why? Why not just help me? Together we could have taken her—"

"There is no *her*," he said tensely. "There is only *you*. Anything that happens to one happens to both. If you hurt her, you hurt yourself. If you kill her—"

"But we're inside your head! My head. Something. Anyway, none of this is real!"

"It is to your brain, and it will react accordingly."

"Meaning what?"

"I do not fully understand all the implications myself," he said, turning back to meet my eyes. The cold had whipped up some color in his face, and his hair had come loose from its confining clip and was flying everywhere. A strand blew into his mouth and he spat it out, before pulling it behind him and tucking it under the collar of the long coat he'd somehow acquired.

And then pulled off and put around my shoulders, when he noticed I was shivering.

He was wearing an old-fashioned tux underneath it—white tie and tails—but I didn't bother to ask why. "Give it your best shot," I told him.

"Your father did not have much time to explain. But it has to do with the fact that your brain controls your body—your breathing, your heartbeat, your autonomous nervous system—"

"Could I have the condensed version?"

"If your brain thinks you are dead, you are dead."

I stared up at him for a moment, hoping this was a bad joke. But those sapphire eyes were doing that guileless thing again, the one that always threw me because vampire eyes didn't look like that. Unless they were Louis-Cesare's, which right now were open and honest and worried and utterly serious.

"Let me get this straight," I said, clutching the fine wool of the coat. "If I die in here, I die. But if I fight her—"

"You also die."

"Then what the *hell*—"

"Mircea needs time. He has to find a way around the blockage, to get you back into the physical world."

"And what do we do in the meantime?"

"We disappear," Louis-Cesare said grimly. "I thought it would be easier to do that in my memories. She does not know them as she does yours. We merely have to avoid her until Mircea fixes this."

I stared at the icy boards under our feet, and didn't say anything. Because hide-and-seek wouldn't work, not for me. Not with Marlowe probably putting two and two together right now. But then, there wasn't only me to think about, was there?

Louis-Cesare had been so insistent, back in the consul's library, that my victims hadn't been victims at all. Maybe because he hadn't been there. Hadn't woken up surrounded by corpses time and time again. Hadn't seen people flinch or in some cases run screaming as soon as I came into town.

Because they thought I was her.

He hadn't been there; he didn't understand. And even if he did, even if I could convince him that she'd kill him to get to me, it wouldn't do any good. Would probably do exactly the opposite, in fact. Louis-Cesare wouldn't just abandon me. I knew that, as much as I knew anything.

So I had to avoid her until Mircea brought us back. And I had to keep my mouth shut in the meantime. Because Louis-Cesare might be crazy enough to oppose Marlowe if he knew the deal, and that wouldn't end well. Not when one man fought fair and the other . . . didn't.

Get back, then deal with the fallout, I told myself. Somehow.

"So it's hide-and-seek," I said, as the deck moved under our feet. Louis-Cesare didn't answer. I looked up to find him leaning against a column, looking spooked, and vaguely ill. "Are you all right?"

"I . . . Of course," he told me stiffly.

"Then why are you green?" It didn't go so well with the hair.

He swallowed. "I . . . do not care for ships."

"You're a *vampire*. You can't get seasick."

"That is not the issue."

"Then what is?" I asked, just as a heavily muffled woman decided to hell with the tour of the Arctic we seemed to be on and went back inside. And left a bare spot on the wall. Or what would have been bare had a life preserver not been hanging there, taking up space.

A life preserver that said—

"We must go," Louis-Cesare told me, taking my arm.

"Why don't you like ships?" I asked shrilly, looking over my shoulder as he hustled me away.

"I had a bad experience once."

"A bad experience?" I shrieked, just as the deck lurched, hard enough to cause a bunch of chairs and a guy in a sailor suit to go sliding by.

It rocked again before I could get my balance back, and Louis-Cesare lost his grip on my arm when a woman staggered into him. Which would have been fine if sailor-boy hadn't grabbed me at the same moment, trying to get back to his feet. And ending up dragging me off mine.

And despite being only a memory or a figment of Louis-Cesare's imagination or what the hell, he felt real enough, and his grip was hard with desperation. And the angle was steep and the deck was icy and once we started sliding, we just kept on going. Picking up momentum and knocking stuffy types out of the way left and right, heading straight for—

"Oh, shit."

A churning mass of water, like waves breaking against a shore, boiled up beneath us, coming our way fast as the deck suddenly went from slanted to *slanted*. And I found myself being pelted by the avalanche of people now pouring down from above. They were screaming, and the frigid spray was drenching us, and the sailor was panicking and using me as a shield, with the arm he'd thrown around my neck threatening to choke me.

And then Louis-Cesare, who had somehow gotten ahead of me and grabbed a railing, flung out a hand. "Dory!"

I grabbed for it, and would have caught it, if three people going crazy fast hadn't chosen that second to toboggan in between us. He jerked his hand back to avoid getting swept away and I went sliding by, elbowing the sailor and throwing him off and then wrenching back and reaching—

And finally grabbing Louis-Cesare's hand because he had lunged for me at the same time, his feet hooked under the rail, his body dangling headfirst, like a lifeline.

It was a pretty impressive bit of acrobatics, and apparently everyone else thought so, too. Because suddenly people were barnacling onto the only handhold available by grabbing whatever part of him was closest. Including something that made his eyes pop and his face go crimson and—

And then an angry cloud of darkness loomed up behind his head, blotting out the stars.

Tag, you're it, I thought but didn't say, because he couldn't have heard me over the yelling and the crashing and the ship's horn. But it must have shown in my face, because he wrenched his neck around and took a look—

And then he let go of the rail.

It wasn't so much a slide this time as a fall. The ship was fast approaching the perpendicular, leaving us tumbling and flailing helplessly into a dam of people and furniture around a wrecked lifeboat. And then *over* it, as the impact threw us into the air and through some spray and into—

A big steel door that hadn't been there a second ago.

And neither had the dark street and the cracked sidewalk and the shiny black, bulbous car that rain was pattering down on the top of.

"Word?"

I went from looking dizzily at the street to looking dizzily at the large guy with the nicotine yellow teeth who had appeared behind a small window in the door.

"Titanic," Louis-Cesare told him grimly, and the door opened and we were through.

There was a pretty Asian hatcheck girl in a tight red dress on the other side, but we didn't have any hats. Or shoes, in my case—not that anyone seemed to notice. Maybe because the place was so smoky; I could barely see my hand in front of my face, much less my foot.

But I could still talk, so I did, pulling Louis-Cesare— who was now wearing a standard black tux for some reason—over to the wall. "What the hell are you *doing*?"

"Trying option two."

"What?"

He licked his lips. "Once we realized that I could not take you out, your father told me to evade until he could come up with a plan. He said there were three ways to do that."

"Which are?"

"Hide—"

"Which didn't work out so well!"

"No." He grimaced. "We are therefore attempting to lose her. If she isn't right on top of us when we transition from one memory to the next, or if she becomes distracted by what else is happening, she will not know where we went."

"But if she figures it out?"

"Then we go to option three."

"Which is?"

He said something that I didn't hear because the door opened again and a fat cat with a bunch of squealing girls blew in. Along with a gust of rain and the sound of lightning. And Louis-Cesare took the chance to pull me into the main room.

It was loud, with someone playing bad jazz and someone else trying to sing over the sound of drunken laughter, the call of a croupier and the *click click* of a roulette wheel. It was all utterly, completely real, like my first mind-trip to the wharf. Only there were no disturbing holes in this picture.

There hadn't been any on the ship, either, but I hadn't been in a headspace to notice it then. *Maybe it was because vampires' senses were better?* I wondered, staring at the silver shimmy of a showgirl's costume on a small stage. So maybe their sense memory was, too. Or maybe he was filling in the blanks?

Or maybe I was nuts for thinking about this now.

Yeah, that sounded about right.

Louis-Cesare had snagged two glasses off the tray of a passing waiter, and handed me one, which turned out to be straight bourbon. "You might want to drink that now," he said grimly, and bolted his own.

I didn't even ask. I just threw it back, managing to choke most of it down before a bell rang out, harsh and discordant. And had me jumping reflexively and spilling the rest.

And I wasn't the only one. On all sides, people jerked to attention, glasses sloshed, cigarettes fell from holders and hands disappeared inside coats. And then everything stopped—music, talking, gambling, drinking. And every head in the place swiveled around.

And looked at us.

"Now what?" I muttered to Louis-Cesare, who had gripped my arm.

"Rien."

"Then why are they staring at us?"

"They're not," he said, pulling me to the side as a fist started pounding on the door.

It was loud enough to cut through the din and make me jump again, although I'm not a jumper. But my nerves were a little frayed at the moment. A fact that wasn't helped when a line of bullets suddenly strafed the door from the other side.

"So I guess we're going with distraction, huh?" I yelled, as the room went wild.

Louis-Cesare didn't answer; he just grabbed my hand and pulled me through a horde of waiters beating it with trays of illegal booze, good-time girls fighting croupiers for cash and tough guys pulling guns. And then the door gave way and a bunch of blue-coated cops burst in, yelling orders we couldn't hear over the din.

Louis-Cesare grabbed my hand and pulled us onto the stage along with the ensemble, who had packed up their instruments and were disappearing behind a cheap red curtain. And down a hall. And behind a set of stairs.

Until we got hung up behind the bass player, who couldn't get his huge instrument through a narrow exit.

I looked behind us, but there was nothing there. Not even the cops, who had probably assumed that the curtain fronted a wall. "I think we lost her," I told Louis-Cesare breathlessly, who didn't look convinced.

Maybe because the lights took that moment to flash out.

"Shit!"

He didn't say anything. He just picked up the bass, with musician still attached, and threw it behind us. And then jerked me through the doorway. And then on a breathless trip through a stream of memories that went by so fast, they made me nauseous.

I found that the only way to deal was just to concentrate on my feet, which were running over surfaces that changed between steps: scuffed hardwood to mossy stone to cigarette-strewn concrete to inlaid marble to rocky seashore to—

Fire-lit dirt?

I looked up, blinking, when the scene stayed constant for a few seconds. And saw a slur of dark greenery and bright stars that didn't make sense because I was dizzy and really confused. Like part of my brain was still trying to catch up.

"Where are we?" I slurred, grabbing Louis-Cesare for info and balance.

And got neither. He didn't answer, and then we lurched and almost went down. I stared at him stupidly for a minute, because Louis-Cesare was a master swordsman; he didn't stumble. The man practically looked like he was dancing just walking across a freaking room.

Or going to one knee.

Or leaning heavily against me.

Or crumpling to the ground in my arms.

Chapter Thirty-six

I let him down to the ground, and went into a defensive crouch over him, looking wildly around for our attacker. But all I saw was a tree-strewn hillside under a huge black sky, the Milky Way glittering overhead like a starry rainbow. A small, tumbledown shack stood near the bottom of the hill, and a bonfire was burning at the top. But nothing moved, except for a cool breeze rustling the treetops, a rogue meteor burning up along the horizon and the firelight flickering down the hill.

It looked like we'd outrun her—for the moment.

The bonfire was a ways off, but it was still bright enough to send shadows to play over Louis-Cesare's face, giving the illusion of movement. But that was all it was. Because he just lay there, even when I shook him.

I pushed up his shirt, which had gone from fine linen to rough homespun, thinking maybe she'd caught him between one transition and another. It doesn't take much time to slip a stake between the ribs, or to run a knife edge over a neck. And it wasn't like she hadn't had enough practice.

But there were no wounds, no blood. No obvious problems at all that I could see. I ran my hand around his throat, then down through the lacings on the front of his shirt. And encountered only fine, unbroken skin. And sat down abruptly, feeling dizzy again from sheer relief.

For a second, I thought seriously about passing out. But I couldn't afford to do that. Not when it looked like he'd beaten me to it.

Which made no sense. Master vampires didn't pass out. Master vampires kept coming until you chopped them into little pieces, and sometimes even then. But people didn't go running around in other people's memories, either, so tonight was obviously about new experiences.

I looked up again.

There were people circling the bonfire. I could see their bodies if I squinted, silhouetted against the light. Could hear their laughter when the wind was just right, feel the reverberations of their feet if I concentrated. They were pounding out a rhythm to the accompaniment of drums, a flute and what might have been a lyre. It was almost hypnotic: dark figures whirling around a tower of flame, sparks flying high into the sky, a riot of color and light and movement on an otherwise dark hillside.

It didn't look like something that should be in Louis Cesare's memories. Or even in the consul's. It looked like a pagan kaleidoscope, something that predated history: violent, primitive, dangerous, raw.

It didn't make me want to go up and say hi.

And I didn't know what they could do for him if I did. Vampires healed themselves, for the most part. There were potions that could counteract the effects of curses, and low-level necromancers that could speed up healing in the case of particularly nasty wounds. But neither of those was likely to be available here, and anyway, they didn't apply. Louis-Cesare hadn't been cursed or wounded. Louis-Cesare was just out cold.

Which left me in a mess.

I couldn't transition us out of here, because I didn't know how. And with my guide unconscious, I had no way to contact Mircea and find out. Besides, I'd been a good girl and avoided snooping, so I didn't know Louis-Cesare's memories any better than my other half did. Even assuming I figured things out on my own, the only place I could take us was back into my memories.

Where she'd be onto us in about a second.

I closed my eyes for a moment, and just breathed.

I'd had a plan, at the beginning of this crazy ride. It

wasn't much of one, admittedly, but it was the best I'd been able to come up with under the circumstances. And it still was.

Get him out. All the rest of the hundred or so things clamoring for attention could wait. Just get him out.

Get him out before she found him.

Get him out before she killed him.

Just fucking Get. Him. Out.

I opened my eyes.

We needed to get moving, to put some space between us and where we'd come in. It didn't matter where—just so the bitch would have to look for us, instead of stumbling over us. Somewhere I might get a few seconds' warning when she showed up. And somewhere under cover, so I could stash Louis-Cesare out of sight.

I knew where he was; if she came, I'd leave him here and run, because it was me she wanted. If I got away, I could tell Mircea where to go to retrieve him. And if I didn't ...

Well, I'd have a really good incentive to make sure that I did, wouldn't I? Or to hope that Mircea could find him anyway. Or that he'd wake up on his own and figure a way out.

None of which was going to happen if she found him first.

I got my hands under his arms and started dragging him backward, toward the shack.

It wasn't far off, and it was downhill, thank God, over a path made of trampled grass that was slick enough to minimize the friction. It should have been a pretty easy trip, despite the six feet four inches of pure muscle I was dragging. But it wasn't.

Either this mental stuff was exhausting or the week I'd had was finally catching up with me, but I was panting like a steam train and sweating like a pig. And that was before we'd made it halfway there. I stopped for a rest, crouching in the dirt, wishing to God I had something to use as a—

I stopped, cursing myself for being an idiot. The damned place looked so real, it was easy to forget that it was *in my head.* I could dream up a stretcher—hell, I could dream up a freaking wheelchair, if I wanted—and save my back and legs and thighs, all of which had started seriously to protest.

Only I couldn't.

I tried again, and again got nothing. I couldn't remember what I'd done before, but staring at the ground and hoping really hard obviously wasn't it. *Of course not,* I snarled, and grabbed Louis-Cesare again, preparing to continue with my old buddy the Hard Way.

So much for dreaming up a bazooka if anybody threatened us.

Like the monster in the tall grass, for instance.

I froze, hoping it was a trick of the light. Because I was pretty close to crazed right now, and didn't need yet another problem. Especially not one with two huge, narrowed eyes peering at me from the side of the path. But there they were anyway—evil, dark and soulless—reflecting the bonfire light like the flames of hell.

And then slowly crossing.

Okaaaay.

I carefully lowered Louis-Cesare to the ground again. No reaction. I edged around him and slowly moved to the side of the path. No reaction. I gradually put out a hand. No reaction.

I jumped forward and parted the grasses—

And had no freaking idea what I was looking at.

It was lying on its side, big and brown and lumpish, and vaguely donkey-like, if donkeys were the size of Clydesdales. And covered in dreads. And simpleminded, because it was not only crossing its eyes but grinning, the massive lips pulling back from equally massive teeth and a lolling tongue.

And then it noticed me looking and it farted.

I just stared for a moment, bewildered.

"Baudet de Poitou," Louis-Cesare said hoarsely from behind me.

I whirled around. "What?"

"An ancient breed of donkey. We called him Jehan after his bellow—and the local drunk."

I licked my lips, swallowing my heart back down. "What's wrong with him?"

"*Rien.* He did this every year." Louis-Cesare got an arm underneath himself. "Someone would clean out the vat and dump the residue under the tree."

I belatedly noticed that the path diverged, with one branch going to the shack and the other to a large, round wooden tub with suspicious stains around it. Reddish purple ones. Like those ringing the donkey's mouth like badly applied lipstick.

"It made him useless for days," Louis-Cesare added, looking disapprovingly at the great creature.

"Because it made him sick?"

Louis-Cesare looked surprised. "*Non.* Because it would ferment." His lips pursed. "I suppose you could say he is now . . . drunk off his ass."

Jehan bellowed agreement and let out another fart. I squatted down on the path and put my arms over my head. And just stayed there for a minute.

"What happened?" Louis-Cesare finally asked me.

"You passed out."

"I did not." It was said with such conviction that I almost believed it.

I turned my head and looked at him through the gap by my elbow. I debated arguing it, but decided I wasn't up to it right now. "Okay. Then what do you remember?"

"Only that it was becoming . . . difficult."

"It?"

"The transitions between memories."

I raised my head. "But that's not hard. We do it all the time. Normally, I mean."

"This is not normal."

And on that, at least, we could agree.

He'd struggled back to his feet while he spoke. I hadn't helped because something told me it wouldn't be appreciated, and because I was feeling a little unsteady myself. But he let me put an arm around his waist as we finished hiking to the shack, supporting me as I supported him. And when we got inside, he quickly made the acquaintance of a blanket-covered pile of straw on the floor.

I looked around, not that there was much to see. A table but no chairs. A dirt floor. Three stone walls, old and rough and more or less supporting a thatched roof. Which was kind of irrelevant since it was letting in starlight through no fewer than five different holes.

But at least I could see. Between the stars and the light from the bonfire flickering across the stones, I could pretty much make out everything. And for a tumbledown shack in the middle of nowhere, it was stocked pretty well.

"Did you do that?" I asked Louis-Cesare, eyeing the spread laid out on an old table.

It wasn't anything fancy—coarse brown bread, wine, cheese, butter. And it looked like a lot of it had already disappeared, judging by the greasy wooden platters littered with crumbs and the empty wine barrel lying on its side. But still.

Louis-Cesare shook his head, and then stopped, wincing. "No. It is too difficult. I do not think I can imagine anything into existence at the moment."

"You don't think you can?" I repeated, my heart sinking.

"No, why?"

Because I'd kind of been counting on that bazooka. "Because I can't, either."

He frowned. "But this is your mind."

"But it's *your* memory."

He peeled off his now-filthy shirt, which had gotten the worst of the path outside. It left him in rough brown trousers that laced up the front, a greasy bandanna around his neck and a pair of scuffed boots. "But you are gifted. Like your father."

"No," I reminded him sourly. "*Dorina* is gifted. And thankfully, she's not here." I glanced around again. "Wherever here is."

"France," he told me, reclining against the hay. "About ten miles from Saumur. Near the village where I grew up."

"And the bacchanalia going on outside?"

"Vendanges."

"The grape harvest?"

He nodded. "When I was young, before . . ." He licked his lips. "Before it was decided to send me away, I lived on a farm in the country. Every year, the local vineyard would hire young people to help pick the grapes, and to stomp them into wine. And once harvest was over, they threw a party."

"That's one word for it." I turned back to the table and started loading up a tray, because it might be only imaginary food, but I was hungry.

"It became customary for young couples to leave early," Louis-Cesare agreed. "And find one of these. The farmer had four or five scattered about the vineyard to make processing easier. The grapes did not have so far to go."

"Just as well," I said, eyeing Jehan through the missing wall. Who stared the stare of the completely blitzed back at me. But at least he didn't cut wind again.

I guessed that was something.

I joined Louis-Cesare, and put the tray between us. Surprisingly, the blanket didn't smell. Except of hay, which must not have been harvested too long before this. Because it gave off only the scent of earth and flowers, which blended well with the vinegary reek of the wine.

"How long until Mircea pulls us out?" I asked, slathering some butter on bread.

"He . . . was not sure."

"Can't you just ask him?"

His face answered that for me.

I sighed. "*Why* can't you just ask him?"

"As soon as I entered my memories, I lost contact with your father," he admitted. "Of course, the opposite may not be true, considering his skill. He may be able to take us out from here, once he fixes the problem."

"Or he may not."

"If he does not, then when I . . . in a little while, we can return to the wharf and contact him from there. He should be able to assist us, or at least give us an update."

Yeah, as long as we manage to avoid evisceration first,

I didn't say, because it wouldn't have helped. "But until then we're on our own."

"Yes."

Louis-Cesare rested his head against the wall, his eyes closing. And I ate in silence for a while, my thoughts going to all those back-to-back transitions he'd made. Which hadn't been too healthy, but may have been worth it. My evil twin might have inherited Mircea's mental gifts, but how much experience could she have had chasing people through somebody else's memories?

Maybe we were okay.

Maybe we'd lost her.

Or maybe she was just taking a while to follow the trail. How long had it taken her to show up on that ship? Ten minutes? Fifteen? I wasn't sure. But I didn't think it had been longer than that. And how many transitions had we made on the way here?

I did the math, and didn't like the answer. I thought it had been six, maybe seven. I couldn't be sure because the first few had been blurry. But that was close enough.

So say ten minutes apiece, or fifteen, assuming she wasn't getting better with practice and shaving off time....

I scowled.

I hoped Louis-Cesare rested up fast.

He was watching me when I looked up.

"So this was like May Day around here," I said, to take my mind off it.

"Something like that," he agreed.

Of course, in May, you had a nice pole to dance around, I thought, watching the shadows leap and whirl. A nice phallic symbol to piss off the church, which hadn't liked the obvious symbolism. Or the fact that a large number of the local teens would be slipping off into the woods to celebrate the return of the earth's fertility in the time-honored way.

But I guessed a bonfire and a vat of wine worked, too.

Louis-Cesare didn't deny it. "There were a number of children with birthdays every year, nine months from now."

I bet.

I took a sip of the wine I'd found in a pitcher that had somehow been overlooked. It was harsh, bright and tart in a way that modern wine never was, but packed with fall fruit that gave it a hint of sweetness. Like a French version of sangria. I liked it.

"And how often did you bring someone back here?" I asked, licking my lips.

"I didn't."

I looked at him over the cup, and raised a skeptical brow. Because sure.

"It is true," he insisted.

"And how old were you?"

"Old enough."

"Then why . . ."

He shrugged. "I was considered . . . different. No one knew the truth of my birth, but they knew that much. Most people guessed that I was some noble bastard who had been quietly removed from sight."

"I thought most noble bastards were kept around, put to work."

He raised an eyebrow. "Where did you hear that?"

"My own grandfather was born on the wrong side of the blanket," I reminded him, in between crunching bread. It was good, coarse but crusty, and nutty with barely cracked grain. "And he did okay. Ended up as an errand runner for the Hungarian king, who loaned him an army to conquer the throne he couldn't win by birth. So it all worked out." I thought about it. "Well, for a while."

"Ah, but he was a man's bastard, yes?"

I nodded.

"It worked a little differently for the women," he reminded me. "Particularly in France."

"The good old double standard."

"*Oui.* Most of the noblemen had mistresses, the kings even official ones. But their women were expected to be pure as new-fallen snow."

"And when they weren't, they pretended."

"And removed the evidence."

I looked at the evidence, and wondered how anyone had ever found him a burden. "That sucks."

He reached past me for the wine, a ripple of fine muscle under finer skin. "Not . . . entirely. But my birth did make me stand out."

"How did anybody know?"

He shrugged. "Rumors had spread of a fine lady who came to see me, all muffled up, a few times when I was a child. And then there was the money that was sent, every month, to pay for my schooling. It was thought that I was being educated for a reason, and that someday I would be summoned. And go away."

"And the girls didn't want to go away with a handsome sort-of prince?"

"It was not a matter of what they wanted. Their fathers had put the fear of God into them. For the best, as it turned out."

He didn't elaborate, but he didn't have to. I knew what that was like, to live with a group but never really be part of it. To have people find you useful but also strange, foreign. To have them automatically exclude you, suspect you, dismiss you. To stop talking when you came near, not because it was anything important, not even because they were afraid you might tell someone.

But because you were different.

What was weird was to think that somebody like Louis-Cesare knew it, too.

I glanced around the unprepossessing little shed again. And wondered about the young man who would remember a place like this so vividly, and for so many years. And about the foolish, foolish girls who had gone off with someone else.

And turned back to find him watching me again.

He was lying in a beam of firelight leaking around the side of the mostly missing wall. It was bathing that part of the room in an eerie ginger twilight. It bathed him, too, haloing his hair, darkening his eyes, warming his skin to damp golden velvet. I licked wine off my lips and watched his eyes follow the movement.

"Is there a reason you brought me here?" I finally asked.

"As living beings we stand out against the background

of the memories we visit," he said softly. "To someone gifted in the arts of the mind, it is as if we were in color and everyone else in black and white. But the more we sink into a memory, the better we blend in. If we sink far enough, Mircea thinks it may allow us to appear as part of the background, and so be overlooked."

"That was option number three," I guessed.

He nodded.

I drank wine. "And how do we do this fade thing, exactly?"

"I . . . did not have time to get complete instructions." I looked at him. "Or any," he admitted.

"But you have an idea."

He finished his own wine in one long swallow. And then he got up and bowed slightly. And damned if he didn't pull off courtly despite being dirty and half naked and covered with hay.

"If you allow, I would be honored to show you."

And he held out a hand.

I stared at it.

An hour ago, I wouldn't even have hesitated. An hour ago, I'd have just said no. Because it was what I always said, what I'd always had to say. So I wouldn't hurt anybody, so I wouldn't get hurt myself. No, you can't have that person; no, you can't stay in that town; no, you can't live that life.

No, no, no.

An hour ago, I'd have reminded myself that I wasn't going to be with someone who was with me for the wrong reasons, and whose life I was likely to screw up to a gigantic degree. I'd have pointed out that we probably didn't even need to do this, because I'd been along for that crazy ride and I couldn't have re-created it, so how could she? I'd have told myself to relax, to have another drink, to wait for Mircea to work his magic.

But things had changed in that hour, hadn't they?

I'd gone from thinking I might someday find a way to conquer my demon, to having it almost conquer me. From struggling to finally get my life together, to watching it all fall apart. From yearning to be alone in my skin, to wondering if I was about to live my oldest nightmare, trapped in a prison of my own mind, unable to get out, to stop her, to—

From having a future, to living on borrowed time.

And suddenly a lot of things didn't seem so important anymore.

I stared at the hand. It was fine-boned for such a large man, long-fingered and slender. A fencer's hand, if there was such a thing, a duelist's hand. Louis-Cesare's hand. Waiting. Offering . . .

A chance that might never come again.

I drained my wine. Screw it. I'd had a lifetime of no. And can't, and shouldn't and don't. I was sick of no. Tonight, just for once, I wanted a little—

"Yes," I told him, and locked my fingers with his.

Chapter Thirty-seven

I thought the whole standing and bowing thing was just Louis-Cesare being, well, Louis-Cesare. But no. He grabbed the carafe of wine and the blanket and out the missing door we went. Jehan gave me a knowing smile as we passed, like he'd seen it all before. And then we were through the trees and into the next field, and up a gentle incline carpeted with clover.

The Milky Way was a river of silver overhead, glittering in between dark clouds laced with distant lightning. The clover was soft and cool, and so thick we could have left the blanket behind. The dancers were still flickering around the fire, orange-red shadows on the hill above us, like darker flames. But I thought there might be fewer of them.

Like we weren't the only ones to slip away into the night.

But the musicians seemed to have gotten a second wind, or possibly a second barrel, and were really going at it, pounding out a throbbing beat that made the stars seem to pulse, the flames to leap, the shadows to jump, as if the whole hillside were dancing. It reminded me of that night in Claire's garden, only that had been fey magic. And whatever was here tonight . . . was not.

Primal, earthy, human, there was nothing otherworldly about it. Or even necessarily magical, at least not in the way humans defined it. But I knew better. The people here were glorying in the simple things: not grand mansions and fine clothes, but food in their bellies, the taste of new wine on their lips, and a lover beside them, under them.

And there was no greater magic than that.

It was all I'd ever wanted, and had somehow never managed to find: a place of acceptance, peace within myself, someone to love. I might never get the first two, not now. But tonight . . . tonight, I had the third. And I intended to take full advantage.

I pushed Louis-Cesare down to the hillside.

He looked a little surprised, like he'd expected to run things. And then he tried, pulling me down on top of him. I pulled back. He started to follow but I pushed him down with a foot on his chest.

No. My night. My way.

He settled back again, watching me with fire-lit eyes.

His shirt might have gotten dirty, but his skin was clean. It looked incongruous next to my dirty toes, but it felt good, and the thudding heartbeat below felt better. I kept the foot in place as I unbuttoned my jacket.

It was short-sleeved with no shirt required, a Jackie-O-in-the-sixties kind of thing. But it did have those gloves. I paused to strip them off.

And Louis-Cesare made a disappointed sound in his throat.

I arched an eyebrow, but kept them on.

They were the only things I did.

Jacket, bra, skirt—I had to move my foot for the last, because it was a pencil-type and I couldn't get it off otherwise. Just as well. Easier to wriggle out of the panties that way.

He reached for me again, before I'd even finished, but my foot was back in place and I stopped him. He stared up at me with dilated eyes and a fading smile. Good; he was beginning to understand.

"My way," I told him roughly, and pushed him down again.

I picked up the jug of wine and stood over him with it, straddling his thighs while I dipped my fingers inside and took out the wine-soaked fruit. Sweet with the sharp tang of liquor, sun-warm from a long afternoon in the sun, warmer from my body.

Rivulets ran down my arm, dripped off my elbow, spotted the material of his trousers like blood. I took some time to lick wine from my palm, my wrist. Then I nudged his waistband with my heel. "Off."

His hands were shaking slightly as he undid the laces. Or maybe I was imagining things. Louis-Cesare was a duelist; his hands didn't shake. But it seemed to take him a long time to get free, maybe because I didn't move. He arched up to push the trousers down to his thighs, and then leaned forward to strip them down his legs.

He didn't make it.

He stopped, his face next to my hipbone, and the heavy lids over his eyes fluttered closed. And he *breathed*. Not the way humans do, to take in oxygen, because he didn't need that. But the way a vampire does, a breath that was almost touch, almost taste, almost sight, and gave more information than all three. He stopped and just breathed me in.

My hand came down, tangling in the mane of hair that was spilling, unconfined, over wide shoulders and down his back. I'd always had a problem with his hair. There was too much of it, it was too long, and the slight curl ensured that it was constantly escaping the discreet clip he used to confine it. I had often wondered why he didn't just cut it off.

A lot of the older vamps didn't, but it seemed that the dueling champion of the European Senate might have found it a hazard in battle. And after all, it was a small thing, this satin river gleaming red in the firelight. But I was suddenly, perversely, glad that he'd kept it.

My hand tightened, wanting to feel the softness I grasped, and his face turned into the gesture. A moment later, warm lips found the buttons on the inside of my wrist, undoing them without moving the strong hand he'd curved around my calf or raising the other. One, two, three buttons, undone by a deft tongue, and then a kiss placed on the inside on my wrist, where the pulse beat hard and fast.

Harder now, as he kissed down the smooth grain leather over my palm, as he bit the mound under my thumb, as he sucked a single digit into his mouth. And then white teeth clamped onto the skin-warm material and *pulled*. And stripped it off me in a single motion.

I swallowed, and felt my knees try to buckle.

He kissed his way back up my heat-damp skin, but left the other glove in place; I wasn't sure why. Maybe he liked the contrast, black leather against pale skin, or maybe it was some kind of fetish. We'd never talked about those, never talked about anything to do with the intimacy we hadn't had. But I must have been doing something right. When he suddenly looked up, his eyes were glazed, a little strange, and a little wild.

I wasn't sure what had put that look on his face, I just knew I wanted to keep it there as long as possible.

I pushed him back, without allowing him to free himself from the trousers still knotted around his legs. I spent a second just taking him in: naked strength, flexing muscles, already half hard. And then I knelt, straddling his body, pushing the hand he'd looped around my leg to the ground along with the other. And pinned them both with my knees.

"My way," I told him again, this time a little breathlessly.

He didn't answer. But his eyes blazed up at me. I wasn't sure if it was out of passion or frustration, but I doubted that Louis-Cesare was used to being ordered around. I imagined Christine never did that; her type of manipulation had been far more subtle. On the surface, she'd been the perfect elegant little vampire, all sweet and soft and obliging.

Too bad. Because I wasn't soft. I was rarely sweet. And as for obliging . . .

Well, it depended on how you defined the term.

I pressed down, knees hard against the palms that cupped them, making my point about who was in charge.

Louis-Cesare's eyes flashed again, dangerously, but he didn't move. I took that as a good sign and grabbed the carafe.

Another dip inside, another handful of wine-soaked fruit. I ate it while he watched me with hot eyes, while the drumbeat shivered our skin, while the juice dripped down my chest and onto his stomach. But I made sure to flex my thighs, keeping myself hovering just out of reach. Like the fruit I didn't let him have.

Another handful and the wine was running in rivulets across his chest, along the dips made by his abs, into his navel. It should have looked strange; it didn't. He matched the night now, the revelers up above, the festival that, I was willing to bet, had been old when the local church was a pagan grove attended by dark-robed priests. And defended by painted warriors.

Louis-Cesare would have made a fine ancient warrior, with the firelight playing over the high cheekbones, the proud nose, the sensual lips. Even the hillside seemed to think so. A wild vine had twined itself through the fiery hair, like a fey crown.

But no. He was too muscular for a fey, too solid, too broad. For some reason, the sheer size of him wasn't usually apparent, despite the fact that he had inches on most other men, and more than a foot on me. It was something in how he carried himself, or how he stood or . . . I didn't know. But sheer size wasn't everything. And right now, I had the advantage.

I intended to keep it.

His body was warm and heavy, scarred and strong, and I learned it with lips and tongue and fingertips. Memorizing it for later as his breathing sped up and his skin flushed and pebbled and his abdomen tightened in helpless little jerks. But he didn't move. Not even when I eased back, when my hands took the place of my knees, barely holding him down as I lapped at the spilled sweetness below his belly button.

He groaned, but didn't move, even when I stopped the pretense and let go of his hands. He could have broken my hold at this angle anyway; hell, he could have done it before, if past experience was anything to go on. But he seemed determined to take whatever I could dish out.

I smiled against his skin.

I could dish out a lot.

More fruit, more wine dripping on the bare expanse of Louis-Cesare's stomach and abs and chest and chin, because I ate it as I crawled back up his body. And then I paused, a few inches above his flushed face, to lick the residue from my palm. His mouth was open, his tongue flicking out again, like the strange little flutters in his abs, the ones he couldn't control.

I decided to indulge him—slightly—leaning down to that perfect, smeared mouth to share a wine-soaked kiss. He tried to deepen it, but I pulled back. Not yet.

He needed to learn some patience first. Needed to writhe and squirm and moan. My gloved fingers dug into his hip as I moved down again, letting my mouth go where it would, tracing every muscle, every line. Because I wanted him *to remember this*.

No matter what happened, no matter if I ended up as little more than a memory in some recess of Dorina's crazed mind, I wouldn't forget this. I wouldn't forget *him*. Hard muscles shining in the firelight, gleaming with the spilled wine, my red-stained kisses on his skin. Everywhere.

And something in his eyes I'd never thought to see from anyone. And I suddenly found that I didn't care why it was there. It was there. It was enough.

I trailed the leather-gloved hand across his stomach, down his hipbone, then traced the length of him. I wasn't holding him down anymore, but he stayed in place, watching me with half-closed eyes. Determinedly still.

Until I slowly followed the stains my finger had left with the tip of my tongue, licking them away.

And then his breath caught, and he gasped something and his body arched—but not enough. Because I drew back as he rose up, staying just above him, only my breath touching him. And either the wine was a lot more alcoholic than usual, or I was getting drunk on the whole experience. Because I laughed suddenly, low and elated, and reached for the carafe once more.

And somehow ended up on my back instead.

It happened so fast, I never even saw him move. But between one blink and the other, I was lying on the soft clover. And he was—

Standing over me, heavily muscled and solid as an oak, and barer than I was, since I still had on a glove and he was somehow wearing nothing but firelight. It shone in his hair, played over the hard body, darkened his eyes. But I didn't have much time to enjoy the scenery. Because he scooped up the jug of wine, and then slowly, gracefully, went to his knees over top of me.

And he was more generous than I had been, scooping out a wine-soaked offering, holding it to my mouth. I opened it automatically, even though it felt like I'd already had enough. *Maybe a little too much,* I thought, as I felt the world shift beneath me.

And then it happened again, that strange connection we'd always had, clicking into place even though this wasn't that sort of wine. But right now, I didn't seem to need it. Maybe because I was already in his mind, or he was already in mine? Didn't know. Didn't care, caught in the floating, surreal feeling of feeding and being fed, all at the same time.

I felt soft lips part, brushing fingers that were both mine and his at the same time. Felt the heat of my own tongue as it curled around a finger, saw myself in a flash—dark eyes shining, face flushed, lips full and red-stained and opening hungrily again.

"More," someone said. And I wasn't sure if it was him or me.

But he was the one who sat back, showing me the whole long line of his body, almost every inch displaying signs of my possession. A bite mark on his left shoulder, which he deliberately wasn't healing. Twin outlines of my hands, like the ochre-colored impressions found in cave paintings, on his pecs. A perfect imprint of my lips, caught in the middle of an openmouthed kiss, on his lower stomach.

Mine, I thought, but didn't say. Because he wasn't. Except for tonight. And if this was all I had, all I would ever have, then I needed to *touch—*

My fingers flexed under his knees, but he didn't let up. It should have infuriated me, but instead I felt something in me twist, uncoil, release. I felt drunk on more than wine, as his thumb ran along the curve of my mouth, chasing some wayward juice, and received a nip of teeth instead. A silent order for *more.*

And more there was, more fruit, more wine, more strange double vision, showing me my own face superimposed over the flames dancing in blue, blue eyes. More emotions, most of which I couldn't, or wouldn't, name. But behind the heat was a strange vulnerability that was all too familiar, and a terrible sympathy that raked my soul, without stirring up the sharp-edged pride I carried like a shield.

Because he *understood.* What it was like to be unwanted, to be abandoned, to be shunned. Our isolation might have been caused by separate things, prejudice on my side, politics on his.

But the result . . . the result had been the same.

And it was suddenly too much, like something was cracking open inside. I let my eyes flutter closed, but I could still see through his, although I almost wished I couldn't. Because my lids might have been shut, but my face was open, too open. He cupped my jaw, and I turned into his palm. And when he leaned close enough to lick the wine from my cheeks, I tasted it right along with him, and the faint edge of salt beneath the sweetness.

My voice sounded strange when I spoke, harsh and raw, and so low I could feel it in my belly. "More."

He took a handful of fruit, bringing it to his mouth, before bending over me, one fat, wine-soaked strawberry held between hard white teeth, dripping a trail of bloody drops across my torso, my throat, my—

I took it from his lips although it wasn't what I wanted. Not anymore. But the kiss that followed—yes. *Yes.*

It was slow, sweet from more than wine, and gentle, but not careful. I licked the taste of crushed berries from his mouth, finding Louis-Cesare beneath the wine. I wanted to kiss him until what passed for morning, to lick away every taste but my own. I moaned around his tongue and the sound made him kiss me harder. And I discovered that when he lost control, Louis-Cesare kissed the same way he fought, wild and passionately, and with his entire body. He kissed like he was never going to stop—

Until he suddenly did, leaving me gasping for air, while smooth lips and rough hands and soft hair trailed down my body. I could feel my heartbeat loud in my ears, at my groin, fluttering in the bottom of the foot I'd pressed against his thigh. He was marking me now, too, leaving prints and streaks on my skin as he worked downward, as he parted my legs, as he . . .

I breathed his name as he settled between my thighs, stroked his cheek, buried my hands in cool, silky hair as a warm tongue went to work. And I could swear his strokes matched the pulse of the stars, the beat of the drums, the sounds of the night. All of which became louder, brighter, more real as I was ravished by hard hands and soft lips and wet tongue.

I let my hands grip his head to steady myself, rather than to guide him where he needed to go. Because he already seemed to get that, judging from the way my breath was coming faster and my body was quivering and my thighs were clenching uncontrollably. And my fingers were digging into the muscles of his shoulders where they'd dropped when the hillside started to shake and the stars to spin.

To the point that I barely noticed when a storm spread across the horizon, blotting out half the sky.

It was sweeping this way, on wide, tattered wings of night, but it didn't seem to matter. Not in comparison to the fingers digging into my hips, or the sounds Louis-Cesare was making in his throat, or the warm tongue dragging over me. And then I threw my head back and—

And saw the sky crack open.

Not with lightning, or thunder, or anything else that

would have made sense. But slashed. As if a giant talon had caught the edge and ripped its way across the stars.

It was about the time the storm swept over the landscape, gobbling up the hill, the dancers and the bonfire. And then heading straight for us.

"I think . . . I think she found us," I gasped, only to have Louis-Cesare grip my face, turn it to his.

"No!" Blue eyes locked with mine. "See me, see *me*."

And he kissed me, even as we were plunged into a torrent of slapping wind and wailing outrage. And it was a damned good kiss. My stomach did a weird, tilting cartwheel, my hands tightened reflexively on his shoulders, and one of my legs went around him, pulling him to me, *in* me, as what sounded like a thousand banshees wailed by overhead.

I barely heard them. If falling into the moment helped us to gray out, then we must be almost invisible, I thought, as he growled and covered me with his body. Taking me as he'd stripped off the glove earlier, smooth and sure, in one long thrust.

It hurt, to be stretched so abruptly, filled so completely. But the sheer animal satisfaction I took was greater. This was *mine*, the hard body above me, the sweetness on my tongue, the hands bruising my hips. And I met him stroke for stroke, arching up as he flexed into me, in deep, powerful motions that sparked coiling warmth in my gut, melted my spine.

Mine, I thought deliriously, as a shadow swept over us, like a cape had been thrown over the sky.

Mine, as my hands stroked up that strong back, velvety and warm, where every dip and line of muscle fit sweetly into my palms.

Mine, as the storm trembled in the air around us, and shook the earth beneath us.

"Mine," I murmured, as blue eyes met mine, wide and startled. And then closed again as he *took* my breath in a kiss so consuming that I barely noticed when the storm continued on toward the horizon, the midnight wings showing vague starlight through in patches as it passed overhead.

As it missed us.

"Yours," Louis-Cesare groaned, pushing his face into the crook of my neck as his movements turned erratic inside me, as my body clenched around him, as the storm banked and turned, like some great bird, somehow zeroing in on our location despite everything.

And then the hill cracked open, the earth fell away beneath us, and we were falling.

Chapter Thirty-eight

I landed on my own, Louis-Cesare being torn away in the plummet. And I landed hard. I slammed into what felt like concrete, only to hear the pop and feel the sandpaper grind of bone on bone beneath me.

It was my hand. And of course, it was the right one. Not that it mattered, since I wasn't being given a chance to go on the attack anyway.

A blow caught me as I tried to rise, and a kick to my ribs had me retching. And then that damned boot was back, visible for a split second before making contact with my skull. The impact was hard enough to send me tumbling, and instinct had me putting out my injured hand to break my fall.

Not the best idea, I realized, as a sickening wave of pain hit me.

Come on. You're better than this! I told myself harshly, as I stumbled trying to rise. But I didn't appear to be listening. Maybe because something, either the crack to the head or the mental powers I was really starting to envy, was adding another layer of hell to the fight. Suddenly, even blinking took an effort, and anything more ambitious felt like I had a two-hundred-pound weight attached to every limb.

Unfortunately, my assailant didn't seem to have that problem. She was kicking me over and over in the ribs, in almost the same spot, because I was too winded and in too much pain to move out of the way fast enough.

Not good, I thought, as the stabbing pain of a broken rib suddenly cut into my side.

I snarled and kicked out with a foot, catching what felt like the softness of a stomach. But it bought me maybe a second at best, which wasn't even enough to get back on my feet. And then another rib went, and another, and I lashed out again—blindly, because I couldn't see a damned thing. The darkness was complete, as much as if I really had fallen into a pit in the earth, and the only things I saw were the stars exploding behind my eyes.

Until a single spear of light shot through the darkness.

It was tiny, like the glow of a very dim flashlight, but I started crawling toward it anyway. Until a hard kick to my chin had me flipping over, and another destroyed a kneecap. And if I hadn't managed to roll to the side, the boot that stabbed down where my chest had been might have killed me.

Although that outcome was looking pretty inevitable right now anyway. Because I just plain couldn't move fast enough to avoid the blows that were quickly beating me to a pulp. I cried out again, in pain and sheer fury—

And the pinprick of light turned into a flood.

I blinked, barely able to see past the glow, but managed to make out the figure of a man. "Louis—" I began thickly, reaching out—

But it wasn't.

The dark silhouette was tall but not that tall, broad but not that broad, familiar . . . and even more familiar. Dark hair, dark suit, but eyes that were glowing even brighter than the illumination behind him. Like twin stars in the gloom, brighter than I'd ever seen them.

Mircea, I mouthed, because I couldn't seem to draw a breath. But he started walking forward anyway, slightly off course, but in the right general direction. And every step he took parted the darkness more, like a curtain being drawn back on a stage. Until I could see again.

The light behind him resolved itself into the dim view of the harbor that I was really beginning to hate. But it was also the only way out. And if I could reach it . . .

And maybe I could. Because, suddenly, I wasn't being attacked. I struggled up on my good arm, broken, bleeding, peering around for an assailant that wasn't there anymore.

Maybe because she had found a new target.

I looked back at Mircea, just in time to see him stumble. And a bloody slash, like the cut of a sword, appear on the front of his formerly white shirt. He ignored it, moving forward another few feet, only to be hit again. And again. I watched, horrified, as gashes that looked almost black in the strange light appeared on his face, his hands, on the arm he held out in front of him, across his eyes.

And then a massive blow sent him staggering.

"Mircea!" It was barely a whisper, practically inaudible, even to me. But never underestimate a vampire's hearing. Because his head jerked up, and the wedge of light around him narrowed, focused—and spilled all around me.

It was the most beautiful thing I'd ever seen, a glistening pale blue lifeline.

Or maybe not.

Because Mircea wasn't getting much closer. He should have been able to cross the distance between us in a heartbeat. Instead, he was barely walking forward, and getting shredded in the process, his coat already a tattered mess, his shirt drenched red. And a panic gripped me like nothing I'd ever known.

Because I'd never seen him injured so easily. Because it didn't look like he could see me, or knew exactly where I was. But mostly because he wasn't fighting back.

And then he stumbled again, going down to one knee.

"Go!" I croaked, because I couldn't scream. But if he heard, he gave no sign. And he wasn't leaving.

Of course he wasn't, I thought savagely, dragging myself to my feet. When had he ever been anything but a stubborn son of a—

My knee collapsed, dumping me on the floor. Stupidly, I tried to stand again, and for some reason, it worked that time. Every step was agony, my ears were ringing too loud to hear anything and I couldn't fucking *breathe*. And the light from the small wedge that Mircea had opened kept moving around, like it was playing keep-away, although that was probably more from my wildly zigzagging course.

But I was up.

I was moving.

And so was he.

How he was doing it I didn't know, but hearing wasn't the only thing you should never underestimate about master vampires.

Or dhampirs, I thought, gritting my teeth while spots danced in front of my eyes and one of my own ribs stabbed me in the side and the damned leg collapsed again. So I crawled, because there was nothing between me and my goal but pain and *fuck* pain. Because Mircea might not be defending himself, but he was doing a good job of keeping the bitch's attention on him.

Too good of a job, I thought, as he collapsed to both knees, his clothes a bloody mess, his face unrecognizable.

I didn't cry out again, because I didn't have the breath and because it wouldn't have helped and because I wasn't going to give her a warning. I was just going to kill her. I didn't care what it did to me, I was going to *fucking kill her*, I thought viciously, as the light flickered and the wedge narrowed and Mircea didn't look at me.

He still didn't, even as the most savage beating I'd ever seen continued, throwing him around the sparkling blue light, crushing limbs and shattering bone and sending splatters of blood arcing into the air like rubies as I crawled and slipped and closed the gap. But not completely. Not before the bitch somehow got a clue, a dark shadow turning my way as she suddenly remembered that, oh, yeah, I wasn't dead yet.

Not yet, I snarled to myself, getting my good leg under me as she flew my way. And then falling and rolling and lunging and grabbing—

A hand slick with blood and cold, too cold.

And then falling again, into nothingness that suddenly bloomed into light so bright that it tore a gasp from my throat.

Or maybe that was Radu. I couldn't see him because there was something in my eyes, but I identified his cologne. And then he was pulling me back and I was flailing and fighting and not getting anywhere because I had no strength.

Until he abruptly let me go, and I dropped like a sack of sand, hitting my chin on something I identified as the edge of the bar. But I managed to swipe a shaking hand over my eyes in time to see Louis-Cesare, lying unconscious on the floor; Marlowe, yelling at the half dozen guards who had just flooded the room; and Mircea—

Mircea in a widening pool of blood—eyes, mouth, ears, nose, all gushing bloody streams onto his dark suit and the pale sofa and—

And for a minute, I thought he was dead.

And I think Marlowe did, too, because as soon as he'd cleared the room, he grabbed Radu's arm. "Let up," he said, his face terrible. "Wait for the healer—"

And then Radu—*Radu*—jerked Marlowe up and *threw* him at the window, sending his body crashing through the heavy drapes and the glass behind them. It set the curtains swaying, back and forth, like the pendulum of a ticking clock, intermittently highlighting the tableaux on the sofa in beams of light-filled dust.

"Hold him," Radu snarled at me, the voice nothing like his usual dulcet tones.

I was already moving as he spoke, scrambling across the floor, because my leg seemed to work now. Unlike my brain, which could only focus on that pale face. But I grabbed Mircea, who like me, seemed to be whole physically. But the blood—God, so much blood—and he was deadweight now—

"Pay attention!" Radu snapped, jerking at his sleeve as Marlowe vaulted back into the room.

And stopped, because he'd figured out what was going on the same time I had.

"Will he?" I breathed, my voice strange in my ears.

Radu ignored me. And then he bared an arm that looked nothing like its usual plump, well-toned self. It was corpse-pale, with ropy muscle and prominent veins running purplish blue under the surface. And fingernails that were suddenly a lot more pointed, a lot more talon-like, than the perfect manicure he'd had a second ago. Like the face that was suddenly older, more gaunt, and the hair that was finer, duller, with wide streaks of silver striping the brown.

I stared at him, and then around at the room, because it was that or look down. And I didn't want to look down. Didn't want to see that usually so-poised face splattered with blood, the sharply intelligent eyes closed, the fine mouth slack and agape. It would make it all too real, this strange, dust-filled room, with the ticking clock and the swinging drapes and the tasteful furniture I didn't need to remember because nothing was going to happen in here of importance today. *Nothing.*

And then Radu sliced his arm open from elbow to wrist, using one of those knifelike nails. Blood welled up, not red like a human's or a young vampire's but dark, dark, almost black, with dull crimson glints when the intermittent light hit it. It didn't gush like human blood, either, but seeped down his skin, molasses-thick with age and power.

He held the bloody limb to his brother's pale lips, pressing them tight around the wound, forcing the fluid inside.

Blood of family, I thought dizzily, my own blood icing in my veins. The last resort for a dying vampire. Mircea's own strength, distilled in the body of every vampire he'd ever made. And reinforced in Radu's case by five hundred years of love, shared pain, struggle and sacrifice—

None of which did him any good if he wouldn't take it.

"His mouth was full of blood already, I don't know if . . ." someone babbled, and I snapped my lips shut when I realized it was me.

"Drink," Radu rasped, a taloned hand digging into his brother's shoulder. *"Drink!"*

But Mircea didn't.

Marlowe stood by the couch, staring. Face white, eyes dark and burning. For once, the mask was gone, and he looked as stunned as I felt. And as horrified. And something else that I finally recognized—belatedly, because I'd never seen it on that face before.

He saw me looking and blanked again, but his voice was rough when he spoke. "How?"

"I . . . He wouldn't defend himself," I said, my voice still sounding strange. High and weak—and shrill with fear. But unlike Marlowe, I couldn't seem to mask it.

Nothing, I told myself savagely.

"Against what? What did this?"

"Dorina." There was no point in denying it now. "She was after me, but he got in the way—"

"No," Radu said, not looking up from his brother's face.

"What?"

"Mircea said it wasn't you—her. It was almost all he managed to say before—"

"Then why didn't he defend himself?" Marlowe demanded, before I could. "If he wasn't worried about hurting—"

"That is one of the reasons for using a guide," Radu told him abruptly. "Even a gifted master cannot hold open such a connection and also defend against attack. It takes too much concentration—"

"He *had* a guide!"

"Louis-Cesare was knocked unconscious," Radu snapped, gesturing at him. Where he still lay, because no one had bothered to help him.

Somehow I didn't think he'd mind.

"He was never trained for this," Radu added. "And it is not easy, in the best of times. And what he did—I am surprised he lasted as long as he did."

"Then Mircea should have damned well waited until he woke up!"

Radu looked at him angrily. "Dory was under attack—"

"*We're* under attack. The whole damned lot of us! We can't afford to lose him, Radu!"

"As he could not afford to lose her." Radu smoothed down his brother's hair. "We have lost too many, through the years."

"She was the one attacking him!"

Radu looked up, eyes glowing in fear or anger or pain—or all three. "You heard him. He said no."

"He would," Marlowe said, looking at me. And making me wonder if this hadn't all been a waste. If I would even make it out of here alive.

Right now I didn't care all that much. I didn't care about anything but the blood dripping onto the sofa. Unused.

"It wasn't you," Radu said softly, turquoise eyes meeting mine.

"Then who?" I asked, my voice weaker now.

Because I was bleeding, too. I'd barely noticed, but slippery trails were trickling from my ears, down my neck, soaking the once fine material of the suit. More was filling my eyes, along with something else that I blinked away.

"Then who?" I demanded, louder.

"Mircea didn't know," Radu said softly, gaunt hand covering mine, where I gripped his brother's shoulder.

No. My *father's*. Where I held my *father's* shoulder, I thought angrily, grasping it tighter. And somehow managing to be furious at myself, at everyone, at no one, all at the same time.

"He said he thought someone was using you for an anchor," Radu told me. "That they were narrowing in on you as if you were their guide. In order to attack you."

"What? How?"

"He didn't say. He was concentrating on finding you; his reports were ... sporadic. I'm sorry, Dory; I don't know any more. When he wakes—"

"If he wakes," Marlowe said, and then stopped.

As if there was nothing left to say.

No. *NO*, I thought, and shook the limp body in my arms, causing the head to fall back onto my shoulder. Tears splashed his face, mingled with the blood, streaked the perfect features that were marble-like in their beauty. And in their coldness. The tears were mine; I didn't care.

"Drink," I begged him, as the room grayed out and the rushing in my ears got louder and he just lay there, draped across my lap, Radu's blood cascading down his chin.

So much power, so much life, *right there*, and he wouldn't take it.

My anger suddenly found a target, and it was the man bleeding on the sofa. "Marlowe's right. He should have left me," I said harshly.

"You know he wouldn't do that," Radu admonished.

"Then he's a fool." My head was spinning, my temples pounding, but I didn't care. I only cared about the man on the sofa. And the anger. So much anger bottled up for so many years, and finally spilling over.

"Coward," I spat. "Fool and coward!"

"Dory!"

"It's the truth. Five centuries of life, of fighting and conniving and scheming and clawing and *this*? This is how it ends?"

Nothing.

And it utterly enraged me. Like all those years, loving him and hating him and being drawn to him but being afraid to get too close, because it always, always ended the same way. With him leaving. Either physically walking away, or withdrawing behind an icy facade until I did.

And now he was doing it again.

Now he was doing it permanently.

But the bastard wasn't getting away with it this time.

I already had him in my arms, and now I shook him. A great clot of blood, his own by the color, fell from his lips, staining my already gory shirt. Like I gave a damn.

"Is this how it ends, Mircea? Is it?"

Nothing.

I threw him down on the sofa, straddled him, slapped him, hard. *"Is it?"*

"Security," I heard Marlowe mutter, behind me.

Fuck him.

"I'll kill the first one who touches me," I snarled.

And then I slapped Mircea again.

"Five centuries, *five fucking centuries*, only to die a

puling coward while this thing gets away. What about revenge? What about pride? Don't you care?"

Nothing.

"So many years, and for nothing," I told him scornfully. "If you were going to die like this, going to just give the fuck up, you should have done it then. You should have died with *her*."

Radu was looking at me, horrified. And then he seemed to remember what he was doing, and stuck the bloody arm to Mircea's lips again. Not that it mattered.

"She waited," I said, staring down at him, the blood pounding in my ears. "You didn't come. She bled out, on one of your own brother's stakes, worse than a damned crucifixion, only it was your name on her lips as she prayed. And as she died, still calling for you. Sobbing, begging . . . but you weren't there. *You were never there!*"

I shook him again, he and Radu together, because as terrified as he was looking, Radu didn't move. "She needed you; you didn't come. Now *I* need you. Are you going to abandon me, too? *Are you going to leave me, too?*"

Nothing, except the tick of the clock and my harsh breathing.

Nothing.

Until . . . a movement. Tiny, tiny. Just a tick in his throat.

Or possibly . . . a swallow.

"Mircea . . . Mircea, *please*," I whispered, as the light in the room, brilliant only seconds ago, dimmed, narrowed to just his face.

Please.

And then nothing.

Chapter Thirty-nine

I tried to push him out, but the Scream had taken all my strength, not that I'd had much to begin with. And he was strong. So strong, this strange creature of light.

"Why are you doing this?" The voice was warm, deep, gentle. Inexorable. "You are hurt and exhausted. And at the moment, weaker than the things you stalk. This is not about the Senate . . . is it?"

I fought back, knowing it to be futile. I didn't succeed in driving him out, but for the moment, he didn't push any further. He was waiting for me to tell him.

I'd be damned if I told him.

But something must have leaked through, anyway.

"The child?" He sounded surprised. And then forbidding. "What do you know?"

I didn't answer.

"Tell me!"

It was sharp, the tolerance completely gone from his mental voice. But I still said nothing. I couldn't.

"Then show me," he said grimly.

And the darkness became dazzling.

The ballroom was a swirl of light and color and sound, stunning, overwhelming. I was almost glad I couldn't see much of it, yet I yearned for more. I dug my fingers a little farther into the lines of mortar between the bricks, hitched my toes a little higher on the faint edge of an ornamental frieze, and stared.

The pose left me clinging to the side of the palazzo like a barnacle on a ship, and hurt after only a very few

minutes. But there were no other safe perches. Gaily cos-
tumed people were constantly coming and going on the
balcony around the corner, or arriving in gondolas at the
pier just below that. And there were lights in every window.

There were no lights here, the shade from another
balcony directly overhead offering a wedge of darkness
in which to hide. I liked the dark. It allowed me to see
others before they saw me. It was cool, comforting, safe.

But the light . . .

The light was irresistible.

They were irresistible, the very things Mircea had
warned me about. Terrible and beautiful, alien and
hauntingly familiar, repellent and oh so seductive. I
could never get enough of them.

And they had taught me things, things he wouldn't. Or
couldn't, for I did not think he knew much about them,
either. My favorite game was called Families, where I
tried to guess how they all fit together.

At first I thought it was easy. Vampires of a single line
all burned with the same unearthly fire. If the master
wore green flames like a cape, then his Children did, too.
Only in smaller, lesser, darker hues: moss instead of emerald, olive instead of jade.

But then I started to notice that that wasn't always
true. Sometimes there would be different colors, some
jarringly so, within the same family line, and it confused
me. Until I overheard a conversation, and realized that
some vampires were adopted into families from other
lines. Or traded or sold or acquired a hundred different
ways.

And although the new master's power bled over into
the old, it never quite erased all of it. So some of the
most formidable-looking vampires had halos of purple-
striped green or red-dotted gray or, my favorite, a stern
old man who walked about with a shining outline of
pink-, blue- and brown-flecked orange.

At first it was funny. And then it made me wonder. My
aura was blue. Mircea's was white. Why was mine not
white, too?

"And what did he tell you?" the voice asked softly.

"That I was part of his physical family, but not of the vampire. No dhampir ever is. Mircea could control me to a degree through his mental gifts, but there was no bond of blood. There was no formal tie."

"And how did you feel about that?"

I didn't answer.

"Vampires are, by nature, social creatures, some of the most I have ever encountered," he mused. "They live in large, active families, constantly in the company of others, right down to the sharing of thoughts. I have never met a lone vampire. I do not think they exist, other than for revenants."

"And dhampirs," I said hoarsely.

The visits to the palazzos had become less and less frequent over time, not due to Mircea's prohibition but to my own pain. The yearning grew as I aged, to the point that it became torture to watch them laugh and dance and scheme and belong in a way I never could. For I was not vampire; I could not make a Child. And the human part of me . . .

"Could not have a child, either," he guessed softly.

"No."

"And so you were alone. Vampires are family-oriented by nature, driven to unite with others, to form binding ties. But that is the one thing you could not do."

I didn't answer, but I didn't have to. I felt him flip through my memories, like someone paging through a book. Scene after scene of failure, of watching lovers leave, friends flee—

"Even the other part of yourself," he murmured. "Cut off. Walled away."

I turned on him, impotent, furious. "Why are you doing this? Does your kind take pleasure in the pain of others?"

"Some do," he admitted. "But I am not among them."

"Then why?"

"I needed to understand you. To know why you wanted the child. And I am satisfied that it was not for a weapon, or for your Senate. But for family, connection . . . loneliness."

"What does it matter?" I asked harshly.

"Because you may be the only one who can help me find her."

I woke in another sumptuous bedroom, judging by the feel of the linens. But it wasn't Louis-Cesare's. I could feel the pressure of the consul's house holding me down, like a dozen hands trying to push me through the bedding, even before I opened my eyes. And then I blinked the room into view and had it confirmed.

It was a nice room, blue and brown and beige, with lots of iridescent satins and thick velvets and a few furs warming up the ever-present marble. All of which my eyes glossed over because they were busy looking at something else. But I didn't feel like getting up, or even moving, so for a few minutes I just lay there.

And watched E.T. float around in my wall.

The expanse opposite the bed was mostly unadorned, except for subtle striations in the marble. And a few pieces of museum-quality art. And some glowy blobs that, yes, kind of looked like E.T.

I turned my head—slowly, because it made the room do some convoluted spinning thing otherwise—to look at the wall to the left. The blobs sort of reminded me of reflections, like people passing in front of stained-glass windows. And having their shadows distorted before being cast on the opposite wall.

There was only one problem: there were no windows.

Not too surprising. Regular old vampires had to make do with regular old houses and modify them to suit. But the consul didn't have to put up with that crap.

I hadn't had an opportunity to do much exploring last time I was here. But from what I'd been able to tell, her house was built like an onion, with an outermost skin that opened onto long, shallow hallways that kept it from looking strange to anyone who might happen by and wonder why anyone would build a house with no windows. But that's essentially what it was after you penetrated the first layer.

And I guess I was past that. Because all I saw was some shelves and a table-and-lamp combo. None of which could be throwing light shadows, including the lamp, which wasn't on.

I turned my head back again—slowly, slowly—and looked at the wall. But E.T. must have found me pretty boring, because he was gone now. Or maybe my brain had decided not to go *schizo* right at the moment, although I didn't know why. It had done everything else.

Including possibly killing Mircea.

That whole horror scene came back to me in a rush, hard enough to leave me gasping. I abruptly sat up, and just as quickly regretted it when the room telescoped and threatened to collapse. But I wasn't going to lie back down.

Not until I found out what had happened.

I threw off the covers and went almost a yard before my knees gave way, throwing me onto a very nice carpet that probably didn't need any puke stains. I stayed down for a moment, breathing, waiting for my head to accept the idea that, yes, *we were doing this*. And then I got to my feet and stumbled toward the door again.

And got halfway there before I realized I was naked.

Of course I am, I thought angrily, and went back to the bed for a sheet. God forbid I actually wake up dressed anymore.

I made a sixteen-hundred-thread-count sarong and wobbled back to the door. And poked my head out. And was immediately glad that I'd had enough working brain cells to think of the sheet. Because there were no fewer than six huge vamps outside, all spit and polish in shiny faux Roman gear, eyes expressionless pools of disapproval even without being exposed to a naked dhampir.

But one of them wrinkled his nose anyway, as if he smelled something bad.

Yeah, well, fuck you, too, buddy, I didn't say, because I wanted to see Mircea more than I wanted to piss them off.

I started out the door, only to have two long spears crossed in front of my face, one from each of the guys framing the door. I looked at them, but they didn't even bother to look back. They were staring straight ahead, just like the two on the opposite side of the hall, who apparently found something fascinating on the door over my head.

"Really?" I croaked, not gesturing at my sheet-covered form or the dried blood flaking off my upper lip or the fact that my eyes kept trying to roll up in my head. Because I was afraid if I let go of the doorframe, I was going to end up on my knees again.

And because nobody was looking at me anyway.

I cleared my throat and decided to try again. "I just want to see my father."

And okay, *that* got a reaction. Not verbal, because I didn't rate that. But the stony look in the vamps' eyes got a little stonier.

"Sorry," I said drily. "I forgot that it's bad taste to mention that *he is my father*, but there you go. And I'm going to see him."

I started to duck under the spears, only to have the two vamps on the other wall suddenly appear in my face. Or, at least, their crotches did. Another day, I would have made a cute remark about heat and leather jock straps, but I wasn't feeling real cute right now. Apparently, they weren't either, because the next thing I knew, the spears were gone, the door was shut and I was back inside the room, despite not being able to recall how I got there.

Okay, then.

I stared at the door, swaying gently, for what was probably a full minute. I would like to say that I was standing there planning my next move, but mostly I was just standing. My head felt really . . . odd. . . . My mouth was dry and I really, really wanted to crawl back into bed.

But I wanted to see Mircea more. And I was going to. Just as soon as I figured out—

My train of thought, such as it was, got derailed at the appearance of another otherworldly visitor. Only this one was a little different. Instead of E.T., it kind of looked like the blobs that used to goop around inside lava lamps, round and unformed and visible in a full-length mirror to the right of the door.

I turned around. It was on the same wall that the bed was facing, the one that held a large, ornate fireplace and a couple chairs. And, at the moment, some fuzzy blue stains that glooped along until they hit the mantel. And then flowed along its massive carved shelf until they fell off the other side.

I blinked at them for a moment, and then wobbled over.

They hadn't waited. By the time I got there, they'd traversed the entire length of the room and disappeared. But before that, they'd gotten a little clearer for a moment. And instead of random blobs, they'd formed themselves into a vaguely person-shaped thing, with a distinct head, torso, and a couple smaller bits that might have been arms or tentacles.

I supposed the former was more likely, but considering where I was, I wasn't ruling out the latter. *But here's hoping,* I thought, and stuck my head in the fireplace. Or, more accurately, *through* the fireplace, because the bastard wasn't really there.

It shouldn't have surprised me—what does a vampire really need with a fireplace? And yet they were all over the building. And now that I thought about it, I vaguely recalled the consul vanishing into one the last time I was here, when she'd thought I was too out of it to notice.

Like I had just done.

It took a moment for my eyes to adjust to the dark, and then to notice that I was standing in a corridor, surrounded by a wedge of hazy light. It was coming from a filmy ward over the surface of a square opening in the wall. The fireplace, I assumed, which was apparently just for camouflage. I could see the whole room from here, including the bed, which was creepy.

But not as creepy as another light monster coming my way.

What is this, Grand Central? I thought, staring stupidly at the haze for a second, which was getting rapidly brighter. And then I stumbled quickly in the opposite direction.

It wasn't exactly a run, because running into utter blackness isn't fun, and I wasn't really up to it right now anyway. The best I could manage was a shuffle, with a hand on the wall for balance. But at least there was nothing to trip over, because nobody had bothered about decoration in here. It was just a concrete floor, cold against my bare feet, and an equally cold blank wall.

Or it was until a reddish light started coming toward me from the other direction. I turned around, but the purple light monster was still there and still coming up strong behind me, judging by the way shadows were jumping on the ceiling. *Well, shit,* I thought, backing up, trying to get a wall behind me.

Which would have worked better if there had been one there.

But my reaching hand found only air, just my ears registered a difference in the echo. I was standing in front of another opening. And then I was through it and into an almost black room.

I threw myself to the side of the opening, hard enough to set my head spinning, so I didn't see much as the blobs passed by outside. Just flickers of different colors strobing in through the opening for a second. And then they were gone and everything was dark again.

Except for something that gleamed to the far right of the room, displacing a tiny bit of dark.

My eyes fixed on it, and after a moment, it came into focus.

It was a candle.

I felt my spine relax, and I let out a breath I hadn't noticed I was holding.

It was sitting on a small table by a bed. The bed was big and old-fashioned, with a canopy and curtains to close it off from the cold—and the consul's spy tunnel, I assumed. It was the sort that had gone out of style with humans when things like central heating came into vogue, but had retained its popularity in the vampire community due to offering added protection from the sun.

Of course, that wasn't needed here. A windowless room inside a vampire stronghold was about as far from sunlight as it was possible to get. But the bed was there anyway. So it probably belonged to one of the older vamps, who tended to be more traditional.

And who probably wouldn't be thrilled to wake up and find a dhampir looming over him or her.

I paused, because the last thing I needed was another fight. And if whoever was in there was old, they were probably also powerful and well rested and I . . . was not. So it might not just be inconvenient.

I should go back to bed.

For once, I should just do the smart thing and go back and get some sleep. By the time I woke up, someone would probably be around to tell me how Mircea was doing. Who was probably fine because he was a freaking tank and people had been trying to kill him for five centuries and had usually ended up dead instead. He was fine and I didn't even know that this was his room and he was *fine*.

I moved closer.

What the hell, feet? I thought, but the feet didn't comment. Except to send up happy signals about the squashiness of the rugs and the smoothness of the wooden patches in between them. Which were brief because it looked like somebody had mugged a caravan in here, with a dozen priceless rugs scattered carelessly around.

But at least they muffled my steps, not that I was worrying about it by the time I got halfway across the room. Because along with fine leather and old books and the faint smokiness of the candle was an even fainter scent. Dark and musky and piney and—

"Mircea."

He was lying on his side, pale and cold and white, and for a second, my heart stopped. Until I told myself not to be stupid. He was a *vampire*. And when they rest, they don't always bother to keep up appearances. Especially if they need their strength for other things.

But I didn't breathe again until I bent over him, and brushed fine strands of loose, dark hair off his face. And saw beautiful pale features, which unlike mine had been cleaned up. And vampires don't waste time on corpses that aren't going to rise again. So if he was here—

I felt something in my own chest unclench.

I should have known. Mircea was a master mentalist. He could repair anything to do with the mind.

Couldn't he?

I glanced around. It would help if he had eaten, but if so, dinner had already departed. I frowned at that. What if he woke up hungry? What if his mental abilities were impaired after everything that had happened? Why the hell was nobody here? The guy was a goddamned senator. Didn't he rate a nurse?

I glanced at the door, and thought about raising some hell, even if it got me kicked back to my room. Or into a cell, more likely, because no way was Marlowe just letting me walk out of here. The number of guards had said that much.

But, of course, Mircea *did* rate a nurse, he rated a whole roomful of them. So if he was alone, it was by choice. But I still didn't like it. What if that thing was still around here somewhere? What if it attacked him again?

Only it wouldn't, would it? If Radu was right and it hadn't been Dorina, then it was almost certainly someone with a vested interest in my not recalling what happened on that pier. And that meant if it came back for anyone, it would be me.

I felt my lips draw back from my teeth slightly. Good. It would save me the trouble of having to track it the hell down.

Because I would.

The son of a bitch had hurt Mircea.

And nobody got to do that but me.

I stared at him a moment longer, but he wasn't looking real conversational. I shoved my hand through my hair, then cupped it on the back of my neck. The muscles were so tense there, it felt like I could flick a thumb against my nape and hear it twang. Like I hadn't been able to relax, even in sleep.

What a shock.

But it was calm here, peaceful. Maybe that was why I didn't feel like leaving, even though there was no reason to stay. Mircea was already in a healing trance, judging by the fact that he hadn't woken up as soon as I came in the room. He didn't need medical help, beyond what he could give himself, and as for mental . . .

Well, whatever abilities I had were locked up with my other half, and she wasn't talking.

But I still didn't feel like going anywhere.

Mircea's hand slipped off the sheet, to the mattress at his side. I started to pick it up, to put it back in place. And then I stopped, my fingers hovering a few inches above his.

Even in a healing trance, something like a touch might wake a master. In fact, on some level, he was probably already awake, at least enough to have identified me as not posing a threat. But a touch might set off alarms, might make him wonder if he'd identified correctly.

And I didn't want that. Mircea often managed to run circles around me in conversation even when I wasn't about to fall over. We needed to talk, about a lot of things, about a lifetime of things. But this wasn't the time.

And then there was the fact that this was . . . nice. Odd, because I could never remember being with him without having my hackles up, without being tense and guarded and watchful. I had, of course; that scene in Venice proved that. But it had seemed almost . . . surreal. That girl with her bare toes and her candy-thieving ways and her obvious adoration of her equally adoring father . . . it just . . . I couldn't . . .

I pulled my hand back.

I didn't want to disturb him when he looked relaxed. It wasn't an expression I'd seen very often. Or ever, actually.

But then, maybe he'd never had much to be relaxed about.

I wondered what it had been like for him, in those early years. For someone trained his whole life to be the leader, the provider, the protector, to suddenly be unable to do any of those things. To be a prince without a country, or a treasury, or an army—or even a body he could understand. Because his exile had come at the same time that he'd been dealing with this whole new existence that had been foisted onto him.

He'd gone from having everything to having nothing, almost overnight. And yet, somehow he'd managed. And in Venice, of all places, which had been a snake pit of vampire intrigue, back in the day. And not only managed, but taken care of others at the same time.

I won't always be weak. . . .

And he never had been. He never—

I swallowed and blinked back tears. God, I didn't know what the hell was wrong with me. That attack must have messed me up more than I'd thought. Then I decided to hell with it and leaned over, placing a soft kiss on his forehead.

And heard a softer sound behind me.

I turned abruptly, because I hadn't heard the door open. But it must have, because dinner was waiting on the threshold. Tonight's tasty morsel was young and pale, with messy blond curls and unsettling bright blue eyes. They looked a little unfocused, like she was looking both through me and at me at the same time. She was a little creepy.

She was also useless right now.

"He doesn't need you," I told her, clutching at my sheet, which was slipping.

"W-what?" For some reason, she looked fairly gobsmacked.

"He's sleeping," I repeated patiently. "And I can give him what he needs."

She just stood there, her mouth hanging open. I thought there was a chance that she might be a little slow. "You can go," I repeated. "Vamoose, amscray, make like a tree. Do you get it?"

"Yeah." The voice had gone flat, cold. "I get it."

And then the next thing I knew, I was sitting all alone in the middle of a field filled with mud and some very startled cows. Who weren't half as startled as I was. I got up, slid on a cow pie and went back down, landing in a puddle and splattering mud *everywhere*.

And somewhere far off, like an echo of an echo, I could swear I heard someone laughing.

The *fuck*?

Chapter Forty

A couple hours later, I was driving a stolen SUV past the parking lot of Singh's gutted grocery. I still smelled like cow, due to schlepping across a field full of them courtesy of some witch with a sense of humor. Or maybe I was just crazy; at this point, I wasn't ready to rule anything out.

But I thought I'd stolen an SUV and I thought I was driving it past Singh's, so I was gonna go with that for now. I also thought that a light rain was falling, sending the crime scene tape flapping against the front door and staining the soot-streaked walls a darker hue. But not so much that I couldn't see the two shadows lurking near a Dumpster.

I kept right on driving, only sliding to a stop at a red light down the street.

Two vamps, even two of Marlowe's, would normally have been no problem. Hell, two vamps would normally have been an insult. But tonight . . . tonight, I thought they might be overkill.

Not that killing me was Marlowe's plan—probably. But that wasn't much comfort considering what he likely did have in store. I had the key to this mess locked up in my head and he knew it. And the assault on Mircea had given him all the excuse he needed to hold me until . . .

What? He brought out the thumbscrews and rack, or whatever the Senate was using these days? Or until some other mentalist was brought in to poke around inside my head?

And yeah. Didn't that just sound like fun?

So I needed to hole up until Mircea woke up. And there was only one place I knew of to do that where Marlowe couldn't get at me. Unfortunately, he knew it, too, and he had no intention of letting me back in.

I let my fingers drum on the steering wheel.

Two vamps were bad, but there were almost certainly even more around the house. Making Olga's portal my best bet, assuming it was still there. But just because there were guards on the place didn't mean that Marlowe hadn't shut it down. Or that the fire hadn't destroyed it. Or that the shield we'd just installed at the house wasn't up on the other side, leaving me a very flat dhampir if I—

Damn.

The light had turned green and I hadn't noticed. And now one of the shadows had peeled away from the building and was coming this way, resolving into a dark-suited guy with slicked-back blond hair. He wasn't running— not yet—but he would be in a minute as soon as he ID'd fugitive number one. And with vampire sight, that would only take—

Until about right now.

He turned into a blur, with his buddy right behind him, and I threw the car into reverse, burning rubber flying backward and forcing them to scatter. I'd have liked to turn around, but there wasn't time since I'd only hit one and that had been a glancing blow that had merely provided incentive. I also couldn't take time to get out of the car and make for the door, because if they caught me in my current shape, that would be it.

So I just floored it and kept on going—right into Singh's grocery. And luckily, the fire Scarface and the boys had set had been a good one. The wall disintegrated into a fall of dirty glass and scarred bricks, and a bunch of half-burnt beams fell out of the ceiling, sending a black cloud into the air and obscuring what little view there had been.

I had to aim for the right spot by memory, with zero seconds to get it wrong and—damn. I'd forgotten about the hall. Which was in no better shape than the front of the store, and wasn't quite wide enough for the SUV. Resulting in my plowing through the walls on both sides like a speedboat on the high seas, sending a wave of fake wood paneling bursting against the back windshield and slowing me down.

But not as much as the hand I couldn't see that had just grabbed the front bumper.

Suddenly, everything stopped.

Until I threw the SUV into four-wheel drive and skidded back hard enough to wrench off the bumper, to burst into the salon still wearing the remains of the wall, and to sling around and hit my head on the door as I slammed on the brakes, planning to head straight for—

Nothing. Because the hand that had been on the bumper was now on my shoulder. And it wasn't kidding around.

But neither was I, so I floored it again. And that, plus a vicious elbow to the head of the vamp hanging out the driver's-side window, broke his hold long enough for the SUV to dive through the portal. And out the other side. And I was moving before it stopped, jumping out the door, lurching for the wall and slamming my hand down on—

Ha, ha—yes! The shield slammed shut, slicing through the SUV like a knife through butter. Its crumpled back end remained in the ruined grocery-slash-beauty-shop, while the rest—

Well, damn, I thought, my euphoria fading as the bisected front section peeled away from the wall and crashed to the floor.

The sound was deafening—metal scraping, glass shattering and the radio still blaring Rammstein's greatest hits. For a moment, until the engine gave one last gasp and died from the lack of a fuel tank that was now several blocks away. The headlights winked out a second later, plunging the basement into darkness. And the music faded off with one last, strangled cry.

And, finally, all was quiet.

But not for long, I thought grimly.

It was after eleven, which meant I'd been away more than twenty-four hours without a phone call. I'd expected to catch it from Claire tomorrow, but at least by then I would have been clean, dressed and somewhat prepared. Instead of covered in grass and sweat and reeking of cow shit, in a sheet, and without a clue.

I sighed.

And had it echoed by a small, higher note from somewhere nearby.

My heart leapt to my throat, since it had been pretty close anyway, until I identified the sound: one of Stinky's strange trills. I sighed again, this time in relief, and sagged back against the railing. But only for a second. Claire was probably belting her robe on right now, and while I couldn't save myself, I could rescue a certain midnight miscreant.

I started up the stairs.

Duergars were mostly nocturnal, although that wasn't why Stinky was often found prowling around the house in the middle of the night. That had more to do with his conviction that pretty much everything belonged in his fuzzy little belly, including my beer. Which was less of a concern than some of the potions I kept around that he could easily mistake for a new type of beverage. His Duergar blood made him resistant to poisons, but resistant didn't mean immune, and he was going to learn to *stay in bed*, damn it.

One of these years.

"Give it up, boyo," I told him, throwing open the door. "You know what Claire will say if—"

I froze, my hand still on the knob.

"I do not think your friend will say anything," a polite voice commented.

It was familiar, although I hardly needed it. The light wasn't on in the living room, but starlight streamed through a gap in the curtains, casting an ironic halo around a certain silver-blond head. Narrowed gray eyes met mine, hard as steel, and a faint smile turned up a corner of a sculpted mouth.

Æsubrand.

The stairway was open behind me, since I hadn't even reached the top step. I could slam the door closed, leap down the stairs, hit the shield and dive through the portal. And even in my condition, there was a decent chance I might make it.

I didn't move.

And he'd known I wouldn't, because he hadn't moved, either. Except to tighten one strong hand a little more around his captive's diapered bottom. Aiden, fast asleep and slack-limbed, the silky blond hair tousled and hanging in his face.

And Stinky wasn't far off. He was kicking fretfully in the arms of a woman across the room, but not making any headway. He looked vague, the big eyes half-lidded, one blue sock clinging precariously to a few stick-like toes. Unlike the woman, whose star-like gaze was sharp as a knife.

She was tall, more so even than Claire, with a wave of golden hair that cascaded down her dark blue gown, almost reaching her embroidered satin shoes. She was fresh-faced, pink-cheeked, blue-eyed and stunning. She looked about sixteen.

She wasn't.

Unless I was way, way luckier than normal, I thought I knew why mama hadn't been covering for Æsubrand.

Because she'd been with him.

"We have been expecting you," Æsubrand told me, his mouth quirking as I just continued to stand there.

"This is the creature you told me about?" his mother asked, looking me over. She didn't appear impressed. I wished I could say the same.

"She can be surprising," he murmured, his hand running over the soft baby hair of his hostage.

"How did you get in here?" I rasped, stalling for time. Where the hell were the twins? Or the garden full of dreadful warriors we were supposed to have? Or Claire.

I felt my stomach go into free fall.

Where was Claire?

"C'est pas difficile," a familiar voice said, causing me to jump. But we hadn't had a new arrival. A glance across

the room showed Stinky being held in the same spot, in the same position. But now he was cradled in the arms of an overweight Frenchman in chef's whites.

"My mother is skilled in glamourie," Æsubrand said casually. "And in far-seeing. She has been watching the house through the eyes of one of her bird-creatures, and saw the vampire's servants arrive yesterday. It was simple enough to mimic one of them, and persuade the half-breed to let her in through the wards."

"A weary mother will rarely turn down an offer of help," the woman's voice said, sounding strange coming from the man's throat.

"So you helped her . . . how?" I asked, afraid I already knew. I didn't think Efridís had chosen to impersonate the chef by accident.

"I offered to cook *le diner*," she said, the clear young voice turning amused.

My blood ran cold.

"But this one, he is part Duergar," she continued, glancing at the sleepy Stinky. "Their kind are resistant to drugs."

"Drugs?" I said sharply, not allowing myself to hope. There were plenty of lethal drugs, after all. . . .

"They live," Efridís said shortly, melting back into herself. "My son believes we need your assistance."

"My . . ." I looked back at Æsubrand, who had settled himself comfortably in the big red wingback chair. Like he was here for a friendly chat.

Yeah. That was likely.

But Stinky was still alive, and Aiden. And Claire—

"I want to see Claire," I told him.

He frowned. "We do not have much time. I expected you to return hours ago. There is—"

"I want to see her!" I repeated. And even to me, my voice sounded a little . . . high.

Screw it. It had been a long day.

The two fey exchanged glances, then Efridís nodded. "Come."

I followed her into the hall, and then through an utterly silent house. The place was usually a subtle symphony: light fey laughter from the backyard, the clang of pots and pans from the kitchen, SpongeBob shrieking from the living room, bits of conversation from everywhere, and the country music one of the twins inexplicably liked drifting up from the basement. Tonight, all I heard was the tinkle of a wind chime getting tossed around by a faint breeze as Efridís pushed open the back door.

Outside was more of the same—the porch dark and empty, the garden still except for a fire guttering in the fey camp. There were a few people around it, getting splashed by the low red light, but no one was talking. Or moving.

One of the guards had a stick in his hand, like he'd been using it to poke at the embers. His eyes were open, with reflected flames dancing in the irises. More flames were slowly eating up the stick, the bottom half of which was already black. The next second, it collapsed into nothingness, sifting away on the wind. He didn't flinch.

Not even when a sudden gust of wind caught the back door of the house, slamming it against the old boards like a gunshot.

I jumped, and Æsubrand grabbed my arm. "Are you satisfied?"

"At what?" I demanded harshly. "What did you give them?"

"A fey drug," Efridís said, shrugging. "You would not know of it."

"Then how do I know you haven't killed them?" I'd finally spotted Claire, slumped over one of the picnic tables, her bright red hair cascading over the weathered wood like a spill of firelight. I wanted to run to her, to feel that pulse beating under my fingertips. But that would mean shrugging off Æsubrand's hold, and right now, I wasn't sure I could do that.

And weakness wasn't something he admired.

"If I had wanted them dead, I would not have used poison," he sneered. "It is a coward's weapon."

"That's real convincing coming from someone who makes war on children!"

Silver eyes flashed. "It was not my doing that put the child's life in danger. He should never have been born."

"According to you."

"According to treaty," Efridís said, her voice a sweet note on the air.

"Come again?" I said, trying not to look like I was scouring the surroundings for help. Marlowe should have had a crap ton of his boys around the house. So where the hell were they?

And why do you care? I asked myself bitterly. They couldn't get through the house shields, and I couldn't get to the charm that collapsed them. Not with two fey to watch and lives at stake. I couldn't do anything but stand here, trying not to sway on my feet, and listen. And hope they needed something I had to offer.

Although I'd be damned if I could think of what that might be.

"There was a great war once, between the two leading martial houses of Faerie," Efridís said. "You know of it?"

I nodded. I'd seen a flash of it once, in her brother's mind. A fact I didn't see the need to mention to these two. "I understand it was . . . pretty severe."

"It almost annihilated us both," she said flatly. "But a truce was finally arranged, sealed by a marriage alliance. My brother—Caedmon, as you call him—offered me to Aeslinn of the Svarestri as a bride. Aeslinn accepted, but not merely to end the war. He was hoping for a child who might one day unite all Faerie under one ruler, one throne."

"And this didn't worry Caedmon?"

Efridís smiled slightly. "My brother gambled on my being as infertile as he was himself. He has only ever sired the one child, and that with a human."

"Heidar." Claire's fiancé.

Efridís inclined her head.

"But at his birth, my uncle began to scheme," Æsubrand broke in angrily. "What if he used his half-breed in a liaison with another? Their human blood would render them more fertile than he had ever been himself. And if he could find one who possessed more than half fey blood, he would have a successor from his direct line. And cut me off!"

"Leaving you with only one throne. What a tragedy."

"It may well prove a tragedy—for us all!"

"I find that hard to believe."

"Because you're as shortsighted as the rest of them."

"Say rather ill-informed," Efridís said smoothly, cutting in.

"And you're here to inform me about ... ?" I asked her.

"My husband," Efridís said simply. "I discovered that he was not trying to unite all Faerie merely for dynastic reasons. He is what I believe you would call a religious ... zealot?" She tipped her head charmingly. "Is that the word?"

"It's a word. I didn't know you had religion in Faerie."

"We do not anymore."

"But you did once."

"Yes. That is why the war was fought. The old gods were banished from both Earth and Faerie thousands of your years ago, by a spell maintained by your Silver Circle of mages. My husband wishes to destroy it."

"And thereby to bring his gods back."

She nodded. "He was trying to invade Earth at the time of the war in order to attack your Circle, which was much more vulnerable then, but Caedmon opposed him. The two sides were almost equally matched and the battle was therefore—"

"Wait. Caedmon opposed him? Why?"

Æsubrand said that thing that might be a curse word again and glared at me. "Do you know *nothing*?"

"About this? Yeah. Nothing is pretty much what I know."

Efridís sent him a let-me-handle-this glance, which surprisingly had Junior backing down. It was a little surreal, seeing the titan of the fey abruptly close his mouth when his tiny mama told him to, but that's exactly what happened. Then she looked at me, smiled, and tried again.

"It is . . . complicated. Too much to go into now. All you need to understand is that a generation of fey warriors died for their faith on one side, and for the right to live free of it on the other."

"And you're telling me this because?"

"Because the war you are currently fighting did not start recently. It started thousands of years ago, on that battlefield."

"It started before that, in the war between the gods them—" Æsubrand broke off at another glance from mama.

"Let us keep this simple, shall we?" she asked, with a brittle smile. She looked at me. "The two sides only ceased fighting out of utter exhaustion. Afterward, the pathways between Earth and Faerie were closed, the easy commute of the old days gone forever. And a truce was established, sealed by my marriage, between the two great houses. But truce is all it was. Peace was impossible. For both sides still believed they were in the right. And now, the war is about to be reignited."

"Why now?" I demanded. "What's changed?"

"The number of available warriors. It is what stymied my husband's plans all along. As I have said, the two sides were very closely matched, and try as they might, neither could gain the upper hand. And Caedmon made it clear that if my husband wished to invade Earth in the future, he would have to do it through a Blarestri army."

"Which he'd just proven he couldn't do."

"Yes."

"That's why my father was willing to settle the matter—temporarily—in exchange for a royal Blarestri bride," Æsubrand put in, more calmly. "He assumed that any child that resulted from the union would be able to claim both thrones one day, thus uniting the two most powerful fey armies under Svarestri control. And giving him the numbers he needed to combat your Circle."

"Only that hasn't been working out so well," I pointed out.

"That remains to be seen. But Caedmon's successful

attempt to gain an heir raised the possibility of an unbroken line of opposition. And even had it not, my father was beginning to doubt the depth of my devotion to his dogma."

"You're not a true believer?"

That got a flash from those strange eyes. "I am a *king*, or will be shortly. Not a lackey to a group of beings who could be banished by a human spell!"

Okay, that I could believe. A moral objection I'd have laughed at, since I was pretty sure Æsubrand didn't have any morals. But being king of all Faerie didn't mean much if he still had to bow and scrape and kiss godly butts all the time.

"Okay, say I believe you. Say you're suddenly on our side. Then what the hell were you doing at Slava's?"

"Trying to warn you."

"Warn me? You almost killed me!"

"You were in the way," he said, shrugging off my almost-death. "And I did not mean to warn you specifically, but your people. When I learned that my father was preparing an attack, my mother and I decided to alert the other side. The difficulty was in how to be believed. Due to . . . certain incidents . . . in the past, we felt some proof might be required—"

"You think?"

Pewter eyes narrowed. "—and the vampire had it."

"And that proof was?"

"You should know. You killed him with it."

It took me a minute, because technically, I hadn't killed Slava at all. But I had shot him. And I guess turning into an ice cube hadn't improved his chances any.

"You're talking about the gun."

"The bullets, to be precise," Efridís said. "They are infused with a fey battle spell, giving anyone who wields them the power of a strong fey warrior—"

"Hardly," Æsubrand said tightly. "There is more to being a warrior than a single spell."

"Perhaps, but it is a devastating one." She looked at me. "My husband knew he needed three things for any hope of success: superior numbers, a way around the blockade Caedmon had enacted and allies. He has obtained them all. And he is about to turn them on the Circle's greatest supporter. Tonight, unless you warn them, the six senates will fall. Tonight, unless you stop it, the war may be lost."

Chapter Forty-one

"This is bullshit," Ray said, as Louis-Cesare's chauffeur pulled into the long line of cars waiting to get up the consul's impressive front drive.

"What is?" I asked, trying to drag on a thigh-high in the dark without running it or kicking Ray.

I managed one of them.

"Ow!" he yelped, glaring at me through the neck hole in his T-shirt, which he was in the process of stripping off.

"Don't be a baby. I barely touched you." I looked around. "Where are my shoes?"

"Did you leave them? Tell me you didn't leave them!"

"I didn't leave them." At least, I was pretty sure. It wasn't like I hadn't had about a thousand other things to keep straight.

Like getting here at all. I wouldn't have managed it if Ray hadn't shown up half an hour after our unwelcome guests left. I'd been holding Claire's head in one hand, while she tossed up a couple days' worth of food, and yelling uselessly into the phone in my other when he stumbled through the portal. And bitched me out about the shield he'd had to hack his way through.

He'd come to warn me about the fat bounty that had just been offered for my capture. So he'd been less than happy to hear that I was about to walk back into the arms of the guy who had issued it. He'd been even less happy when he found out I expected him to pay for the privilege.

But there wasn't any other choice.

Despite what Æsubrand seemed to believe, I did not have a large amount of influence over the vampire world. Or, you know, any. What I did have were contacts, including some who might actually listen to the crazy story I had to tell despite the fact that I had exactly no proof to go with it.

Or they would have if they had been conscious.

But Mircea and Louis-Cesare were still out of it, and they'd taken their masters right along with them. A senior master in extremis will pull power from family, and Mircea's need had been dire. Louis-Cesare's masters were wandering around in a stupor, looking like they'd been hit by a large truck, but Mircea's weren't even vertical.

That left Radu as the only other person I knew who might be able to force someone to listen. Luckily, he'd been emancipated from Mircea's mastery centuries ago, so he wasn't in a dead faint. Unluckily, where he was, along with the rest of the vampire world, was at the fights.

Why he was at the fights, I didn't know. Yes, this was the last night and, yes, they were choosing new senators this evening. But I'd have thought he'd have had better things to do right now. But apparently not. And that put him behind the consul's massive wards, which rendered electronic devices as dead as their owners.

So, if I wanted to get his attention, I was going to have to go to him. And that meant walking straight through the consul's front door. With no one to pull my ass out of the fire if she objected.

Sometimes I really thought I needed my head examined, only that hadn't been going so well lately.

Like this shoe hunt. Where the— There.

"Ow!" Ray and I went for them at the same time and knocked heads. Hard.

"At this rate, the bad guys aren't going to have to take us out," I said, rubbing my newest knot.

"There are no bad guys!" Ray said, jerking on a white dress shirt. "It's bullcrap. How is somebody gonna attack *that*?"

He gestured at the huge edifice above us, which was blazing with light from every window. It was glittering off an acre of expensive marble and a mass of silken banners and an army of golden breastplates on the chests of the double row of honor guards who were lining the sweeping staircase. It was a ridiculous over-the-top display that nonetheless managed to be damned impressive.

And to make my palms sweat.

Of course, they were doing that anyway. Just like my knees kept trying to buckle and my hands kept wanting to shake, and if the plan had been to fight, I'd have been in trouble. Fortunately, that wasn't on the agenda.

At least, I really hoped not.

"Nothing's gonna happen," Ray said, as if he'd heard me. "You're being paranoid."

"Okay," I said, getting the other stocking in place. "Then what about Æsubrand's story?"

Ray rolled his eyes. "What story? Ancient war, blah, blah, something about some gods, blah, blah, fey army coming to kill everybody, blah, blah, blah. No. Just no."

And yeah, I knew how it sounded. Which was why the only one of Marlowe's boys I'd been able to reach by phone had hung up on me. But what Æsubrand said had answered a lot of questions.

"What he said answered a lot of questions," I told Ray, who was fighting with his cuff links.

"Like what?"

"Like what the deal is with all those hybrids we keep finding. Crossbreeds like Stinky have been turning up everywhere—weird ones that don't make sense. There were a bunch at that auction where I found him, and the Senate has a whole collection—"

"Slaves run away all the time," Ray said dismissively. "And there's occasionally some sicko trying to cross-breed 'em, to get stronger specimens for the fights. Like the ones Geminus used to run."

"And maybe that's where he got the idea," I pointed out. "He was weapons master for the Senate. It wouldn't be too much of a stretch for someone like him to wonder what would happen if you combined human and fey magic—"

"Only you can't," Ray interrupted crabbily. "Everybody knows that. It's why you don't see the mages going into Faerie without permission and an escort—half the time their spells don't work, or they're weak as water when they do. And the fey don't come here much, because their spells take, like, ten times the strength that they do back home."

"Which is my point. Æsubrand said that the experiments were about crossing human and fey magical creatures to come up with one whose magic worked both places. And then to harvest its abilities—"

"If it was that easy, why didn't somebody do it a long time ago?"

"The fey didn't do it because the only reason you'd try such a thing is if you were planning on fighting a war here," I told him, striving for patience. "Something that most of them had no interest in. The Svarestri were the only ones who did, and they were the bigots of Faerie. They thought that everyone, especially everyone from Earth, was inferior and they never interbred with them, much less experimented—"

"And our side?" Ray demanded. "The Circle's had plenty of spats with the fey, but nothing ever comes of 'em because humans can't fight there and fey can't fight here—"

"I didn't say it was easy," I interrupted, because patience isn't really my thing. "And the Circle didn't have a thousand-year-old necromancer working for them!"

"I'd still have to see it to believe it."

"Well, I did see it," I said curtly, brushing ruthlessly at the tangles in my hair. "And the gun I lifted off that mage at Slava's was frightening."

Ray didn't reply to that, but his forehead wrinkled. Like he was actually thinking about it for a change. I took the opportunity to slide on the gleaming patent leather stilettos Louis-Cesare's tailor had provided.

They matched the low-cut, black chiffon evening gown with little fluttery bits that I was wearing. They were supposed to move when I did, creating a flowing effect "like the ocean at midnight." Or so he'd said, after Ray and I showed up pleading for help, since neither of us had the wardrobe for something like this. He'd seemed like a nice guy, so I hadn't informed him that dark water hadn't been real lucky for me lately.

But at least it fit. Unlike Ray's outfit, because even vampire tailors balk at whipping up a bespoke tuxedo with all of five minutes' notice. And there hadn't been anyone on staff with one the right size. In desperation, the guy had cut down one of his own, but the result was . . . less than perfect.

Ray scowled and jerked the jacket on, which he barely managed to button.

Good thing vamps don't need to breathe.

"Yeah, well," he finally said. "Say they did come up with some kind of super-weapon. Somebody's still got to use it, don't they? And how you gonna get an army here from Faerie with nobody noticing? Especially a *Svarestri* army?"

"What difference does it make what kind it is?"

He rolled his eyes. He was going to make himself dizzy at this rate. "You just said it. The Svarestri don't like Earth; think it's beneath 'em. So they almost never come here. So how you gonna hide a few thousand people who don't speak the language, don't know the laws, can't drive a car and dress completely crazy?"

"In New York? Check them in at the Y."

He glared at me. "We're being serious, all right? And seriously, how do you hide something like that right underneath the Senate's nose?"

"You don't."

Ray nodded, looking smug. "That's right."

"You bring them over all at once."

His smile faded. "What?"

"Æsubrand said the idea was to use Geminus's portal network to bring everybody over on the night of the attack. But then he was killed, and suddenly nobody knew where the portals were. Well, except for Varus, and he wasn't talking."

"And how do you know that?" Ray demanded—angrily, because this was starting to sound plausible and he didn't want it to be true, any of it. "He'd have had to be in on it. He was Geminus's second!"

"Yeah, but being a crook and a traitor are two different things, and it's possible that cagey old Geminus hadn't told his buddy exactly what he was planning to bring in. Either that, or Varus got cold feet. Either way, we know that because Varus stalled and contacted the Senate, once he understood what was going on."

Ray started to say something else, and then stopped. "But Varus wasn't gonna tell 'em any details until he got a deal," he said slowly.

"Only somebody got to him first, used him to set up the only guys likely to stumble across this whole mess, and then killed him and dumped him in a portal."

"Not knowing it was one I'd hacked."

I nodded. "So instead of going someplace he'd never be found, he floated over to Olga's. But a dead body didn't tell us much, and someone has been doing a damned good job keeping me from remembering whatever I saw at the wharf. Giving the bad guys time to find another way to bring in their army."

"But they *couldn't*," Ray argued. "None of the other bosses knew where Geminus's portals were, and you can't use what you can't find!"

"Right. Which was why they decided to use yours."

I could almost hear the record scratch as Ray slowly looked up from pulling on a pair of dress socks, and stared at me. "What?"

I nodded. "Yes."

"No."

"Yes."

"No, damn it! This . . . none of this has anything to do with me!"

"Well, of course it does," I said impatiently. "How many people do you know who have a portal network to Faerie? It's not like they had a lot of choice!"

"But I . . . nobody ever . . . I wasn't contacted—"

"Because you were in the Senate's loving embrace.

Nobody could get to you. Which was why they had to attack Central."

"They—" He stopped and just blinked at me for a minute. "You know, people are always saying that you're cuckoo. Looney Tunes. Off the freaking edge. But I tell 'em, no, she's okay. She's just got some . . . anger management issues. But you know what? They're right. You're nuts."

"Frequently. But that doesn't change the fact that the bad guys went into Central to get you."

"They did not!" Ray said, the anger now mixed with a healthy dose of remembered fear. "That was Radu! Everybody knows the guy is some kind of crazy genius. If anyone was gonna figure out what they were up to—"

"It might have been 'Du, yeah. But think about it. Radu came and went to Central via the portal system. He never used the front door. He had a hard time even telling me what level he was on that night, because he'd almost never been in the elevators. So it wouldn't have been possible for them to know if he was there or not."

"They could of . . . assumed." Ray scowled.

"Attacking Central was a one-time deal. Whoever they were going after, it had to be someone they *knew* was there. Not suspected. Knew."

"But I *wasn't* there," he pointed out. "Or I wasn't supposed to be. I'd been released—"

"And gone running to me. And the first time we left the wards around my house, what happened? What *immediately* happened? We were attacked."

"By *Zheng*."

"Who works for your old boss. Who, as you told me, is a major player in the smuggling trade. *And who wanted you to bring in something big*."

Ray had been unfolding the tux pants, but he paused to look at me incredulously. "Something big like a bunch of crates. Not big like an army!"

"Well, naturally he would say that."

Ray shook his head furiously. "It isn't like I have any loyalty to the guy, you know? But Cheung . . . he don't play that way. It's like you said, there's a difference between a crook and a traitor, and he's no traitor."

"He's a smuggler and a triad leader."

"Yeah? So am I. Or I was. Now I'm freaking Batman—"

"I thought I was Batman."

"Yeah, right. Who shelled out like a year's profits to the scalpers tonight, huh? Bruce Wayne had the money; Bruce Wayne bankrolled the operation. And Bruce Wayne was the Batman."

The Batman currently had a knee on the seat and his ass in the air, trying to get the tux trousers on without putting any more wrinkles in them. Which left me staring at a bony butt covered in gaily striped red and blue silk. I didn't know what kind of underwear The Batman wore, but I was betting that wasn't it.

"I told you, I'll pay you back for the tickets."

"Sure, like you got that kind of money. Like you got *any* money. Hell, I should be subsidizing you."

"Hey, that's right. If I'm your master, don't you owe me—"

"Nothing. That's not the kind of deal we got."

"I don't remember us specifying what kind of deal we have."

"Exactly."

We were nearing the front of the line, where the light from the house was starting to illuminate the car's interior, even through the tinted glass. So as soon as Ray zipped up, I pulled him back down. "Okay, say Cheung isn't a bad guy. Say he was just offered a ton of money to let some people use your bastardized portal system."

He nodded. "That I might buy."

"Okay. So when he failed to come up with you, his clients were going to want to know why, right?"

Another nod.

"And Cheung probably told them that he couldn't get at you, because you were back under the Senate's control. He must have had people watching the house, waiting for another chance to grab you after Zheng failed. And they saw you drive off with Marlowe. Who took you back to

Central. Which was when the bad guys decided that they were just going to have to go in and get you."

"Attack Central. For me." Ray still didn't believe it.

"Yeah."

"Then why did that creepy-ass necromancer say they wanted Radu?"

"Because they needed someone to get them through the portal, of course."

Ray slowly leaned over, rested his elbows on his knees and put his head in his hands. "I know I'm going to regret asking this," he said. "But what portal?"

"The one at Central. The one that connects here."

"No."

"Yes. Look," I said, forestalling another argument, because we were running out of time. "They needed a way to get their army here from Faerie, and a way to get it into the consul's home without getting fried by the wards."

"Stop. Just . . . stop. Okay?"

"No. And in fact, it wouldn't surprise me if going in through Central wasn't the plan all along. It was a little too well thought-out to be a seat-of-the-pants kind of thing. And with the focus on the consul's home and the games, it wasn't as well guarded as usual, and would be a much easier target than fighting their way in here."

"I'm not listening to this."

"And with a senator on their side . . . well, hell. They might not have had to fight for it at all. Good old Geminus could have offered to have his boys staff the place on the night of the finals, as a favor to the guys on duty. So they could watch the fights. And then just order his people to stand aside as a fey army waltzed in the door."

"Do you hear yourself? Do you?"

"So maybe his death was a blow for more than one reason. But his allies figured another way to get inside, and it must have seemed like a dream that the Senate was actually keeping you *right there*. Sure, it was a hiccup when you were suddenly released, which was why they contacted Cheung, thinking he was still your master and you'd be handed over to him. But you came to me instead, and then Marlowe took you back—"

"I'm begging you."

"—and so everything was in place once again. You to bring their army in, and the portal to get it into the consul's home. All they had to do that night was find you. And Radu, of course."

I paused to check my makeup, and then stuck my compact in my little black beaded evening purse. If we wanted to blend in with the type of people who could shell out the price of a private jet for a ticket, I had to look halfway decent. Which would have been easier if I hadn't tried to put on mascara during the bumpy ride over here.

"Geminus must have had the password," I added. "As a senator, there would have been no reason not to give it to him. But he was dead. And it's changed weekly, so even if he'd shared it with his allies—which I doubt— the one he'd had wouldn't work. But as the senior person there, they assumed Radu would know the new one."

"But you just said they didn't know Radu was gonna be there that night!"

"But somebody had to have it, right? A portal isn't much use if nobody can use it."

"So why not get the password from the lead guy on duty?"

"They'd probably planned to. But he must have been killed in the initial assault, possibly vaporized when they went through the floor. But somebody told them Radu was there, or one of the zombies saw him—remember, the necromancer could see through his puppet's eyes—"

"Yeah." Ray shuddered.

"—and so they went after 'Du."

"But they didn't get him. They didn't get either of us. They tipped their hand and got nothing!"

"Which is why they're trying again tonight, at least according to Æsubrand."

"And I don't suppose he said how?" Ray asked sarcastically.

"He didn't know." I frowned at him, but not for the attitude. I was getting used to that. But because we were third in line now and he looked ... well, less than a model of sartorial splendor.

Way less. His hair was sticking up in the back, his jacket sleeves almost covered his hands, and then there was that tie. That tie Would Not Do.

I grabbed it and pulled him forward.

"What?" he said, pulling back for a second, and then giving up. "You mean Mr. Know-it-all didn't know the one thing we need to stop this? How convenient!"

"The bad guys weren't the only ones to tip their hand last night," I reminded him, trying to remember if it was over-under-over or the reverse. "Æsubrand did, too, when he showed up at Slava's—"

"And ruined everything! If he wanted to help, he should have just let us have the fat bastard."

"He said he would have, but he assumed I was there to assassinate him, and he needed Slava to back up his story. So he ... intervened. And now he's out of the loop."

"And so are we. We have no freaking clue what they're up to!"

Ray looked pissed, and I couldn't blame him. Walking in there at all was bad enough; walking in with no real plan was ... not bright. But the only clues were inside, and if I was going to figure this out, that was where I had to be.

And pray for inspiration.

"You don't know what you're doing, do you?" Ray asked.

It took me a second to realize he was talking about the tie.

"Women don't wear these things," I reminded him.

"Yeah, but their men do."

I thought back to all the one-night stands, most of which hadn't been with the kind of guys who owned tuxes. And none of them would have been likely to let me anywhere near their throat, if they had. Unlike a certain auburn-haired vampire, whose only reaction to my lips at his neck had been to hold me closer.

Before I fried his brain, that was.

I closed my eyes. He was going to be okay. He was Louis-freaking-Cesare. He was the ex-Enforcer of the European Senate, the only guy in memory to keep another first-level master as a servant, the guy who made other badasses suddenly remember their manners. He might look ornamental, but he was tough as nails and he was going to be okay. And so was Mircea. Because if things went south, I fully intended to grab them both and run like hell. Fuck the Senate; I was here for family.

"They didn't stick around long enough for me to learn," I said abruptly, and let him go.

And the next second, the chauffeur was opening the door and we were there.

Chapter Forty-two

That was the longest stair climb of my life. I didn't look left; I didn't look right. I don't know what the hell I *was* looking at, because nothing really registered. If I hadn't seen it from the car, I wouldn't have even known which direction to go. All I could manage to do was to put one foot in front of the other and *push*.

Against POWER, like nothing I'd ever experienced. This wasn't ants crawling over my skin, or even a few extra atmospheres. This was an unrelenting tide beating down on me, slamming into me, wave after wave and more with each step, until all I could do was focus on my feet and try to stay upright.

I noticed when Ray slid a hand under my arm, like an attentive date—and one who was exerting a lot of upward pressure to keep me from falling on my face. I didn't know what he was feeling; maybe not that much, since he was a vamp, too. But I always felt like I'd picked up a pair of hundred-pound weights every time I got near this place, and my exhaustion tonight only made things worse. I was going to face-plant any minute if the damned stairs from hell didn't *end already*.

Annnnnd they didn't.

I faltered, but Ray caught me halfway down. "Are you okay, *dear*?" he asked, but with an edge that made it into "Get up or I'm leaving your ass here, I swear to God."

I got up.

"Fine," I croaked. And on we went.

And on. And on.

But it was like we'd somehow stumbled onto a down escalator. Because no matter how far we climbed, the top never seemed to get any closer. And it was beginning to feel less like stair climbing and more like mountain climbing, one of the really tall ones with no oxygen and no Sherpa to help carry the load.

And then I suddenly found the Sherpa, and he was riding on my shoulders. Along with a couple of his friends and maybe a yak. Because the consul was an anal-retentive *bitch* and she'd arranged the guards by rank.

That left the weaker ones, relatively speaking, at the bottom, and at the top . . . well, it explained why the blasts of power coming from both sides were no longer washing over me. They were slicing right on through and meeting inside my skull. And threatening to *rip it apart*.

I gasped at a particularly strong gust, and Ray's grip tightened. "I told you not to wear those shoes," he said, his voice strained. And then, "I'll get you a drink when we get inside."

"Sounds good," I croaked, even knowing that it was a lie. Inside was an illusion that had never existed and never would because life consisted only of this infernal stairway and *he had to be kidding me with inside*.

But I gritted my teeth and pushed on, since there were exactly zero other options, fighting my way through air that didn't feel like air anymore, but liquid. First water and then molasses and then something that was fast approaching a solid. And then I wasn't moving at all, and was so far gone that it took me a second to realize that I'd just hit something.

It turned out to be Ray, who had abruptly stopped in front of me.

"A moment, dear," he said, giving a little whinny of a laugh. "I have to give the man our tickets."

I nodded, trying to look nonchalant . . . and then realized that I didn't need to try. The ticket thing should have worried me, because it meant that we were no longer just two faces in the crowd but were being individually scrutinized. This was the moment of truth, when I was going to be recognized or not, depending on who was on duty, something I had absolutely no control over. It was the sort of thing I hated, the random chance in every mission that usually had my spine stiffening and my pulse racing and my fight-or-flight response kicking in big-time.

Except for tonight.

Tonight, I just stood there, too exhausted to care about a scrutiny I couldn't see properly anyway. I looked around, because it would have seemed weird to do anything else in the face of a spectacle like that, but my eyes weren't working right. All I saw was a blur of dark red and flashing gold and gleaming white and pitch-black. Until we started moving again, and the black abruptly changed to dazzling light.

And I stumbled, but for a totally new reason.

"Oh . . . oh *God*," I gasped in dazed wonder, as Ray dragged me away from what I guessed was the front door.

"This way, this way, this way," he chanted through clenched teeth, as I wafted around, feeling like I might just float away. Because the pressure, the horrible, horrible pressure, was suddenly just . . . gone.

"Stop it!" Ray hissed, as we found a wall somewhere.

"Stop what?" I asked thickly.

"That!" And he pointed me at something that turned out to be a mirror. And I guess my eyes worked now, because I managed to identify myself, looking slick and soigné and faintly French—and drunk off my ass. I was flushed and bright-eyed, grinning like a loon and still weaving a little. And the only reason we hadn't already been nabbed was the sheer number of people who looked pretty much the same.

The place was packed.

"What—" I began.

"Spell to make the mages more comfortable," Ray said, standing beside me and pretending to fiddle with his cuff links. "They can feel vamp power if there's enough of us, and it makes 'em . . . jittery."

"Mages?"

"Silly girl. You didn't think vamps were the only ones

who want to see the fights, did you?" he asked, still in
character, because yeah, we couldn't talk now.

Not that I was up to it. I was busy catching my breath,
and watching the throng ebb and swell behind me, like a
glittering tide. I was seeing them in the mirror, although
it was a little unnecessary. The whole place looked like it
had been dipped in varnish in the hours I'd been gone.
The walls and floors and ceiling gleamed, almost mirror-
bright, reflecting chandeliers brilliant as diamonds overhead, stretching in a long line down the wide main corridor
to the ballroom.

The consul's house usually looked like something out
of the end of the eighteenth century, when Greco-
Roman had been forcibly married to Baroque, in a shotgun wedding that did neither any favors. But tonight it
was stunning. Which made it a marked contrast to a good
portion of the crowd.

I hadn't worn a disguise because I'd assumed anti-
glamourie charms would be in effect for security reasons. And I had assumed right. Because the crowd was
looking . . . a little scary.

The mages were okay; about what you'd expect, with
maybe a few more wrinkles and blemishes than usual.
The vamps, though, were another matter altogether. The
clothes were couture, the jewels were dazzling, the hair
a stylist's dream. But the faces . . .

Ray looked pretty much the same, except for a big zit
on his nose, possibly because he hadn't been covering up
much. But that wasn't true for the guy passing behind us,
who must have been starved at some point like Radu.
Only either it had been for a longer duration or he hadn't
had a brother with serious healing skills, because he
looked . . . well, like a corpse. A dessicated, dried-up stick
of one with a sunken neck and eyes, discolored, mummy-
like skin, ropy muscle, and a puff of grizzled hair erupt-
ing from his skull—what was left of it.

The humans were scattering ahead of him, looks of
ill-concealed horror on their features, a fact that was not
lost on the vamp. A corner of one leathery lip raised, in
sardonic acknowledgment of their fear. Or maybe in the

knowledge that he could have any one of them outside these walls, where a moment's work would return him to youthful beauty.

Although he'd probably do okay without it, I thought, as his power hit me, like the train on his sweeping emerald robes. And despite the spell the consul was using to keep her mage guests from melting through the floor, and despite the fact that he wasn't even *trying*, the force of it was like a backhanded slap. I had to clench my teeth to keep an undignified yelp behind them until he passed on, and his power dissipated into the background buzz of the rest of the room.

"Hassani," Ray muttered. "African consul."

Great, I thought, swallowing, and feeling a little like a squashed bug. Thankfully, he didn't know me. Unfortunately, that wouldn't be true of others.

We needed to get moving.

"Where are our seats?" I asked Ray.

"Nowhere. We're standing."

"Standing?"

"Hey, I was lucky to get anything this late," he said, as we merged with the flow heading down the main hall.

And we weren't the only fashionably late arrivals—the huge corridor was shoulder to shoulder. Or shoulder to head, in my case, and elbow to head, and knee to thigh, since the jostling crowd tended to top me by at least a foot. If it was like this inside, I didn't know how we were supposed to find anybody.

Ray wasn't doing any better, getting knocked all to hell across from me, until I grabbed his arm, pushing him into a stairwell. "This isn't going to work. I need to be able to *see*."

"Well, yeah, but that's what everyone else wants, too," he pointed out.

"There's got to be someplace—" I looked up at the stairs. "Where do these go?"

"To the box seats, I guess. But our tickets don't let us—"

He stopped, because I was already moving, under a velvet rope and up the stairs, which unlike the cattle call below, were completely clear. And then around a bend and up some more. Until I was stopped by two guards lounging in a marble hallway leading to a row of little rooms. The box seats, I assumed, judging from the flash I got of one as a man came out.

A very familiar man.

It was Radu's latest boy toy, a blond hunk whose name escaped me but who didn't seem to have that problem himself. "Dory?" he asked, in disbelief.

"That would be me. And this is Ray." I shoved him forward. "Sorry we're late."

"I . . . you . . . yes . . ."

"But we made it, so that's what counts," I said, starting forward. Only to find another hunk in my way, this time of the vamp variety. An apologetic-looking one, because anyone who might belong here rated the white glove treatment.

"I am afraid I will need to see your ticket, Miss . . ."

I ignored the hint for my full name, since I didn't think it would be popular. "Oh yes, that's right. Give him the tickets, Ray," I said, and dodged around the vamp. Who let me go, because it was that or tackle me, and he wasn't ready for that.

Yet.

"Tickets, I . . . yeah, where did I put those?" I heard Ray say weakly, as I slid through a red drape of curtain. And into what must have been the family box.

Mircea was absent. Louis-Cesare equally so. I hadn't really expected them, though. But considering Gorgeous George—or Ted or Harry or whoever—outside, I had expected Radu.

Who wasn't there, either.

A bunch of other people were, however, who had been talking and drinking and gossiping and who were now silently staring at me, as if I had suddenly grown two heads. I ignored them in favor of turning to the blond, who had just come in behind me. "Radu—"

"Was asked to stand in for your father in the consul's box. For the opening ceremony."

"And the consul's box would be?"

He blinked at me, like I might be slow. "There."

I followed his gaze across the railing, and the width of the huge gleaming oval below, to the far wall. Where a massive balcony ran the length of all the box seats on our side. It was still mostly empty. A lot of shadows were moving around in an arched alcove, talking and drinking and waiting for the hoi polloi to settle before taking their seats, but only a few had drifted out onto the actual balcony. Radu wasn't one of them.

But guess who was?

Marlowe looked about the same, even without whatever glamourie he usually used. A little paler, maybe, and there were tired lines at his mouth and dark circles under his eyes, probably because this was something like his fifth straight day awake. But his servants must have finally tackled him out of sheer desperation, because he was currently wearing a perfectly cut black tux without a wrinkle in it. It looked a little incongruous next to the still messy brown curls and the gold earring shining in one ear, but it perfectly matched the sharp, dark eyes, which were busy scanning the crowd below.

But despite the fact that we were in each other's line of sight, he didn't see me. I suppose the people in the boxes were regarded as safe, more or less. I only hoped he continued with that thought, because this was the best vantage point I was likely to get.

And there was plenty to see.

The great mirror at the far end of the room reflected back the huge crowd assembling at the other. Although "assembling" isn't quite the word for being packed into the standing-room-only area like sardines, with no regard for expensive clothes and delicate feelings. Or danger, because the overflow was being channeled along the sides of the wide-open area of floor where the action was soon to start.

If it had been me, I'd have wanted a splatter shield.

But nobody was looking worried, maybe because they were busy looking up—at the balcony, where Ming-de had just emerged from under one of the arches. The empress of the Chinese court was surrounded by attendants, every single one of whom dwarfed her tiny four-foot-eleven frame. But there was no question who was in charge: she was encircled by a rush of power like a tornado.

It was currently keeping several fans aloft, fluttering around her head like jeweled butterflies, which matched the moving splendor of the rest of her outfit. Bright blue dragons coiled around her wide cuffs, white tigers prowled around her hemline, ebony tortoises gleamed on either shoulder, and a brilliant red phoenix preened its feathers at her waist. I knew enough to recognize ancient symbols of imperial power, although not what they meant.

And then there was the stark contrast offered by Hassani, coming up on her left, his elegant movements at odds with the tattered ruins of his face. They were making small talk as their attendants jostled about in the background, jealously staking out space for their respective masters. Some of Hassani's were also exotically pretty, in jewel-tone silks and ropes of pearls. They were rushing around, bringing up piles of pillows to cushion the already overstuffed chaises the consuls had in lieu of regular old chairs. But the rest . . .

Hassani's more . . . interesting-looking . . . servants weren't running around and they weren't wearing silk. They'd also apparently declined tuxes, suits or even the elaborate costumes of the consul's vamps. Instead, they remained in what looked like their everyday attire—stark, hard leathers, old and scratched and vaguely dusty, over thin cotton shirts and trousers and discolored boots. They didn't go with the decor or the surrounding splashes of gleaming fabrics and bright jewels. They did go pretty well with the rifles slung over their backs and the swords at their waists. And the looks on their faces as they hedged the boss.

And for the first time I seriously started to doubt myself.

It would be suicide for any group to try to fight their way in here. Even assuming they got past the outer wards and the inner wards and the guards bristling with weapons, what then? There would just be more hell awaiting them in the form of the crème de la crème of the vampire world.

The original plan had relied on surprise: a rush through the portal, a strike with overwhelming force on a largely civilian crowd, who could be relied on to go nuts at the first sign of danger and run amok. That would complicate any attempted counterstrike by the consul's guards for a few vital minutes, during which the other side might be able to gain the upper hand. It was a gamble, but one with decent odds.

Unlike this.

I suddenly started wondering what I was doing here.

Not that it looked like I'd have that problem for long.

"I told you, I must have dropped them on the stairs," Ray was saying, as he was shoved unceremoniously through the curtain.

There were two guards now, and they didn't look so obsequious anymore. Although, amazingly, neither seemed to have recognized me yet. It was only a matter of time, though, and if there was nothing more to see from up here, there was no reason to—

Ray came into my line of sight, looking rumpled and put upon and as crabby as ever, flanked by the two guards.

And outlined by the silver gleam of the great mirror behind him.

You know, the one that masked the consul's portal.

And just that fast, I understood.

"I know we checked, but I'm telling you, somebody must have picked them up," he was saying, glaring at the vamp with the hand on his arm. "Don't you have cleaning staff? Have you checked with them? Because you're making a big mistake here. I'll have you know that Lord Mircea and I, we're like this." He held up a hand with crossed fingers. "He gave me a ride in his limo just the other day, and I was telling him . . ."

I didn't hear whatever story Ray had dreamed up, which didn't appear to be working on the guards anyway. One of whom grabbed my purse, I guess to check for tickets. I let him have it in favor of gripping Ray's arm. "The password," I said tightly.

He just looked at me.

"For the *portal*. You said Radu guessed it."

"Yeah, so?"

"So the bad guys were *right there*. What if they heard—"

His eyes got big, but before he could answer, the guards stiffened. And one glance to the right showed me why. It seemed that Marlowe did look up now and again, after all. Because he was practically hanging over the balcony, staring straight at me. And I finally understood the saying "If looks could kill. . . ."

Only they didn't have to, because his boys had just been instructed to do it for him.

"Shit," Ray said, and slammed his elbow back into the gut of his vamp.

I kicked out at mine, heard something crunch, and saw him go staggering at the balcony. And then Ray was jerking me through the door and toward the stairs, only to do a fast one-eighty and drag me through the curtain of the next box instead. "More, coming up fast," he told me quickly, as Radu's blond spoke from the hall.

"They just jumped over the balcony," he told someone laconically. "They're back downstairs now."

There was the sound of booted feet hitting marble, but only some of them. Others started checking the box seats, because they hadn't been born yesterday, and that included this one. Which I'd just noticed contained only two people.

One of whom was making down gestures at me.

I grabbed Ray and dove behind a low-slung couch, just about the time the metal curtain holders shlincked along their rod. And, presumably, a guard poked his nose in. And saw what I just had, namely the hairy leg and thigh of the flagrantly naked man on top of a pretty brunette senator whose name escaped me, but it had once been linked with Geminus's.

Only it looked like she'd traded up. Because the guy

continuing to move lazily against her was none other than Anthony, the European consul. Who obviously had his own way of celebrating, and it didn't involve hobnobbing with a bunch of his rivals.

Fortunately, scaring the crap out of intrusive guards had made the list. Or maybe he was just returning a favor I'd once done him. Either way, he was giving a good glare over the back of the chaise.

"Yes?" he drawled, voice dripping with the privilege of a few thousand years.

"I . . . uh . . . I . . ." Well trained or not, the guard had obviously been thrown for a loop. I guess the consul's place was usually a bit more straitlaced—an adjective that had never once been applied to Anthony.

Who suddenly smiled at the flustered vamp. "If you stay here any longer, I am going to assume you want to join in."

The guard fled.

Anthony looked at me. "Having fun?"

"Not even," I said, scrambling back to my feet.

Only to have Ray grab me. "You've got it wrong."

"How?" I demanded—hopefully. Because nothing would make me happier right now.

"They weren't that close," he said quickly, because neither of us was under the impression that Anthony had bought us much time. "We got the portal open before you came around the last bend, but you couldn't hear us 'cause it was so loud in there. So Radu had to go get you. They couldn't have heard—"

"*Vampire* zombies," I reminded him grimly. "Their strength and speed doesn't vanish, even after they start to decay—"

"Don't remind me."

"So why should their hearing? And the necromancer heard everything his puppets did. Remember the half-missing guy upstairs?"

"I said don't remind me," Ray hissed, and then: "Marlowe's probably changed it by now, anyway."

"Changed what?"

"The password! You know how paranoid the guy is—"

"I also know he hasn't slept in five days and has about a thousand other things to watch. He can't—"

"Can I say something?" Anthony asked mildly.

"What?" Ray and I both demanded in unison.

"He's standing behind you."

Chapter Forty-three

I always wondered what Marlowe would look like if he ever really lost it. I found out. He gave a very nonhuman snarl and jumped me, sending a brazier tumbling and the hot oil inside it sloshing and Anthony and his pastime running butt naked out into the hall when the oil caught their chaise on fire.

Marlowe didn't even appear to notice. His eyes were fixed on me, and they were blacker than I'd ever seen them. It was like staring into two black holes, only not as friendly.

"Wait," I said.

And then I was airborne.

Which might not have been so bad, but Marlowe was, too. I got a split-second impression of him launching himself over the balcony I'd just sailed across, and then my back hit the floor of the arena. Hard.

And oh, yeah. That's what I needed tonight, I thought, rolling over. And thereby missing the vampire who landed on light cat feet right beside me. And getting squashed by the one who smacked into me like a sack of potatoes a second later.

"Okay, okay," Ray said, from atop my butt. "Let's not be—"

And then he was sliding backward, too, like a toboggan, only without the sled, across the shiny floor. And I was jumping back to avoid the fist of an enraged master vampire. Who seemed to have forgotten that he needed my brain intact in order to probe it.

"Is this the first match?" I heard someone say, as I ducked and dodged and tried to explain what was going on, only I didn't have the breath.

"Tell him!" I gasped at Ray, who ran back up as I bobbed beneath an iron fist.

"Dory's here because she thinks the bad guys got the password to the consul's portal," he said quickly. "And that they're about to bring a fey army through. Tonight," he added, since Marlowe didn't seem real impressed.

I nodded, and darted behind a confused-looking guy who was consulting his ticket.

"Am I in the wrong place?" he asked me.

"No, you're fine," I breathed, avoiding the blows Marlowe was aiming to either side of him. And then dropping to the floor and scurrying behind some startled bystanders, when Marlowe growled and picked the guy up, setting him aside like he weighed nothing.

"Only I'm trying to tell her that they don't. Have the password, that is," Ray added. "Or that it wouldn't matter if they did."

"Wouldn't *matter*?" I asked, stopping to glare at him through some chick's legs.

Only to have Marlowe dive between them and grab me around the neck.

Well, that was fast, I thought resignedly, when the girl's outraged date—who clearly didn't know who he was dealing with—kicked Marlowe in the head. It didn't do much more than distract him, but my patent leather stiletto was a bit more forceful, and his grip slipped. And I slithered away with only the loss of a few chiffon bits.

They don't make evening dresses like they used to, I thought, as Ray caught my eye.

"It doesn't matter because nobody's getting back into Central," he yelled at me. "It's on a major lockdown, so they don't have access to the gate. They couldn't use the password if they had it!"

"Yes, they can!" I insisted, furiously dodging through the crowd. And yet somehow meeting Marlowe coming the other way.

Crap.

"And just how do you expect them to do that?" Ray demanded, as a hard hand grabbed me around the throat.

But not so hard that I couldn't talk.

"What if Cheung happened to mention to his would-be employers just how you got your network?" I asked Ray, as I was jerked up. "And what if they decided to take a page out of your playbook? You said it yourself—it's easy enough once you think of it, only nobody ever does. . . ."

Marlowe's hand tightened, almost to the point of strangulation. Which didn't stop him from demanding information. "What are you saying?"

I looked up at the mirror, looming huge at the far end of the room, and a shiver went up my spine. Or maybe it wasn't just me. Because for a second, it looked like the whole room was shivering. And then I realized why, when another ripple—tiny, tiny, like a single drop of rain on the surface of a lake—shimmied across the supposedly hard glass.

"I'm saying . . . what if they hack it?" I gasped, just as the whole surface exploded outward.

Marlowe threw me to the ground and fell on top of me, as hard shards of glass erupted across the combat oval, tearing at my skin and sending the crowd into panic mode. Or maybe that was more about what was coming through the now quite visible portal. From under Marlowe's arm, I watched five huge, shaggy creatures break off from the horde and make straight for us.

They looked kind of like werewolves—in the same way that saber-toothed tigers look kind of like kitties. They were huge—at least twice the size of normal werewolves, but with none of the elegant lines and dignified bearing of the Clans. Who would probably have run screaming at the sight of them.

I kind of felt like that, too, until Marlowe threw out a hand.

And their heads exploded, one after another, like gory firecrackers.

The bodies thudded to the ground, still sliding forward on their own blood and past momentum, almost reaching us before Marlowe jerked me back. "How sure are you?" he yelled, to be heard over the screaming and the yelling and the whoosh of the vampire guards descending on the rest of the horde like a blurry wave.

"About what?"

"The *fey*!"

"Pretty sure. But—" I looked at the more immediate problem. "What are *they*?"

"Cannon fodder," Marlowe said grimly. "The real army will be behind them."

"And when it gets through?"

"It won't. I have a group on the way to the basement now. Stay out of the way; this won't take long."

"The basement—what?" I asked, but he was already gone.

I didn't have a chance to pursue him, because I had to hit the deck again to avoid the chandelier that came crashing down like a ball of ice. Literally, I realized, as it shattered against the floor, and some of the pieces flew up and hit my arm. And left marks on my skin, because they were cold enough to burn.

And I didn't have to ask why. Bullets were flying everywhere, prompting me to jerk Ray to the ground as several whistled by overhead. Because a new group had joined the party. And if I'd thought the other Weres were strange, they were nothing compared to the new arrivals.

They looked like Hollywood's idea of the wolf man, with grotesquely elongated hands, talon-like claws and weirdly distorted faces. And vaguely human bodies, because I guess it's hard to carry that much hardware in full wolf form. And they were armed to the teeth.

Fortunately, cannon fodder didn't seem to aim too well. Unfortunately, it didn't matter. Because every place one of their rounds landed turned into a winter wonderland.

The floor was suddenly mostly ice, crackling around my shoes and threatening to freeze my feet through the soles. Mirrors cracked and shattered on all sides, fissures appeared in the walls where marble slabs had been adhered to the surface, and a few slid off to detonate in thunderclaps against the floor. The consul's balcony was hit, carving off a chunk, and causing one of Ming-de's servants to abruptly meet the ground. And to then shatter into a hundred pieces, because he must have been caught in the spell, too.

The fey spell was wreaking havoc, but the wards were doing exactly bupkes about it. So either they were down, which seemed impossible this fast, or the spell was so alien that they didn't recognize it. And either way, we were—

"Come on!" Ray said, tugging on my hand. "There's nothing we can do. We gotta get out of here!"

"How?" I yelled, to be heard over the din.

It was already threatening to become a mass stampede, with the people who hadn't slipped on the icy floor starting to trample each other in a desperate bid to get out. This wasn't helped by the late arrivals, who obviously didn't realize what was going on. They were still pushing from the opposite direction, trying to get in before they missed the excitement and managing to create even more.

And then the lights blew out, and everything went dark.

The crowd issued a collective scream and panicked. And the resulting chaos made it impossible to hear any directions that might have been given. Not that anybody appeared to be bothering.

I could still see, after a moment, due to the glistening blue light coming from the portal. It wasn't much, but it lit the consuls, who were watching the events occurring below as if they were spectators at a play. A not very interesting one.

Hassani looked bored and vaguely irritated, and wasn't doing anything that I could see, although a few of his vamps were using the creatures for target practice. But Ming-de must have been annoyed about her shattered servant. Because she was peering over the edge of the balcony, a slight smile on her pretty features as she watched her apparently knife-edged fans decapitate creature after creature.

For his part, Marlowe had delegated some of his boys to try to corral the crazy by the exit and to hunt down the creatures who were thrashing around here and there. The rest were grouped around the portal, systematically decimating the cannon fodder still coming through. Most of which weren't even making it completely out before being cut down.

Despite the initial pandemonium, things were slowly getting back in hand, and I breathed a brief sigh of relief. It looked like maybe Marlowe had been right after all — this wouldn't take long. Someone even seemed to have gotten the lights back on, although they must have been the emergency variety, because they were blue, too.

Blue and swirling, I realized, a second before I threw Ray to the icy floor and dove after him, as what looked an awful lot like another portal opened up almost on top of us.

I jerked him back, into the maybe three-foot gap between the portal and the wall, as a wash of slime started vomiting out the other side.

"What the hell is *that*?" Ray shrieked, which might have been a problem if the things pouring out in front of us had had ears. But they didn't — or hands or feet or anything except gelatinous, squid-like bodies that squirted around underfoot harmlessly for a moment, to the point that I wondered what they were even doing here.

Until one of them a few yards away began to quiver. And to shake. And to explode, sending a familiar burst of acid-laced pus shooting into the air and setting a nearby guard's clothes on fire.

And it was only the first, like the initial kernel in a bag of popcorn. A minute later, gelatinous bombs were going off everywhere, setting little fires across the dark. Which would have had normal vampires in hysterics, but the nearby area was mostly filled with guards, who had been better trained than that.

Until they realized that the fire didn't go out.

As bad as the blood of Slava's vamps had been, the gel-like bodies of the creatures were worse. Because they stuck like glue, and the fire burned like phosphorus, and any guards who couldn't whip off a piece of affected clothing before the poison reached their skin began to burn like living candles.

One ran past us, screaming and flaming and flailing—and slamming straight into the crowd. Which was also largely composed of vampires. And although he was tackled by two of his fellow guards a split second later, it was too late. "Panic" wasn't the word for what broke out, with crazed people even jumping for the consul's balcony in their terror, only to be smacked right down again by the guards.

Until one of Hassani's men smacked a guard in return and somersaulted over the balcony, decapitating a Were with one sword stroke and grabbing a nearby girl who had been about to be lunch. He threw her up to one of his fellow soldiers, and then started grabbing random guests, plucking them off their feet and tossing them after the girl, with no regard for fine clothes or hurt feelings. Not that anybody seemed to be complaining; in fact, after a second he was all but mobbed, although his fellow soldiers didn't look real interested in—

"Dory!"

The voice came from above, and I looked up to see Radu's blond hanging over the edge of the balcony, dangling something. It was red and twisty—the curtains, I realized, a split second before I grabbed it. And then Ray grabbed me and a moment later, we were airborne again.

We were hauled over the side of the balcony, not by the blond, but by Anthony. He was back in his clothes, a bright purple toga in this case, and back in charge. "Go, go, go!" He had a sword in one hand and used the other to slap the shoulders of a double line of vamps pouring over the side of the balcony and into the fray—the guards from outside, I assumed.

He caught my eye. "Having fun yet?"

"No! What the hell is going on? I thought we only had one portal to worry about!"

"So did I. I just sent Radu's man after him to make inquiries. Radu knows about portals."

"And what about you?"

"I know about killing things," he said, before being plucked off his feet by the talons of a huge birdlike creature that came out of nowhere.

Anthony's sword flashed, gutting his ride halfway across the arena, and then he and it both fell. I didn't see what happened after that, because of the darkness, and because the fighting had just increased by about a thousand percent. And then Ray was dragging me off to the side.

"We don't need Radu," he told me quickly. "I know what's happening."

"That makes one of us," I said, grabbing a sword off a wounded vamp. It looked like somebody had designated the private boxes and the hallway and stairwell behind them as the triage area, because lower-level vamps were running up the stairs with makeshift slings filled with casualties. Most looked like other low-level types, along with some humans in evening attire—people caught in the stampede, as a guess.

I didn't see any masters.

But then, other than the guards, I hadn't seen many masters in the fight at all.

So what the hell were they doing?

"It's the shield," Ray was saying. "The place was secure until it went down. After that, anything goes."

"Come again?"

He sighed. "The shield . . . Look, it doesn't just protect a portal. It shields an area *of a line*. Because a portal is just a tunnel cutting through a ley line, and without a shield—"

"They can cut as many as they like."

"Yes."

"Then why were they so concentrated on *this* portal?"

"Because it was the only way through the shield. It's like . . . a gateway in a wall, okay? Why do you think those old castles always went to so much trouble to shield their gateways? Because that's where they were vulnerable. The wall—or the shield in this case—keeps the bad guys out. But there has to be a door for the good guys to get in."

"And our door is the portal."

He nodded. "That's why they call it a gate."

My head hurt. I wasn't good with all this metaphysical crap. I was like Anthony; I was good at killing things. Or rescuing things, only I had no idea where Louis-Cesare was, and I'd never even seen Mircea's room from the outside. It could be anywhere in the labyrinth of corridors running through the interior of the consul's house.

And even if I could find them, they might be better off where they were. Rather than being dragged unconscious through the thick of the fight by someone who wasn't likely to be much protection right now. Especially with a sword that my arm didn't feel strong enough to wield.

I passed it to Ray and took a gun from a guard who had just been brought up—the first master I'd seen. Something had all but bisected him, and yet he was still trying to crawl off the pallet, to get back to the fight. Unlike the rest of them.

Where were they?

"Stay down," someone told him, and I looked up to see the brunette senator Anthony had been with earlier. She'd found her clothes, too, only to have the front of her pale blue evening gown smeared with dark blood, since she seemed to be the one serving as hospital manager.

"You are Dory?" she asked.

I nodded.

"Kit said to tell you that the men he sent to the basement earlier have not reported in. He wants you to check on them."

"He wants . . ." I looked at her incredulously. "What is going on? *Where are your masters?*"

"Those sworn to the North American Senate are in the fight, those who were here, in any case. And more have been summoned. But they cannot use the portal, and therefore will take time to arrive."

"And the other senates? What are they doing—sitting on their hands?"

"Yes," she said, bitterly. "Except for Anthony's. But he had few masters with him, as most of his were knocked out of the competition early. He is doing what he can, but he does not have the numbers—"

"But there's a metric ton of master vampires here!"

"Belonging to other senates. Who do not wish to waste their resources on a fight which is not theirs."

"Not . . . Then whose fight is it?" I demanded. "The fey are coming to slaughter them, or didn't they get the memo?" Marlowe would have had more than enough time now to flash a thought around, telling everyone what was going on.

"They heard, but they do not believe. The fey have never attacked us, they say; why should they do so now? Undeclared?"

"Because that's the best way to win?"

"They do not believe a king of the fey would be so dishonorable."

"Then what do they think is happening?"

"That our consul is staging this, to force them to do what they have been avoiding, and to put their forces under her control."

I just looked at her for a moment. *"What?"*

She nodded. "Our kind can sometimes be too suspicious. It has hurt us before."

"Fuck hurt; it's about to kill you!" I snarled, before Ray dragged me away.

"I think I know what's in the basement," he told me.

"What?"

"The shield's power source. Marlowe must have sent his people to reactivate it, once the other side brought it down."

"But they haven't." And I couldn't think of a single reason for that that didn't involve something nasty.

"No. But as soon as they do—or as soon as someone does—the shield goes back up."

"Trapping us in here with the mutant squad!" I pointed out.

"But keeping out the fey army," he pointed out right back.

He won.

And even better, this was something I could do. Exhausted or not, I could activate a freaking shield charm. We had one in the basement; it wasn't hard.

"All right, I'm going," I told him. "Stay—"

"*We're* going," he said, cutting me off.

"You—" I stopped checking the master's pockets for ammo. "You don't have to do that."

"Yes, I do," he said, crabby as ever. "What if there's a problem with the shield? You don't know anything about that stuff. But I can jury-rig something out of almost nothing."

That was true.

"It could be dangerous."

"Like this isn't?"

"Okay, it could be *more* dangerous."

Ray crossed his arms and narrowed his eyes at me. "I'm coming." It was flat.

It was also something else.

I thought about all the senior masters, sitting on their hands or taking a few potshots here and there, and refusing to join in the fight. I thought about how much more power they had than a small, chubby, low-level little guy who was nonetheless willing to put his neck on the line. And then I thought that maybe the Senate's method of choosing new members was screwed.

"I guess maybe you are Batman," I told him roughly. "Come on."

Chapter Forty-four

We'd reached the bend in the stairwell when Ray suddenly grasped my arm, his grip tight enough to bruise. "Wait."

I froze, looking around for a danger I didn't see. Just bare marble walls, with what sounded like an epic battle raging on the other side. "What?"

"Just . . . hold on. . . ." He was fumbling around in his coat with his free hand, and finally pulled out his wallet. And from that he took—

"What's this?" I asked, staring blankly at the mushed-up granola bar he gave me.

"Just eat it."

"Why?"

"Did you have dinner?"

"*Dinner?*"

"Yes, dinner, dinner! Did you eat?" He waved a hand. "No, don't bother to answer that. I already know. You never eat."

"The food at my house was drugged!"

"Yeah, you always got an excuse. But then you end up bottomed out of energy and we almost die." He pointed a slightly shaking hand at the bar. "Eat it!"

I ate it.

It was good.

I held up sticky fingers. "Happy?"

"Not for longer than I can remember," Ray said fervently, and gave me a little push. "Let's go."

We went.

And found portals opening everywhere when we hit the great hall, and I do mean everywhere. One appeared in the floor almost under our feet, even before we managed to exit the stairwell, swallowing up the last few steps and almost swallowing us. We leapt across as creatures started crawling out, clearing them by inches, only to hit the ice rink the floor had become and slide into the thick of the fight.

Which, ironically, was the only thing that saved us.

Marlowe's boys had been fighting back-to-back against a mob of the bird-type things that had attacked Anthony. They were losing, which I couldn't understand since they seemed to outnumber the creatures. Until one of the guards turned my way.

I froze, partway to my feet, staring into the face of a vamp wearing the shoulders of a golden breastplate. It was all he had left after what looked like giant talons had ripped away the rest, and most of the flesh underneath. His heart was gone, his chest just a raw cavern of broken ribs and shredded lungs, his throat savaged.

Yet he was on his feet.

But not due to his own power.

"Dory!" Ray cried, and jerked me back. But Ray couldn't get any traction, and I still had the damned heels on because I'd been afraid my feet would freeze to the floor otherwise. So instead of getting away, we hit the ground again, just as the zombie lunged—

And had a thrashing mass of Weres fall on his head.

Judging by their expressions, I don't think they'd expected their portal to open over a sixteen-foot drop. And startled Weres have exactly one reaction. They demonstrated it by attacking everything in sight, giving our guys a moment to regroup and us a chance to scramble out of the way. And duck into a dark alcove, because there was nowhere else to go.

Busts and statues were cracking and falling in huge chunks. Lights were bursting and raining down glittering glass. Bullets were whizzing around thick and fast, and creating an impossible-to-navigate obstacle course down the whole length of the corridor. And then there were the portals, which worried me more than the rest, since there seemed to be no rhyme or reason to them, no way to predict where the next one would show up.

Because it didn't look like the other side cared.

One sprang into existence in front of the wall just down from us, which would have been bad. Except it was maybe a foot away from the marble and *facing it*. That left the vaguely lizard-type things inside scrabbling uselessly against the flat, shiny surface as more and more tried to push through, until the ones in front finally turned around and tore into the ones threatening to crush them from behind.

None of them made it out.

But the creatures in a second portal had it worse, when their doorway on the world opened in what would have been a prime spot in the middle of the hall—if another portal hadn't already been occupying it. And no, I'd never stopped to wonder what would happen if a portal tried to open inside another one. But I would have guessed that maybe you ended up with two metaphysical "tubes" running one inside the other.

Only apparently not.

What you got instead was a blur of color as the two portals met, but didn't meld. The currents started fighting it out, which in turn began pulling them out of shape, distorting the usual round openings into odd and conflicting shapes. Which probably wasn't good for them but was even worse for the creatures trying to come through.

"Duck!" Ray screamed, as a slurry of bones and fur and mangled flesh was suddenly flung around, like someone had stuck a knife in a blender.

But other than for dropping into a squat, we didn't move, because there was simply nowhere to go. If a squad of master vampires couldn't break out of this corridor, Ray and I sure as hell weren't going to do it. But the odds on getting back to the stairs weren't looking that great, either, since the battle had shifted and the fighting was taking place right in front of them now. But we couldn't stay here much longer without—

I stopped, my thoughts skidding to a halt as a third portal caught my attention.

Not because of what came out this time, since it was already open.

But because of what went *in*.

Nothing much. Just a couple of the hundreds of spent casings rolling underfoot, which had been kicked this way in the scuffle. And which had fallen into the portal, because the bottom of it was intersecting the floor.

Fallen in and hadn't come back out.

I looked at Ray. "Did you see—"

"No."

"But I think it's—"

"I know what it is!" he said feverishly. "And we're not jumping into some random portal when we don't know where it goes. We are not ending up any-freaking-where! We are not doing this, do you understand? For once we are not going to take the craziest possible—"

I didn't try to convince him. I didn't have to. The Senate's men had been getting pounded by an army of creatures whose abilities they couldn't have known about because they weren't supposed to exist. And by the steadily worsening odds, as portal after portal spit out reinforcements that our side didn't have. And by the fact that every time they lost a colleague, he or she abruptly ended up on the other side.

Facing them.

Marlowe's boys were well trained, but they weren't used to having to hack apart the bodies of their fallen friends. Or to being abandoned by their own kind. Or to having a portal full of gelatinous, acid-filled creatures open in the ceiling directly overhead and start to rain down fiery death.

The first sizzling lump had barely squelched against the floor when they broke and ran.

I didn't blame them.

Only they couldn't retreat, because of the mass of civilians behind them, most of whom hadn't made it out of the ballroom. So they surged forward, running into the minefield of portals ahead. Because they'd last longer there than they would standing in a rain of unquench-able fire.

And they took the creatures they'd been fighting right along with them.

There was no hiding from those kinds of numbers, no standing and facing them. There was only one option that didn't equal certain death, and I guess Ray felt the same. Because when I jumped for the maw of the suspicious portal, he jumped right along with me.

Something snatched at my arm, something else tore my dress, and a breath hot as fire skimmed along my neck—for an instant. And then the portal grabbed us and threw us around and spit us out. Onto a long, rectangular balcony in what looked like some kind of cave, with a line of fiery blue swirls dotting the side of a rock-cut wall beside us.

And a bunch of men and fey who looked kind of surprised to see us there.

For a second, we looked at them and they looked at us, and yeah, they were Svarestri, all right. At least the fey were. The war mages with them were typical—old leather trenches, ass-kicking boots and a crap ton of weapons. They looked a little grubby next to the fey, with their silver eyes and silver hair and haughty expressions, though the last were kind of overwritten by shock at the moment.

"Well, I don't know what I expected," Ray said blankly.

And then we were diving back into the portal, the wrong way around because there was no time to turn—or to avoid the hail of bullets that came after us. But we landed as we'd fallen—on our backs—less than a second before the barrage whizzed by overhead, one bullet cutting through my hair on my way to the floor. Then I was rolling and jumping and getting back on my feet—

And slamming back down, because they were shooting on this side, too.

We'd ended up back in the great hall, just as a new group of guards appeared from the ballroom. They started laying down a deadly salvo ahead of them, which flew over our heads since we were hugging the ground.

But that wouldn't be a huge help in a second, because they were coming our way.

And they didn't look like they planned on stopping.

Ray and I dove back inside the portal as a solid wave of heavy-booted feet pounded toward us, since friendly fire kills you just as dead as the other kind. We found the same group of bad guys standing about three yards ahead of us on the other side. Only they were facing away from us this time, having an animated conversation, I guess on the assumption that we wouldn't come back out the same portal.

And you know what they say about assumptions.

I dropped three of them with the vamp's gun before the rest even turned around, and then we threw ourselves backward, hoping like hell that the charge was over.

It was, only it didn't look like it had been too successful. Because the vamps were now coming back this way, chased by what looked like half the corridor, and that same trick wasn't likely to work twice. I guess Ray didn't think so, either, because he picked me up and *threw* me out of the way, which would have been great if I hadn't hit the consul's marble wall quite so hard.

And if he'd been able to get out, too.

And he might have—if four fey hands hadn't reached out of the portal and dragged him back again. *No, I don't think so,* I thought savagely, hugging the wall as guards and things pounded past, ignoring me in their rush. And then lurching for the portal again.

Only to find something in my way.

A big something. I looked up to see a handsome, blood-flecked face with dark eyes and hair and a tiger prowling around the side of it. Zheng.

"Where do you think you're going?" he demanded.

"In there," I growled, trying to push past, but he grabbed me with one huge, overmuscled arm. I could see it because he'd lost his tux jacket and his shirt had taken a beating. But not as much as he was about to. "Let me go!" I told him furiously. "They have Ray!"

"Who does?"

"The fey!"

"Whcre?"

"In there!"

Zheng looked at the portal. "Son of a bitch."

And then he let me go and we were both diving in headfirst. We hit the ground and rolled back to our feet to find the same bunch, minus three, *facing away from us again*.

Because some people never learn.

"Surprise, motherfuckers," I snarled, and grabbed my vampire.

"About . . . time," Ray choked, because one of the mages had been trying to chop his head off. He hadn't succeeded sincc it had been sewn on prctty well tlie last time, and because heads don't just pop off.

Not that Zheng seemed to be having any problem.

"That was really satisfying," he told me, as three more mangled bodies hit the floor.

And then we hit it right after them, courtesy of Ray, who had just jerked us both down.

"Shh!" he said, looking desperate.

"What—"

"Shh! Shh!"

I looked around, searching for a reason to panic. But I didn't see one. Just the drop-off, with a bunch of what looked like murky caves beyond, an arched doorway on one side and the portal wall washing us with alien light from behind. And some old, iron-barred cages I hadn't noticed before, because they were swaying in the air overhead, occasionally dripping some of the nastier bodily fluids down on us and the already badly soiled floor.

I didn't have to wonder what had been in them, since they reeked like the creatures we'd just been fighting. It looked like there was some sort of pulley system that brought the cages down to the level of the wall, where they could be opened right into a portal's mouth. I guess the fey didn't like dealing with their experiments any more than we did.

But the cages were empty right now, having already

had their contents sent through. And while there was another line behind them, snarling and spitting in the air over the edge of the balcony, it was far out of reach. So I didn't see the problem.

"What's the prob—" I began.

"Don't you know what *shh* means?" Ray hissed. "And *that's* the problem!"

His eyes went across the ledge.

It was a wide one, and since I was almost nose to filthy floor, I couldn't see anything beyond it. I couldn't hear anything, either, but not because the place was silent. The roar of what sounded like every ocean ever bounced off the walls, serving as damned good white noise.

So I decided to check it out.

I heard Ray curse behind me, but Zheng didn't say anything. And the next thing I knew, he was right beside me, slinking over the rough-hewn floor in a liquid motion that belied his size. And then Ray was there, too, I guess on the assumption that there was strength in numbers.

Only we weren't the ones who had them.

"Aiyaaaa," Zheng said softly.

And if that meant "holy shit," I agreed.

A stone floor spread out maybe twenty feet below us, covering what looked like about an acre. Which wouldn't have been all that remarkable. Except that it was packed with a solid mass of helmeted heads.

I felt goose bumps break out on my arms, because the heads belonged to fey. Row after row of them, crammed tight together in shiny black battle armor and drawn up in front of a huge wall on the right. A wall lined with massive portals.

The gaping blue maws could easily accommodate two or possibly three people at a time. And there had to be at least twenty of them, maybe more. It was hard to tell, given the flickering light sending waves of color rolling over a crowd that looked to be two, maybe three thousand strong.

The only good news was that it didn't look like anybody was moving through the portals yet. So maybe gateways hadn't been cut through to the other side. But as soon as they were . . .

"We're fucked," Zheng breathed.

Yeah. That pretty much summed it up.

We were barely holding our own with the trashed experiments and ragtag mercenaries and bio weapons that the fey had thrown at us in the first wave. We wouldn't last ten minutes with this bunch, not even if the consuls finally got off their asses and ordered their people into the fight. There were just too many and they were better armed, and even a consul might have a hard time fighting after being turned into an icicle.

So yeah.

Fucked.

"Come on," Zheng whispered, and began crawling back toward the much smaller line of portals behind us, just a dark shadow in the flickering light. Ray and I were less impressive, but we made it because nobody was paying attention to where the riffraff were being launched.

Except possibly the shadows leaping on the wall under the arch, as if someone with a light was coming up some stairs.

"Crap," Ray said, freezing in place.

"Grab the bodies," Zheng ordered, flinging two at the portal. Ray and I looked at each other, and then we did the same, snatching one each and dragging them with us into the wild blue yonder. Zheng followed with a corpse tucked under each beefy arm, dumped them on the floor of the great hall and turned on me.

"What the *hell*?" he demanded.

"You ought to know. Or did your boss get cold feet?"

"Lord Cheung didn't have shit to do with—"

"Told you," Ray said.

"—whatever *that* is—"

"What does it look like?" I asked.

"It looks like a damned invasion force! But who cuts a two-way portal into their staging area?"

"Somebody who made a mistake," I said, thinking of the other problem portals we'd seen.

"That's what you get for allying with idiots," Ray said,

stripping the nearest dark mage. And passing me a bunch of potions I didn't know what to do with, and a gun and bandolier that I did.

"Well, it's a mistake that's gonna cost them," Zheng said viciously. "We—"

"Cost them *how*?" I asked, draping myself in lead. "Even if we could get a group together, we'd just die there instead of here. There's no way we have the people to—"

"Then we'll die on the offensive!"

"Like that's an *improvement*?"

"Given the alternative! I'm not staying here and being slaughtered like—"

"Help us and you won't have to! Marlowe wanted me and Ray to check on the guys he sent to get the shield back up, but we can't get down the damned—"

Zheng cursed. "You and *Ray*?"

"Yeah, why?"

"You're barely able to stand and Ray's . . . Ray! Where the hell are Marlowe's boys?"

I gestured around. *"Busy?"*

"The ones he sent!"

"He doesn't know," Ray said softly. "He can't contact them."

"And we know what that means, don't we?" Zheng asked viciously.

"We won't know until we find them," I snapped, panic eroding my already tenuous patience. "Maybe they fell into a portal; maybe they're too injured to respond—"

"Maybe they're dead! Face it—if Marlowe's boys couldn't get the damned shield back up, when they know every inch this place, we're not going to. And if we waste time trying, the fey will be through—"

"You aren't *listening*. They're coming through whenever the hell they want! Did you see—damn."

That last was in response to a group of pissed-off things, mostly Weres, that had started our way.

And equally quickly regretted it.

"Damn, it feels good to be a gangsta," Ray muttered, watching Zheng let out some frustration.

"You're a smuggler."

"Close enough."

But good as Zheng was, the odds weren't great. And they were about to get worse as the smell of fresh meat got the attention of more of the Were-things. A large group down the hall had just finished savaging something on the floor, and now they turned hound-like heads toward us, red-stained maws wet and dripping.

"Call for backup!" I yelled, trying to lay down some cover fire as they charged, but they were too fast and there were too many of them. Plus, bullets didn't do much more damage to them than to Zheng.

"There *is* no backup," Zheng growled. "Marlowe's fucked in there as it is."

"*And what's your assessment of us out here?*" I demanded, as they surrounded us in a space with no portals.

"Been better," he said, shoving me behind him, because vampire bodies handled damage a lot better than mine did.

But I didn't know how much longer that was likely to last, when six jumped him and another one came after me and Ray, and I emptied two guns into it at point blank range. It flew back, only to be replaced by another gaping maw full of teeth that snapped at me as I jumped back—and hit the wall because there was no damned room to maneuver in here. Only that didn't seem to bother the Were much. I rolled to the side and he hit the wall where I'd just been, slashing and biting at the marble, before turning on me with liquid speed, faster than I could bring up a gun—

And then suddenly stopped.

And made a very strange face.

And crumpled to the ground like a busted toy.

A toy with no head, I realized a second later when it came off and rolled a few feet away. And despite the fact that there were bones and tendons and veins and assorted other things in there, the wound was so clean that it didn't even bleed at first. Like a rapier had sliced through a candle.

And then heads were popping off everywhere, all around the circle, and bodies were falling and I was wondering if the consul had some wicked new ward I'd never heard of that didn't like Weres.

But no. Because a moment after the last huge shaggy body collapsed on the pile, a very familiar redhead staggered out of absolutely nothing. It was like he'd stepped out of a portal, only there was no portal there. Just a shimmy of air and then a very confused-looking master vampire.

His hair was everywhere, he was barefoot and swaying slightly, and he appeared to be wearing only a blue bathrobe. But he was holding a rapier so thin and sharp that it was barely even bloody. *And okay,* I thought.

I guessed I knew what Louis-Cesare's master power was.

He looked at me, pupils blown huge and dark and vague, like his vampires' had been earlier. "Who . . ." He swallowed, and finally managed to focus on my face. "Who am I?"

He sounded a little desperate.

"My boyfriend, come to get me out of this?"

Louis-Cesare blinked. "That's right."

And then he pulled me to him and kissed me.

For a second, until Ray pushed us apart. "Can you do that again?" he demanded.

Louis-Cesare looked at him haughtily. "Of course." And he gave me another kiss, this time with tongue.

"No! I meant that thing you just did."

"The Veil," Zheng added enviously.

"Yeah, yeah, that. Can you do that again?"

Louis-Cesare looked up, blue eyes narrowing. "Why?"

"Because I think I have an idea."

Chapter Forty-five

The balcony was occupied when we slipped back through the portal, but only by a couple of mages. They were looking surprised at not seeing anyone there. But not half as surprised as when they did.

"All right," Zheng said, after they hit the floor. "Let's hear it."

Ray licked his lips, suddenly looking less sure of himself. But then he straightened his shoulders and met Zheng's eyes. "Okay," he said briskly. "The fey have to go through the portals to get to us, right?"

"Obviously."

"But they haven't cut them all the way through to the other side yet, or we'd have been seeing a lot of gates with nobody coming out of them, and I haven't."

"Of course not," Zheng said impatiently. "They don't want to telegraph where they're coming, in case we booby-trap the area."

"Right. Which is what gives us a chance."

I was looking at Louis-Cesare, who was still swaying and appeared slightly cross-eyed.

He caught my eye. "Where are we?"

"Somewhere in Faerie. Svarestri lands, I think."

"Oh."

"What chance?" Zheng was demanding. "Unless you can collapse a bunch of portals on the fly—"

"Well, yeah."

"What?"

"Closing a portal is easy," Ray said impatiently. "It's

cutting it to begin with that's hard. But that won't do no good, because if we close 'em, they'll just open more. They gotta have the people here to do that, given how many—"

"*Pardon*," Louis-Cesare interrupted politely. "But you did say *Faerie*?"

"What's wrong with him?" Zheng demanded.

I sighed. "He's brain-fried. He shouldn't even be here."

"That makes two of us." Zheng looked at Ray. "Get to the point."

"I'm trying! Look, destroying the portals won't work, 'cause then they'll know something's up and just cut more. But what if we reroute 'em?"

"Reroute them how?"

"With this. I—"

Zheng snatched the little device Ray had just pulled out of his wallet. "What's this?"

"My own invention," Ray said, snatching it back. "I use it to cut into portals. *And to link them.*"

"Holy shit," I said, catching up.

The little thing didn't look like much. Just a basic charm, like the kind people used for everything from opening warded doors to hanging around their necks for a quick glamourie: flat, gold, vaguely roundish, like an old-fashioned watch fob. Only this one had a couple metal prongs sticking out of it.

Ray was looking smug. "I cut into the Senate's line, remember? To link up some of my portals. So it's in my network, so to speak."

"So you're going to do what?" I asked, wanting to be sure I got this.

"The same thing Olga does when she wants to make more than one stop on the same line," Ray explained. "You gotta tell the portal which destination you want, don't you? Or you could end up at any gate along the line."

"So you're going to use that thing to tell the fey's portals to let out ... somewhere else?"

He nodded.

"Like where?"

"Do you *care*? Somewhere that isn't Earth, okay? I got a lot of locations preset—"

"Wait," Zheng said, his forehead knitting. I didn't think it was from lack of intelligence; he'd always struck me as fairly bright. But it didn't look like portals were his thing any more than they were mine. "You're saying you can link the fey's portals ... and then ... reroute their army somewhere else?"

Ray sighed. "For like the third time. Yes, that is what I'm saying."

Zheng looked skeptical, but he nodded. "Okay. Go for it."

"Well, I can't do it from *here*," Ray said, as if it was obvious.

"Why not?"

Ray rolled his eyes. "Do you see that line of portals? There's gotta be twenty of them—"

"Twenty-four."

"—so I'm gonna need all the juice for linking them, not for straining across half an acre of space. I have to be close."

"How close?"

"The closer the better. Preferably right next to one."

"Right—" Zheng looked at him like he was crazy, which, okay. Couldn't really argue with that.

"We can't get over there," I told Ray, wondering how this wasn't apparent. "The fey are *facing* the portals."

He scowled. "Like I don't see that? What am I, blind?"

"No, but you intend that they should be," Louis-Cesare said, sounding slightly more alert.

Ray nodded. "See that? The crazy guy knows what I'm talking about."

"There'd be a reason for that," Zheng muttered.

"I am not crazy," Louis-Cesare told Ray. "But your plan may be."

"But you just said you can do it—"

"I can—for a limited amount of time."

"Wait," I said, looking at Ray. "You want him to work that thing for you? When he's never done it and in his condition?"

"No, I want him to get me over there so I can!"

"Which is the problem," Louis-Cesare said. "I can shield another, but it decreases the amount of time that I can hold the Veil even further."

"How much?" Ray asked, starting to look worried.

"Under the circumstances?" Sculpted lips pursed. "Thirty seconds."

"Thirty—"

"Perhaps. Certainly no more."

Ray looked outraged. "Well, what the hell kind of a master power is that? What good is that to anybody?"

"In a duel?" Zheng asked sardonically. "A lot."

"Yeah, but we're not in a duel! And we're not gonna be, even if they see us. A massacre would be more like—"

"How much of the thirty do you need?" I cut in. Because this was no time for Ray to get going.

He looked at me incredulously. "How much? Like *all* of it? If I can even—"

"It could work," I said, looking from Zheng to Louis-Cesare and back to Ray. "Just."

"How?"

I told them.

"I don't know who's crazier," Ray muttered a few minutes later. "You or me."

"Me."

"Then why am I doing this?"

"Because you're the only one who knows how?"

"God. I hate being useful."

"First time for everything," Zheng said.

Ray didn't even bother to reply, which was how I knew he was bad off. And I really couldn't blame him. "Just . . . concentrate on what you're doing and leave the rest to us," I said, trying to sound confident.

"Yeah, sure. I'll . . . I'll do that," he said, as Louis-Cesare got an arm around him. And then Zheng got one around them both. Because there was no obvious route down to the portals from here, and no time to traverse it if there had been.

Ray needed the optimum amount of time at the gates, and we were going to give it to him.

"Just . . . try to land quietly," I told him, and got a vicious look in return.

"The Veil masks sound," Louis-Cesare said.

I looked up. "Really?"

He nodded. "It would be little good otherwise, vampire hearing being as it is. But when under the Veil, I cannot be seen, heard or smelt. Even wards have difficulty perceiving me. I have heard it speculated that it places me slightly out of phase with our world, and that is why—"

"Can we just *do* this?" Ray asked tightly, clinging to Zheng's already slightly elongated arm. Because Louis-Cesare wasn't the only one with a master power around here.

"Let go," Zheng told him. "I'm the rubber band; you're the spitball. And spitballs don't hold on to rubber bands."

"Die in a fire," Ray told him savagely. But he let go.

And Zheng's analogy was, for all its strangeness, pretty apt. He grabbed hold of a protrusion in the rock near one of the portals and braced himself, and I slunk over as near to the drop-off as I dared, holding his hand from something like six yards away. And then Louis-Cesare started backing up, at what would have been the elbow if Zheng had anything left that looked like one anymore.

Instead, it suddenly felt like I was holding on to a thick rubber hose with a hand-shaped glove at the end, neither of which was giving me a lot of traction. The idea was to use Zheng like a human slingshot to launch Louis-Cesare and Ray over the heads of the fey and to the line of portals. But to do that, we needed tension—a lot of it. And there wasn't anything else to provide it but us.

That wouldn't normally have been an issue, but right now I was sweating and struggling and still barely holding my position. And then I almost lost it anyway. Because we suddenly got a new complication.

The portals occupied maybe the bottom quarter of the huge wall, with the upper having been empty just seconds ago. But I guess it was showtime, because a long rectangular image had just appeared on the rock face. It was as big as an old-fashioned movie screen, but if there was a projector, I didn't see it.

What I did see was the interior of the consul's ballroom, where a massive number of portals had just burst into being on all sides.

And it looked like something had finally gotten the other consuls' attention. Because Ming-de's little fans zipped back to their mistress, and Hassani rose to his feet, his eyes narrowing and his hand gripping the hilt of the blade at his side. The other consuls were there now, too, and they were also rising: a South Asian guy dressed like a Bollywood maharaja, and a Spanish-type in enough velvets and laces to give Radu a run for his money. I didn't see Anthony, but I didn't have a view of the whole room.

And it wouldn't have mattered if I had.

Because the consul had just come out onto her balcony, and it was suddenly impossible to look anywhere else.

She was in gold, head to toe, in an outfit that made Liz Taylor's Cleopatra look like a pauper. And I finally understood how she'd managed to successfully lead a Senate for centuries, when plenty of other, stronger vamps had failed. You might not like her; might even detest her. But there was something there. Call it what you will—authority, command, leadership—it was that indefinable thing that makes men throw themselves at impossible odds because their commander tells them to. And she had it in spades.

Of course, she also had something else: vamps have never had the same problem with bribery as humans. It's considered everything from a performance enhancer to a loyalty inducer, depending on the size of the gift. And the consul had one of the biggest in history.

And she knew it.

Hard, cold, sublimely beautiful, she coolly surveyed the scene. And then those dark eyes flashed, and the perfect lip curled. And the low, sibilant words got right to the point. "If you wish a seat on my Senate, then bring me the head . . . *of a fey*!"

And just that fast, it was on.

An army of fey rushed through the portals; an army of vampires met them. And I turned to catch a split-second glimpse of two more vamps shooting into the fray, Louis-Cesare tucking into a graceful somersault and dragging a very freaked-out-looking Ray right along with him. And then they were gone, shimmering away into nothingness between one heartbeat and the next.

It was impressive, but not half as much so as the number of fey streaming through those portals. I guess Zheng must have thought so, too, because he was suddenly behind me. "Too many getting through."

"Ray will have the portals rerouted in a few seconds." I hoped.

"We don't *have* a few seconds."

"Yeah, but what can we do?"

"This," he told me, and the next time I blinked, he was holding a fey warrior.

I hadn't even seen him twitch, much less snake a long Gumby arm down into the pit and snare one, like a guy fishing off a dock. I saw it the second time, though, and saw the two fey go limp and collapse, their hair a bright spill against the dark rocks. Zheng had grabbed them by the neck, and he hadn't bothered being gentle.

Neither was I as I frisked them for the weapons I knew I'd find: suspiciously human-style guns, because they were far better at delivering a payload in hand-to-hand combat than bows and arrows. Especially when complete with three rounds each of what I could only assume were spelled bullets. At least, I really hoped so, because this was going to look pretty stupid otherwise.

It didn't look stupid.

I fired off a shot at the portals, and suddenly that whole end of the room was engulfed in a blizzard that—

"Whoa," Zheng said.

"I guess the fey didn't trust the help with the good stuff," I said, watching blinding bands of snow lash the fey lines. "Too afraid it might fall into our hands."

"Yeah. That'd be a shame," Zheng said, and fired a round directly into the wall just below us.

We didn't get a blizzard that time, but the effect was pretty spectacular just the same. The whole long expanse of rock iced up, like we were suddenly perched on top of a glacier. And sent the couple dozen blonds who'd spotted us, and started scaling the cliff like mountain goats, sliding right back into the crowd.

Zheng got another salvo off after them, but I didn't see what good it did. Because I had to stop and deal with a group coming through the archway. *You really can't fault their reaction time,* I thought, and shot the leader square in the face.

His skin turned blue and he staggered back, which I'd expected. And then an ice storm started up in the close confines of the hallway, which I hadn't. In all of a second, the whole door had iced over, with a bluish white slab so thick that it looked like a glacier had suddenly decided to park itself there.

I laughed, because if you're crazy, you may as well live up to it, and turned back to Zheng. Who didn't appear to get the joke. Or maybe he was just concerned about the fact that fully *half the freaking army* had just broken off and were coming for us.

Because yeah, they couldn't see us and didn't know how many were up here, I realized, as Zheng fired his last bullet directly into the crowd.

Who, without missing a beat, raised long, shiny black shields above their heads, like they'd been expecting it. And maybe they had. Because the shields locked together, creating a slick, solid surface that gave the ice nowhere to go but out. And it did, spreading like frost over the dark water of a pond and creating an almost flat, hard surface.

Which another group of fey promptly jumped on top of.

"Shit!" Zheng said, grabbed my gun and fired again.

But not at them. Because even though they were climbing fast, something else was more urgent. Louis-Cesare and Ray were in trouble.

I could tell because I could see them, not clearly, but in fits and starts, little glimmers like a couple of ghosts, if ghosts made "oh shit" faces on the one hand and agitated French gestures on the other. And that sort of shit wasn't going to go unnoticed for long.

Aaaaand it didn't.

One of the fey in line for the portal nearest them let out a very inelegant squawk, and pointed. And Louis-Cesare and Ray looked up from arguing over Ray's device to stare at the soldier in shock, as if they hadn't realized they could be seen. And yelled at. And shot at, only the latter didn't go so well because of Zheng's bullet, which hit the floor near the line of soldiers the pointer was standing in and—

Yeah, that's better, I thought, as a new blizzard tore through the lineup.

Except for the fact that that had been our last bullet. And that the fey below us had now achieved something that looked like a cheerleaders' tower, composed of three tiers of black-armored warriors with death on their faces. And that the blizzard that was supposed to be helping Louis-Cesare and Ray was fizzling out for some reason, just like the other had.

I didn't understand why until I noticed the shields of the fey clustered around them. Which instead of being shiny black, were now a blowing, snowy white, as a blizzard raged—beneath their surfaces. Somehow they'd trapped it, or most of it. The crazy winds and snow of a second ago had lightened to a few thin bands blowing across my vision, which did nothing to obscure the sight of Louis-Cesare and Ray fighting for their lives.

Louis-Cesare was showing the fey that he hadn't been the European dueling champion for nothing. His form was fluid grace, liquid motion. If it had been slower, it would have looked like an exotic dance. But at speed it was easy to see the moves for what they were, violence doled out with deadly precision.

But it wasn't enough, even though the fey hadn't just shot him. I don't know why. Maybe they didn't want to waste the ammo or maybe he was too close to the portals, and they didn't want to risk more going out of commission.

Or maybe they just didn't want to admit that a single warrior could hold them off.

But he couldn't, not forever. There were just too many and it didn't look like he could manage that disappearing trick again. He was already defending instead of attacking, dodging and weaving and twisting, yet finding no opening because there was none to find. Just a solid wall of shields closing in, and swords flashing and—

And Louis-Cesare looking at me, searing me with his stare, for a long second.

Before he fell.

A cold wash of disbelief tore through me, like the blood had suddenly left my body all at once. And if I'd ever had any doubt about how I felt, it was gone in that second. When I couldn't do a damn thing about it but scream my head off, a hopeless, horrified sound that hurt my own ears with the intensity of it.

But not as much as it seemed to hurt everyone else's.

Suddenly the whole room went quiet. The portals were still running, still murmuring to themselves, like two dozen rushing rivers. The thin bands of ice were still blowing, making *shush-shush* sounds against the stone. But nothing else talked—or fought or moved. Even the fey coming over the precipice, the ones who had been about to swamp Zheng, were frozen in place, as if they'd all been hit by one of their own weapons.

But I didn't think so. They weren't cold and blue; they were simply stopped. Or stunned, I realized belatedly, as one of them fell off the wall and crashed to the floor, and just lay there, looking up with portal light gleaming in his wide-open eyes.

I stared at the fallen fey for a second, and then at Zheng, who was just as unmoving by the wall, face set in a snarl, fist raised. And then I *moved*. Over the wall and down what felt like a fun-house slide, three bumps of slick, icy shields and then a spray of snow over a cold, cold floor. And then through an army of frozen obstacles, not one of which was less than seven feet tall, with helmets that made them even taller.

It was like being in a shiny black forest, one that could suddenly come to life and kill me at any second, because I had no idea what I'd just done or how long it would last. But something told me to *hurry, hurry, hurry*, to the point that I was pushing soldiers over, jumping past their bodies, fighting and clawing and—and finding them. Both of them, Louis-Cesare bent over Ray, still trying to defend him, even with no fewer than five swords sticking out of his body.

But none were through the heart; none had slit the throat. He would live if I could just—

And I couldn't. If I'd been weak before, it was nothing to how I felt now. That scream had taken every bit of energy I had. And even if it hadn't, Louis-Cesare was a column of solid muscle and I couldn't budge him. And then there was Ray. . . .

"What the hell just happened?"

Somebody growled behind me, and I spun, hands still on the shield I was trying to get in place for a travois. But I didn't need it now, because Zheng was there and—

"Grab them!" I told him desperately, even as eyelashes started to flutter around us and limbs started to twitch. And to his credit, he grabbed them, without asking further questions that I couldn't have answered anyway.

"We'll talk later," he threatened, throwing Louis-Cesare over one burly shoulder and snatching Ray up under one arm, like a package he was carrying home from the store. And then we were moving, back through the crowd that was more like a forest than ever, but the wind through these treetops was sighs and groans and vague, slurred words—

And then action, as the forest came alive even as we neared the not-so-fun slide. Which had been easy coming down but was a bitch going up even for me, and I wasn't carrying two. But Zheng's boots were made for walking—

and stomping and kicking—and we made it up the first level, and then the second, before our footbridge realized what was going on and all hell broke loose.

But by then Zheng was able to unceremoniously dump his two burdens over the edge of the rock shelf, and then it was just about getting the two of us over. Although that was harder than it sounds with a mountain of fey disintegrating around us. And then surging up underneath us as Zheng caught the ledge and swung us over, arcing just ahead of the grasping hands—

That caught us anyway.

But they caught us at the top of the arc as we fell onto the ledge, not over the side, and that made all the difference. Or it would if I could—

There! I wrestled the vampire's gun out of its holster just as someone grabbed my leg. And jerked me back, trying to pull me off the ledge or himself up, I wasn't sure which. And it didn't matter, because either was equally bad for me and equally not happening. I twisted, trying to line up a shot, while it felt like I was being torn in two.

"GO!" I yelled, as Zheng threw off three fey who had jumped him, sending two over the ledge.

His head whipped around at me, and then at the two bodies lying so still on the floor. But they were on the floor by the portal because Zheng wasn't stupid, and he'd thrown them as far as he could. And now he dove after them, because we both knew I couldn't drag them through with me or protect them on the other side if I did.

But he threw his last attacker into mine as he went, buying me maybe two seconds of freedom in the process. But not to run. Because running wouldn't help, just like the few regular old bullets I had left wouldn't do much against the dozens of fey now surging over the ledge.

But something else might.

I rolled onto my back, took aim and fired—at the cages just above the ledge. I'd almost forgotten about them, despite the fact that the contents had been rattling their bars and howling. And I guess they'd slipped the fey's minds, too, because they looked a little surprised whcn a wave of snarling, slashing hate fell on them as soon as the locks popped open.

I didn't wait to see who won. I didn't even turn around. I leapt back into a circle of blue, even as the third fey Zheng had thrown off recovered and twisted and lunged—

And missed.

Because the portal's familiar jerk caught me.

And I was gone.

Chapter Forty-six

The consul's place was a disaster area.

Of course, it had been well on its way before. But after another hour of fighting, which was what it took to clear the house and lock up the fey who had gotten through the portal but had avoided being gutted, the place had finished its descent into an expensive heap of rubble. Not that that seemed to bother Zheng.

He tossed what might have once been a quality settee aside, and searched through the debris underneath. And emerged with—

"Don't you think you have enough?" Ray demanded.

Zheng ignored him and dusted off his find, before severing it from its remaining tether and adding it to his collection. "She said—" he began.

"I know what she said," Ray interrupted testily. "And it was *a* head. Not seven heads!" He regarded with loathing the collection bouncing along at his former associate's waist, tied there by bloody silver-blond hair.

"Yeah, but she don't like me so much," Zheng pointed out. "And it don't hurt to have insurance. Not that I oughta need it after saving the senates' collective—" He broke off as a younger vamp sped by, clutching a gory trophy tightly against his chest.

And then looking around in shock when he realized that it suddenly wasn't there anymore.

"Oh, come on!" Ray said, as the young vamp caught sight of his golden ticket being tied securely onto Zheng's waist.

Zheng grinned at him. The younger vamp's shoulders slumped, and he sped off.

"He wouldn't last a day against the competition anyway," Zheng said. "Anybody who don't get a seat and thinks they ought to have, will be challenging for it for weeks, maybe months. There's a lot of fighting ahead." He looked pleased.

Ray looked skyward—literally, since that part of the roof was missing. "I wasn't talking about him!"

"Oh? Then what?"

"*You* saved their collective asses? I thought I had a little bit to do with it, too!"

"Oh, yeah." Zheng grinned. "That was pretty good. Where'd you send 'em, anyway?"

"This swamp I know," Ray snapped.

"Swamp?"

"In Faerie."

Zheng looked disapproving. "That don't seem so bad."

I had a brief flash of that vision Ray and I had shared once, about a primeval-looking quagmire straight out of Jurassic Park, and begged to differ.

Only I didn't have time, because Anthony staggered out of a hole in the wall, hugging a pretty blonde in one arm and an amphora of wine in the other. His toga was gone, his tunic was bloody and he was sporting what looked a lot like an old-fashioned shiner. But he seemed happy.

He looked around at the spotty fires, the drifting clouds of smoke and the tumbled marble of what had been a beautiful atrium only hours ago.

"She really knows how to throw a party," he told me, with apparent satisfaction. "You have to give her that."

He staggered off.

Zheng shook his head, frowned and looked around one more time. "I think that's all of 'em."

"What?" Ray asked. "There had to be, like, a couple hundred fey who got through before we hijacked their portals."

"Yeah, but the consul cheated. Her sandstorm scoured

half of 'em, and then Hassani's fire cooked most of the rest and then Ming-de got hold of what was left—"

We collectively shuddered.

"—and then she has the nerve to say she won't take 'em unless they're in good shape." He clucked over his collection, all of whom looked pretty good to me.

For severed heads, that is.

"Yeah, but I still don't get it," Ray said fretfully.

"What's not to get?" Zheng asked. "She wants people who'll fight for her. What's the use of Senate members if they won't do anything?"

"No, I mean I don't get *this*," Ray said, gesturing at their surroundings. "I know how the fey hacked through the shield, okay? But it shouldn't have mattered. It should have been back up in minutes—"

"And it woulda been, if somebody hadn't offed Marlowe's guys. You heard him, all five ended up—"

"Dead, yeah. And that's my point. Who killed them?"

"Whaddya mean, who killed them? The damned fey killed them. Or their mutants did. Those things were strong—and fast. Did you see—"

"Yes, I saw," Ray said sharply. "I saw a bunch of . . . things . . . come through the portal. But Marlowe spoke to Dory just after that—like less than a minute after— telling her that he'd sent guys to the basement. So he must have sent them practically the second he saw anything come through."

I nodded. "He told me he had people taking care of it."

"But they didn't take care of it. And a couple minutes later, he had Halcyon ask you to check on 'em, because the shield wasn't back up and they hadn't reported in."

"Yeah." I was starting to see where he was going with this.

"So the mutant things are back in the ballroom and then a few minutes later, they start showing up in the hall. But Marlowe's boys are dead by then, because you and me, we're already on the way to check on them. So again, *who killed them*?"

"It couldn't have been Jonathan's experiments," I said slowly. "Marlowe's boys should have been ahead of them."

Ray nodded.

"Unless a portal opened down in the basement," Zheng pointed out. "We wouldn't have seen it, so we wouldn't know."

"Okay, say it happened that way," Ray replied. "Say somebody figured Marlowe would be sending a group to fix the shield, and opened a portal down there before we even realized they could do that. That still leaves a bunch of other things unexplained."

"Like what?"

"Like Slava's." He looked at me. "It's been bugging me since our convo in the car. The bad guys, they got this perfect plan for getting into Central, right? But that requires us arresting a bunch of Slava's guys and taking them back there. They got in so easy because they were *let* in, and they were let in *because they were expected*."

"You're wondering how the fey and their allies knew we'd be showing up at Slava's," I said, wondering why that hadn't occurred to me.

Ray nodded. "They couldn't just wait around, hoping you'd get there sooner or later. It was too elaborate a plan for doing on the fly. And anyway, Slava was known as a pimp, not some big-time conspirator. Why would they think Marlowe would go there at all?"

"He went there because of the yacht," I said slowly, my headache getting worse. I was too tired for this, too tired to think. But Ray was right; something was ... off. "Mircea saw it in my head, and then Marlowe tracked it down from the description he gave. And discovered that it belonged to Slava."

"Yeah. So if it was in your head, who else could have known?"

"Whoever Marlowe told," Zheng said.

Ray rolled his eyes. "Yeah, because we all know what a forthcoming guy he is, right?"

"Nobody was in the kitchen when he told me but us and Louis-Cesare's cook," I told Ray. "And I somehow can't see Verrell being involved in the conspiracy."

"Neither can I, but that still don't explain how the bad guys *knew*."

"You need to let Marlowe know there might still be a problem," I said. "Some loose end somewhere."

He nodded. "I'm going to if I can ever find him. He's probably off interrogating the fey—"

Zheng nodded. "I heard they're bringing in Jack for that. Should be fun."

"—but, yeah, I think we got a problem. I mean, that attack itself was a little weird, too, if you think about it. Who shows up and attacks Central and just assumes they're gonna find the password? What if the senior guy on duty gets offed by your crazed killing machines? What then?"

"We know what," I pointed out.

"Yeah, we do. A total screwup. If they hadn't overheard us using the password, and if Marlowe hadn't failed to change it—"

"You heard him." Zheng said. "He'd just changed it the day before. On a hunch."

"—then they'd have been SOL. It seems a really slipshod way of doing anything."

"Well, you know the Black Circle," Zheng said, obviously losing interest. "Anyway, I'm gonna go turn these in. What about you?"

He was looking at me, but Ray answered. "I'm going to go find Marlowe. And some different shoes. These have been killing my feet all night."

Zheng was still looking at me.

"I think I'll hang out for a while," I said, going for nonchalant.

It didn't work.

He grinned. "That healer's gonna have your ass, you go back again before morning."

"Louis-Cesare will be fine," Ray told me irritably. "Well, physically, anyway, I don't know what you did to his head. I still don't feel so good."

Me, either. I had a headache that wouldn't quit, and I was so tired it felt like I was drunk. Which is probably why Zheng took pity on me and led Ray away, still fussing.

I looked around. That doc had been a bastard, but he had a point. The makeshift clinic had spilled out from the box seats into the charred remains of the ballroom, and usable space was at a premium. And since Louis-Cesare was in a healing trance, I couldn't do anything at the moment but sit at his side and be in the way.

I thought maybe I'd go do something useful, and get a little sleep—if I could find a bed that was still intact. Or a couch. Or a chaise. Or considering how I felt right now, any flat surface that wasn't covered in rubble and broken glass would—

Some sixth sense had my thoughts breaking off, had me turning. And that was all the warning I got before something slammed into me with an almost audible *whummmp*, knocking me off my feet and sending me sliding.

Into a horribly familiar scene.

Suddenly, the atrium's half-destroyed walls were replaced by gleaming skyscrapers, the steaming piles of rubble became water lapping against the sides of boats, and the haze of smoke and dust in the air turned into silvery moonlight flooding over—

No.

No! I jumped to my feet and whirled around, hoping I was hallucinating. And maybe I was.

Because somehow I was back in my head once more.

And worse, I was back at that fucking pier.

This time there was no Louis-Cesare, no Radu, no Mircea. There wasn't even a mysterious assailant trying to gut me. But there was a group of men standing on the bloody concrete, with flashlights in the hands that weren't holding smoking guns.

Or not, I thought, staring. Because one of them wasn't a man. Which might explain why I was suddenly looking at a memory that didn't seem familiar.

And hearing a mental voice that wasn't mine.

"Hurry up," the idiot in the dark overcoat said urgently. *He was looking around, gun in hand, tensed as if for a fight. And no wonder.*

Black scorch marks marred the concrete, and burnt gunpowder hung in the air like a cloud. Even muffled gunshots are far from silent and this wasn't exactly remote. The fools had probably woken half of Manhattan.

It was typical of the "Black Circle," Lawrence thought viciously. A bunch of the biggest stoners and losers he'd ever encountered, too strung out on magic to remember the simplest of instructions, and too incompetent to carry them out if they did. He gave the man the response he deserved—none—and knelt by the girl.

She was lying on her side, bloody and crumpled, and for a moment he thought they'd fucked up everything. His fangs dropped, sensing their blood, their fear, the heartbeats that sped up as they watched him. The decision was instantaneous. If they had killed her, they died.

But then he saw it, a faint, ever-so-gentle aspiration, and he unclenched the hand he couldn't remember closing. He pushed her over onto her back and checked out the damage. Two bullet wounds, a few too many contusions— damn it, he'd told them to avoid the head! But she would live. Long enough to do the job, anyway.

It was about time something went right.

It had been the perfect plan—his plan—calculated down to the last detail. Others had played their part— Geminus had come up with the idea for the weapons, the damned Black Circle had put him into contact with the man who could bring the idea to life, the fey had provided the army to use them. But he had been the one to stitch it all together, the one to watch Kit like a hawk, the one to steer the investigation away from their activities for what felt like forever.

He who was poised to pull off the greatest coup in vampire history.

But the sheer moronic incompetence that surrounded him was threatening to bring it all down. Geminus managing to get himself killed after two millennia of avoiding it, just when the lazy son of a bitch was actually useful for something. Then Varus suddenly gaining a conscience and Mircea—devil take him—being put in charge of the Senate's smuggling investigation instead of Kit.

Mircea, whose family Lawrence didn't know and over whose actions he had no influence. Mircea, whose skills with the mind rivaled his own, and whose secrets were closed to him. Mircea, who had charmed away the best investigators from a dozen families and formed them into a unit that was closing the noose tighter every damned day . . .

Sometimes Lawrence thought it was a wonder he was still sane.

The only thing that kept him going was the thought of what he was going to do to his allies once this was all over. He felt his face crack into a smile, felt the men tense and shift uncomfortably. And then he slid into the girl's mind as smoothly as a fish into water.

The easy pathways and uncomplicated patterns of the human brain opened up before him, like an unfolding flower. Such a relief after the twisty, dark paths of the vampire mind, where barriers were everywhere and hidden traps could suddenly lunge out and grab you, threatening to shred your consciousness if you weren't nimble enough to get away.

Like Varus, who had proven impossible to read. Or Mircea, who had almost trapped him the one and only time he'd ventured into that quagmire of a brain. He thought it fitting that the freak Mircea had sired and inexplicably continued to shield was Lawrence's way out of the mess her bastard of a father had made. All Lawrence had to do was to plant a few memories, adjust a few others and—

What the hell?

Lawrence stopped abruptly, gazing in disbelief at the . . . thing . . . at the center of her mind. If "mind" was even the right word. But all of the others—"maze" and "jungle" and "labyrinth"—that he'd used to describe some of the more unusual minds he'd encountered fell completely short. It was a gigantic snarl of impossible patterns and massive barriers and odd dark places and strange duplicated synapses and . . .

And it was like nothing he'd ever encountered.

It wasn't human. It wasn't even vampire. He didn't know what the hell it was, or how she functioned with it at all. It was . . . insane, he thought, horrified.

And then jumped at the feel of a hand on his physical arm.

He pulled back abruptly, the jumbled-up mess retreating, to be replaced by another mess, in the form of one of his allies' faces. "Are you almost done?" the idiot asked, looking anxious.

Lawrence reminded himself that he couldn't kill him. Not yet. "If I was done, I would have said so," he hissed instead.

"It's just . . . you're needed at the third site. Jonathan's having trouble with one of the masters."

Lawrence glared at the man, furious. "I instructed him to wait for me!"

The man shook his head, and glanced at his partner. "Jonathan doesn't take instruction well. Not from anybody. He does what he wants."

"Then he's a fool, and he can die as one. Danieli has mental gifts. He'll resist the compulsion."

"He is resisting. That's what I'm trying to tell you. You gotta get over there or this is all going south—tonight."

"As it will if I leave the woman's memories intact!"

The man's partner, who was slightly more intelligent, if no more capable, uttered an expletive. "What is taking so long? You said she wouldn't be a problem."

"She isn't."

"Then what—"

"Her father," Lawrence said viciously. Of course it had been Mircea; of course it had. Cobbling together some form of bastardized consciousness for his pet. Why, Lawrence couldn't even begin to imagine. The man gave him the fucking creeps sometimes.

"That vamp isn't here," the partner said sharply, challenging him.

And causing Lawrence to have to clench a fist to keep from dropping the SOB, then and there. "He's done something," he said shortly. "Something I've never seen before. I don't know what it is, or how to counter it."

"You're saying you can't manipulate her memories?"

"I'm saying I can't do it right now, in some hatchet job

on a pier!" Lawrence retorted, shoving damp hair out of his eyes.

Half of it was salt water, the other half blood splatter from the girl mixed with his own, because this had to look real. Ten to one, Mircea would be extracting her memories, and he would recognize a wholesale implantation. So Lawrence had had to take a few bullets, after already taking a portal to one of the nastier hell dimensions. And now he learned it might have all been for nothing?

God, he wanted to kill something.

"But she has to remember the ship, or they won't go to Slava's!" Idiot #1 said. "And that you died, or Marlowe will change the passwords and then we'll really be screwed—"

"We're going to be screwed anyway if you don't come on," Idiot #2 said, a phone to his ear. "Jonathan says now."

"Jonathan can—" Lawrence cut himself off. Soon. Very damned soon, he'd deal with Jonathan and the rest of them. He would deal with them slowly. He stood up. "Take her."

"Take her? Take her where? If she's no use to us, we gotta clean the scene. We gotta—"

Lawrence shoved the man's hand away, the one he'd raised with the gun in it. "We need her!"

"Not if you can't—"

"Put her in one of the labs. The girl got off a call for help, right at the end. I have to wait here for a few minutes, in case anyone comes, and then bail out that fool of a necromancer. Then I'll deal with her."

"And if she wakes up before then?"

"She won't. And even if she does, she'll be weak from blood loss and mentally confused. I did enough when I knocked her out for that. She won't be going anywhere until we release her."

"But she's supposed to be found here," the man argued. "Bleeding out. If we take her away, how are we supposed to explain—"

"Leave that to me! Do as you're told; I'll handle the rest. This is a minor setback."

"And it would have been," Lawrence said, shivering into existence beside me. "Except for you and your father. And my old master, who changed the damned passwords anyway, for no reason!"

"He has gut feelings sometimes," I said, cursing myself.

I don't read minds, much less those of powerful mentalists. I should have known I wasn't picking somebody else's brain on my own. Should have realized that Lawrence was showing me the scene on the pier, the scene he'd withheld for so long, for a reason.

So he'd have time to find me.

"I'll gut him," Lawrence said cruelly. "Just as soon as I finish with—"

Me, I assumed, judging by his expression. At least, the one he'd had a second ago. Before the gun I'd thought into existence blew it away.

He'd forgotten that I'd learned that much, at least, from our former encounters. Or maybe he hadn't noticed, since I hadn't been able to use it very effectively. And it didn't look like that had changed, because he was healing before he hit the ground, make-believe bullets apparently not carrying quite the punch of the real thing. Or maybe he knew some kind of trick to minimize his damage in here.

Too bad I didn't.

And he didn't give me time to come up with anything. In a liquid movement that blurred my vision, he surged to his feet and caught my wrist. And then broke it so viciously that I thought for a second he'd ripped my hand off.

He hadn't, but the pain was so excruciating that the whole wharf wavered as I emptied the clip into him anyway, as I stumbled back, as I stared around for somewhere to run—and came up empty. I didn't know how to access Louis-Cesare's memories, and besides, that hadn't worked so great last time. And there was nothing else in sight except the scene on the wharf, frozen in place, and the skyline with its missing chunks of sky and—

And the rift.

The breech in the wall between Dorina's consciousness and mine was still there, and still frightening. But I didn't hesitate, because things couldn't get any worse. I threw the gun at him and ran, straight into the enveloping clouds around the entrance. Straight past the gaping pink maw, a fluttering tentacle brushing softly over my face. Straight through the flickering scenes of a life I had lived but didn't know. Straight into—

Darkness.

Chapter Forty-seven

It wasn't wholly dark.

The pinkish light from before had faded, but other, brighter sources had taken its place. Pieces of memory flickered against the gloom, but not like last time. Before, they had been vague, washed out, wavering oddly. Like a hundred projectors turned onto someone's laundry. Now it was more like walking down a dark street in Chinatown, assaulted by glowing neon signs on all sides. Or maybe holograms would be a better analogy, because they floated in the air as well as clinging to the rift, like flattened portals to other places, other times.

And there were more of them—a lot more. I glanced behind me, trying to spot Lawrence, and saw bits and pieces I recognized, as well as a lot I didn't. It looked like the memories were colonizing this new ground, washing in from both sides to jumble up in the middle, creating an obstacle course of ever-changing light and shadow.

A little too much light, all things considered, with the brighter scenes shedding a haze of illumination for several feet around them. But it was still better than outside. I darted behind the darkest one I could find, slammed back against the skin-slick wall of the rift, and watched a younger me crawling through a trench, knee-deep in muck.

The visual was stark, almost like a film shot in black and white, although it wasn't. That's just how the place had looked: dark coils of barbed wire pushing up into a washed-out sky. A dead tree. And an unburied bone, possibly animal, possibly human, poking out of the mud.

Flanders, First World War.

And no, no way was I hiding in that one.

Or in any of the rest of them. What had Radu said? Something about people getting lost in their own minds, wandering around aimlessly from memory to memory, trapped forever in their past?

I swallowed, feeling an involuntary shiver ripple over me.

My past hadn't been that great, frankly.

"Nice try." Lawrence's voice filtered to me in strange echoes. "But bullets don't have quite the same effect on me as on most of my kind."

No, I didn't guess so. Like it wasn't a problem to fake death when you came apart anyway. Son of a *bitch*.

But there'd been more than just the one reason to suspect him. Mircea had told me that Lawrence had three master's abilities, but I'd seen him use only two: the Hound senses and the dissolving trick. I had never thought to wonder about the third, despite Marlowe's saying that mental abilities had gotten Lawrence out of trouble before.

And me into it.

"You may as well come out." Lawrence's voice came again, sounding so close that it had me whipping my head around violently. Only to see nothing there. "You can stall all you like, but you forget that we're *in the mind*. Outside time is meaningless. Weeks could pass for you here before anyone even realizes you're in danger."

I didn't answer. He could be telling the truth, for all I knew. But he could just as easily be lying. I didn't know how this mental stuff worked. I just knew I needed to stay near the pier, or as close as I could manage, where Mircea might eventually come looking for me. If I went too far in—

"And then there's the small fact that you don't have a choice," Lawrence informed me. "Neither of us does. I am your only way out, just as you are mine."

Okay, that got my attention. But he didn't elaborate.

Even when I waited he didn't. He was going to make me ask, going to try to use conversation as a way to zero in on my location.

I didn't give much for his chances. The walls seemed to trap some sounds and magnify others. His voice was simultaneously nearby and distant, with some words so far off I could barely make them out, while others sounded like they were coming from only a few feet away. It was spooky as hell—but it might also be useful.

"Meaning what?" I demanded harshly, and heard my own voice coming back at me in receding echoes.

"That neither of us has a guide; neither of us has a way to resurface. Unless one of us dies."

"And then the survivor wakes up."

"Yes. As would have happened last time, if your father hadn't cheated and come after you," he said, sounding annoyed.

And for a second, all I could see was Mircea's bloody face, stony and white and resolute as he let this bastard carve him up to give me time to get out. All I could see was Louis-Cesare lying on the floor, unconscious and worse, because he might be Europe's champion but he didn't know how to fight this way.

Neither did I, but I wanted to. I felt my fangs drop, and for the first time, it didn't bother me. It felt good, like his flesh would feel under my teeth, the way his blood would taste on my lips, the way his screams would—

I swallowed and looked away.

"But it didn't matter. He had to be removed in any case," Lawrence added, and stopped again.

Baiting me.

I told myself to *shut up*. To concentrate on finding a way out of this. Only I didn't see one.

Even if Lawrence was lying, and a competent mentalist could have brought me out, where was I supposed to find one? The only one I knew about was Ming-de, and I had no way to contact her. Or reason to believe that she would help if I did.

And say he was making that stuff up about time being perceived differently in the brain. I could still lie there in the rubble a long time before anybody noticed me. And even then, if my rescuer wasn't one of the handful of people who knew me, he'd just assume I was one of the human guests and put me wherever they were keeping the others. It might be hours before anybody realized I hadn't just been knocked out cold.

And I didn't think I had hours.

"Was that your job? To betray the Senate?" I asked, taking the bait. And starting to search the shadows for the one searching for me.

"Betray?" Lawrence's voice was mocking. "Was it betrayal for those fools to gut each other nightly on the arena floor? Fools fight; winners think."

"So you planned to get on the Senate this way?" I asked in disbelief.

"No, I planned to rule the Senate this way," Lawrence said. Because he was obviously crazier than I was.

"If you're so strong, you could do that anyway," I said, watching a shadow slink along a wall. "Challenge the consul. As far as I know, she isn't a mentalist."

"No, but your father is."

"Ahh." Things started to make sense. The consul could fight her own battles, but she could also call for a champion when challenged. And obviously, Lawrence didn't think he could take Mircea.

So he'd just decided to murder him instead.

"Is that what the fey promised you?" I rasped. "The consulship?"

"No, that is what they promised Geminus. He'd discovered that a Senate seat is merely another form of slavery. The only way out of bondage in our world is to *rule.*"

"And that's what you think you're going to do?" I demanded. "Rule? Because I got the impression that's what the fey want. And their godly buddies."

"The fey care about Faerie, not Earth. And what gods?"

"The gods the fey plan to bring back! Or didn't they share that tidbit?"

He laughed. "Oh yes. I think it was mentioned a time

or two. But you forget—the gods are not here. And will not be here until the Circle falls."

"And isn't that the idea? Take out the Senate, then destroy the Circle?"

"That's *their* idea," he said condescendingly. "Mine is to remove the consuls and to consolidate rule of the six senates in my hands. Once I have it . . . Well, both sides will need my favor then, won't they? And with the odds in the war nearly even, the vampires will be poised to make the difference."

"And you'll throw your weight behind the Circle," I said slowly.

"Who will then owe me their victory, further cementing my position."

"So this is just another vampire power play." It shouldn't have surprised me. Mircea had guessed as much, and it was certainly nothing new. Where vamps were concerned, it was the oldest story in the book and I'd seen a thousand examples. But for some reason, this one seemed particularly—

I belatedly realized that memory-me had started climbing out of the trench she'd been slogging through. And that the trench had been in shadow and outside was a whole lot brighter. And suddenly, so was I, as light from the scene spilled over into the surrounding area.

"*The* power play," Lawrence said, materializing out of nothing right in front of me. "And even for a novice, that was pathetic."

Behind him, memory-me made an "oh shit" face and launched herself back into the trench.

"Really? How's this?" I asked, and kicked him viciously backward.

Because I might not be strong enough to kill Lawrence myself, but I had plenty of lethal memories that might.

As he was discovering.

I saw him fall into the scene, saw him land in a splash of mud and blood and half-rotten donkey parts. But I didn't see him get up. Maybe because a barrage of artillery fire ripped across the scene a second later, whiting out everything.

Or maybe because I was running like hell.

Not back for the entrance, but farther, further in. Dodging around, looking for other memories, worse ones, because the son of a bitch wasn't dead yet. No, not yet, or I'd be out of here. I ran past strafing gunfire and a stampede of horses and a crashing surf and—

And straight into the fist that came out of nowhere.

It looked a little different than it had a moment ago, blackened and bleeding, with bare knuckle bones protruding from ruined flesh. It matched the face above it, which was almost unrecognizable. Demon red eyes looked out of a mask of charred skin that had partially flaked off, including the part that had once covered the now hairless skull. One cheek was split open, the guard uniform he was wearing was smoking, and half of the breastplate had melted to the burnt torso.

It looked like Lawrence hadn't come apart fast enough this time. But he hadn't died, either. A fact he demonstrated by sending me staggering back against the floor. He tried to shove a boot through my skull next, but I grabbed it—*hot, melting rubber, shit*—and *twisted*. I heard his knee pop before I felt it, before he screamed and grabbed my hair, jerking me up and throwing me face-first into the wall.

Right before I whirled and kicked out with everything I had left, sending him flying back into another memory. Of an earthquake-fueled rock fall that had very nearly caved in my head once, a few hundred years ago. And then I turned and scrambled away, trying to look ahead and behind at the same time, my eyes watching half a mountain slough away into billowing dust, while my feet—

Splashed down in a puddle.

The puddle was on wet cement. The cement was in a warehouse. And the warehouse looked to be on the edge of what passed for civilization.

Shit. I immediately spun back around, looking for the

way out, because I must have accidentally fallen through one of the flickering memories that formed the obstacle course outside. But there was no door, no square of boiling darkness, no furious pursuer.

Just a drab, water-stained wall, a couple of broken pallets and the puddle. The puddle was water. I looked up.

And a great drop of tar-laced rain hit me square in the face.

Great.

I looked back down, holding my eye and wondering: *Now what?*

I honestly had no idea. I was panting with exhaustion, my wrist was on fire, and now I was half blind. I wasn't going to win a fight like this. If Lawrence found me, I was toast.

Of course, I probably was anyway. I didn't recognize this place, so it must be one of Dorina's memories. And since I didn't even know how to navigate my own, the chances of figuring a way out of hers didn't seem so great. So I went in instead, because it was either that or wait around to die.

Although it smelled like something already had.

Maybe a lot of somethings, judging by the stench. But it wasn't the old, familiar stink of putrefaction that caught my attention as I passed behind a wall of crates. It was the fact that whatever had died in here wasn't exactly—

Human.

I stopped abruptly, staring at the remains of what looked like hundreds of creatures, stacked against the far wall in cages three and four high.

Most were various species of fey I had encountered through the years, along with what might have been shifters. Others . . . I didn't know about the others. And I doubted that anybody else would have, either. The monsters who had engineered these crossbreeds hadn't been concerned with viability or quality of life or anything but their intended outcome.

I wondered how many creatures they had killed along the way.

I wondered if those hadn't been the lucky ones.

Because it looked like they had just abandoned this place, once they'd finally achieved the result they wanted. Or maybe the Circle had gotten too close, and the conspirators had decided to walk away, leaving us another cache to find. Only we wouldn't have learned much from this one.

Because they hadn't bothered to open the cages before they left.

And the contents hadn't managed it themselves. There were signs that a number had tried, biting and clawing at the bars, before succumbing to hunger or thirst. Or in a few cases, to their fellow experiments. But it didn't look like any had made it out.

Or maybe I spoke too soon.

A bunch of boxes formed a tall line facing the cages, blocking off the view of at least half the wall of horrors. That was true even when I got close, drawn by morbid curiosity and a weird sense of hope. And found a woman kneeling on the floor.

Her head was bowed, but not in shadow. A beam of moonlight was filtering down from a high window, illuminating her like a spotlight. As a result, her face was mostly still visible.

And her face was mine.

I had a killer on my trail and, given his track record, he wouldn't take long to find me. I should get moving, should try to find a defensible position. Should try to figure out how to fight something that could dust away to powder in the blink of an eye.

But I didn't move. She didn't seem to notice me, or even look up. But I . . . couldn't look anywhere else.

She looked like a vampire.

I don't know what I'd been expecting, but we weren't twins, despite the superficials. She had my short dark hair, my features, my height, even my basic style of clothing. At least, the kind I wore when I wasn't going to the party from hell: black jeans, a black tank top, a black leather jacket. She had on rubber-soled shoes instead of my usual ass-kicking boots, maybe because she didn't need any help in that department.

And yet, if I'd seen her from across the room, I'd have sworn she was a vampire.

It was something in the way she held herself, so preternaturally still. Something in the way she squatted there, effortlessly balanced on just the toes of her feet, in a pose a prima ballerina would have tired of very fast. Something in the way she didn't seem to breathe or blink quite the right number of times per minute.

Although the latter might have had something to do with the silent tears rolling down her face, unnoticed and unchecked.

I'd never seen a vamp cry before. And even though I wasn't seeing it now, it looked like I was, and it threw me. Like this night, like this whole week, hadn't done that enough already.

I was beginning to wonder if you could get so far off balance that you'd never quite make it back to true. I was starting to feel like that, and then she looked up. But not at me.

She was cradling something I hadn't noticed because my eyes hadn't left her face. Something with thin blond hair, soiled and tangled, a slight form, a dirty blue shirt or dress. Something—

*Some*one.

Child.

The images slammed into me, most of them too fast to process, but I got the gist. She'd found the girl; she'd lost the girl. And had been looking for her ever since. Searching the underbelly of the city, places like the one where she'd found her, places like this. And cutting a swath through an entire chain of slavers, smugglers and Black Circle members in the process.

There hadn't been a civil war in the smuggling community. They hadn't savaged each other and then thrown the bodies into the portals. That had been Dorina on a rampage, every time I went to sleep, looking for the child she'd lost.

And finally found.

"Too late," I mouthed along with her.

She clutched the girl harder, and her face was so open,

so easy to read. More so than mine ever was. She didn't mask her feelings, didn't hide behind sarcasm or bad jokes. Didn't pretend. She hurt; she cried.

And I felt the earth shift a little more under my feet, centuries of preconceptions crumbling beneath the foundations.

I didn't know who I was anymore. Didn't know who she was. It was strange to be facing the end of my life, and realize that I'd never really known myself at all.

Or the memory I was suddenly seeing.

The golden footsteps I had followed across the city ended at her body.

She was crumpled on the floor, near the line of cages where she must have collapsed. I did not know why she had come here. Perhaps hoping to free the others? If so, she had been too late.

Like us.

"Not quite," the creature with me murmured, his long wings sweeping the ground as he knelt a few yards away.

And held out a hand.

And from the body rose . . . a golden child, happy and laughing and skipping over to the shining one, who opened his arms for her.

I stared as he picked her up, this creature made of light. Like him, I realized. I didn't say it aloud, but he nodded.

"They stole her from my people."

"Why?" I asked, my voice hoarse.

"For the same reason they stole all of these." He glanced around. "They wished to make a weapon, to give themselves an edge in a war. They needed something that would work in Faerie and on Earth. But there are few things that walk the Divide well enough for their purposes."

"The Divide?"

"Earth is the highest of the hells; Faerie is the lowest of the heavens. My people originated in one realm and . . . moved . . . to the other. Therefore our magic works in both."

I didn't understand. I just reached for the child, but he kept a hand on her arm. She looked up at him, bright-eyed, curious.

But he shook his head. "She must return to her people."

"Then . . . she is not dead?"

"The body is. But she will one day be strong enough to make another, since her essence was not scattered. Thanks to you."

I didn't understand that, either. I didn't understand anything. Except that the child would not be here.

She would not be family.

"You have a family," he said softly. "More than you know."

I shook my head. I couldn't speak. The child didn't, either, but she pulled away from him. And this time, he let her go.

She came over to me, and looked down at the body I still held. And then up at me. And smiled.

And placed a soft kiss, light, light like air, on my cheek.

"To help you bridge your own divide," the Irin murmured.

I looked at him, hurting, defeated. "I don't understand," I cried.

"You will."

Something clattered to the floor behind me, loud in the silence. I jumped and spun—and saw no one. Just an echoing, dark warehouse, cold and empty and completely still.

And the same was true when I turned back a moment later.

And found myself alone.

The woman—Dorina—was gone. And so were the child and the Irin. No sign of them remained, not a scent, not even an impression in the dust. I stared, wondering if my fevered brain had dreamed them up.

Like the hubcap that suddenly clattered to the floor at my feet, shiny and metallic and reflecting—

"Damn."

I started moving just as the whole towering line of boxes began to tip over, coming after me in wave after wave of cardboard. And falling machine parts, which seemed to constitute most of the boxes' contents. Parts that were glittering in the moonlight and striking off concrete and about to cave my head in if I didn't get out of the way.

Which would have been easier if they hadn't been coming from both directions.

I stopped, turned, and went back the other way, but found no escape. Except for one. I dove into an empty cage, trying to avoid seeing what was on either side in favor of watching what was in front. Because I knew who was going to be coming through that fall of destruction, and I needed to be out of here before he trapped me in—

And then it wasn't a problem anymore. When he suddenly materialized out of nothing in front of my makeshift bunker and snatched me out. And while his face was still a blackened mess, he must have been busy healing the important stuff. Because my feet weren't even touching the ground.

"I just want you to know," Lawrence said amiably, "when I am consul, your father will be the first to die."

"Then he'll live a long time," I gasped, because the hand holding me was around my throat. "The Senate remains."

"For the moment," Lawrence said, frowning, because I guess I wasn't on script. I was supposed to be cowed and begging or awed and overcome by his brilliance.

Instead, I decided to go out as I'd lived, a bitch to the very end, and materialized a stake into my hand. Only to get thrown at the remaining boxes. Which hadn't budged because they contained what felt like solid rock.

I slid off and was jerked back within striking range, because Lawrence wasn't afraid of me. And why should he be? I was beat-up, bruised and bloodied, and had the use of only one hand. Even if I managed to slip the wooden sliver into that cold, dead heart, there would be no way to slice his throat before he snapped mine.

And he knew it.

A smile cracked those burnt lips, causing a little blood to ooze down his chin. "I think this is what they call checkmate."

And it would have been. Except for the figure who

suddenly rose up behind him, very real in the darkness. With black, black eyes that met mine.

And locked.

I swallowed, and Lawrence eased up slightly, waiting for my final pleas, I suppose.

He would wait a while.

"I don't think ... that's a game ... for three," I whispered, and saw his eyes go wide.

Right before he threw me away, trying to get space to turn.

But the boxes that hemmed me in did the same to him, and there was nowhere to go. I hit the ground, but turned in time to see a shining blade slice cleanly through his jugular. He knocked his assailant away, sending her sailing halfway across the length of the warehouse, but I was already moving.

I lunged off the ground, ducked under a fist that disintegrated before it could touch me, as Lawrence's patented trick rippled inward from the extremities. He was disintegrating, but not as quickly as before, his injuries taking a toll. And the target I needed was still solid. He stumbled back, trying to buy himself another second, even as his legs foamed away into nothingness.

Even as I fell on him, snarling.

And slammed my stake home.

Epilogue

It was amazing what twenty-four hours could do, I thought, gazing out over the now pristine ballroom.

Not that there weren't still signs of the battle. Tapestries were draped around the walls, hiding missing marble panels and weapons' fire, and lending the room an odd Gypsy vibe. Potted plants had sprouted here and there, too, covering gaps in the floor where broken tiles had been pried out and not yet replaced. And one of the great chandeliers was missing, obviously too damaged for repair, leaving a strange patch of dimmer light in the center of the floor, where I stood.

That was okay, though. That was actually my only saving grace. Not that a shadow did much to conceal me from the hundreds of sharp vampire eyes scattered around what remained of the ballroom, but it was better than nothing. Especially since I had the vague impression I might be listing slightly to the left.

I straightened up, trying to look nonchalant, and caught an eye roll from Ray in the family box.

He was easy to spot because he was hanging over the side, dressed to kill in a tux so sleek it simply had to be bespoke. I didn't know where he'd gotten it, but I suspected that Louis-Cesare's tailor was being taken advantage of. I didn't know, though, since I hadn't seen Ray. I hadn't seen anybody much, since I woke up an hour ago, after apparently being out of it for most of a day.

And I pretty much still was. I'd been woken up, still half asleep and dreaming about little golden footprints leading me out of a long, dark tunnel. And then dressed in a scarlet, bias-cut gown that was far too attention-getting for my taste, only nobody had asked me.

They hadn't asked me when they dragged me in here, either, surrounded by a bunch of guards I didn't need except as props to keep me on my feet. Only then, the guards had disappeared, blending back into the crowd and leaving me alone. And facing a balcony stuffed with new faces.

The new senators had been inducted while I slept, I guessed. I recognized the old crew, the ones too wily or too strong or just too damned hard to kill for the war to have removed them. There was Marlowe, looking like a guy on his way to a fancy dress ball, in full-on Elizabethan regalia. Or maybe Stuart era; I always got the styles mixed up. But the velvets and laces didn't make him look any less deadly, maybe because of the searing look he was sending me.

It wasn't his usual glare; I didn't know what it was. I looked blearily back for a minute, then decided I didn't care. Because right next to him was Louis-Cesare.

He was in a tux as fine as Ray's, probably because the same guy had made it. It was a break with tradition, assuming he was on the Senate again—which is what it looked like to me, ban or no. He was in one of the crimson-backed chairs everybody was using, the ones that looked more like thrones. There were twelve of them on the balcony, six on either side of the consul's massive no-doubt-about-it throne.

He was also looking a little . . . antsy. His hands kept clenching and unclenching on the carved arms of his chair, like he was hyped up on caffeine or something. Only it couldn't be, because caffeine had no effect on vampires. I didn't know what did affect vampires, but it looked like a lot of them had had it. Not on the Senate, but in the crowd, which was looking less than perfectly composed. The crowd was actually looking kind of like fans in a football stadium right before the deciding points are scored—jumpy, anxious, breathless.

It would have made me nervous if I hadn't been about to fall over.

The consul wasn't on her throne yet, and two of the other chairs were empty. But all the other senators seemed to be in place. And I guessed Cheung and Zheng had made it, because they were both there, and both looking smug as hell.

The former gave me a small nod, which was probably all he could manage in his getup, which I guessed was medieval Chinese pirate chic. Or something. Tooled leathers and bright silks and a gleaming sword, anyway. Zheng, on the other hand, opted for a modern tux. And he was the one to break tradition and shoot me a grin.

Nobody else seemed so inclined. Which was fine, since Jack, the euphemistically named Persuader, creeped me out even with a poker face. He was sitting on Cheung's left, next to a pretty Asian woman I didn't know, but who looked like she smelled something bad. Possibly Jack, considering he was wearing some rotting velvet thing that looked like he'd stolen it off one of the corpses he played with. Or possibly me, considering she was giving me a death glare.

I gave a discreet sniff.

Nope, must be Jack.

The other senators were unknown to me—except for Anthony's diversion: Halcyone, Ray had called her. I guessed they were either new or just lofty types who didn't talk to dhampirs. But somebody was about to be in serious trouble, because the spare chairs were still empty, and Herself had just walked out onto the balcony.

The already-simmering excitement ramped up a notch, with an audible murmur running through a group that didn't need to talk aloud. And I had to admit that she was worth it, a glittering column of pleated gold lamé that should have looked tacky as hell but somehow didn't. But despite the bling, I barely noticed.

Because Mircea walked out at her side.

Radu was with him, a hand on his arm, despite the fact that nobody else had a servant on the balcony. And nobody said anything about his being there, which was just as well, 'cause Radu wasn't taking any shit. The beautiful mask was back, in all its breathtaking perfection. But the expression ... the expression said, *I don't care who you are, touch my brother and I rip your face off.*

And one look at Mircea told me why.

He settled onto the Senate seat to the consul's right, looking more than a little delicate. It was nothing I could put a name to—the sleek hair, the expensive tux, the family-crest cuff links were all the same and were all perfect. But his face was drawn and his eyes were pained as he looked down at me, and there was a strange expression on his face: defiance and fierce pride and something that looked like wonder, all jumbled up.

And suddenly, I wanted to stab Lawrence all over again.

I killed him for you, I thought, staring upward.

"I know."

The consul took her seat last, which seemed backward to me, but what do I know about high court protocol? Or much of anything else, like what the hell I was doing here. I really wished they'd hurry up and tell me about whatever-it-was, because I really, really needed to sit down. Or kneel. Or just fall on my face on the shiny, shiny marble.

I look a little rough, I thought, staring at my reflection in the floor.

Damn, what did they polish it with to get it to look like—

Someone cleared her throat, and I looked up, blinking. And saw the consul staring down at me. At least, I guessed so, since there didn't seem to be anybody else around.

Suddenly, it got very, very quiet.

I licked my lips, wondering if I was in trouble. I couldn't actually remember doing anything ... well, *so* bad. Of course, the way my head felt, God only knew what I'd forgotten. I wondered if I'd accidentally offed any good guys. Like maybe somebody the consul was fond of. Because she was looking a little . . . fierce . . . and not in the usual supermodel kind of way. But in the I-might-hang-the-lot-of-you kind of way, and that probably wasn't a great—

"*STOP.*"

The sound echoed through my head like a spoken voice. Like the consul's voice, only I didn't think she did that mental stuff. Unless it was with another high-ranking vamp and, of course, that let me out. But maybe somebody was giving her a boost, or maybe I was just hallucinating. And really, I wouldn't put it past me right—

"*Dorina, please.*"

That was Mircea. Looking half amused, half appalled, which was weird. Because his expression never gave that much away. But then, he didn't usually get his brain *Roto-Rootered* either, so—

"*You're projecting.*"

I stopped, blinking. Was I? Huh.

I didn't know I could do—

"I find myself in an unprecedented situation," the consul said grimly, speaking aloud. "Before me stands a dhampir, one long regarded by our kind as little better than a revenant. Powerful, but incapable of being controlled by a master's voice, and subject to rages that threatened the lives of countless of our Children. Such creatures were hated, mocked and often put down on sight."

I bit my lip. Shit. Whatever I did must have been a real—

"*But last night,*" the Consul forged ahead, glaring at me, "this outcast fought and almost died in our defense, while many of our supposed supporters stood aside and did nothing. She came here to warn us of our enemies' plans, despite the risk to herself in doing so. She found a way into their stronghold, which none of our people managed. She helped a small group of our *loyal*"—the stress on the word was vicious—"servants to close the breach our enemies had created through our defenses. And then she killed, *in mental combat*, the traitor who had made much of this possible."

A rustling had gone around the room at the "mental combat" comment; I wasn't sure why. But Ming-de, seated with the other consuls in solitary splendor to the left of the balcony, suddenly sat forward. The long, jeweled nail covers she wore made a small sound on the marble balustrade as she looked over at me.

And smiled.

A chill ran up my spine hard enough to make me flinch.

Luckily, nobody noticed because the consul was speaking again.

"It has occurred to us that the traditional understanding of the dhampir being may have been ... flawed. It has been suggested that, perhaps, instead of being half human and half vampire, as was always believed, they are instead two creatures in one: a fully human consciousness residing alongside a fully vampire one."

And okay, that got the attention of the crowd. It didn't get mine, at least not as much as it deserved, because I suddenly felt metal-tipped nails gliding gently, gently through my hair, and over my skull. And then *through* it, as if they could stroke the brain matter itself. I felt like shuddering, but didn't get the chance before a slash of crimson splattered across my vision, and the nails were rapidly withdrawn.

I blinked, and put a hand to my forehead, expecting to find myself bleeding profusely. But there was nothing there. Nothing except clammy skin and sweaty hair, which went pretty well with the tiny tremors my body had started making.

Okay, they really need to hurry this shit up, I thought. Because I wasn't going to —

"And now I find myself faced with a dilemma," the consul said quickly. "On the one hand, I have a creature whom I have been assured is the equivalent of a first-level master, who was sired by a trusted counselor, and who has useful connections to our allies among the fey. On the other, I have a number of first-level masters who did nothing while she fought and bled and almost died for us. And between them," — she made an elegant gesture with a long brown hand—"I have the last Senate seat."

I'd heard the phrase "You could have heard a pin drop" many times. But I'd never really understood what it meant. Until now.

The entire room, which must have held a couple thousand, at the least, went suddenly, deathly quiet. And nobody does quiet like a vampire. Not a breath was exhaled, except for my labored ones. Not a piece of clothing rustled, except for the almost inaudible *swish, swish* of my hem brushing the floor as I swayed slightly from side to side. Not a foot scraped the ground, except for my heels, as I fought to stay upright.

And to figure out what was going on, because clearly now, I was hallucinat—

"After careful consideration of the fact that we are at war, and that, in wartime, loyalty, ability and courage are more to be prized than all other factors—"

And that was as far as she got. The room erupted furiously, and the wash of sound and thought hit me like a fist, causing my already tenuous grip on the upright position to wobble. I saw Louis-Cesare rise from his chair, saw Mircea lean forward. But nobody knew how to grab attention like the consul, who cut through the bedlam with just seven words.

"Come and take your seat, Lady Dorina."

And okay, I thought. That's it. If I was going to hallucinate, I might as well do it on my damned face.

So I did.

I woke to darkness puddling in the corners of a high ceiling, a low-banked fire chasing shadows along the wall, and a naked vampire in my bed.

One of these things is not like the others, I thought vaguely, and swam slowly back to consciousness.

I was naked, too—of course—but for once, I didn't mind. I did kind of mind the weird, fuzzy, strung-out feeling I was having, though. So I just lay there for a few minutes, too groggy to do much more than stare at the elaborate molding on the ceiling.

After a while, it got a little better, and I rolled over and watched the vampire instead. He was more interesting— a lot more, I decided, as the firelight danced over fascinating hills and valleys, hard muscle and soft creases, and picked out fiery glints in the dark mass of his hair. And in the brilliant blue eyes that slowly opened to blink at me.

An arm reached out and tugged me over, and I went grinning, sprawling on top of him bonelessly. And pleased to discover that, yes indeedy, he wasn't wearing anything except a satiny comforter. Of course, that was kind of a problem, too, because silken sheets and satin bedding and sleek vampire turn out to be kind of slippery. I started to slide off the other side, but hands came up to grip my waist. I smiled sloppily at their owner.

He smiled back for a second, a brief, sardonic twist of his lips, until I decided to sit up. And then the smile faded, replaced with something else as his eyes slid down my body. That glance was warmer than the fireplace heat on my back, although I guess my body didn't think so, judging by the way certain things perked right up.

He closed his eyes in what looked like pain.

I bent over him. "Howdy," I said, feeling friendly.

Those sapphire eyes fluttered open again. No man should have lashes that long, I thought, or a bottom lip that tempting. It was just wrong. It deserved to be punished, to be bitten . . . really . . . hard. . . .

I finally noticed that it wasn't getting any closer, despite my best efforts. Maybe because his hands had come up from my waist to my biceps, holding me in place. I tried pushing against them, which did no good at all. And for some reason I found that just really sexy.

Of course, that pretty much applied to everything right now.

"Dory." He swallowed as I writhed around on top of him, sending his Adam's apple bobbing deliciously. I had a sudden strong urge to bite it, too.

"Hmm?"

"We can't."

"Can't what?" I was still watching that little bump, I

don't know why. His pecs were works of art, the washboard stomach rising and falling gently under my ass was completely lickable, and then there were those lips. They were supermodel lips, Renaissance angel lips, and I fully intended to get around to them. But right now, they weren't what I wanted.

"I'm going to bite you," I warned him, and felt him groan.

"Do that again," I said because it had resonated in interesting places.

"We can't," he repeated instead.

I suddenly realized what he was talking about, and laughed. "Wanna bet?" I challenged, and wiggled back a few inches.

Oh, yeah. No problem here.

"Don't," he said tightly, grasping my hips before I could manage to arrange things properly. Which was a bit of a disappointment, but then I realized that delicious throat was unprotected. I went in for the kill.

Well, not literally; I even made sure not to use fangs. And after the first bite, it was really more of a sucking motion, because I liked the way it vibrated under my mouth when I—

Hard fingers dug into my hips and that was more like it.

"Dory, *please*."

Or maybe not. I paused to look up at him. "Give me one good reason why not."

"Any moment, you are going to remember. And once I begin to pleasure you, I do not intend to be interrupted."

I frowned, and sat back. "Remember what?"

And then it hit me.

"That," he said sardonically, as I stared down at him.

For a long moment, I didn't say anything. And then I tried hopping up, intending to make for the door because I'd really lost it this time, and I didn't need to be around people when—

Louis-Cesare tackled me.

My back hit mattress, and my front hit vampire, or I

guess he hit me, because he landed on top. "You're not crazy," he told me, as I fought, and kicked and bit—

And ended up immobilized with my arms over my head and hot, satiny muscles sliding along—

Okay, that was unfair.

"Not crazy, huh?" I demanded, as he deliberately slowed down. And started kissing my neck.

"Mmm."

"Then why do I think I just got appointed *senator*?"

"Possibly because you did."

"Now you're just as crazy as I am," I told him, as those lips slid lower.

"No. I am sure of it. I am on the Senate, too. They require that we know these things."

"And I require that you stop being an ass! What the *hell*?"

He looked up from licking his way around a nipple. "Do you see why I did not wish to start this?"

"Just tell me."

He rested his chin on my sternum and smiled slightly. "It is true. Extraordinary, I grant you, but then, these are extraordinary times. And the consul was not pleased at the reaction of most of the masters who had come to vie for the open Senate positions. This is a wartime Senate; it needs warriors. Yet, when it came down to it, it was as she said. Few were willing to put their lives on the line without certainty of reward."

"Yes, but . . . I'm *dhampir*. I'm not even a person in vampire law!" Why was I the only one who seemed to get this?

"You are not. But your father was able to successfully argue that Dorina is. And since you are inseparable . . ."

"Dorina." I stopped, and felt my skin go cold. "That's it, isn't it? They want her and her mental abilities."

He nodded. "They are rare and, based on Lawrence's fate, it would appear that you have inherited much of your father's skill."

"Then . . . are they going to try to bring her out?" I gripped his arms. "Are they going to try to—"

"Dory." He gripped me back. "You *are* Dorina. And

she is you. You may feel separate at the moment, because you have been cut off for so long from the other side of yourself. But you are one person."

"But Mircea said—"

"He made the argument he did because it was the only one most vampires might accept. Our kind are notoriously xenophobic; they needed to see you as one of them."

Yeah, like that was likely.

"And because the consul told him to."

"What?" Now I was really lost.

His mouth screwed up in a scowl, but I didn't think it was for me. "You were right—your abilities are rare, and highly prized. The consul wanted them on her side, before you were snapped up by a rival. She also wanted your connections to the Blarestri, whom it appears we now need badly. And she wanted a Senate firmly under her control, something much less certain with some of the other leading candidates."

"But . . . a *Senate* seat . . ." It was not just crazy. It was completely impossible.

"If it makes you feel any better, it is for the duration of the war only. As is mine. Then my century-long ban will go back into effect, and you . . . Well, you may do as you like. Of course, you can do that now, if you insist. I cannot recall anyone turning down a Senate seat, but it should technically be possible. . . ."

I lay there, no longer fighting, since my head was spinning too much. And because I wasn't going to win anyway. And because I kind of liked the feeling of sensual captivity, at least by this particular jailer.

Soft hair and warm lips trailed downward, and I stared up, at a fat cherub on the frieze around the ceiling who was smirking at me. He knew I didn't belong here. Knew it couldn't last.

But I wanted it to. I curled my fingers in Louis-Cesare's hair, clenching them unconsciously, because I didn't want to let go. *And maybe you don't have to,* some insidious voice insisted. If you are on the Senate—crazy, stupid, *absurd*—you would be equals. And no one told senators *no* and *can't* and *shouldn't* except the consul. And does she really care who her people are sleeping with ... ?

I could have him, I thought, and it seemed more unreal than anything else that had happened lately. I could have him—

Yeah, for how long? another, slightly saner voice asked. Remember *Christine.* Remember how he really thinks of you. As some kind of replacement for her, as someone he can save—

"Is that what you think?" I looked down to see Louis-Cesare resting between my thighs, but with a massive scowl on his face. "Is it?"

"How did you—?" I asked, confused.

"You're projecting," he said angrily. "Mircea said it is a result of having half your mind flooded with this new power all at once. Or new to it—" He shoved the explanation away. "It will come under your control in time."

"Good to know." Or I could foresee a lot of trouble ahead.

Like right now, for instance.

"Did you mean that?" he demanded again.

"I—it's what I heard—"

"From whom?"

"I don't—"

"Verrell," he hissed, and I winced.

"Stop that!"

"He is—" Louis-Cesare cursed harshly in French, before getting himself under control. "He is a good chef. He is *not* my confidant!"

He got up abruptly and began pacing, giving me a hell of a view, but I didn't enjoy it. It looked like I'd really managed to step in it this time. There was anger written in every line of his body.

"I have existed four hundred years. I have lived"—he spun back around—"I have lived very damned few! Tucked away in the country like a dirty little secret; imprisoned when I didn't thoughtfully die of some plague before coming of age. Years locked away, before escaping with Radu—who promptly left me before I could learn how to live this new life of mine. Having to figure it out for myself, and once I finally did, once I began to build a family, once I began to think that finally, perhaps the future would be brighter—*Christine*. Just another sort of prison!"

"And now me." Because I sure as hell hadn't made his life any easier.

"You are nothing like Christine!" he said, in my face. "She was a *responsibility*, a mistake I made when young and foolish, and from whom I came to believe I would never be free!"

"Then what am I?" I challenged, staring up into blazing sapphire eyes.

"A joy."

His mouth crushed mine, parting my lips in a bruising kiss that I returned with equal intensity. My hands caught the sides of his face, digging into that ridiculous hair. All eight pounds of it, soft and shiny as a woman's, that I'd started out hating and somehow grown to love. Just like I loved—

He jerked back, and the expression in his eyes told me I must have been projecting again. I found I didn't mind all that much. I found I liked it. Like the mouth pressed into the curve of my throat, my breast, my pelvis, the teeth and tongue altering between laving and nipping, while I stared at the ceiling and wondered if I really had gone mad.

When I let myself think about it, how much had changed, how much was changing, it terrified me. We weren't what we had been, not any of us. And I didn't know what we would be by the time the war ended, or even if we'd still be alive. But right now, I wouldn't trade it. Wouldn't trade any of it.

I didn't know that he heard me that time, didn't know if I was still coherent enough mentally for my thoughts to make sense. All I knew was that he did things I didn't even know how to put a name to. Until I was writhing and begging and threatening and—

He took my fingers and brought them down to his lips, and then further, to spread me open just that much more, for him. I slid in knuckle-deep, so ready—I had been ready. And then, his eyes never leaving mine, he pulled my fingers to his mouth and licked them clean.

It felt like something broke inside, but I couldn't look away. Couldn't even say please anymore. Just curled my fingers in his mouth and *reached* for him with the hand he was no longer holding. I grabbed and pulled with no real strength, but he came, crawling up my body, letting that glorious hair drag against me, the tacky sweat on my skin amplifying the friction.

Until he settled against me, pulled my thigh over his hip and ground, in little movements that had me sobbing and blinking at the ceiling like I had forgotten what it was, and had him groaning and talking into my neck. I couldn't understand a word, not a word, because everything around me had become white noise; the ebb and flow of his movements counterpointed with my own so that I honestly couldn't tell which were mine and which were his.

Until he slid in two inches and stopped.

"W-what are you doing?"

"I will only ever do this the first time physically once," he told me, apparently serious. "I want to remember everything, every movement, every scent, every sigh...."

I growled and flipped us, seating him completely, all in one movement, the burn just the way I liked it. "Believe me. You'll have plenty of reminders."